THE SEX THERAPIST
NEXT DOOR

What Reviewers Say About
Meghan O'Brien's Work

Infinite Loop

"…This has become one of my favorite 'give me good feelings about life' books."—*C-Spot Reviews*

The Three

"In *The Three* by Meghan O'Brien, we are treated to first-rate storytelling that features scorching love scenes with three main characters. …She hits her stride well in *The Three* with a well-paced plot that never slows. She excels at giving us an astounding tale that is tightly written and extremely sensual. I highly recommend this unique book."—*Just About Write*

Thirteen Hours

"Meghan O'Brien's writing style is entertaining. She is creative and her story isn't the typical romance. It was a lovely little story with the elevator being the highlight of the story. If you want a long and very sexy foreplay then this book is for you."—*The Lesbian Review*

"Ms. O'Brien has a knack for erotica and she sure isn't shy in showing it off!! Goodness this was a scorcher. I finished it about 24 hours ago and am still blushing, burning and wanting."—*Prism Book Alliance*

"[The] main characters, were well written and I could feel the pain and hope in each of them. As a former US Marine, I usually have a difficult time with books that try to discuss military concepts, philosophy, and events but I didn't feel that way with this book. There were plenty of things in this book that I could relate to."—*C-Spot Reviews*

"Meghan O'Brien has given her readers some very steamy scenes in this fast paced novel. *Thirteen Hours* is definitely a walk on the wild side, which may have you looking twice at those with whom you share an elevator."—*Just About Write*

"Boy, if there was ever fiction that a lesbian needs during a bed death rut or simply in need of some juicing up, *Thirteen Hours* by Meghan O'Brien is the book I'd recommend to my good friends. ...If you are looking for good ole American instant gratification, simple and not-at all-straight sexy lesbian eroticism, revel in the sexiness that is *Thirteen Hours*."
—*Tilted World*

Battle Scars

"As a former US Marine, I usually have a difficult time with books that try to discuss military concepts, philosophy, and events but I didn't feel that way with this book. *Battle Scars* is a quick read that drew me right in and didn't let me go. Both Ray and Carly have had emotionally devastating experiences but this book is about love and hope and dogs. Wonderful, supportive, loving dogs."—*C-Spot Reviews*

Delayed Gratification: The Honeymoon

"Anyone who has read O'Brien's other work knows her talent for writing scorching hot love scenes. She doesn't disappoint..."—*Lunar Rainbow Reviewz*

"*Delayed Gratification* is written well and the sexy times are hot when you get there."—*The Lesbian Review*

Wild

"I love Meghan's take on shapeshifters. ...The story has great pacing and keeps you on the edge of your seat until it's heart pounding end. I can't wait for sequel."—*BookDyke.com*

"I truly enjoy shifter stories but I have never had the pleasure of reading one so well written or so hot. Even for a Bold Strokes Book it was erotic and exotic!"—*Prism Book Alliance*

"[O'Brien] knows how to write passion really well, and I do not recommend reading her books in public (unless you want everyone

to know exactly what you are reading). *Wild* is no different. It's very steamy, and the sex scenes are frequent, and quite erotic to say the least."
—*Lesbian Book Review*

The Night Off

"*The Night Off* by Meghan O'Brien is an erotic romance that is not for the faint of heart. But if you can handle BDSM that includes hard spanking, humiliation, and anal play, then you'll be rewarded with a beautiful, emotional romance. If you've been looking for an erotic romance that is super dirty but has big, big feelings, you won't find anything better than *The Night Off*. Meghan O'Brien is the queen of lesbian erotic romance, and this book is an absolute must."—*The Lesbian Review*

Lambda Literary Award Winner The Muse

"Entertaining characters, laugh-out-loud moments, plenty of hot sex, all wrapped up in a really fun story. What more could you ask for?"—*The Lesbian Review*

"[A] fun read, well-written and with incredibly hot sex scenes."—*Just Love–Romance by Any Definition*

"Emotionally, this books takes you on a roller coaster ride which definitely begins immediately with the thrill of the first big drop and the thrills don't stop till you're pulling into the gate at the end of the ride. ...Meghan O'Brien, I give you five stars for *The Muse*. It was a joy to read and if I'm ever stranded, kidnapped or imprisoned, I hope I have this book with me."—*Stone Soup*

Lambda Literary Award Finalist Camp Rewind

"Romance is on fast forward at Camp Rewind. ...Alice's awakening is beautiful to watch as Rosa tries to protect them both from online scrutiny. This is a quick, satisfying read for those longing for the nostalgia of a summer camp romance."—*Publishers Weekly*

"*Camp Rewind*, Meghan O'Brien's latest offering, has the sexiness we've come to expect in her fiction, with more of a contemporary romance feel. The sex is hot and varied, as expected, with the overt, enthusiastic consent that is rarely seen elsewhere. More time is spent than usual on just making out, and wow, does that ever pay off when they hit the sheets (or the sleeping bag)."—*Curve Magazine*

"The sex scenes were off the chart, which is normal for a Meghan O'Brien novel. Boy does she know lesbian sex and eroticism. I'm still blushing but how I love it!"—*Les Rêveur*

Her Best Friend's Sister

"Meghan O'Brien has written some of the steamiest books I've ever read, and *Her Best Friend's Sister t*ops them all. I think part of why her erotic romances are so satisfying is that they're as heavy on the romance as they are on the erotic."—*The Lesbian Review*

"*Her Best Friend's Sister* is definitely one of the hottest lesfic books to come out this year, if not THE hottest. If you like your erotic romances to equally balance the erotic and romantic sides, definitely check this one out. It's as sweet as it is sexy."—*Smart Bitches, Trashy Books*

Visit us at www.boldstrokesbooks.com

By the Author

Infinite Loop

The Three

Thirteen Hours

Battle Scars

Wild

The Night Off

The Muse

Delayed Gratification: The Honeymoon

Camp Rewind

Her Best Friend's Sister

The Sex Therapist Next Door

THE SEX THERAPIST NEXT DOOR

by

Meghan O'Brien

2018

THE SEX THERAPIST NEXT DOOR

ISBN 13: 978-1-63555-296-6

This Trade Paperback Original Is Published By
Bold Strokes Books, Inc.
P.O. Box 249
Valley Falls, NY 12185

First Edition: November 2018

CREDITS
Editor: Shelley Thrasher
Production Design: Susan Ramundo
Cover Design By TY Justice

Acknowledgments

First and foremost, I need to thank my wife, Angie, for letting me spend so much time alone with my characters. It would be easy to get jealous, but you're legitimately great when it comes to sharing me with horny, make-believe ladies. Yet one more reason we're so well matched.

I'm also grateful as ever to Shelley Thrasher, who never fails to make the editing process a true joy. If only I could stop overusing clichés and finally conquer the difference between lie vs. lay, maybe you'd feel like you were finally getting somewhere with me. For everyone else at Bold Strokes Books: thank you for the support and the community. It feels good to be part of this team.

And now the obligatory note to my beloved family: Kathleen, the cover may have already tipped you off, but you'll need to keep your students the hell away from this one, too. Sorry. Maybe next time? Mom and Dad, this applies to you as well. If ever you can't help yourselves and choose to read one of my books despite my dire warnings not to, for the love of God, please…don't make it this one. (If I had to choose…*Battle Scars*, perhaps? Just skip the naked parts.)

Dedication

For those brave enough to keep trying.

CHAPTER ONE

Roused from the couch by an insistent knock on her apartment door, Jude Monaco prepared to dismiss whichever friend or former lover had decided to drop by unannounced. Instead, she fell into stunned silence at the sight of her next-door neighbor Diana— the beautiful, relatively older woman for whom she'd been carrying a particularly lusty torch for the past thirteen months—anxiously shuffling her feet on the welcome mat, elegantly dressed and openly distraught. Her vivid blue eyes lit up at the sight of Jude, which made Jude's heart sing. She opened her mouth to offer Diana an effusively friendly hello, barely thinking to wonder why someone she'd rarely spoken with except to trade casual pleasantries in the laundry room or at the mailbox would knock on her door this late on Saturday afternoon.

Before Jude could attempt a charming greeting, Diana broke the ice with an awkward wave. "Hi." She cleared her throat, so overtly nervous that Jude's stomach churned in empathy. "I'm not sure if you remember me, but—"

"Diana. Of course I remember you." Opening the door wider, Jude leaned against its blessedly sturdy frame and attempted a carefree smile. "How's it going?"

"Hi." Diana repeated, somewhat unnecessarily. "And, well, it's…" She took a deep breath and dodged the subject. "You're Jude, right?"

"That's me." Jude folded her arms across her breasts, wishing she'd worn a bra to the door. If she'd known who was on the other side, she would've stopped to throw one on. "What can I do for you?"

"Well…" Diana grew redder with every second of uneasy silence she allowed to stretch out between them. After an unbearably long hesitation, she muttered, cheeks aflame, "You know what? This suddenly feels like a really terrible idea. I think I should…" She moved a half pace to the right, clearly flirting with the urge to flee toward the safety of her own apartment. "Sorry to bother you."

"Diana." Jude stepped into the hallway to catch her neighbor by the wrist. "What's going on? Did you need something?"

Diana jolted at the contact, so Jude let her go and allowed her gaze to drift to Diana's luxuriously thick and shiny hair, which fell just above her narrow shoulders and boasted a smattering of gloriously silver strands woven throughout the natural dark brunette. Flustered by the thought of how often she'd masturbated herself to sleep with Diana in the starring role of one of her go-to mature, older-lover fantasies, Jude struggled not to reveal how attracted she was. It had always seemed painfully obvious that Diana considered her a bit of a kid. Probably even a wild child, given that they shared the wall of Jude's busy bedroom and its revolving door of sexually liberated—and frequently vocal—women of every age, shape, and color.

Of course Diana looked at her and saw her as a child. How could she know what Jude *really* wanted? Who she *really* was? Jude didn't share those hopes and dreams with just anyone. Not even the women who graced her bed.

Diana managed a tense smile. "To be perfectly frank, I came over to ask you for a completely batshit, wholly inappropriate favor…a request that would have almost certainly resulted in you slamming the door in my face. Which I would've totally understood, actually. I'm not sure why I ever thought…But I wasn't sure what else to do, so—"

"So ask me the favor." More intrigued than intimidated after that rambling disclaimer, Jude beckoned for Diana to follow her into the apartment. "How about you come inside and sit down first? Maybe it'll be easier that way."

Diana scoffed and shook her head, yet drifted closer. "I'm not so sure about that."

"Believe it or not, I *am* a pretty friendly person. Once you get to know me." Jude held open the door, grinning as Diana tentatively walked past. "I promise not to be offended, regardless of how inappropriate this favor turns out to be."

Diana stopped just inside the entryway and released an explosive sigh. "You sleep with women, right?"

Jude closed the door behind them, glad she'd thought to suggest taking their conversation somewhere more private. Her intrigue had become stark fascination. Emboldened by the nature of Diana's query, Jude quipped, "Sleep usually isn't all that high on my agenda, but…" She winked, then extended her arm to entice Diana even farther inside. "Yes, I date women. Why? Are you looking to set me up with someone? Because I should warn you, I'm not necessarily in the market for a serious relationship right now. Unless you happen to be matchmaking for Michelle Pfeiffer. Then maybe."

Twisting her hands in front of her, Diana glanced at the couch Jude was attempting to usher her toward but seemed reluctant to move away from the door. "Sorry. Not here on Michelle's behalf." She chuckled, studying Jude with seemingly renewed interest. "I'm thinking she's too old to be your ideal match, anyway. You can't be more than, what, twenty-three or twenty-four?"

"Twenty-six, actually." Tired of waiting for Diana to relax, Jude strolled to the couch and sat at one end. "For the record, Ms. Pfeiffer is fifty-nine, sexy as fuck, and I don't believe in setting age limits on attraction."

Diana's eyelashes fluttered, gaze drifting to the floor in apparent recognition of Jude's effort to drop a hint—even if their own age difference ran closer to ten or fifteen years. After a drawn-out silence, Diana took a seat at the opposite end of the couch. She angled her body toward Jude's and looked her dead in the eyes.

"I'm not quite sure how to start, so…I guess I'll tell you a little more about myself first." She inhaled. "My full name is Diana Kelley, and I'm a trained psychotherapist—a sex therapist, specifically. Mostly I work as an educator…of a sort. I, uh…" She fidgeted, making Jude wonder if she wasn't doing an adequate job of appearing nonjudgmental.

"That's so awesome." Jude flashed Diana a big, everything-is-cool smile. "I mean, I love sex. It'd be amazing to get paid to talk about it on a daily basis, let alone teach people how it's done."

Her vapid response seemed to loosen some of the tension in Diana's delicate shoulders. She returned Jude's smile, maintaining eye contact despite her now-perpetually flushed cheeks. "Most days, I absolutely love my job. Tonight? Not so much." Diana took another steadying breath, then pushed on before Jude could offer more reassurances. "I've been hosting these couples' workshops for women. Each week I cover a different topic—usually a new technique or position, or fresh ideas for foreplay, like spanking or role-play. The goal is to offer erotically charged sexual instruction for women in a safe, judgment-free environment…with the hope that my students will leave inspired and dormant fires will be rekindled."

Jude couldn't help but squirm excitedly at the image of Diana instructing a classroom full of horny women on the best ways to make each other come. Before tonight, she'd only seen Diana as a person who treated their elderly, wheelchair-bound neighbor Gwen kindly, always taking out her trash and regularly walking her small, scruffy dog. To discover this new aspect of Diana's personality exhilarated her. Far more turned on than she would've ever anticipated possible—especially with an entire couch cushion separating them—Jude cleared her throat before attempting to respond to the bombshell revelation about her not-so-mild-mannered neighbor. "Sounds fun. And like noble work."

Diana chuckled, yet also seemed pleased. "Noble, huh? I can't say I hear that very often. At least from non-clients." The corners of her eyes crinkled adorably when she smiled, making Jude's clit jump. "But you're right. The work can be very satisfying. Not always, but often enough to keep me going."

Deciding Diana had to feel at least *slightly* more at ease after her demonstration of respect, Jude surrendered to impatience and begged for the answer to her most burning question. "Please, *please* ask me your favor. After that disclaimer, I'm willing to bet it's not anywhere near as inappropriate as what my perverted brain has conjured up."

"Oh, I wouldn't be so sure about that." Diana attempted a brave smile, but her hands were shaking. "You'd be surprised."

Jude's heart raced. "So surprise me."

Diana pulled her phone out of her jacket pocket, glanced at the time, then shielded her eyes with her free hand and sighed wearily. "These workshops…I have this friend, Ava, who usually assists me. And her assistance is essential because, well…I employ a hands-on teaching style. My classes are meant to be interactive. With one's partner, of course. Ava…plays the role of my partner. So I'm able to…demonstrate what I'm telling my students."

Jude barely resisted the urge to pinch her own arm. She wasn't dreaming, but she also wasn't entirely convinced that what seemed to be happening was really…*happening.* Afraid to speak—hell, afraid to *move*—she impersonated a statue and simply listened.

"I'm not sure I want to know what you must be thinking." Diana peered between her fingers, wincing sheepishly at Jude's wide-eyed stare. "About what I do for a living, about why I've told you all of this as a precursor to the inappropriate favor I never should've come here to ask—"

"Yes." To hell with waiting to hear the details. After all this buildup, she couldn't fathom *not* doing anything Diana asked. "I'm in. Whatever you need from me, I'll do. Enthusiastically."

Diana's breath caught, an almost inaudible hitch that elevated Jude's ardor to ever more dizzying heights. "Maybe wait to hear what you're agreeing to first."

Shivering, Jude murmured, "All right. Why don't you tell me what you need, Diana?"

Diana delighted her with a full-body shudder. "Ava called about an hour ago. She fell and hurt her back seriously enough that she's at urgent care having images taken to assess the damage. She says she's okay, not to worry about her, and please don't cancel tonight's workshop—which is the very last thing I want to do, believe me, since I would hate to disappoint sixteen clients, refund all those registrations, and lose the rental fee for the space. But as my students signed up for a highly specific type of experience—an experience I can't easily provide without a partner of my own—I'm not sure I have any choice *but* to cancel. I can't very well ask these women to expose their bodies, their *sexuality*, to the group without doing the same. Not to mention, certain concepts are much easier to show than tell. Especially for the more visual learners."

Amused by the attempt to rationalize her insanely arousing teaching method, Jude took a chance and leaned across the empty cushion to rest a hand on Diana's rapidly bobbling knee. "You came over to ask if I'd fill in for Ava tonight, didn't you? Because you happened to notice that I sleep with women, a lot."

Diana appeared stricken, flooding Jude with the momentary terror that she'd somehow managed to get this wrong. She removed her hand from Diana's knee, then sucked in a startled breath when Diana caught her by the wrist and tangled their fingers together. Awestruck that she was literally *holding Diana's hand* after pining for months in secret, Jude struggled to stay focused, to avoid getting swept away into a lurid fantasy that would further embarrass one or both of them.

Diana gave her an affectionate squeeze. "That *is* why I came here, yes, but I realized my mistake the second you opened the door. I can't in good conscience ask a much-younger neighbor to bare her body for a roomful of strangers, let alone allow me to touch her sexually, just to save myself a few thousand dollars."

Jude raised her eyebrows. "A few *thousand?* Are you kidding me? Sure you can. Ask away."

"Jude…" Diana exhaled at length, then stared up at the ceiling for a few beats before turning her attention back to Jude. "Tonight's workshop is on cunnilingus. You would have to let me go down on you in front of sixteen women—most of whom will be at least a decade older than you, if not two."

Jude tilted her head, genuinely perplexed by the last part of her disclaimer. "Why are you so focused on my age? I already told you, that part doesn't matter to me. Or rather, it doesn't *bother* me." She stroked her thumb over Diana's, teasingly. "On the contrary, I've always wondered what it would be like, the touch of a more mature, more *experienced* woman."

Diana laughed, looking equally flattered and taken aback by the bold admission. "Is it my imagination, or are you trying to tell me you're the right girl for this job?"

"Admittedly, volunteering to have my pussy eaten by a gorgeous sex therapist slash guru hardly counts as a selfless sacrifice." Jude raised their hands to her mouth and kissed Diana's knuckles, noting how she shifted in her seat. "But also, I legitimately hate to think of you losing all that money. Especially since I've got nowhere to be tonight, anyway. So… yeah, since you brought it up…" She arched an eyebrow. "You bet your ass I'm the right girl for this job. As in, I've never been self-conscious about showing my body to people, I positively *adore* oral sex—both giving and receiving—and this wouldn't exactly be the first time I came for an audience." She smirked at Diana's subtle reaction to her disclosure, an easing of her posture that signaled an acceptance of Jude's sincerity— and clear relief at her exhibitionistic tendencies.

"This *would* be a job, by the way." Clearing her throat, Diana disentangled her hand from Jude's and combed her fingers through that wondrous hair. "Meaning, I'll pay you. Only five hundred, unfortunately, but—"

"Five hundred *dollars?*" Jude's head spun at the thought of making almost a third of her former bi-weekly salary in a single evening. For having an orgasm…with her fantasy lover.

"I could go up to six hundred, but that's—"

"Whoa, whoa." Jude waved her hands to stop Diana from reducing her profit margin any further. "Five hundred dollars is more than enough, given all you're really asking me to do is lie back and let you lick me." She lowered her hands and narrowed her eyes. "*Is* that all you're asking?"

"Basically." Diana folded her hands on her lap, coming across far more prim than should've been possible. "I'd appreciate a little verbal interaction during the lesson, along with vocal feedback from you during the act—you know, to offer the students some idea about how well my techniques work."

"I highly doubt that'll be a problem." Surprised by the mild heat crawling up the back of her neck, Jude admitted, "I'm, uh…not exactly shy about letting my satisfaction be known."

"Perfect." Diana gave her a careful smile. "How do you feel about letting me penetrate you with my fingers? To be clear, it's not a deal breaker if you'd rather—"

"You can put your fingers inside me." Jude shifted her weight, keenly aware of how wet this conversation—and Diana's proximity—was making her. Her neighbor's hesitation was palpable, but pointless. Jude couldn't envision saying no to anything Diana offered. "Especially if you want to make me come faster."

Diana swallowed, throat rippling in a way that made Jude's mouth water. "Good to know. Beyond that…yes. All I'm asking is for you to let me perform cunnilingus on you in an educational setting, for six hundred dollars."

"Five hundred. I don't feel right taking any more than that." She barely felt right accepting money at all. Having the chance to play out this stunningly kinky older-woman fantasy in real life—with the sexiest older woman she knew, no less—was compensation enough. She stuck out her hand, waiting for Diana to shake and close the deal.

Instead, Diana hesitated. Glancing from Jude's hand to her face, she said, "You don't think this will complicate our relationship? Meaning… you're a good neighbor. Despite the occasionally loud fucking at all hours of the night—"

"Sorry." Jude winced, remembering a particularly voracious screamer she'd brought home around a month ago. "I'll be sure to start covering their mouths after midnight."

Diana ran her tongue along her top lip, then bit back a smile. "That won't be necessary. There *are* worse nighttime soundtracks than two women having mind-blowing sex."

Wait—had Diana ever masturbated herself to sleep with fantasies of *her*? Jude loved that such a possibility even existed, whether or not it had actually happened. Forcing her mind back to the question she'd been asked, she said, "No. I don't think this needs to complicate our neighborly coexistence. We're talking about a simple business transaction, right? You need to hire a last-minute substitute assistant, I'm more than qualified for the position, we've successfully negotiated a salary…nothing complicated about that. Sure, you're hiring me for sex, but that doesn't mean things have to get weird between us. We both know what this is. You're looking for someone to bail you out, and I'm looking to spice up an otherwise boring Saturday night—and earn some much-needed extra cash. Seems straightforward enough to me."

Diana reached across their buffer cushion for a brisk handshake. "Okay, then. Class starts at seven. I can either text the address to your phone or you can hitch a ride with me—your choice."

"I'll ride with you." Startled when Diana hastily stood, Jude followed with her eyes as she hurried toward the door. "What time do you want to leave?"

Diana swiveled to face her. "Six? I prefer to get there early so I have time to set up before the students arrive."

"Six it is." Jude rose from the couch as well, mentally planning the remainder of her now-busy afternoon. "That should give me plenty of time to shower and, uh, groom."

"Great." Halfway through her turn toward the door, Diana stopped. She met Jude's eyes, gazing at her with more kindness than she was used to seeing from anyone—*ever*. "But please don't go crazy with the grooming—at least not on my account. Do whatever makes you feel comfortable and attractive, by all means, but…" She smirked. "Well, I've read your generation is more likely than mine to feel compelled to shave themselves bare. I want you to know that as far as I'm concerned, pubic hair is a natural, functional, perfectly lovely feature of the feminine landscape. Its presence won't impede my appetite in the slightest."

Shaken by Diana's perceptiveness, Jude managed a nonchalant smile. "Noted."

"All right, then. See you at six." Diana put her hand on the knob before looking back at Jude one last time. "And thanks. For saying yes, of course, but also for being open-minded. I was afraid you'd be offended that I would think to ask you at all. But I have to say, this turned out to be much easier than I ever expected."

Jude grinned. "You mean *I* turned out to be much easier than you ever expected."

Chuckling, Diana opened the door and backed into the hallway. "More charming, too."

"And older!" Jude followed Diana into the hallway, watching as she stopped in front of the next apartment. "A whole three years, remember?" She answered Diana's playful eye roll with a toothy grin. "Twenty-six, not twenty-three."

Diana shook her head and opened her door. "A bona fide grown-up. I remember."

"You're about to find out exactly how grown up I can be." Thrilled by the verbal foreplay, Jude kept on teasing. "Aren't you?"

"I suppose I am." Lips quirking, Diana moved halfway into her apartment, then tipped her head in farewell. "Go on, then. Take your shower—and get ready for school."

CHAPTER TWO

A little over four hours later, Jude sat perched atop a sturdy, blanket-covered platform, wondering what the hell she'd gotten herself into. Clad in a thick terry-cloth robe from Diana, she surveyed the sixteen rosy-cheeked, partially dressed women who surrounded her on all sides. Their eyes roved Jude's body anxiously, and their quiet whispers set her nerves even further on edge.

She didn't understand her rising trepidation. Granted, this would be the first time she'd ever gotten naked in front of so many people—the audience she'd mentioned to Diana had been more like a small crowd, if you could even call three people a *crowd*—but the prospect of disrobing wasn't responsible for the uneasy knot in her stomach. While her body was far from flawless, naturally, she'd never felt much shame about its imperfections. Deep down, she wondered if her reticence had more to do with the idea of being touched by a woman she'd wanted with utter desperation—for too many long, lonely nights—while all these strangers looked on.

What if she made a giant laughingstock of herself and came instantly? Or accidentally burst into tears of joy as she mentally scratched oral sex from Diana Kelley off her sexual bucket list?

Diana rested her hand on Jude's bare knee, shaking her from her haze. "Ready?"

Steeling herself for what was about to occur, Jude gave a resolute nod. "Ready."

"You sure?" Diana squeezed her knee, a gesture that triggered an involuntary shiver that both began and ended between Jude's thighs. "I won't be upset if you've changed your mind. Honestly. We'll move forward only if you're still comfortable enough to try."

Unable to imagine a potential embarrassment that could make her feel worse than canceling their demonstration surely would, Jude conjured a brave face and a broad grin. "I'm fine, promise. A little nervous, but… who wouldn't be, right?" She batted her eyelids playfully. "I'm also *super* turned on. Like…*super*. Hope you're prepared for that."

Diana's blue eyes sparkled with what Jude read as genuine delight. "I make it a point to always come to class prepared. Tonight is no exception." She squeezed Jude's knee a second time, then stepped away from the platform to address the class.

"All right, ladies. Good evening, and welcome to Cunnilingus 101— or for the less clinically inclined, Intro to Pussy Eating. Now, while I do recognize quite a few of your faces, I know we have a few newcomers tonight. Welcome, one and all. My name is Diana Kelley, I'm a licensed sex therapist, and my goal for this workshop is to help you and your partner rediscover at least a little of the passion and intimacy that initially drew you together. I'll do that by sharing my favorite tips on how to give excellent head, by answering any questions you may have about one of *the* most intimate sexual acts you can perform on a lover, and by inviting you to watch an erotic, live-action demonstration of my tried-and-true techniques."

She pivoted to make eye contact with the other half of the room. "To those of you who currently enjoy an active sex life—congratulations. Keep up the good work!" About half the women chuckled proudly; two bumped fists. Diana continued. "To those who came here tonight hoping to reintroduce some heat into a relationship that's cooled for one reason or another—*bravo*. Bravo for taking the initiative, *together*, to recognize how important physical intimacy is in a romantic relationship and for choosing to repair a crucial bond that far too many long-time couples fail to nurture. Either way, regardless of why you're here, I hope this lesson inspires a whole lot of mind-blowing sex. Tonight, and in the future."

Everyone clapped, including Jude. Transfixed by Diana's warm introduction, by the rich, impressively professional timbre of her voice, and by her students' rapturous gazes as they watched the commanding performance, Jude failed to suppress a gasp of surprise when Diana's hand found her knee once more, then slid higher up her thigh.

Diana smiled at Jude, then the class. "Please extend a warm welcome to my beautiful young friend Jude, a real trooper who very graciously agreed to make her classroom debut here tonight despite being asked to fill in at the last minute. This will be my first time working with Jude in any capacity, so while she and I did discuss boundaries prior to class, you'll be hearing me check in with her on a fairly regular basis. Even more than I do with Ava, simply because I don't know Jude as well."

Jude's attention drifted to a stocky brunette on her left, whose deep frown creased an otherwise unlined forehead. "Diana, if you don't mind me asking…where *is* Ava? I mean, she's all right…right?"

"Not to worry, Sadie. My lovely assistant tweaked her back this morning and didn't want to test her luck by attempting to withstand the earth-shattering orgasm I had scheduled for her tonight." Diana's hand crept closer to the juncture of Jude's thighs. "Sadly, that means poor Jude has to shoulder this burden instead."

Amidst the light chuckles of her peers, Sadie's concern gave way to amusement. "Sure. Poor Jude."

Licking her lips, Jude attempted a pithy remark of her own—to prove she was actually in possession of a personality, and a sometimes appealing one at that. "Call me crazy, but I'm not exactly disappointed about the turn my Saturday night has taken."

A woman who sat across from Sadie—blond, middle-aged, and sporting a seemingly perpetual smile—winked at Jude, calling out, "I'd call you crazy if you *didn't* drop everything for this gig. Diana sure knows her way around the female anatomy."

Jude fought back a whimper as she pondered the blonde's insight, yet failed to suppress a low moan when Diana's fingertips brushed across her bare inner thigh. Closing her eyes so she wouldn't have to see the reactions from the peanut gallery, Jude bit the inside of her lip as Diana withdrew her hand from beneath the robe to take hold of the belt knotted around her waist.

Diana spared her from having to invent another wisecrack by launching into the introductory speech she'd outlined to Jude during the drive over in an effort to obtain her explicit consent once she'd explained its purpose. Like everything else about this situation, what seemed doable in the abstract felt daunting in the moment. Jude focused on Diana's spiel, bracing for the impact of having her body exposed to those breathtakingly blue eyes.

"Each and every one of you should make it your personal mission to master your own partner's anatomy. Wasn't it Confucius who said 'she who masters her lover's pussy rarely stays in the doghouse for long'?" When Jude opened her eyes to join in with the good-natured laughter, Diana flashed her a reassuring smile and wrapped up the lighthearted portion of her lecture. "While I can't guarantee the skills you'll learn here tonight will be the ticket to endless get-out-of-jail free cards, I *can* assure you that satisfying, not entirely infrequent sex will almost certainly bring you closer to your partner. That's because great sex doesn't simply end at the physical pleasure you're giving and receiving. Having lots of great sex helps bring about emotional wellness, both individually and as a couple. It enables the healing of emotional wounds. Perhaps most critically, it's a way to have fun with someone you care about, largely by making sure they feel amazing and *extremely* desirable."

Won over by the impassioned sales pitch for consistent fucking, Jude almost stopped breathing when Diana moved directly in front of her and stared into her eyes. "Jude, sweetheart, would it be all right if I opened your robe?" Her right hand toyed with the knot at Jude's waist while the left skimmed up her inner thigh, so high she expected Diana's fingers would come away wet. "I want to see that gorgeous body I've been imagining all night."

Jude shivered, wondering how much of Diana's verbal seduction was for her, how much was for show, and whether she meant anything she was saying. Ready to find out, she maneuvered her hands beneath Diana's to untie the belt on her own. "Yes."

Diana held the robe closed for another moment—to study Jude's face and grin faintly at whatever she saw there—before pulling it open to reveal Jude's painfully hard nipples to her sweeping gaze. "You're stunning," Diana murmured, and deliberately pushed the robe off her shoulders, then down her arms, until the material fell from Jude's body and pooled around her waist, baring her completely.

Grateful for Diana's decision to mostly shield her from view, Jude battled an uncharacteristic wave of self-consciousness. Not because of the sixteen pairs of eyes currently straining for a peek at her tits, but because Diana—*Diana*, the goddess next door—seemingly had no reservation about drinking in the sight of her nudity like they were the only ones in the room. Jude mustered a shy "Thank you," then gathered the will to plant her hands behind her hips and lean backward to offer a better view. "I really am fine with this," she whispered, hoping to encourage Diana onward. "In case you were wondering. Feel free to let everyone look." Jude flushed when Diana's gaze lingered on her chest. "If you want."

After a drawn-out pause, Diana's attention drifted lower, down to Jude's naked lap, and she gave her lips a sensuous once-over with her tongue. "*Absolutely* stunning. Delectable, too, no doubt."

Jude's awareness of the world narrowed to only Diana and the thundering of her own heartbeat, lulling her into the seductive illusion that they were alone, together. In awe of the mindless anticipation coursing through her veins—of how *alive* she felt, waiting for Diana's touch—Jude eased her legs apart to show off the sparse, downy covering of pubic hair she'd left mostly untouched to disprove the suggestion that she was yet another form-over-function millennial. Astonished to find her voice while Diana's intoxicating blue eyes drank in the sight, Jude tossed off a flirty retort—anything to keep Diana moving. "I'm happy to let you have a taste. For science."

A radiant smile broke across Diana's face. She lifted her eyes to Jude's, winked, then faced their rapt audience. "When it comes to licking pussy, my motto is 'Always Start Slow.' That same advice applies to anal sex, by the way—an act for which ASS is, admittedly, a more suitable acronym." As Jude chuckled along with everyone else, Diana reached blindly for her thigh, landing mere centimeters from her lap. "Now when I say slow, I mean *slow.* Like, don't even consider touching her below the waist for the first five minutes...minimum."

Jude groaned unconsciously, dismayed to hear she would be made to wait for the first touch of Diana's tongue to her labia, let alone her clit. When a few women giggled at her vocal disapproval, Jude reverted to her class-clown days, doubling down on the performance of impatience in a bid to gain control over everyone's amusement so it wouldn't be at her expense. Locking eyes with an attractive, pleasantly round middle-aged woman to her right, Jude flashed a goofy grin. "Can you blame me? A situation like this doesn't really require much foreplay." She looked at the woman's snickering partner. "I'll be honest with you guys. It's been almost a year since a woman's gone down on me. Now that dry spell is about to end, purely for your gratification. So, like...come on, right? Cut the last-minute substitute assistant a break."

The woman whose gaze she held raised an amused eyebrow. "Personally, I think you should listen to Diana. She knows what she's doing. Just...enjoy the anticipation."

"I appreciate your confidence in my sexual judgment, Yolanda." Diana stepped aside, angling her body toward Jude's to allow their audience an unobstructed view. Before Jude could complain about the injustice of delayed gratification, Diana molded her palm against Jude's clavicle and stared into her eyes. "Do you like having your breasts touched?"

"Yes." She'd already answered the same question earlier, in the car, but gladly obliged Diana's eagerness to illustrate the erotic potential of explicit consent. "Very much."

Diana lowered her hand, smoothing over the slope of Jude's right breast, then gingerly rolling the nipple between her fingertips. "What if I wanted to kiss them? Would you let me?"

Dizzied by the way Diana's sultry tone further blurred the line between her fantasies and this increasingly surreal version of reality, Jude nodded dumbly. She leaned into the thrilling contact, desperate for *something* beyond that simple caress, but soon understood that nothing else would happen without her definitive permission. Swallowing, Jude uttered, "Kiss them, *please.*"

Diana bent to place her lips on Jude's left nipple, tenderly. Her fingertips continued to tease its twin, wrecking Jude's ability to linger on any single, rational thought for more than a millisecond. She couldn't predict what she would do when Diana finally ventured between her legs. What if she passed out? Or spoke in tongues? Or otherwise acted like a real dumbass in front of all these nice ladies?

Jude cried out, ecstatic when Diana's searing tongue finally skimmed over the puckered flesh of her areola. Transported by the sensation of skillful, insistent lips sucking her breast into the wet cavern of Diana's now-wide-open mouth, Jude arched her back, then hastily thrust her hand into the narrow space between her thighs. Finding her labia *soaked*, she cast a furtive glance around, keenly aware that her every action was subject to scrutiny. Luckily, just about everyone was too preoccupied with the task of undressing themselves and their partners to notice her self-pleasuring. Jude left her fingers exactly where they were, greedy for even the subtlest friction near her clit.

"Ah, ah, ah." Diana latched onto Jude's wrist and yanked her hand away. "At least five minutes, remember? That goes for both of us."

Jude failed to suppress a pout, despite not wanting Diana to see her as even more of a relative child. "No fair."

Diana straightened to murmur next to her ear. "My poor, sweet darling." She dragged the tip of her tongue along the sensitive earlobe, triggering multiple contractions of Jude's vaginal muscles so that she very nearly climaxed prematurely. With a deep, longing sigh, Diana shifted to nibble on Jude's other ear. "I never promised fair. Only *good.*"

Diana hadn't even touched her pussy yet, and already Jude knew that "good" was a woefully inadequate descriptor for this sex therapist's expertise. Overwhelmed by the strength of her desire, Jude checked the crowd once more, this time spotting a few fleeting glances in the process. It was then that she realized the worst of her self-consciousness had eased. Scorched away by her mindless arousal, she assumed, along with any sense of shame she'd possessed before today. Jude flexed the wrist Diana still held, hissing when the already firm grip tightened.

Pulling back, Diana grabbed Jude's free hand and pinned both her wrists against the platform, next to her hips. Jude gasped at the forceful move, caught off guard by how perfectly Diana channeled the confident, sexually dominant older woman of her dreams. This experience would do nothing to extinguish the massive torch she carried for her next-door neighbor, contrary to the lies Jude had been telling herself all afternoon. Obviously, this decision to quench her thirst was going to backfire. So long as Diana continued to outshine even her most salacious forays into the land of make-believe, Jude's crush would grow and grow. She might even fall in love.

Trembling with want, Jude begged, "I'll behave, Diana, please. *Please.*"

Diana kissed Jude's neck, then her shoulder, without releasing her hands. "I know you will." She bent to take Jude's nipple between her teeth, laving the tip with her warm tongue. The grip on her wrists remained firm, even when Jude squirmed restlessly in a halfhearted attempt to break free. Diana quashed her faux resistance by stopping altogether, then murmuring, "You must like being held down." Her fingers loosened ever so slightly. "Is that it? Do you like having control taken away from you? Or do you just need to be licked *that* badly?"

"*Yes.*" Jude thrust out her chest in a mindless bid to force her nipple back into Diana's mouth. Diana smirked, easily avoiding the lame ploy with a well-timed retreat. Recognizing her utter powerlessness, Jude clarified the non-answer to entice Diana's willing return. "I like when you take control, and I *do* need to be licked. *So* badly." She repeated, beseechingly, "Please."

Diana brought her mouth to the breast she had yet to suck but didn't make contact. Instead, she tightened her grip on Jude's wrists. "Does it make you wet to be teased like this?"

Jude blurted the first thing that came to mind, which also happened to be the truth. "*You* make me wet."

Diana moaned and licked around the turgid nipple. Once…twice… and then, distressingly, she backed away yet again. A knowing grin on her pink lips, Diana rose to her full height and made eye contact. She waited for Jude to squirm, then closed the distance between their faces for a brief, exceedingly amorous kiss. Jude was still catching her breath when Diana mumbled against her mouth, "Open your legs, sweetie. Show me *how* wet."

Jude obeyed without thinking, parting her thighs until she felt cool air hit her molten center. She tensed in anticipation of the first, exploratory caress, but rather than deliver, Diana returned her attention to the students. "Once you've spent a decent amount of time tormenting—I'm sorry, *exciting*—your partner, I recommend you make a game of 'checking' to see whether she's ready to be licked. No doubt she will be, but that type of foreplay will get her even hotter for the first touch of your tongue."

"If you don't drive her fucking bananas first." Jude relished the scattered laughter from their audience—interspersed with hushed whispers and muffled moans—but she was only halfway joking. She'd never wanted anyone this fiercely. It *hurt*. "Take it from me. Your partner has been hot for your tongue this whole time. So *give it to her* already."

Diana patted Jude's knee, smirking at the crowd. "If you've done your job right, as it appears I have, your partner should be begging for more by this point—all without you having gone anywhere near her pussy." She winked at Jude. "Until now."

No longer concerned with modesty, Jude spread her legs as wide as they would go—until it felt downright obscene—and showed her sopping center to everyone who cared to see. Once a few pairs of eyes had strayed in her direction, including Diana's, Jude said, "I'm more than ready, but go ahead, check anyway."

Diana swallowed, throat tensing visibly. Encouraged by the minor hint that she wasn't alone in her desire, Jude threw back her shoulders, meeting Diana's gaze head-on when the older woman dragged her attention up to Jude's face. Shaking her head, Diana said, "Just look at the mess you've made. *Bad* girl." She pressed her lips to one corner of Jude's mouth, then the other, before initiating a deeper kiss. Their tongues instantly established an ardent rhythm, dancing together as though they'd made out dozens of times before that moment.

When Diana's hand crept up her inner thigh, fingertips gliding suggestively over her slick, exposed labia, Jude broke away with a gasp. The fingers deepened their exploration, pushing between Jude's sensitive folds to ghost across her labia, then forge a slow, winding path up to her clit. Jude rested her forehead on Diana's shoulder and closed her eyes, overwhelmed by all she was being made to feel.

"You *are* ready, aren't you?" Diana massaged her more firmly, spreading around the hot juices that poured from Jude like a waterfall. "Ready for me to lick you clean?"

Nostrils flaring, Jude attempted to not sound quite so out of her mind as she felt. "Yes, ma'am." The response was automatic, a phrase she'd uttered countless times within the context of her "dominant Diana" fantasies. She stiffened while awaiting Diana's reaction, embarrassed by her deference. *So much for convincing her I'm a grown-up.*

Diana swirled her fingers around Jude's opening one last time, then withdrew. Seconds later, she laid her hand flat against Jude's chest and pressed her down onto the platform. Jude went willingly, grateful to be free of the responsibility of holding herself upright any longer. Being able to stare at the ceiling was nice, as well—and far easier than facing the witnesses to her seduction. Jude moaned when Diana's hands slid up the insides of her thighs, then held her breath as careful fingers opened her labia and displayed her arousal to the room. Although Diana had already obtained permission to incorporate her body into this tutorial, Jude wasn't sure how she was going to endure such a blatant examination without bursting into flames.

"Oh, my. Would you *look* at that mouthwatering sight?" Diana held Jude open with one hand, using the other to rub up and down her hypersensitive folds. "Remember our motto, ladies: *Always Start Slow.* That means stay away from her clit in the beginning, until you've driven her right to the edge of 'fucking bananas.'"

Jude uttered a tortured moan, driving a few of the women to even heartier laughter. Clamping her eyes shut, she shivered at the scrape of wood on tile as Diana dragged a chair in front of the platform and sat down. Jude listened to the distinct soundtrack of women lost in pleasure playing out in the background, a provocative melody composed of murmured endearments, strangled moans, and the occasionally lewd slap of two bodies coming into contact. Diana repositioned her hands at the crease of Jude's thighs, using her thumbs to stroke the tiny hairs that covered her vulva.

Jude's toes curled painfully at the first, steamy breath Diana blew across her dripping hole. She cried out when Diana followed up with another slow exhalation, one that washed over her clit and left it throbbing, and reached for her own breasts to give the nipples a vigorous tweak. Already she was dangerously close to orgasm, and Diana had barely even started. Wishing for leverage, Jude lifted her hips to seek out the source of that tantalizing warmth, frantic for the end of Diana's interminable foreplay.

"I recommend licking her outer lips first. Softly." Diana paused to do exactly that, trailing her tongue down one side, then up the other. "In my experience, the best way to send a woman to heaven on earth is by taking the time to appreciate each part of her body—especially those spots that don't usually get a whole lot of attention." She planted a string of kisses across Jude's vulva, nuzzling the short hairs with her nose. "Don't make the mistake of going for her clit too early. Get her quivering first. Make her *beg.*"

"*Please,*" Jude keened, angling for some way to fast-track Diana's process. "See? Begging already. *Pretty please.*"

Diana fitted her smiling mouth against Jude's slit, then poked out her tongue to casually delve between the slippery folds. She released a goose-bumps-inducing groan at her first taste, unleashing a renewed flood of arousal that Jude could feel slowly trickle between her ass cheeks. She went to reach for Diana's head, then stopped. It didn't feel right, somehow, to resort to her usual assertive methods or, really, to try to assume control of this encounter in any way. Diana was in charge here and presumably hadn't hired Jude to contradict the lessons she sought to teach.

"Good girl." Diana captured the hand still hovering in the air above her head, guiding Jude's wrist back to her side. "Do as I say, and I promise you won't be sorry."

"Yes, ma'am," Jude said again, not quite under her breath.

Diana rewarded her with a long, languorous lick that started at Jude's opening and ended just below her clit. "You know I'll take care of you, don't you?"

"*Yes.*" Jude hissed at the careful probing of her labia by Diana's talented tongue. Her hips came off the platform when the insistent muscle pressed deeper to lap at her sensitive inner folds. It was everything she'd dreamed, and more. "Fuck, *yes!*"

Perhaps to punish her enthusiasm, Diana scooted her chair backward and to the side, leaving Jude not only bereft, but exposed. Jude shuddered, driven that much closer to release by both the denial and the knowledge that everyone could see exactly how wet Diana made her. A gentle rap on her thigh pulled Jude's attention to the shiny, openly amused grin of her tormenter. "Sweet, sexy Jude. I can't remember the last time I feasted on a pussy *this* juicy."

Jude's stomach muscles tensed as Diana's fingers inched closer to her vulva. Lacking a suitable rejoinder, she muttered, "I…can get *crazy* wet."

"The glory of youth." Diana winked indulgently at Jude before directing her next words at the class. "Before I turn my focus toward making my unbelievably *delicious* temp assistant come all over my tongue, I want to offer you a friendly reminder: Eating pussy isn't just about making your lover come. It's about making her feel things nobody else can. Not like *this*. I mean craved. Desired. Sexy." Her voice softened. "But, above all, *accepted*."

Though she hadn't forgotten their audience, Jude startled at an unfamiliar voice from somewhere beyond her line of sight. "Excuse me, Diana? My name is Liz, and I, um…well, the truth is…I don't know how to get over my insecurities when it comes to receiving oral sex. I mean… it's not that I think there's anything *wrong* down there, exactly—"

A second voice cut in. "Because there's not. You're perfect."

"I know that's what you say, but…" After a hesitation, Liz asked her question in a more tremulous voice. "How do I overcome this?"

Unable to see the couple who'd stalled their momentum, Jude watched the smile they'd elicited transform Diana's already beautiful face. "Believe me, it's not uncommon for women to feel self-conscious about their genitals—for one reason or another. If you're concerned about your appearance, all I can say is *don't be*. Every woman is unique, and despite what the media tells you, there *is* no standard you need to meet. There's beauty to be found in every aesthetic—something that's especially true when you're gazing upon the body of a woman you love."

"And I *do* love you." The partner's voice wavered with emotion. "You know I do, sweetheart."

"I know." Liz sounded even more choked up than before. "And I love you, too. But that doesn't change the way I feel about my body."

Jude tried not to groan when Diana kicked into therapist mode, turning away from her completely to establish eye contact with her struggling clients. "I said it before, and I'll say it again. Cunnilingus is one of the most intimate sexual acts you can give *or* receive. It requires an immense amount of trust to allow your lover to put her head between your legs. Some women find it downright impossible to be in a position that vulnerable, that exposed. To be clear, there's absolutely nothing wrong with feeling that way."

Diana delivered the reassurance without any hint of judgment, in a calm, compassionate voice of authority. "Never force yourself to do something that doesn't make you feel good. Sexually, at least. Sadly, the IRS doesn't share my opinion when it comes to filing your tax returns in a timely manner." She waited for a few semi-distracted chuckles to subside. "On the other hand, if you genuinely want to enjoy having your pussy licked, all I can tell you is that practice makes perfect. Take whatever steps you can to boost your confidence beforehand. Put on an outfit or some lingerie that makes you feel extra sexy. Keep the lights dim, or turn them off altogether, if that will help alleviate your anxiety. Maybe make a ritual of bathing together first, so no one's worried about her taste or smell. And—as a bonus—washing your lover serves as rather potent foreplay."

"We can attest to that!" A different woman called out from the opposite side of the room. "I always know when my wife is planning a trip downtown because she invites me to take a hot bath. At some point she'll rub her fingertips along my clit and labia, back and forth, to clean me. It's so erotic, to know she's preparing me for her tongue."

"Indeed." The huskiness of Diana's reply caused Jude's inner muscles to tighten, then contract, igniting an ephemeral burst of pleasure that ripped a girlish moan from her aching throat. Diana's eyebrow shot up at the outburst, and she turned toward Jude. "Poor thing. I have you all worked up, don't I?"

Thankfully, Liz delivered Jude a little mercy by interjecting, in a more relaxed voice, "Sorry, Diana. I didn't mean to sidetrack us from the lesson at hand. Keep going, please." She snorted. "For poor Jude's sake, if nothing else."

Jude held her tongue, not trusting her ability to speak with Diana's clever fingers on either side of her clit. The unabashedly gratifying caress felt like Diana praising her for a job well done, a concept that thrilled Jude more than she cared to admit. Indeed, when Diana rolled her chair back into position, she stared at Jude approvingly. The electricity of their shared look coaxed another whispered plea from Jude's dry throat. "*Please.*"

Diana's smile widened. "Yes. Poor, poor Jude. It's time to reward her patience, isn't it?"

Jude raised her hips off the table, chasing Diana's hand as it drifted away from her pussy to resettle on her upper thigh. "Way past time," she groaned, only half kidding. "Remember how I'm doing you a favor here?"

"Touché." Diana nudged Jude's thighs farther apart and lowered her mouth to hover over her straining center. "Thanks for filling in tonight." Without breaking eye contact, she dragged her tongue from Jude's opening to the sensitive spot right above the hood of her clit. Diana's eyes sparkled at the full-throated cry Jude didn't even try to hold back. She echoed Jude's pleasure with a satisfied hum of her own, sending intensely satisfying vibrations throughout Jude's taut body. Moving lower, Diana sucked lightly on her labia, then nibbled the tender flesh for long, taunting seconds before flashing Jude a wicked grin. "I really do owe you one."

Jude's limbs shook, the muscles no longer under her control. "Pay up then," she whimpered, plaintively. "Seriously, Diana...*I beg you.*"

Diana covered Jude's labia with her open mouth, then undulated her tongue so the tip only *barely* grazed her slick opening. The feeling was so exquisite Jude nearly allowed her eyes to slip shut again. She was able to keep them open only because she couldn't bear to miss even the smallest detail of this experience. The bliss of Diana's mouth on her pussy, the confidence of the hands pushing her inner thighs apart, the healthy luster and shine of the hair she hung on to while trying not to come right away— Jude memorized every sight and sensation so she could revisit this event whenever she wanted. Diana was ushering her toward a true sexual awakening, unparalleled by anything Jude had felt in the decade since receiving her first orgasm from someone else's hand.

Diana's oral talents sent her to another plane of existence, a utopia where nothing existed except the diligent tongue on her pussy and the firm yet gentle grip of warm hands on her quivering thighs. Jude tried valiantly to delay the inevitable, not prepared to end their lesson quite *yet*, but it was useless. Once Diana latched onto her clit and began to suck— head bobbing, eyes glittering—Jude was a goner.

Urgently, she whispered, "Fuck. Gonna come."

Diana gave her an encouraging caress, stroking her thumbs over the tender juncture of Jude's hips and thighs. She intensified the suction without altering her rhythm, then—right as Jude hit her peak—grabbed her right hand and held on tight. Grateful for the anchor, Jude reluctantly let go, allowing the tremendous pleasure to seize hold of her body for endless, earthshaking seconds. Uncontrolled moans and whimpers— along with other noises she'd never heard herself make before—escaped from Jude's open mouth throughout the lengthy duration of what had to be the greatest orgasm she'd ever experienced. Diana moaned with her, turning an already overwhelming climax into a true test of fortitude.

Muscles shaking, Jude fought to withstand as much of Diana's mastery as her body would allow, but eventually her left hand rebelled, sinking into Diana's lush hair to push her away.

"Stop," Jude breathed, hating herself for giving in. "*Fuck.*"

Diana placed one final kiss on her labia, then pushed back her chair and stood. "Come here," she murmured, slipping an arm beneath Jude's shoulders to help her sit. Heavy with exhaustion, Jude fell forward into Diana's open arms and buried her face in the soft, fragrant neck of the woman she secretly adored. Diana rocked her lightly, swaying their upper bodies from side to side while smoothing her palm up and down Jude's spine. "You did great," Diana whispered, making Jude snort. "Thank you."

Jude straightened to meet Diana's slightly unfocused eyes. "Thank *you.*" Noticing the clear arousal in her smoky gaze, Jude very deliberately brought her mouth to Diana's for a quick but passionate kiss. She groaned at the taste of her own juices on Diana's gorgeously full lips and pressed her tongue deeper, breaching the intoxicating heat of her shockingly adept mouth. Jude tightened her hands on Diana's shoulders and locked her legs around her thighs. They kissed for at least a full minute, which wasn't nearly as long as Jude wanted. She suppressed a disappointed frown when Diana broke away and expelled shaky, surprised laughter.

"Come back here." Urging Diana forward using the ankles she'd crossed behind her calves, Jude initiated another kiss. This one was shorter than the first but every bit as passionate.

Diana retreated, full of palpable regret. "Jude…" She hesitated, then gestured toward their audience. "I'm sorry. I wish we had more time to cuddle, but…"

Afraid to appear clingy, Jude waved off the apology. "Don't be silly. Of course. You have a workshop to run."

Diana spent a moment searching her face, then gathered Jude into another fast hug. "Let me check in with everyone. I'll be right back."

Embarrassed, Jude said, "I'm all right, you know."

"You're more than all right." Diana embraced her one last time, planting a friendly kiss on her cheek. "You're *magnificent.*"

Breathless at the compliment, Jude was almost relieved when Diana turned to face the group. She barely registered Diana's speech to the class, too fixated on the fact that she'd been licked to orgasm by the indomitable Ms. Kelley to focus on the educational takeaway of their encounter— the encounter that had changed her life forever. Blinking, Jude flitted her distracted gaze from student to student—none of whose names she remembered anymore—wondering if anyone in the room understood how powerfully shaken she was by all that had occurred before their eyes. Probably not, given how distracted everyone was by their respective partners. Right as Jude's attention drifted back to Diana, the older woman planted her hand in the center of Jude's bare chest.

"The class seems to be doing a fine job of keeping themselves occupied, and we still have forty minutes on the clock." She pressed lightly on Jude's clavicle, urging her to recline. "Why don't you lie back and let me demonstrate the multi-orgasmic magic of sex between women?"

Tempted as she was by the notion of an encore, Jude wanted something even more. Resisting Diana's attempt to maneuver her down onto the platform, she fingered the hem of her neighbor's form-fitting blouse, then tugged on the waistband of the linen pants she filled out to perfection. "Or you could grant me the privilege of reciprocating." She caught her bottom lip between her teeth, suggestively wetting the bruised flesh with the tip of her tongue. "You can show me how you like to be licked."

Diana's throat tensed, then bobbed. "Jude, I didn't ask you here tonight—" For the first time since they'd arrived at class, her easy confidence flagged. Looking past Jude, she said, "No reciprocation necessary. This workshop isn't about my gratification."

"Is it about mine?" Moving past the momentary sting of Diana's rejection, Jude clung to her certainty that the chemistry between them wasn't purely one-sided. "If so, please know that absolutely nothing would gratify me more than having you in my mouth." When Diana inhaled to answer, Jude interjected one more reason for her to say yes. "Besides…" She affected an exaggerated pout. "How will I ever learn unless you teach me?"

CHAPTER THREE

Diana was making a big mistake, and the worst part was she knew it already.

A massive mistake, she lamented—before her gnawing guilt all but disappeared at the first, tentative touch of Jude's tongue against her labia. Moaning, Diana used the hand not tangled in Jude's shiny brunette locks to brace herself against the edge of the platform upon which she knelt over her temporary assistant's head. She settled her weight more heavily onto Jude's sexy mouth, wiggling her hips while she reveled in the girl's white-knuckled fists and the impossibly stiff, highly suckable nipples she couldn't seem to stop touching.

She's your next-door neighbor, *for goodness' sake. Your entirely too young, more than likely emotionally immature neighbor. What happens when this little arrangement of ours goes pear-shaped?* Diana threw her head back and gasped, astounded by how quickly Jude had worked her into a state of pure, desperate need. She wouldn't beg, of course. Even if she wanted to.

What if she asks for sex outside class? Diana wasn't normally the conceited type, but she got the distinct impression that Jude had *really* enjoyed her orgasm. Living in such close proximity, it seemed inevitable that Jude might request another encounter at some point. A private one, on their own time. That would be a disaster. Diana was only three months away from turning forty, far too old for an eager, young fuck-buddy in the midst of such a vastly different stage of her life.

Granted, Jude *was* damn good at eating pussy—even better than expected.

"How will I ever learn unless you teach me?"

Diana groaned at the memory of Jude's seductive plea and her own pointed response. *"I can't believe you don't already know your way around a woman's body. In fact, I'm certain you do. I've heard as much through our bedroom wall."*

Jude had given her the greatest smile, one that made it impossible for Diana to say no. *"Grade me, then. Give me your final exam."*

So now here Diana hovered, bare from the waist down, over the busy mouth of the lively young seductress who'd somehow obliterated all her good sense with a single bat of her eyelashes. Those impeccable tits hadn't helped, either, being the prettiest Diana had ever kissed—an impressive distinction given her own prolific sexual history. Jude's ever-changing roster of overnight guests reminded Diana of her own freewheeling youth, before she'd made the foolish decision to commit to a woman who would go on to treat her like absolute shit for nearly five of the six long years they were together. Her ex-girlfriend Janine had taught her the value of caution in her interpersonal entanglements, an important lesson that grew somehow hazier and less relevant with every stroke of Jude's enthusiastic tongue.

It wasn't like she hadn't noticed Jude over the past year. She'd even fantasized about fucking her, more than twice, during some of the loneliest of her increasingly solitary nights at home. She was only human, after all. Jude wasn't just undeniably luscious in appearance, but she was also the proud owner of an abundant sexual appetite—one that had provided inspiration for Diana's self-pleasuring sessions ever since her first night in the building. Even if she'd wanted to ignore the girl next door, it would've been impossible. Jude had become a semi-frequent sight during Diana's trips into and out of the building where they lived their lives side by side, always with a smile on her face and a warm, casually flirtatious greeting to offer. Their brief interactions had provided Diana with more than enough material to assemble the occasional "sexual mentor to a younger woman" fantasy. They were also the reason she'd immediately thought of Jude after Ava's phone call.

So…yes. She'd been curious for a while. At least now that curiosity would be satisfied—even if she'd ruined their politely cordial relationship as a result.

Diana shuddered, then sat on her heels to let Jude heave for air. She ran her nails down the center of Jude's scalp, smiling. "That's nice, sweetheart. Really nice."

Jude's brow furrowed. *"Nice?"*

Clearly the compliment hadn't come across as intended. "Really, *really* nice." Diana rose onto her knees, then used her fingers to spread her labia apart. Jude's attention drifted to the sight and locked on. "You're making me very, *very* happy."

Jude rewarded her with a sweetly pleased grin. She turned her face to the side, licking Diana's inner thigh. "Then let me keep going. Let me make you *come*."

Such an unbelievably big mistake, Diana told herself for what felt like the hundredth time. Then, frustrated by her overactive sense of caution, she switched off her brain and let her body answer instead. "Yes."

In the car after the workshop, Diana kept her eyes on the dark highway stretched out ahead of them, too afraid to catch Jude's gaze to risk even the sneakiest of sidelong glances. She was pushing hard against the speed limit, eager to get Jude home and pay her the rest of the money she was due so they could slip back into their previous roles of somewhat friendly near-strangers. Sex with Jude had been spectacular—beyond her wildest imaginings, in fact—but Diana feared that what they'd done had altered the dynamic between them to a degree she'd never intended. Case in point, the wide-eyed crush Jude had apparently fallen victim to.

Despite the pointed remarks about finding older women sexy, Diana couldn't fathom why Jude would be interested in a woman her age. If her ears were to be trusted, Jude regularly entertained an entire harem of frisky young sex kittens. Even if tonight's cunnilingual exchange *had* been nothing short of magnificent, Diana didn't see any reason for Jude to get starry-eyed over a middle-aged neighbor she barely knew when she had a bustling city full of sexually active young women at her fingertips. *Literally, I'm sure. What do you want to bet she uses one of those silly phone apps to meet girls?*

Jude cleared her throat. "So, that was fun. Thanks for inviting me."

Diana smiled evenly, wishing she didn't feel so awkward in the aftermath of her self-made mess. It would be cruel to punish Jude for bailing out her judgment-impaired ass, especially by turning cold. "Thank *you* for being home—and willing."

"Oh, I'm pretty much *always* willing," Jude purred. Her sweet, low voice elicited a shiver that Diana failed miserably to suppress. "Part of my long-standing policy to try almost anything at least twice."

"Lucky me." Diana wanted to be unaffected by the flirtation, but how could she when her fingers still carried Jude's scent? When she could still taste the delicate flavor of that terrifically responsive pussy on her tongue? When she had yet to recover from the thundering climax Jude had so effortlessly sucked from her finicky clit?

Jude's impressive prowess probably shouldn't have surprised her—and didn't, for the most part. It was her own susceptibility to it that felt so unlikely. Over the past year or so, Ava had been finding it more and more difficult to reliably finish her off in front of the class, a development that led Diana to conclude that the easy access to bone-rattling orgasms she'd enjoyed in her youth was fading with age. But Jude was a time machine, taking her back to the sexually voracious days of her youth. She'd come before she'd wanted to, cursing while she continued to ride Jude's tongue because she knew her loss of self-control had brought an end to the greatest head she'd received in years.

Unaffected? Yeah, right. But Diana pretended to be, all the same. "You were really brave tonight. I know it couldn't have been easy to be so exposed, particularly in that setting."

Jude snorted. "Brave? Yeah, I don't know..." She raked a hand through her hair, enticing Diana to steal a tentative peek at her jubilant face. Jude's bright eyes instantly darted over to meet hers, and her grin widened. "Honestly, who *hasn't* fantasized about being the demonstration subject for a sex-education class?" Even with her attention now fixed on the road, Diana detected a hint of self-consciousness in Jude's answer to her own rhetorical question. "Plenty of people, I'm sure. But even if it's weird, that's one of the first fantasies I can remember having. I guess I've always been sort of kinky."

Ignoring their basic sexual compatibility would be a whole lot easier if Jude didn't insist on being so damn dirty in all the right ways. Pushing aside her curiosity about the other scenarios that comprised Jude's repertoire of fantasies, Diana gripped the steering wheel more tightly before offering a response she hoped wouldn't lead her into any further trouble. "I wouldn't have chosen to teach a hands-on workshop, let alone offer live demos, if I didn't also find aspects of that concept appealing."

"Which would be a crying shame. Like, seriously. You have a real gift for what you do."

Diana flexed her fingers as a droplet of sweat slowly tracked its way from her damp hairline to settle at the base of her neck. Its conspicuous, tickling journey caused her to flush even hotter. "That's sweet of you to say." In a knee-jerk bid to reestablish some professional distance, Diana redirected their conversation toward the least-suggestive topic possible. "By the way, don't let me forget to transfer the other two hundred dollars to your bank account before we head upstairs. I can do it in the car, on my phone."

"No worries."

In her peripheral vision, Diana caught a glimpse of Jude's slim hand creeping closer to her thigh. She stiffened, terrified by the prospect of Jude deciding to touch her. *Please, sweetheart. Don't.* They'd had a fun evening together, despite her unspoken fears, and she hated to ruin it now with a rejection. Scrambling to clarify their situation, Diana said, "Of course I'm worried. I want to make sure you're adequately compensated for sacrificing your Saturday evening. If not for Ava's accident, who knows? You might've gone out and met the girl of your dreams instead."

"Diana." Jude opened her mouth, but nothing came out. When she finally spoke, Diana sensed she'd amended her original response. "Nothing about tonight was a sacrifice. Let's be real. In exchange for three hours of my life I would've otherwise spent on the couch, you lavished me with pure, decadent pleasure—*and* paid a decent chunk of next month's rent. You have to admit that's a pretty sweet deal, with or without any more of your money."

"I'm glad you think so, but I insist on paying you the rest of what you're owed." She had to. This would become entirely too complicated if Jude waived her financial obligation. "I'm sure you could use the extra cash. I know I always did, at your age."

"I won't refuse to take your money." Jude's hand drifted to rest on her own lap, successfully averted from its dangerous path. "In case you were concerned that's what I was saying."

Diana forced a smile far lighter than she felt. "I'm not concerned." She engaged the turn signal, grateful for the distraction of a lane change. "I just want to be sure the terms of our collaboration remain crystal clear. For both our sakes."

"Of course." Jude's heavy sigh sent a shard of regret through the center of Diana's chest. "On that note, you know who to call if you ever need a stand-in for Ava in the future. I'd be happy to sub for you anytime."

"I'll keep that in mind." Diana thought ahead to the class she had scheduled for the following weekend—vaginal massage for couples. She envisioned caressing Jude's firm young body from head to toe with her oil-slathered hands, then sliding two fingers deep inside Jude's snug, impossibly wet vagina to stroke her into a zen-like state of absolute bliss. It alarmed her how tantalizing she found that particular flight of fancy. Afraid of where her raging libido might lead, Diana strove for both kindness and honesty in her measured response. "But—no offense—my hope is that Ava will be back in peak fucking condition before our next workshop. Not that you didn't do a wonderful job in her place, because you *definitely* did. It's just…I think our lives will be simpler as neighbors."

"As opposed to?" Jude asked the question like a dare.

"Neighbors who fuck. Even occasionally, on a professional basis."

"Got it." Jude tried rather obviously to hide the hurt inflicted by Diana's blunt response, but the audible quaver in her voice gave away her disappointment. "Well, it was nice while it lasted. I'm a huge fan of uncomplicated, no-strings-attached sex with women mature enough to know exactly what they want—something that's not always easy to find. That's why this was the perfect gig. Not to mention a crazy awesome way to earn dollars on the side."

"If I *do* end up needing someone to fill in for Ava, you're first on my list to call." Diana shot Jude a more genuine smile, hating that she'd dampened the ebullience of her afterglow with the reality check. "Promise."

"Cool." Jude folded her arms over her stomach and leaned back in her seat. "And just so you know, I won't get all clingy if you do." She chuckled with convincing ease. "I may be younger than you, but I *am* a big girl. Would I jump at the chance to do this again? Hell, yeah. You're hot, your pussy tastes like berries and sunshine, and I'm not sure I've ever come that hard from being eaten before. But does that mean I'm going to pester you to take me out to dinner or have sleepovers or make some sort of commitment? Fuck no. You don't want that." She hesitated, albeit only long enough to inhale. "And *I* don't want that. Therefore, there's no reason for things to get complicated. Agreed?"

Diana questioned the wisdom of allowing Jude's assurances to lower her guard, but at the same time…why on earth *would* a hot young thing like Jude eschew the sexual smorgasbord of early adulthood to chase a woman thirteen years her senior? A woman who had nothing to offer in return? Diana willed her shoulders to relax, then offered an amiable nod. "Agreed." Embracing the theory that polite small talk would feel less uncomfortable than silence, she assumed control of the conversation before Jude could. "So what do you do for a living? Not a schoolteacher, I assume."

"Absolutely not. I'd need to be a bigger fan of children to choose a career *that* extreme."

"You'd also have to be willing to forgo the sort of publicly lewd and lascivious behavior we got up to tonight." Diana smirked. "So, priorities to consider."

"Exactly right." Jude drummed her fingers on her thighs. "Wouldn't be worth it, even if the pay *is* better than my current salary."

Diana frowned. "Sounds like I was right about you being able to use the extra cash."

"It's not so bad. I'm currently eight months into two years of savings I've set aside to focus on my writing. At the moment, mainly freelance. But I'm also working on a novel, and a more autobiographical work of nonfiction…" Jude's drumming reached a sudden crescendo, then stopped. She nervously tucked her hands beneath her bobbing thighs. "Right now the freelancing is what mostly gets me by. Some months are better than others. Depends on how many pieces I'm able to sell, and to which outlet."

Wincing, Diana asked, "Does that mean I just paid to be turned into fodder for one of those millennial confessional essays about the author's wild and crazy sexcapades? Please say no."

She regretted the question the instant she heard Jude's affronted tone. "Nice try, but I don't write shit like that. I know you think you've got my generation pegged, but Diana? You don't have the first clue who I am or what I'm about. If you did, you'd damn well realize that I'm not the vapid, slutty child you've written me off as." Her voice, having steadily risen in volume, dropped to a sullen mutter. "Shit, if only you could see past your ridiculous, age-based stereotypes, you might even figure out I'm moderately likable as a human being."

Chastened, Diana squeezed the steering wheel until her hands ached. "You're right. I apologize." While she felt compelled to offer an explanation for her anti-social tendencies, she struggled to decide how much she wanted to reveal about her less-than-stellar personal life. "I'm sorry if I've been rude. The irony is that despite constantly preaching the importance of sexual intimacy within a committed relationship, my own personal history precludes me from ever wanting another situation like that for myself. I don't even date. There's no point anymore. I'm afraid my social skills have suffered as a result."

"Sounds lonely."

"Maybe, but I'd choose loneliness over total misery any day." Wishing she didn't care what Jude thought, Diana added, "Besides, I have Ava. When I want someone to talk to, I call her. When I need a warm body to fuck, she's usually available. What we have works for me precisely because it ends exactly where it should, at friendship."

Jude waited a beat before speaking. "Whoever hurt you must've been a real nightmare if she convinced you to give up on love altogether."

"That she was." No bones about it. Not wanting to discuss Janine, Diana rushed to the point she'd been trying to make. "Anyway, I'm sure that's why I've been abrupt with you. So as not to lead you on. It's not an excuse, but it is the reason."

"That's your 'back off, I'm not on the market' vibe?" Jude extracted her hands from beneath her thighs and folded them on her lap. "I can dig it. But like I said, don't worry about me. I'd enjoy having more sex with you, but I'm also perfectly content to return to trading hellos at the mailbox from time to time. I'll leave the future up to you. Either way, tonight was a fantastic time." She lowered her volume as Diana pulled off the exit and the hum of the freeway traffic diminished. "You knew exactly how to turn me on. It was incredible."

"To be fair, I *have* had a lot of practice at that sort of thing." Hoping to downplay their undeniable chemistry, Diana added, "And you weren't exactly subtle about what you like."

"Still. You were *good*."

"So were you." The truth slipped out of Diana before her brain could put the kibosh on her mouth. "It's been forever since I came that fast from oral alone."

"Oh, yeah?"

Jude's obvious pride made her feel marginally better about having just admitted something she probably should've kept to herself. "But don't tell Ava. I wouldn't want to hurt her feelings."

"Cross my heart." The confession appeared to have at least partially restored Jude's swagger. She sat up straighter, turning toward Diana to stare heatedly at a spot somewhere north of her tense jawline. "I have to say, I'm thrilled to hear it was also good for you. That's all I wanted, to give you a real orgasm."

"You did *very* well." Even as Diana scolded herself for her wantonness, she couldn't help but offer one final tease. "But you already knew that, didn't you? You're the one who licked me clean after I came all over your pretty face." Jude's shaky inhalation alerted Diana to her own hyper-aroused state, rapidly snapping her back to reality. "Sorry. On to another topic." She blinked, doing her best not to notice the barely perceptible rocking of Jude's hips against her seat. Needing a graceful escape from the hole she'd dug for herself once again—and after she'd just insisted she'd rather die than hold a shovel, let alone move dirt— Diana experienced an immense rush of potentially premature relief when she noticed they were only a few short blocks from home. "Look where we are. How's that for perfect timing?"

Jude snorted. "A couples' sex therapist who can't talk about sex. Who's afraid of *love*." She reached over the center console, explicitly telegraphing her intentions before giving Diana's knee a tender pat. "You really ought to see someone about that. A professional. I say this purely as a friend."

Diana snorted, too grateful that they'd reached the driveway of their building's private parking lot to let Jude's commentary disturb the protective armor she'd long ago erected around her emotional state. In fact, she *had* seen a therapist after breaking up with Janine. Her conclusion? Some issues aren't worth fixing. "I appreciate the unsolicited advice."

"I don't mean to offend you."

Diana threw the car into park, already hunting through her purse for her phone. "I'm not offended."

"It just makes me sad to think of you being alone for the rest of your life."

"Why?" She echoed Jude's earlier point—the one that had left her so chastised. "You don't know anything about me either, Jude. What makes you think I don't *relish* being alone?"

Jude shrugged. "Maybe you do."

"I absolutely do." Diana turned on her phone, then opened the bank app to complete the two-hundred-dollar transfer into Jude's account. "Nobody steals my blankets at night, or eats the last of my chocolate-chip-cookie-dough ice cream, or forces me to watch televised sports and awards shows. I can stay up late reading without having anyone scold me about turning off the light and getting enough sleep. I always get to pick the music and what's for dinner."

"Sounds like you've really thought this through."

Transaction complete, Diana returned the phone to her purse and fixed Jude with a placid smile. "Like I said, priorities to consider."

"Indeed." Jude put her hand on the door handle and gestured with her chin. "Shall we?"

Diana flinched, hit by an unexpected wave of sorrow in the wake of Jude's cool acceptance of her desire for solitude. But why? Jude was giving her exactly what she'd asked for, what she wanted.

Wasn't she?

Confused, even terrified, Diana could only manage a dumb nod before she threw open the driver's side door—and got the hell out of her Dodge.

CHAPTER FOUR

Early the next morning, Diana used her spare key to enter Ava's sunny, oversized studio apartment, calling out, "Sweetie, it's me. Are you up?"

Ava's strained voice answered from the other side of the room. "Pretty sure I'm never getting up again."

Frowning, Diana made her way across the clothing-strewn floor to stand over Ava's unmade bed. Her best friend's motionless body rested in the center of the mattress, stiff-limbed and in obvious pain. Alarmed by how badly Ava seemed to be suffering, Diana hurried to inspect the orange bottle of pills on her nightstand. "Is it time for another painkiller?"

"Fuck those things," Ava seethed through gritted teeth. "Goddamn opiate *bullshit*."

Diana put the bottle back in its place. "Okay, then." She turned to face the bed, taking note of the way Ava continued to stare resolutely at the ceiling. "Shall I roll you a joint instead?"

Ava's eyes softened ever so slightly. "I'd love you forever if you did."

Diana knelt to retrieve the necessary tray of supplies from beneath the nightstand, then perched gingerly on the edge of the mattress while she prepared Ava's preferred form of pain relief. "What the hell happened? You fell?"

"Off that ladder." Ava indicated it without moving, but Diana was too busy grinding a fresh batch of flowers to follow her gaze across the room. "The pain was unbearable."

Diana raised her eyes to Ava's, choking up at the catch in her friend's voice. "Why didn't you call me?"

"At some point during the excruciating lifetime I lay paralyzed on the floor, I settled upon this batshit theory that trained paramedics would be able to offer more relevant aid than my sex-guru bestie." Ava gritted her teeth while minutely shifting her weight to the side. "Well-intentioned though she may be."

"I had no clue you'd injured yourself this severely." Diana licked the seam of the joint to seal it closed. "You should have told me. I would've canceled class and taken care of you."

"Which is exactly why I didn't. What could you have done, exactly? Besides lose a small pile of cash." Ava beckoned for her medicinal herb, grimacing. "Light that bad boy and hold it to my mouth, will you?"

Diana sparked up the lighter, burned away the twisted paper at the tip, and took a hearty drag to start them off. Without exhaling, she flipped the joint around to insert the unlit end between Ava's parted lips and kept it there while Ava inhaled a long, careful drag. She held the smoke in her lungs for a good five seconds, then cautiously exhaled without a single cough. Diana released her own cloud of smoke, grateful for Ava's practiced finesse. "Nicely done," she said, giving Ava another hit. "Hopefully this helps."

Ava closed her eyes after the second exhalation. "It sure as hell doesn't hurt."

"What did the doctor say?" She kept the smoldering joint within Ava's reach, just in case. "How long until you recover?"

Ava's face crumpled. "I don't know."

Diana curled her free hand around Ava's, giving the cold fingers a soothing caress. "Sweetheart, you're going to be okay. Even if it takes weeks, or months, you *will* heal."

Tears streamed from the corners of Ava's tightly shut eyes. "Doc said it's a spinal fracture. Exacerbated by the fucking early onset *osteoporosis* she diagnosed me with. So there's that."

"Oh, Ava." Diana nudged the joint against Ava's lips once more. Once she'd taken another long drag, Diana set the smoldering roach in Ava's favorite bedside ashtray and stretched out to lie alongside her. Realistically, she had no idea what such a diagnosis meant for Ava, so she didn't dare suggest she might be overreacting. *Listen to her fears. Validate them. Present an alternate point of view.* "I'm sorry. I know that must have been hard to hear. Getting old sucks enough without a chronic disease to worry about."

"You're telling me." Ava managed a wry smirk. "Cherish your relative youth, Diana. It'll be over before you know it."

Diana flashed back to the supple perfection of Jude's luscious curves, her flawlessly smooth skin, and the endless river of liquid heat that flowed from her tight little pussy. Osteoporosis was one way to feel old. Finger-fucking a twenty-six-year-old was most definitely another. "I'll try. At least for the next few months."

Ava opened her eyes with an exaggerated roll. "No more complaining about turning forty. Not to me." She lifted her hand off the bed, waving for another toke from the joint. "Never again."

Diana obliged, glad for some way to ease Ava's discomfort. She remained silent for the span of three lengthy inhalations, until Ava indicated that she didn't want any more. Then she tossed the roach into the ashtray and sighed. "You're right. That was insensitive. And while I *do* understand why you're upset…even if your bones are brittler than they used to be, you're still every inch the sexy beast who took my virginity in college."

Ava snorted, finally delivering a genuine smile. "*After* college, thank you very much. I have a very distinct memory of waiting until the idea of bedding you no longer felt unforgivably unethical, but merely…sort of creepy."

"Oh, come on." Diana rose up on her elbow to grin down at a decidedly mellowed Ava. "Popping my cherry wasn't *creepy*. I was never enrolled in any of your classes. I may have been a student at the college where you taught, but you were never *my* professor."

"A technicality that ultimately convinced me to give in to your seductive ways." Ava's eyes welled with renewed emotion. "Thank goodness."

"Kind of a shame we made better friends than lovers, isn't it?" Diana turned wistful as she reflected on their brief, ultimately unsuccessful romantic entanglement and the years of friendship that had followed. "No one has ever been there for me like you always have."

Ava angled her face to press her lips against Diana's forearm. "Like I always will." She resumed her original position with a muted whimper. "I love you, Diana. Even if I can't picture actually sharing a life and a home with you."

Diana would've been more offended if she didn't agree. As much as she adored Ava as a human being, her freewheeling, scatterbrained ways would bring the wrong kind of insanity to their hypothetical romantic partnership. "Ditto." She rested her hand on Ava's stomach and rubbed gentle circles over the thin material of her camisole. "What else can I do to make you feel better?"

Ava chuckled humorlessly. "Oh, I don't know. Uncover the fountain of youth? Cast a magical bone-density-restoration spell?"

Diana attempted a flirtatious eyebrow-waggle. "I meant more along the lines of favors that require my very specialized set of skills."

Ava met her offer with a blatantly disapproving stare. "You've got to be kidding."

Chastised, Diana gave a helpless shrug. "Orgasms release endorphins. Endorphins kill pain. I only wanted to help."

Ava studied her through narrowed eyes. "What *did* you end up doing last night? I hope you didn't have to cancel the workshop." Her entire countenance grew even more tormented. "I felt awful for putting you in that position. You *and* your students."

Diana shook her head, glad to be able to assuage Ava's guilt, yet wary to reveal her confusion about the substitute she'd recruited. "No worries. Believe it or not, I found someone to take your place."

Ava's eyebrow popped, a sure sign she was properly intrigued. "Oh, really. Maya?"

"Now *you've* got to be kidding."

"What?" Ava shot her a pointed look. "I'm sure she'd have said yes."

Diana shifted her gaze over Ava's head, to the far wall. "Probably so, but I stopped seeing Maya for a reason. You don't think it'd be unspeakably cruel to lead her on by offering paid sex after she was so clear about wanting more than I'm willing to give?"

Ava sighed. "Maybe I thought you'd decided to reevaluate your stance on romantic commitment. If you *were* to give love another shot, Maya would be a great choice. Smart, funny, sexy—an amazing cook, to boot. With one fantastically bang-able ass." She caressed Diana's cheek, pulling her focus back to the face she loved most in the world. "Listen, I know how you feel about dating since Janine. And I understand. I mean, I don't *exactly*…but I think I can imagine. It must be scary as shit to think about trusting someone new when the last woman you loved turned out to be a mean-spirited, abusive asshole who kept you in absolute misery for six long years."

"But also, I'm happy being single." Diana spoke calmly, as though Ava's decision to traverse this well-trod topic yet again didn't bother her in the slightest. "Simple as that. I do what I want, when I want. I eat what I want, sleep when I want…watch only the television shows I want." Rattling off the standard rationalizations, she bared her teeth in a mock predatory grin. "If I feel like getting laid, I've got you. Or one-night stands. Or my hand." She snuck her fingers beneath the hem of Ava's camisole, stroking the soft skin of her belly. "Why complicate my life when I already have everything I could possibly need?"

Ava's mouth turned down at the corners. "What happens when Lucy Lawless finally comes to sweep me off my feet? You *do* understand it's entirely possible I won't always be available to play the role of best friend with benefits."

"What? Lucy can't share?" Diana gazed down at Ava's troubled expression. "Listen, we're not together. You're under no obligation to continue fucking me if someone else comes along. I'm content to savor you while I've got you, but beyond that...well, maybe one day I'll put myself back on the market. I'm not close to there yet, but who knows?" She lowered her hand to brush across the alluring swell of Ava's panty-clad vulva. "Maybe seeing you and Ms. Lawless together will inspire me to give true love another chance."

"Seeing us *together*, together, or..." Ava bit her lower lip as Diana scratched two fingernails up the length of her concealed labia.

"You can't expect me not to demand front-row seats for the spectacle of my best friend bedding *Xena*." Diana kissed the corner of Ava's mouth, treating the body beneath hers as though it were made of glass. "Hopefully Lucy will be cool with it, too."

Ava braced her palm against the center of Diana's chest. "Down, girl. Stop trying to distract me from the topic at hand."

"What topic would that be?" Settling at her side, Diana laid her hand atop the damp crotch of Ava's panties to delight in her obvious arousal. "I thought we were making you feel better."

Ava groaned. "I feel *much* better, thank you. But I'm dying to know who took my place last night."

Further evasion would only suggest she had something to hide. Diana said, "Remember my hot little next-door neighbor?"

"The wild child?" Ava raised both eyebrows, apparently surprised—perhaps even tickled—by the revelation. "Young Miss Sex in the City Junior, who fucks for hours on the other side of your bedroom wall?"

"Her name is Jude. And yes."

Tittering, Ava covered Diana's roving hand with her own. "I know her name. God knows I've heard it screamed often enough during our sleepovers."

"Precisely why she was the sole option who came to mind. Though I almost didn't ask. I nearly chickened out right after I knocked on her door. But…she seemed so open. And extremely intrigued."

Ava laughed. "I'll bet."

"Everything worked out. She was a bit nervous, as you can imagine, but enthusiastic. *Very* enthusiastic." Hopeful she'd shared enough to sate Ava's curiosity, Diana rubbed more firmly against the thin satin barrier keeping her from the swollen folds she could feel beneath her fingers. "Even so, I hope you'll feel up to joining me at next weekend's workshop. It's only a yoni massage. Remember? All you have to do is lie there and soak in the pleasure."

Ava's nose crinkled. "I don't know, Diana. I hate to put you in a bad spot, but I'm not sure when I'll be up for something like that again."

Hating herself, Diana said, "Our students really missed you, Ava. *I* missed you."

"And I missed having my pussy licked, but…" Ava inhaled audibly, clutching Diana's hand tighter when she traced an exploratory circle around the hidden but prominent clit under her fingertip. "As much as I want to, believe me, I'm quite certain my body isn't up to the task."

Diana attempted to withdraw her hand, but Ava held on, keeping it in place between her legs. Embarrassed by her uncharacteristic pushiness, Diana first made eye contact, then lowered her face to convey the shame that emanated from her every pore. "Some friend, huh? Contrary to how it must seem, I didn't come here intending to pressure you into sex you don't want."

"Hey." The kindness in Ava's voice made it clear that she'd not only noticed Diana's mortification, but also that not all was well in her world. "I told you, I want to. It's just that I truly am in a tremendous amount of pain. Maybe not at this *exact* moment, thanks to you, but if I were to let you stick your fingers inside me? Well, I know where that leads, and the associated muscular contractions and bodily movements are by nature quite uncontrollable. It's only been twenty-four hours since the accident, Diana, and…I'm afraid I'd pay for it later."

"I understand." Diana smiled, and Ava allowed her to remove the hand from between her thighs. "I'm sorry I even went there. Obviously I have a problem."

"Yeah, you're lonely." Before Diana could rebut that misdiagnosis, Ava shifted the conversation back to the subject she'd most wanted to leave behind. "I'm surprised the sex kitten didn't wear you out last night.

Unless…wait, you didn't let her reciprocate, did you?" Her lips pursed. "It would certainly change my opinion of her to learn that she didn't even offer."

"She offered, I accepted." Opting to stay as honest as possible, Diana shifted her effort toward conveying nonchalance. "It was lovely. I sat on her face and came in her mouth. After that I paid her what I owed her and sent her on her way."

Ava snickered. "Sounds like an ideal Saturday night from your perspective."

"It was fun enough." Diana put her hand on Ava's, which lingered at the juncture of her thighs. "I still prefer working with you, of course."

"You know I love being your faithful sidekick. Unfortunately, my mobility will be severely limited for the eight to ten weeks it'll take for this fracture to heal. Only *then* will I be able to get started on physical therapy and the real recovery."

Diana's stomach dropped. "Wait. Are you saying it'll be eight to ten weeks before you're ready to come back to work?"

Eyes shimmering with what appeared to be sincere guilt, Ava whispered, "At the very least, yes. Unless something changes or I heal much faster than expected…" Her voice caught. "I'm so sorry to do this to you, Di. Maybe Jude would be interested in supplementing her income for the next few months? She might not be me, but hiring her would prevent any financial hardship on your part. We both know you can't exactly afford to wait for me to get better."

Diana was barely listening by that point, too immersed in the puzzle of how to move forward without Ava to pretend that losing her trusted assistant, even temporarily, was no big deal. "Shit."

"Are you worried Jude won't be interested?" Ava watched her closely. "Assuming she's comfortable being watched, I can't imagine she didn't have a great time working with you. You have an insanely talented tongue."

Diana confessed the partial truth. "No. I'm worried Jude may have already developed a mild crush on me after last night. If that's the case, asking for more sex is *not* the right way to handle the situation. Even if I've misread her feelings, it strikes me as a terrible idea in general to further complicate our…acquaintance."

"You don't think it'll work to set your boundaries in advance?" Ava's piercing gaze cut straight through Diana and left her feeling naked. "I could be wrong, but Jude doesn't strike me as the clingy type. She clearly doesn't have any trouble finding regular sexual partners, and—no offense—it seems unlikely that a young lady who appears to prefer her social life casual will suddenly decide she wants to settle down with… such a mature woman."

"Ouch." Diana pinched Ava's knuckle. "While you're probably right, she did drop multiple hints about being attracted to older women."

"Because older women *are* attractive." Ava turned her hand over, lacing their fingers together. "I have no doubt she wants to fuck you, sweetie. You're objectively gorgeous and only seem to improve with age."

Diana narrowly avoided rolling her eyes, a response that would've drawn a swift rebuke. Ava was being sincere, of course, but it had been ages since Diana last believed in her own appeal. The years of cruel insults and gas-lighting from Janine had eroded the effortless self-assurance she'd once possessed, back when she was Jude's age and still bought into the fairy-tale notion of perfect, everlasting love. "Thank you."

"How was it, going down on her? Did you enjoy yourself?"

Diana succumbed to a wolfish grin. "You've seen her. She tastes every bit as delicious as she looks."

"Lucky bitch." Ava winked. "Maybe I'm doing you a favor."

"Maybe." Except that every cell in Diana's body screamed that to ever touch Jude again would be a serious mistake. One that could all too easily upset the fragile inner peace she'd finally achieved. On the other hand, Ava *did* have a point. Wasn't it unforgivably arrogant to believe a stunning young lady in the midst of her indulgent, carefree youth might actually desire more from her cynical, soon-to-be middle-aged next-door neighbor than no-strings-attached sex? "It would definitely be safer to ask Jude than poor, sweet Maya."

"That's for sure." Ava gave her fingers a weak squeeze, then relocated Diana's hand back to her side of the mattress. "Now be a dear and roll a few more. I have a feeling this will be a long, hard few months for both of us."

CHAPTER FIVE

Hoping to arrive early for the first coffee date she'd made since Diana Kelley ruined her for the rest of womankind, Jude threw open her apartment door to find the woman she was desperate to forget standing on her welcome mat. Diana held a large paper sack in the hand still poised to knock, and a bottle of wine in the one hanging stiffly at her side. Jude noted with amusement that Diana looked every bit as shocked to see her as she was to see Diana, an observation that would've tickled her even more if her heart weren't about to crash through her chest wall. "Diana, hello," she said, impressed by her ability to vocalize coherently. "How are you?"

Diana scanned the length of Jude's body before raising her vibrant blue eyes to study her flushed face. "I'm well—but a master of bad timing, it seems."

In a daze, Jude glanced down, instantly recalling her strategic decision to present tonight's random right-swiper with all the cleavage she could safely display in a public venue. Provocative attire had always been one of her go-to strategies for getting laid, as showing off her tits usually increased the success rate. Five days past the best sex she was ever likely to have—courtesy of the woman who secretly owned her heart yet wanted nothing to do with her—Jude had decided to test her theory that the most efficient way to get over a stupid, unrequited infatuation was meaningless sex with a hot stranger. Whatever pleasure she could find through a smartphone app was all but destined to be a pale imitation of the real thing, but she needed to do *something* besides fantasize about the unattainable.

Of course, if staying in with Diana was now an option, then to hell with getting over anything.

Jude smiled, pretending she wasn't nonplussed about this apparent reversal of Diana's policy covering fraternization with neighbors. "Not at all." She stepped aside with a sweep of her arm. "Would you like to come in?"

Diana paused at the threshold. She took a deep breath, then met Jude's eyes. "I meant what I said about not dating, about staying away from relationships. But I need to talk to you about something. And..." She lifted both the paper sack and the wine into the air with an awkward shrug. "I feel like I owe you dinner. At a minimum. You know, after I..." She released a slow, somewhat unsteady breath. "After I ended Saturday night rather abruptly. You did me such a big favor, and I repaid you by being a jerk."

Taking mercy, Jude placed her hand on Diana's wrist and squeezed. "Dinner sounds amazing, but please don't beat yourself up on my behalf. You weren't a jerk, and I really *am* a big girl. I was all right with the way we left things."

"Even so." Diana nodded at the food in her hand. "Ever tried that Himalayan place downtown? It's to die for."

"I haven't." Jude again ushered Diana inside. "But I'm sold."

"Great." Diana moved forward half a step, then stopped, frowning. "Wait. You're dressed to go out. Are you sure I'm not interrupting other plans?"

"I'll cancel." Jude kept on waving Diana into her apartment. "It was only a coffee date, and I've never even met the woman. She's not someone I was super excited to go out with, anyway, so believe me..." She caught herself right on the cusp of an admission she'd regret. "If you've got food in hand and something to discuss, I'm happy to cancel. Relieved, even. She seemed like a real narcissist. Selfies galore."

Apparently conflicted, Diana remained paralyzed in the doorway. "You're sure?"

"Positive." Taking a chance, Jude clasped Diana's wrist and pulled her inside so she could close the door on the rest of the world. "Dinner smells *delicious.*" She led Diana into the apartment, to a small wooden dining table in her kitchen and its two matching chairs. "Sit. I'll grab a couple of glasses for that wine—just as soon as I let Madison know I can't make it."

Diana sank down onto one of the chairs with a muted sigh. "Poor Madison. She has no idea what she's missing." When Jude didn't answer, busy composing the most apologetic text possible on such short notice,

Diana added, "Maybe one day. You must've been *mildly* interested to show up for coffee looking like you do."

"Like what?" Jude's thumb flew over the on-screen keyboard for another few seconds before she hit send. Then she raised her face to meet Diana's watchful gaze. "Exactly?"

"Like a gorgeous, sexually vivacious woman on the prowl."

Jude grinned, pleased by the assessment. "I never said I wasn't on the prowl."

Diana coughed awkwardly yet didn't break eye contact. After a beat, she said, "If sex is your goal tonight, I'm not sure I should keep you from the hunt."

"Don't be ridiculous. I've got two hands and an imagination. I'll be fine." Jude discarded her muted phone on the kitchen counter and retrieved two wineglasses from the cupboard, along with a rabbit-style corkscrew for the bottle. "Anyway, I'm not about to pass up the opportunity to get to know my secretly fascinating neighbor a little better." She set the glasses on the table, then smoothly uncorked the bottle to pour them each a healthy serving of social lubricant. "Before you took me to school last weekend—literally—I never would've guessed what you did for a living. How does someone as private and unassuming as you end up a sex therapist? One offering hands-on workshops, at that? You always struck me as more… corporate, I guess. Conservative."

Jude's heart sank when the smile briefly slid off Diana's face. Though she quickly recovered, the comments had clearly struck a nerve. "I started the workshops only three years ago. I also offer sex-therapy sessions for individuals and couples. Strictly talk therapy, though I do assign homework, and the discussions are often quite frank. I've also worked with survivors of sexual trauma, specifically through trauma-focused cognitive-behavioral therapy."

"Wow." Jude sat down even more impressed than before—a feat she'd hardly thought possible. Why did the most compelling woman in her life also have to be the most inaccessible? Groping for an intelligent-sounding response, she said, "You're so accomplished, and at such a young age."

"I'm thirty-nine." Diana arched an eyebrow. "Hardly young. And I wouldn't call myself all that accomplished."

"You seem to have your shit together. You're doing work I assume you must love. That isn't a career path you take unless you believe in the cause, right?"

"Right." Diana pushed a container of food across the table, then another. "Hopefully you'll like what I ordered. There's mixed-veggie tikka masala, brown rice, a mushroom pakora appetizer with three different chutneys, and naan bread, of course."

Jude stared at the food for a moment, then leapt back onto her feet. "I'll get plates and utensils."

"I hope you're hungry."

With the memory of Diana's flavor still haunting her lips, Jude limited herself to a one-word reply. "Starving." Supplies in hand, she strolled to the table and put a plate and utensils in front of Diana, then sat down. "Thanks for the food. I admit, I don't eat as regularly or as well as I should." She dished out a large scoop of rice and veggie tikka masala, then served a small pile of crispy mushroom fritters onto her plate along with a dollop of each chutney. Finally she grabbed a quarter slice of naan bread from within the aluminum-foil wrapping and took a hearty bite that triggered a deeply satisfied moan. "This seriously hits the spot."

Diana watched with what Jude wished was actually the mixture of amusement and minor attraction she thought she saw in those brilliant blue eyes. "I'm glad you're pleased with my choices."

"I already can't wait until the next time I'll get to eat this food." Jude paused her enthusiastic taste-test to display a broad grin. "Thanks for introducing me to my new favorite place."

Having taken a smaller portion of everything available, Diana had a bite of rice and veggies. "It is rather excellent, isn't it?"

"What can I say? You've got great taste."

To Jude's dismay, Diana's smile threatened to disappear once more, but she salvaged her aura of cheerful warmth before it could slip away. "I must. Look who I recruited to assist in Ava's place. Between you and me, I've received three separate emails from students asking if you would come back for another session in the future. Apparently you made some fans."

Flattered, Jude set down her fork and had a drink of wine. If they were going to talk about the workshop, she would need all the liquid fortitude she could swallow. After draining a full third of the glass, she said, "It's nice to hear that my performance was well-received. Though to be fair, you did most of the work."

"I don't know about that." Diana sipped from her own glass. The delicate movement of her throat caused Jude's clit to throb and her breathing to quicken. By the time Diana traded the glass for her fork, Jude was comically wet. "I'd say you got quite the workout of your own."

"True." Jude shoveled another bite of food into her mouth, not because she was hungry, but because she needed to regain her cool while she chewed. Watching Diana nibble on the naan, she fought to vanquish the memory of that incredible tongue inside her. How perfect it felt. How she'd licked Jude's clit and labia so intuitively, so surely, that it almost seemed as though Diana knew her body even better than she did.

Diana broke the increasingly noticeable silence growing between them. "I should probably get right to the point. About why I'm here, that is."

"Sure." Jude polished off the remainder of her wine in one gulp. "What's up?"

"Well…" Diana inhaled. "Turns out, Ava's injury is more severe than I first realized. She fractured her spine in the fall, which led to a diagnosis of early onset osteoporosis."

Jude managed a quietly sympathetic "Ouch," even as her inner horndog exploded with pure, raucous joy. All of a sudden she knew what Diana wanted. "I'm so sorry."

"Yes. She's having a tough time of it. I can't blame her. She's in a lot of pain, and recovery will take months."

"Poor thing. What can I do to help?" Jude held her breath upon blurting the question, afraid Diana would deem it too forward. A blatant bid for more sex. Afraid to hear the answer, Jude clarified her point. "I happen to know an excellent home caregiver. She's also trained in physical therapy. Maybe Ava would like her number?"

Diana sat up straighter, a new light shining in her eyes. "I'm not sure how much Ava can afford to pay, but maybe if I pitched in half…do you think your friend would even be available? Is this someone you trust?"

Thrilled to have piqued Diana's interest—even if only about her cousin Katrina—Jude gave an enthusiastic nod. "I trust Katrina completely. As far as availability…I'll ask, if you'd like. Even if you hired her to stop by for an hour or two every day to check in and help out, I'm sure Ava would appreciate that."

"Katrina doesn't have a problem with medical marijuana, does she? Because Ava's not shy about her pain reliever of choice."

Jude snorted. "I'm sure Katrina would rather watch a patient use a harmless plant than have them popping pills all day long."

"Excellent." Diana popped one last mushroom into her mouth, then pushed her plate away. "Let me know what she says and how much she'd charge to spend two or three hours a day caring for my sweet, funny, currently very depressed best friend."

"Will do." Ashamed of her earlier celebration, Jude regarded Diana somberly. "I feel terrible for Ava. It must totally suck to have a minor accident leave you so helpless. To have your body betray you like that."

"Aging's a bitch." Diana reached for the wine and poured herself another. She moved the mouth of the bottle over Jude's empty drink and waited. "More?"

"Only half a glass. You don't want to get me drunk."

"No?" Diana smirked as she poured the requested amount.

"Not unless you're ready for an even hornier and more uninhibited version of me."

Diana corked the bottle and set it aside. "Thanks for the warning."

"Just respecting your boundaries." Jude raised her glass. "Here's to Ava's speedy recovery."

"I'll drink to that." Diana tapped her rim against Jude's, then drained half her refill in one go. "So listen…with Ava out of commission, I need to hire an assistant to help out at the next six workshops I've got on the schedule. That means through the end of next month, at a minimum. I do have someone else I can ask, so please don't feel obligated to say yes."

"Yes," Jude said, forgetting to stay cool. "I mean…I could really use the extra money. A job like that will buy me another few months of writing time before I hit the point where finding another full-time gig is no longer optional."

"Understood." Diana started to speak, then hesitated, searching Jude's eyes. "I hope this is okay…"

Frightened by her cautious tone, Jude prompted her. "Yes?"

"But I may have done a few online searches, and…" Diana winced adorably. "May have come across some of your published works."

"Oh." Jude felt ready to burst into flames. Had Diana actually *read* her stuff? "And?"

"And you're a fine writer. I mean it, Jude. You have real talent and a remarkably appealing narrative voice…" Seemingly embarrassed—about which part, Jude didn't know—Diana concluded by clearing her throat. "Anyway, I want you to know how delighted I am to help support those efforts. You deserve all the success I know you'll achieve."

"One day, hopefully." Humbled by the feedback, and that Diana had cared enough to seek out her work in the first place, Jude sought to alleviate any guilt over the surreptitious consumption of her words. "It's cool, by the way. That you googled me. I told you I was a freelance writer, so I don't blame you for being curious. Really, I should've expected it... the Internet *does* exist, after all."

Diana tipped her head in gratitude. "It's important to me that whatever arrangement we make be as mutually beneficial as possible." She picked up her glass, noticed it was empty, and lowered it back to the table with a bittersweet chuckle. "It hardly feels right, asking for this."

"You know I don't mind." At the risk of sounding overeager, Jude said, "You also know I love sex for its own sake. Getting paid only sweetens the deal."

"Well, don't sign away your Saturday nights just yet. We need to talk about the roster—and the subject matter. There may be one or two workshops you aren't comfortable participating in. Which would be *fine*, in case you were wondering. No hard feelings whatsoever." After a brief hesitation, Diana grabbed the bottle of wine and poured herself some more. "I'm sorry. I tried to resist, but—"

Jude dismissed the apology, shaking her head. "You don't have to stop just because I did."

"I promise I won't get horny and stupid." Diana paused to take a long sip, then refilled the glass to the halfway point before corking the bottle. "Just more relaxed. I hope."

"Why are you so nervous around me?" Jude extended her leg until her foot brushed against Diana's, delighting in her restrained jolt at the playful contact. "We've already given each other orgasms, for goodness' sake. You've seen me naked. And I've promised you, repeatedly, that regardless of what happens in your workshops, our relationship will remain strictly professional in nature. If not one-hundred-percent platonic."

Diana downed some more wine. Then she met Jude's steady gaze with a wry grin. "You're correct that my anxiety is most likely overblown. On the other hand...of the two of us, I'm the only one currently aware of the wide range of sexual acts I want to pay you to perform."

"Color me captivated." Jude leaned closer. "Go on, please. Tell me what I have to look forward to."

Smirking, Diana folded her arms over her very attractive chest and leaned back in her chair. "First and foremost, I apologize for the short notice. This upcoming Saturday—as in the day after tomorrow—I'm teaching vaginal massage for couples. That's an easy one. All you have to do is lie back, spread your legs, and let me demonstrate key techniques for the students. Many women orgasm from a yoni massage, but that's not necessarily the goal."

Jude's previously advertised imagination was already working overtime to determine how that might look and feel. "Sounds like a kick-ass Saturday night to me."

"I won't actually need you the following weekend. I'm teaching a class about the physical and emotional benefits of solo masturbation, thus no partner needed."

Jude circled the date on her mental calendar. "Got it. What else?"

"Next one's all about role-playing—my intention is to let the class pick the scenario for us, and we'll provide ideas and inspiration about how to run with whatever characters and situations they devise."

"Right-on!" Jude didn't bother to hide her enthusiasm. "I love role-playing."

"I figured you might." Winking, Diana hurriedly moved on. "Then a class on exploring power dynamics, focused primarily on spanking and other disciplinary techniques."

Jude's nose wrinkled before she could suppress the instinctive reaction. "Oh."

"It's all right if you'd prefer to skip that one." Diana searched her eyes. "Spanking and discipline aren't for everyone."

"I don't *want* to skip anything, but to be totally honest…you're right. It's not really my thing."

"Sexual spanking in general, or being spanked yourself?"

"Being spanked, for sure." Jude imagined positioning Diana facedown over her lap, then delivering alternating, increasingly powerful smacks across her quivering cheeks. She grew instantly wetter, proof she wasn't entirely cold to the overall concept. "But I *can* see the appeal of doing it to someone else."

"If you're more comfortable in the role of disciplinarian, I'm happy to be the spankee." Diana patted Jude's wrist, intensifying her arousal tenfold. "We can review the lesson plan beforehand and work together to choreograph a scene you'll feel okay performing. More than anything, it's important to me that you have fun with this job. And that you're satisfied with absolutely everything we do together."

"So far, so good." Without thinking, Jude stroked her thumb over Diana's knuckle in a light caress. "Tell me what's next."

"Wonderful." Diana's easy grin seemed to confirm that the alcohol was doing its job. "Then there's a strap-on workshop, followed by a beginners' class on anal sex—"

"Always Start Slow," Jude said, recalling the multi-purpose motto Diana had shared with the cunnilingus crowd. "I figured you'd get around to butt stuff eventually."

"Tell me about your stance on 'butt stuff.' Willing to give, willing to receive, or not willing to go there at all?"

"I've taken a finger in my ass before. A few times, actually. It was good, I liked it. Of course, there was this one chick who tried to shove in two fingers at once—I stopped her pretty fast." Jude winced at the memory of that awkward, drunken, fumbling encounter, one of far too many that had left her distinctly unsatisfied. "Too painful."

Diana cringed along with her. "I teach my students that pleasurable anal penetration requires time, patience, close communication, and crazy amounts of lube. Skimp on any one of those ingredients, and the result will likely be less than ideal."

"Another benefit of choosing a partner who boasts extensive sexual expertise." Jude licked her lips. The more Diana relaxed, the harder it was to keep her libido in check. "To be honest, I look forward to receiving expert-level ass-play instruction. It's not like I haven't fantasized about butt-fucking for…well, basically forever. I've just never trusted any of the women I've slept with to take it further than a single finger."

"You think you'll be able to trust me?"

"Diana, I already do." Jude didn't know how or why, but it was true. "I can't think of anyone better to be my first. You *are* a trained professional, are you not?" *Also, I kind of love you.* "Will you use your fingers, or a toy?"

"That's up to you." Diana's attention drifted to the nearly empty bottle of wine. Staring longingly, she said, "Ava's a big fan of anal, so she usually has me wear a strap-on with a medium-sized dildo. Don't worry. I'm not expecting the same from you. I'll let you decide how far you want to go, then do my best to take you there as gently as possible."

"What if I wanted to try the strap-on, too?" The mere thought of it thrilled Jude. "Do you think it could feel as good for me as it does for Ava?"

Diana swiped the bottle from the edge of the table, filling her glass with another inch of wine. "Everybody is different, naturally, but I can promise to go very, very slow, and to stop the instant you're no longer having the time of your life."

Jude was ready to ask Diana to take her into the bedroom right then and there, but restrained herself with the knowledge that such overt enthusiasm would only scare her away. "Then I'm in. What else?"

Diana hesitated. "I actually haven't scheduled any workshops past that one. I'd already planned to take a couple weeks off in the spring to visit my brother and his son in Santa Fe, and Ava and I hadn't finalized the summer roster yet."

Jude wrangled her synapses to tally the items on Diana's list of fantasy fodder. "But I thought you needed an assistant for the next six workshops, minimum. I counted only five."

Diana gulped her final sip of wine, then put the glass down before lapsing into a fairly unconvincing moment of epiphany. "Yes. Sorry." She pointed at her empty glass, then the bottle. "This might be going to my head—a little."

"That's all right." Jude angled her lower body away from the table and crossed one silky-smooth leg over the other. The hem of her fitted skirt remained firmly in place two inches above her knee, but Diana stared at Jude's lap as though willing the material to ride up even higher. "This is for sure the most fucked-up job interview I've ever had. I'm guessing you would say the same."

"Indeed." Diana grabbed another piece of naan, nibbling nervously for a full fifteen seconds before she spoke again. "The sixth workshop… it's possible I could simply cancel it, this far out. Or postpone until after my vacation. I think only six people have registered so far. Definitely no more than eight. It would be the easiest to reschedule."

"Is the subject matter *that* kinky? Or is there some other reason you no longer want to hire me for workshop number six?" Jude tried not to take Diana's reluctance personally, but it was excruciating to feel undesirable in the eyes of someone whose approval and respect she craved beyond reason. "Because I'll do anything you want. Or *almost* anything, I guess. Depends on how fucked up this secret class really is."

"It's not fucked up," Diana murmured. "Or secret." Sighing, she tossed the rest of her bread onto her plate and reestablished the eye contact she'd temporarily abandoned. "Thing is, that last workshop is about helping couples achieve genuine sexual intimacy. Literally, it's listed on my website under the title How to Make Love. My apologies if that term makes you cringe."

Jude scoffed at the assumption about her apparently cynical nature. "Why would it? Because I'm young and waste my nights fucking women I meet on shitty hookup apps?"

Tipsy or not, Diana seemed to recognize that she'd struck a nerve. "I didn't mean to offend you. I'm just aware…" She lifted her shoulders sheepishly. "Plenty of people consider 'lovemaking' to be a hopelessly old-fashioned way to describe an exchange of sexual intimacy. I've triggered more than a few cringes with the word, which is why I've developed the habit of issuing a preemptive apology whenever I use it with someone new." To Jude's stomach-clenching delight, Diana leaned over the table to touch her forearm. "It wasn't personal. Truly."

A few seconds passed before Jude could draw the breath to respond. When she did, her voice came out barely louder than a whisper. "I believe in lovemaking." She debated whether to let the wine loosen her tongue even further and almost immediately determined that she was too tipsy to talk herself out of sharing a confession. "I'm just not sure I've ever experienced it. Not the way I'd like to."

Diana briefly held her stare, then lowered her eyes to survey their leftover food. "Perhaps that's another reason to cancel. I can't ask you to pretend in that way. The whole thing would almost certainly feel awkward, and I'm afraid my students will pick up on that."

"You don't think you could teach me?" Jude told herself not to beg, but she couldn't fathom a better conclusion to her temp job than an evening of true sexual intimacy with the object of her unrequited affection. Maybe by then, Diana would like her well enough to consider the possibility of dating on her own time. Despite Diana's protestations to the contrary, Jude had faith that the charm and sexual appeal that served her so well with the rest of the female population could eventually melt even the coldest of hearts. "I am a fast learner, you know. And not a terrible actress."

"I'm sure you're highly capable—on both accounts—but it feels inappropriate to do that class without Ava. She and I have known and loved each other for twenty years. Even if we're not *in love*, we've experienced sexual intimacy together so many times it's natural enough, and easy enough, to do it in front of other people." Diana's eyes shimmered, but Jude couldn't tell whether emotion or alcohol was the culprit. "We have real feelings for each other, Ava and I. That's the only reason we're able to teach a class like that."

Stung, probably unjustly, Jude nodded and cast a pining look at her own empty glass. "Whatever you want. Your schedule, your call. Obviously."

Diana exhaled in a long, loud rush. "I don't know...I'll think about it, all right?"

"Fair enough."

"Great." Diana regarded her anxiously. "That's all I've got. The pay is five hundred dollars per workshop—seven-fifty for the anal class, since that one runs longer to allow for the extra foreplay required." She hesitated. "Once Ava is healed, we return to our former status as friendly neighbors. No drama, no emotions. Only business." Diana thrust her hand out over the table, a polite smile on her magnificent lips. "Are you in?"

In the span of the millisecond it took her to clasp Diana's hand and shake, Jude considered how this decision left her poised for multiple heartbreaks. Diana could shatter her in ways that would leave her aching forever. The pain of rejection would be multiplied a thousand fold when the weeks of fucking Diana suddenly ended, along with these newly familiar interactions.

She considered those possibilities and more, yet could only nod dumbly as a stupid, eager grin took over at the thought of touching Diana again—even one more time. With total disregard for her future mental health, Jude rumbled, "I'm in."

CHAPTER SIX

I'm a complete and utter dumbass."

Katrina snorted, then collapsed onto the sofa next to Jude. "Yup."

Annoyed by the predictable comeback, Jude nudged Katrina with her shoulder. "Maybe wait until I tell you why?"

"Oh, right." Katrina's luminous grin belied her tired countenance and lit up the entire room—Jude included. "Go ahead. Narrow it down for me."

Katrina was her opposite in nearly every way—taller by about six inches, blonder by at least as many shades, and the product of an undeniably happy childhood courtesy of two parents who genuinely loved one another. Her father Peter was Jude's mother's eldest brother, a lanky, brilliantly minded engineer whose compassion for others had inspired him to join the Peace Corps right out of college. That's where he'd met Katrina's mother Iris, a fellow volunteer whose passion for teaching Ghanese schoolchildren immediately won Peter over, to hear him tell it. They married within months, delivering their daughter that same year. Katrina spent the first five years of her life in Ghana, until Peter and Iris decided to return to the place of their birth in search of more and better opportunities for Katrina than they were likely to find while fighting to make the world a less terrible place. Although they'd faced their fair share of struggles after moving back to "the land of the free," Jude had always envied her cousin's happy little family. Their devotion to each other was palpable, like nothing she'd ever received from her own worthless egg and sperm donors.

Whatever jealousy Jude felt coexisted alongside a deep wellspring of gratitude. All that love, acceptance, and stability had produced her emotional rock and the closest friend she'd ever had. Bearing in mind Katrina's cherished place within her heart, Jude resisted the urge to give her another, harder nudge. "You'll love this one, I'm sure."

Chuckling, Katrina folded her arms over her chest and turned her head to meet Jude's gaze. "I hope so. It's been one hell of a day, and I could really use the distraction from my own miseries."

"Is everything all right?" Jude furrowed her brow. "Tales of my dumbassery can wait if you're in need of a friendly ear."

"I'm fine." Katrina patted Jude's knee. "I spent the afternoon with a male patient who suffers from early dementia and increasingly wandering hands. Nothing I can't handle, but it *is* getting old."

Jude's frown intensified. "I don't love the sound of that."

"And I don't love having my tits grabbed, but a paycheck's a paycheck." Katrina's smile became even sunnier, as though to will away the ugliness of what she'd endured. "Anyway, don't keep me in suspense. Why are you a dumbass? This time, I mean."

Jude harrumphed. "This time, huh? Nice."

"Sweetheart, this is hardly the first conversation you've initiated by confessing that you'd either already done or were about to do something regrettable and/or ill-advised. Please don't expect me to act surprised on every go-around." Katrina bit her lower lip, as though to prevent her rising mirth from bubbling forth. "We've been friends for long enough that I'm well aware of your tendency to occasionally play the fool."

Jude gave in to temptation and pinched Katrina's elbow, prompting an infectious peal of full-throated laughter. Even as she attempted a disapproving frown, Jude couldn't help but chuckle along. "Come on. That's so not true, and you know it. You've said it yourself: I'm a remarkably well-adjusted and mature individual, given my age and history."

"Yes. One who sometimes does silly things to impress women." Katrina brought her other foot up onto the couch and sat cross-legged facing Jude. "Unless whatever you're about to share *doesn't* involve a woman you hope to impress."

Jude grumbled under her breath. "I don't even want to tell you anymore."

"Aww." Softening, Katrina sidled closer to lean against Jude's side. She wrapped a strong arm around Jude's back and pulled her into an affectionate hug. "I'm only teasing, cuz. You know I wouldn't want you any other way. Never change, okay?"

Deciding this was as opportune a moment as any to drop her bombshell, Jude went for it. Slowly. "I took a temporary part-time job working for my next-door neighbor Diana. Two hours on five different Saturdays, three hours on the sixth. Five hundred dollars for each of the shorter gigs, seven-fifty for the three-hour class."

"What kind of job?" Katrina backed off to study her face. "That's a generous paycheck, assuming whatever Diana wants you to do isn't *too* taxing or degrading."

"Not *degrading*, exactly..." Jude's cheeks heated. "But you see, she's—"

Katrina's mouth fell open, and she bounced up and down before excitedly blurting out a random guess. "She's an art teacher and asked you to do some nude modeling! I can't blame her. You *do* have a slammin' body. That's crazy money for sitting around while people sketch their interpretations of your bare ass, and to be honest, I wholeheartedly approve. I know you can really use the cash, and modeling is a far cry from...what you used to be into."

Jude shifted away from Katrina, wishing she'd at least pretend not to be disgusted about the high-paying escort jobs Jude had taken when she was newly eighteen and tasked with supporting herself for the first time. Seventy-five percent of her clients hadn't required sex as a condition of her companionship, and the ones to whom she had offered that service were almost solely responsible for funding the extended writing sabbatical she was nearly halfway through. The same work Katrina found so scandalous had allowed Jude to escape a toxic home environment and thrive in the real world without a college degree or any relevant experience beyond talking down violent assholes with misogynist tendencies. It was the one skill her stepfather had ever taught her, not that she'd always been able to use it to her advantage.

"Hey." Katrina clasped Jude's hand to keep her from scooting farther away. "I wasn't criticizing. I was just saying..." She hesitated. "Listen, even if this new job isn't nude modeling, I won't judge you. I *promise.*"

Unconvinced but desperate to talk to her best friend about what she'd gotten herself into, Jude admitted, "It's not nude modeling. Well, maybe it sort of is. But with more...touching."

Katrina's eyebrow popped, yet she managed to hold on to her kind smile. "Touching? Like, sexual touching?"

"Exactly like that." Exhaling, Jude rattled off a rapid-fire litany of facts. "Diana is a professional sex therapist. She hosts workshops for lesbian couples—educational, explicitly erotic classes—to teach different techniques for spicing up long-term relationships. Subjects range from oral sex to light BDSM to role-play to a class on intimacy and making love. Normally she pays her friend Ava—who I gather is *just* a friend— to help demonstrate whatever lesson she's teaching, but Ava fell off a stepladder last weekend and fractured her spine and has been diagnosed with early onset osteoporosis. Of course that means she can't do physical work for a while, and that's put Diana in a tight spot financially. Because our shared bedroom wall is apparently just as paper-thin on her side as it is on mine, Diana was already well aware of how much I love having sex with women, even for free, and—" She ignored Katrina's knowing smirk. "So she asked, and I said yes. I'll take over Ava's role until she's healed."

"Of everyone I know, leave it to you to wind up with a sex-therapist next-door neighbor. Is this the same neighbor you've been crushing on since her move-in day?"

Jude nodded sadly. "That's why I'm such a dumbass."

"How so?" Katrina shook her head in apparent disbelief. "Seems to me you just stumbled into a near-perfect scenario. You get to have sex with your fantasy woman at least six times, no strings attached—and she's *paying* you for it. Generously." She tapped Jude's arm. "I'm aware you think I'm a total prude, but even I can see the appeal of that offer. Especially from your perspective."

Jude met her eyes. "With almost four thousand dollars more than I anticipated having right now, I could extend my sabbatical another three months for sure. Maybe four."

Wincing, Katrina corrected her gently. "It's closer to three thousand, but still. That would be amazing."

"Three thousand seven hundred and fifty, to be exact." Before Katrina could complain about her math, Jude confessed. "Including the workshop I already did, last weekend. Ava fell only a few hours before class was scheduled to begin, which led Diana to approach me out of pure desperation. She wanted to avoid having to cancel at the last minute and lose money on registrations and rental fees. At the time, she didn't realize that Ava would require an extended recovery, so it was only yesterday that she asked to hire me for the rest of the existing schedule."

"Okay, so *why* are you a dumbass?" Katrina shrugged, far more chill than Jude had predicted. "It's not like you've never done sex work before, and getting paid to be touched by a woman you would happily fuck for free—" She clicked her tongue. "Well, that's a smarter career move than subjecting one's self to frequent, nonconsensual fondling by a confused middle-aged man."

Jude clasped Katrina's hands in hers. "Kat, can't you just refer that client to someone else? Seriously. I'm sure you can handle it, but you shouldn't have to." Meeting Katrina's steady gaze, she said, "I never let anyone touch me for money unless *I* want to be touched. If you're uncomfortable with what's happening, put an end to it. Even if it means this man has to adjust to a new caregiver. A big, beefy male one would be my recommendation."

Katrina's stoic mask slipped, and tears gathered in the corners of her eyes. "I know you're right. I just…" She released a quiet groan. "Hate to lose another client. Mr. Lomas passed away three weeks ago from heart failure, and Mrs. Rosenburg's children insist on moving her to Washington State this weekend to live with them. I'm not sure my work schedule can afford any more holes until I fill the ones I've already got."

"Actually, that's great!" Jude brightened, excited to do both Diana and Katrina a solid by facilitating what felt more and more like destiny in action. "It just so happens that Diana is looking to hire a caregiver to check in on Ava from time to time. I'm sure she'll work around your schedule. She and Ava don't have a huge budget or anything, but that would occupy at least an hour or two of your day."

Katrina narrowed her eyes. "You still haven't told me why you're such a complete and utter dumbass. I'm not sure I should agree to work for Diana until I know why you're admonishing yourself for doing the same."

"You don't need to worry about Diana. The issue is me, not her. She's nothing if not professional, and very reasonable to deal with. I trust her to treat you fairly." Jude released Katrina's hands to throw her own into the air. "After last weekend's workshop, I realized my feelings for her go way beyond some silly crush. I guess I can't say I'm *in love* with her, but only because we haven't spent much time together yet. The point is, I could easily love her. I *will* fall in love with her, given any opportunity at all, and that's a serious problem."

"A problem for you or for Diana?"

"For both of us." Jude didn't often admit to the fantastical aspirations of her secretly romantic spirit, but the desire for an outside perspective overrode most of her modesty about harboring such a boring, old-fashioned dream for her future. "This may come as a shock, but I'm more than ready to fall in love and settle down with the right woman. Unfortunately, Diana has already been there and done that, and she's sworn never to go down that road again. Especially with me."

Sounding affronted on her behalf, Katrina said, "Why especially not you? You're a fucking catch."

"Agreed, and thank you, but Diana basically thinks I'm a child."

"A child she's paying to assist at her sex workshops?" Skepticism seeped into Katrina's tone. "How big an age difference are we talking here? Because although I'll admit that twenty-six does seem much younger to me now that I've reached this side of thirty, I'd hardly call you a *child*."

"Right? You're not a kid if you can rent a car is all I'm saying." Jude dissolved into a sheepish grin. "Diana's thirty-nine."

The revelation earned her a whistle. "Damn. That *is* an older woman, isn't it?"

"I suppose, yeah." Jude recalled Diana's sure, practiced hands and the striking confidence of her touch. "Which only makes her that much more spectacular. I'll say this much. Maturity and experience are beautiful things to bring to the bedroom."

"You mean the classroom," Katrina pointed out. "Unless you're already sleeping together on your own time?"

"Not even close. Diana insists that our relationship stay strictly professional. She brought dinner over last night to butter me up before offering me the job, but I'm fairly positive that'll be our last interaction outside of class. She prefers us to remain 'casual acquaintances' as much as possible...despite the fact that she'll be shelling out cash to fuck me for the next couple of months. Does that give you an idea about the level of commitment-phobe I've fallen head over heels for? And why I'm an absolute dipshit of the highest order?" She sagged dramatically against Katrina's chest, cuddling closer when strong arms drew her into a sympathetic embrace. "She's going to break my heart, Kat. I know she will. But I agreed to travel down this road with her anyway—and not just because the price was right. This job is the only way to be with her again, and I *need* to be with her...however she'll allow."

"Thankfully, six weekends should give you plenty of time to discover the flawed human being behind this idealized first impression of Diana you currently have." Katrina kissed the crown of Jude's head, rocking her to and fro. "You'll see she isn't perfect, that she has flaws like anyone else. In the meantime, you'll remind yourself every step of the way that she doesn't even want a fuck-buddy, let alone a girlfriend. You'll recall the words of wisdom I'm sharing with you now: anyone who avoids romance and commitment to that degree isn't worth your emotional investment. It almost certainly means she's broken in some way—that someone, at some juncture, hurt her badly—and to be blunt, you deserve someone without all that baggage. Decide now that Diana is a far superior short-term lover than long-term prospect, and just…enjoy the sex while it lasts. The paycheck, too. All things considered, this sounds like a sweet gig to help eek out additional writing time."

Realizing that she'd expected Katrina to admonish her for returning to sex work in any capacity, Jude felt almost disappointed by her acceptance. Not because she believed being paid to fuck was an inherently bad way to make a living, but rather because she'd hoped Katrina's pleas for her to reconsider would somehow imbue her with the courage to run from the absolute devastation awaiting her in the future. Of course, Jude wasn't certain anything Katrina could've said would've dissuaded her from accepting the vaginal massage Diana had planned for tomorrow's class, so perhaps it was best to be grateful for the support. "I appreciate your faith in my ability to manage my emotions."

"You're head over heels for her already, aren't you? Chances are, by the time she's ready to terminate your working relationship, you'll have gotten the dose of reality you need to feel content with the time you'll have spent together." Katrina released her with a tender squeeze. "I can almost guarantee Diana isn't actually the woman of your fantasies. She's bound to reveal qualities that rub you the wrong way. You know, like a hypocritical inability to form healthy romantic and sexual relationships with others despite literally teaching classes on the subject."

Jude sagged against the arm of Katrina's well-worn leather couch, whimpering like the pitiful creature she was. "But she's so *hot*. And talented."

"Like I said, have your fun. Take her money. Just don't waste your time pining for more than that." Katrina poked Jude's thigh with her big toe. "Plenty of women out there would *love* the chance to tie you down. Hold out for one who wants you as badly as you want her."

Sound advice, but Jude doubted whether she could shut off her feelings that easily. Still, she wasn't inclined to disagree. "You're right. I'll be sure to keep all that in mind while having the best sex of my life—"

Katrina empathically shook her head. "Not the best of your life, I promise. That'll be with someone you love—who loves you back."

The best of her life so far, then. Sighing, Jude grabbed the remote control off the table and switched on Katrina's wide-screen television. "New topic. What kind of pizza are we ordering? And which show should we binge-watch next?"

"Garden vegetable, and I don't care as long as it's funny." Katrina tugged a blanket onto her lap and settled against the other arm of the sofa. "Laughter is the healthiest way to end a shitty day. Don't you agree?"

Jude nodded as she navigated into the comedy section of Katrina's streaming service. "More words of wisdom. Maybe *you* should teach a class."

"Theories in Media Escapism." Katrina pulled a face. "How apropos. You get to show people how to have mind-blowing sex, while I train them to block out their crappy lives by staring at digital screens. Frankly, you may be a complete and utter dumbass, but I still say you're the winner between us tonight."

"Talk to me again in seven weeks," Jude said, then sent a silent apology to her future self for choosing to ignore the heartache ahead.

CHAPTER SEVEN

Stretched out alongside Jude's prone, wondrously nude form, Diana marveled that she was still capable of teaching, let alone speaking, after the full-body massage she'd just performed. A prolonged warm-up to the main event, the instructive rubdown had produced thirty minutes of the most enticing whimpers Diana had ever heard voiced aloud, making it damn near impossible to convincingly downplay her own arousal. That speech still flowed from her at all was a minor miracle, given that her brain had gone off-line the moment she'd first cupped Jude's perky, tight-nippled breasts in her well-oiled hands.

Coherence aside, she doubted she was fooling the twenty women who encircled them. Camped out on individual blankets and in various states of undress, the vast majority of her students watched goggle-eyed as Diana dripped warm oil onto her hand, then onto Jude's neatly groomed vulva. The room had grown so quiet, so taut with anticipation, that Diana imagined everyone had to hear her heart racing, had to notice her fingers tremble as she lowered her palm to rest on Jude's pubic mound. Guiding Jude's thighs apart with her free hand to ensure that the oil she'd just applied would trickle down onto her clit and labia, Diana realized she was holding her breath—and that her inevitable exhalation would surely draw attention to her flustered state.

Shit, what was I saying again?

"No, don't *stop*." Jude's writhing hips nudged her back into action. "This feels *incredible.*"

It did. Touching Jude stirred her in a way it shouldn't, in a way Diana wished it *wouldn't*. She told herself it was because of the firm, youthful body and flawless skin on display, that the attraction was strictly physical.

Even if she'd never chased younger women in the past, she *was* about to turn forty. Maybe Jude was her mid-life crisis in action, because what better way to celebrate a birthday this monumental than some ill-advised lust for the cougar-hungry sex kitten next door? With Jude's plump, steamy vulva nestled against her palm, Diana struggled to recall why she'd sworn off even the most casual sexual entanglements. Surely the euphoria of human connection merited some level of emotional risk. Didn't it?

"Please."

Dragged into focus by the desperation in Jude's whimpered plea, Diana somehow managed to pick up her lesson plan where she'd left off. "Begin by gently massaging your partner's pubic mound." She used her whole hand to demonstrate, pressing down lightly with her palm as she rubbed small circles over Jude's vulva. "Gradually work your way down to her outer lips, but don't touch her clitoris or vagina just yet."

Diana barely noticed whether anyone attempted to mimic the technique, too engrossed in the subtle arching of Jude's back as she ran her fingertips along one labia majora, then the other. Shuddering, Jude spread her legs to reveal the glistening pink beauty of her inner folds. The sight shook Diana like a gale-force wind, once again knocking her off course. The plaintive moan that arose at her hesitation reminded Diana of the next line in her spiel and simultaneously unleashed a rush of wetness to further soak her panties.

Tearing her eyes from Jude to stare over the heads of the most inattentive couple within her field of view, Diana intoned, "There's no rush here. Remember, you have many reasons to give your partner a yoni massage, and orgasm isn't even close to the best."

"Speak for yourself." Jude's wisecrack earned her a predictable laugh.

Without acknowledging Jude—mostly for fear of what would happen if she veered too far off-script—Diana repeated the previous caresses while listing the benefits of what her fresh-faced neighbor was allowing her to do. "Regular vaginal massage will loosen the muscles of your pelvic floor, which may lead to more intense orgasms. It also reduces tension and, perhaps more importantly, increases circulation—which is why doctors recommend this technique to help reverse vaginal atrophy in menopausal women." Having noticed how rigid Jude's posture had become, Diana preemptively addressed what she assumed was her young friend's chief concern. "All of which does *not* preclude the possibility of orgasm. It's entirely likely your partner will climax while you're touching her. Perhaps even multiple times. But this exercise is about creating sexual intimacy, first and foremost. This massage is about connecting with your partner and making her feel wonderful."

"*Orgasms* are wonderful," Jude muttered pointedly. She gasped when Diana lowered the tips of her fingers to graze the base of her clitoris. "Ah. *Yes.*"

Intoxicated by the power she wielded over her poor, overly eager, wholly defenseless assistant, Diana rubbed her thumb across Jude's slick, already contracting entrance. "When you're ready to escalate, go ahead and massage the base of her clit, along with her vaginal opening. We're trying to build arousal. If you're receiving, focus on your breathing—slow, and deep. Both of you, be present in this moment together." Pausing to inhale, she made the mistake of glancing at her young assistant's guileless face. Jude's chest hitched the instant their eyes met, and she drenched Diana's still-moving hand in a fresh torrent of her ever-abundant juices.

Diana sank her teeth into her lower lip and, unable to stop herself, moaned loudly enough to provoke audible tittering from the crowd. Embarrassed, she retreated to tease Jude's outer lips once more. "Push into the skin with circular strokes. Remember to massage what's underneath. Don't just glide across the surface."

A moan even louder than her own echoed throughout the room, easing Diana's tension somewhat. Seizing upon the opportunity to move past her momentary weakness, she asked, "Do you ladies have any questions so far? Concerns?"

A returning student piped up, breathless from her wife's diligent rubdown. "I'm concerned for Jude. How long are you gonna make her wait?"

Rae, the wife, gave Diana a conspiratorial grin. "Willa means how long are you gonna make *her* wait?"

"Great question," Jude said. "Thank you, Willa." She propped herself up on her elbows, straining to catch Diana's gaze. "I know the goal here isn't orgasm, but if we could fast-forward to the part where you loosen the muscles of my pelvic floor and get my circulation flowing, I'd *super* appreciate it."

Diana managed to remain stone-faced, but just barely. Although she'd deny it if asked, she found Jude every inch as charming as her students appeared to. Rather than ignore the comment, she grasped Jude by the shoulders and guided her down to lie flat on the blanket. "Relax. Let your arousal build."

Jude surprised her by doing exactly that, closing her eyes to wait silently for the massage to resume. To reward the unexpected obedience, Diana delved between Jude's engorged inner labia, using her index and middle fingers to trace the perimeter of her well-lubricated entrance. Jude's breathing deepened with each lazy circle she painted, attaining a slow, hypnotic rhythm that threatened to lull Diana into a similarly entranced state. In a voice that sounded like it came from outside her body, she managed to utter the next instruction. "When your partner is ready, I want you to enter her vagina with one finger—gently, please." Noting Jude's swift inhalation at the foreshadowing, Diana pressed the pad of her index finger against the waterfall promising to ease her passage inside. "Ready for that finger, Jude?"

"Yes." Sticking to the submissive persona she'd suddenly adopted, Jude raised both hands above her head as though to prove her willingness to surrender. "Keep going."

Diana eased into her at an excruciatingly gradual pace, torturing them both with the unhurried penetration. Jude's pussy clung insistently to her invading finger, tight and molten hot, already contracting with pre-orgasmic bliss. To distract herself from what she was doing, and to whom, Diana plunged ahead with her scripted lecture. "Massage the inner walls." She demonstrated. "I personally prefer a firm, consistent touch, but be sure to check in with your partner about what level of pressure is most pleasurable for her. Remember, don't rush your partner to climax. Bring her close, then deescalate. This experience is meant to last."

Rather than deliver the quip Diana expected, Jude released a long, shaky exhalation that noticeably loosened the tension in her stiff limbs. Without opening her eyes, she murmured, "I like that."

Such a simple sentiment, yet Diana couldn't prevent the delicious shiver that ran through her at Jude's vocal contentment. "Good." Covering her stupidly blatant desire with a cocky smirk, Diana added, "Just you wait."

"Happily."

Afraid everyone would notice how delightful she found Jude's uncharacteristic compliance, Diana returned to the discussion at hand. "How many of you know where your partner's G-spot is located?" After about half the class muttered positive answers, Diana pushed Jude's slightly bent leg to the side to give them a better view. "Few bodily sensations are more intensely satisfying than a skillful G-spot massage. To locate your partner's 'go button,' insert your finger one or two inches inside her vagina with your palm facing up. Once you're in position, stroke the front wall using a 'come-hither' type motion." She demonstrated outside of Jude's body using her free hand. "You're looking for an area that feels slightly rougher than the surrounding tissue. This spot may be anywhere from the size of your pinkie fingernail to a half dollar."

Gloria, a first-time workshop attendee, exclaimed, "Found it!"

Her wife Frankie gasped ecstatically. "Uh-huh."

Pleased by their excitement, Diana dragged her fingertip across Jude's G-spot to produce a similar gasp. The increasingly heavy breathing around them confirmed that she and Gloria weren't alone in their discoveries. "Stimulating your partner's G-spot will induce intense sexual pleasure, potentially leading to orgasm. With enough stimulation, some women even ejaculate. Regardless of whether you end up climaxing, being touched this way ought to feel nothing short of *marvelous*."

As Diana intensified the pressure and speed of her massage, Jude's tanned thighs quivered, and her hands flew to her chest to pluck the pebbled tips of her own shapely, heaving breasts. Stirred by the shameless display, Diana lowered her gaze to Jude's mouthwatering pink labia, yearning for an excuse to taste her again. She lightened the pressure of her roving fingertip, not yet ready to finish Jude off or to withdraw from her molten center. Resting her thumb against the base of Jude's clit, Diana caressed her both inside and out. She took care to keep Jude suspended in a state of pre-orgasmic ecstasy, hoping to stretch the demonstration for as long as reasonably possible.

The longer she spent touching Jude, the less time she would have to focus on her own needs. She didn't know if Jude planned on offering to reciprocate again this session, but if so, Diana would have to turn her down—something she *really* didn't want to do. She hated to hurt Jude, hated to create any awkwardness with her, and positively *loathed* the thought of flatly refusing sex her body plainly craved.

Setting the stage for her students to continue on their own, Diana said, "I'll leave you all to the task at *hand*." She smiled at the assorted chuckles, grateful for the polite reception of her lame jokes. "Take your time, have fun, and most importantly, savor this opportunity to connect with someone you love. Please be sure to let me know if you have any questions, because I'm here to answer them."

Another returning student, Liz, piped up from somewhere to Diana's left. "Only one question: Exactly how long do you intend to torture that poor girl? I'm actually feeling sorry for her." She shrugged at Diana's raised eyebrow. "I've never been good at the whole denial game myself, but if that's what gets you off—"

Diana gathered her courage and met Jude's hooded gaze. "Shall I stop?" She kneaded the sensitive spot beneath her fingertip more firmly, inducing a head-to-toe shudder that appeared to straddle the thin line between pleasure and pain. "Or give you more?"

"Yes," Jude breathed. "*More.*"

"You don't mind if I go slow, do you?" Diana swirled her finger inside Jude, then rubbed the thumb on her other hand down the length of Jude's perineum. "I assume you want this experience to last a *little* longer."

Jude clutched at her own breasts. "Uh-huh."

"Me too." Diana broke eye contact to watch the sensual undulation of Jude's hips. "Do you like how my finger feels inside your vagina?"

Jude managed to nod, then grunt. Tilting her pelvis to force additional friction, she ground out a strained, "I love it." Then, "*Diana.*"

Diana bit the inside of her cheek until she tasted blood, desperate to stifle her visceral response to Jude's impassioned recitation of her name. It disturbed her, how effortlessly Jude shattered her well-practiced apathy to awaken this long-dormant hunger. Aiming to silence any further dialogue, Diana rubbed the spot even more forcefully.

Jude's reaction was instantaneous. Letting out an incomprehensible shout, she flooded Diana's palm with a fiery stream of liquid joy. Determined *not* to gloat at the uncontrolled convulsions of Jude's delectable body, Diana gradually ceased moving to let her recover.

Jude's face fell the instant she regained her bearings. "I said I wanted it to *last*," she whined, adorably. "Why did you finish me so quickly? I know what I said earlier, but—I tried so hard to be good and hold out!"

"You were *very* good." Taking pity, Diana wiggled the finger still buried within Jude's fluttering vagina. "And there's no need to despair, sweetheart. We're not done."

Jude tightened around her fully embedded digit. "Oh…okay. *Thank you.*"

Diana accepted the gratitude with a nod, all too aware her motivations weren't entirely selfless. "Relax." She coached Jude under her breath. "Close your eyes, revel in how this feels." She dragged her fingertip around the perimeter of the quarter-sized circle on which she'd been focusing.

Jude's shoulders came off the floor and her whole body spasmed, causing her breasts to jiggle so enticingly Diana found it impossible to look away. Made stupid by the sight, she eschewed her better judgment and ducked to capture a rock-hard nipple between her lips for a languorous suck. The impetuous action wasn't scripted, obviously, as it added nothing of value to a demonstration of yoni massage—but when Diana heard the full-throated groan drawn out by her rogue teeth and tongue, she could hardly regret giving her libido full rein. It was only the fear of rushing Jude to a second, possibly final climax that persuaded Diana to sit up and rededicate her attention to the simple task of G-spot stimulation.

Every time Jude neared her peak, Diana stopped moving. Once the perceptible twitching of Jude's increasingly taxed muscles subsided, Diana would start again—escalating from a bare wiggle of her fingertip to the deep, sustained stroking of Jude's most sensitive region. On their fourth go-around, right as Diana took note of the unprecedented quaking of her soft thighs, Jude finally cried out for mercy. "I...can't take much more. It's—ah!" She bucked against Diana's hand. "Please. It's too intense."

Diana went still. "You want me to stop?"

Jude's hips canted off the floor, forcing her finger even deeper inside. "No...I want to *come*. Please, let me. *Please.*"

Checking the wall clock across the room, Diana registered the time with a hearty dose of relief. "All right." She centered her finger on the spot that always seemed to draw the biggest response and her thumb atop the turgid clit poking out from its protective sheath. "Come for me," Diana murmured, very intentionally *not* looking at their audience. She couldn't stand for them to notice how thoroughly gratified she was by the act of pleasuring her new assistant. Rubbing both spots in tandem, Diana whispered near Jude's ear. "Come all over my hand, sweet girl. You feel my finger inside you? *Fucking* you? I want you to squeeze it for me, baby, with that tight little pussy—" She grinned when Jude's inner muscles clamped down hard, trapping her fully embedded finger in a fiery, pulsating vise. "That's my girl."

Jude's orgasm kicked off a violently sympathetic twinge in Diana's vagina, followed by the requisite rush of embarrassing wetness, shame-fueled regret, and bitter self-doubt. She was supposed to be a professional, damn it. Yet she'd lost control in front of her students. Lost control with *Jude*. She couldn't bear to dwell on how fantastic it felt to sate her irrepressible sexual hunger with someone other than her platonic best friend with benefits. Not that the physical intimacy she and Ava shared wasn't perfectly lovely. No one else knew her body so well, or its limits. More importantly, she trusted Ava with a surety that no longer felt attainable—let alone advisable—in her new, post-Janine existence. So why did sex with Ava already compare so unfavorably to sex with Jude? Even one-sided sex with Jude?

Because Jude was novel, and shiny, and likable. Sexy, too. That was all, Diana told herself.

Resolving to do better—or else accept the financial blow of suspending these damn workshops until Ava recovered—Diana squelched her conflicted internal monologue and eased Jude back to earth by steadily reducing the speed and pressure of her touch. But when she tried to withdraw from her still-pulsing depths, Jude slammed her silky thighs closed around Diana's wrist, trapping her in place. "Not yet. Please…"

Torn between denying her desire and waiting out the clock, Diana stayed put. She even conjured a friendly smile. "Take all the time you need. Let me know when you're ready for me to leave."

Jude locked eyes with her ever so briefly, then brought her forearm up to hide her face. "I've never…" She exhaled. "And I mean *never*…felt anything like that before."

Diana couldn't believe how difficult it was not to beam. "I presume in a good way?"

"In the best possible way." Lowering her arm, Jude stared at her with an earnestness that tugged at Diana's heart. "Is it my turn now? Because seriously, if I can give you even a fraction of the pleasure you just gave me, it'll be my greatest sexual accomplishment to date."

Diana almost hated herself for finding the strength to deliver the polite rejection she'd rehearsed in her head. "Unfortunately, we won't have enough time. Class ends in fifteen minutes, and I need to be available for questions before it does."

Jude cast a dazed, somewhat shocked look around the room, as though she'd forgotten about their moaning, entirely distracted audience. Once the short-lived confusion passed, she honed in on the distant wall clock and frowned. "Oh, I…" She paused, then distractedly tapped Diana's wrist. "Didn't realize that took so long. You can…go ahead and pull out, okay?"

"Okay." Diana withdrew from her vagina inch by inch, taking care not to rush in her desire to escape the newly arisen awkwardness between them. "I'm sorry I didn't leave time for you to practice your technique. I should have."

"It's no big deal, Diana. For real." Jude's eyes found hers, their expression more guarded than before. "I can't pretend that I didn't adore absolutely everything you just did to me. Like to the point I wouldn't change anything about this evening, even if I could."

Relieved by Jude's respectful, easy acceptance of a boundary it had genuinely pained her to impose, Diana laid her sticky palm on Jude's inner thigh and squeezed. "I appreciate your understanding."

"Of course." Jude shot her a breezy smile, sitting up carefully. "You *are* the boss. Pretty sure that means you get to decide how I spend the time I'm paid to be here."

Diana was tempted to disagree, or propose some type of egalitarian compromise, but that would be foolish. She couldn't afford any more impetuous missteps, not if she wanted to keep Jude on the payroll until Ava's triumphant return. If that meant enforcing the idea of a hierarchy, so be it. Unwilling to undo the hard work she'd put into establishing this small measure of professional distance, Diana gave Jude an affectionate wink, then turned away from her still-panting assistant to face the women who gave her solitary life its meaning.

CHAPTER EIGHT

Three days after her second Ava-less workshop, Diana keyed into her best friend's apartment, then stopped just inside the door to listen. The worry she'd been battling on and off throughout the morning dissipated at the distant sound of Ava's familiar—albeit recently absent—laughter over the top of a woman's voice Diana didn't recognize. *So that's why she hasn't answered my texts.*

"Hello?" Diana called, in case she'd somehow managed to interrupt an intimate moment. *But with whom?* Hedging her bets, she added, "Is this a bad time?"

"Hello?" A tall, comely blonde crossed the uncharacteristically neat expanse of Ava's studio dwelling to greet her with an outstretched hand and a warm smile. "Diana, right? I'm Katrina, Jude's cousin and Ava's new part-time caretaker."

"She means taskmistress." The less-than-convincing complaint from the other side of the room brought a stunning grin to Katrina's lovely face. "I'll have you know, she keeps making me do stuff that hurts."

Katrina shook Diana's hand, then, sighing fondly, walked to retake her position at the foot of Ava's bed. "So far we've worked on getting out of bed as painlessly as possible—"

"Spoiler alert: nothing is painless with a fractured spine." Although Ava delivered the line in a humorless deadpan, her eyes twinkled with a life and humor Diana hadn't seen in weeks. Heck, maybe even months. Unlike the last few times Diana had visited, her best friend was seated against the headboard and not flat on her back. "Fortunately for Katrina, I have a weakness for charming personalities." Ava winked at her new caretaker playfully. "And pretty faces."

Diana held her breath as she awaited Katrina's reaction to the blatantly flirtatious remark, afraid her uninhibited best friend had already managed to cross a line with Jude's seemingly friendly—but as far as she knew, straight—cousin. When Katrina ducked her head, pink-cheeked and brimming with bashful delight, Diana's shoulders relaxed. Straight or not, Ava's new helper was clearly receptive to her sweet-talking.

"No one said recovery would be easy." Katrina gave Ava's sock-covered foot a brief, mildly therapeutic-looking caress. "Also, weren't you the one who thanked me no less than three times for forcing you into the shower yesterday morning? You said, and I quote, that having clean hair really did make you feel 'a thousand percent better'—and you would be sure to take my advice next time, no arguments."

Ava scoffed, rolling her eyes to pin Diana with a long-suffering smirk. "You wouldn't believe how many times she's brought that up already this morning. In all seriousness, remind me never to admit I was wrong in this young lady's presence again."

"We'll see about that." Chuckling, Katrina glanced down at her phone, then hurriedly leapt to her feet. "Next time, all right? I have another appointment I need to run to…I can't believe it's already past noon."

"Time flies when you're torturing defenseless old women with broken backs, I suppose—"

Katrina burbled laughter at Ava's toothless jibe. "You may be a lot of things, Ms. Gardiner, but 'old'? Not even close." Despite being at least fifteen years Ava's junior, Katrina sounded utterly sincere. "Occasionally grumpy? Sure. Infuriatingly obstinate, somewhat like a toddler? Absolutely."

"Aw, shucks," Ava grumbled amiably. "Stop, before you give me a big head. Also, it's *Ava*…remember?"

"Prone to interrupting? Yes, indeed." A smile tugged at Katrina's lips as she grabbed her jacket from the nearby sofa and zipped it over her chest. "Fortunately for *you,* I'm *also* a sucker for charm—and that's something you have in spades. Despite the grumpy obstinance."

Diana snorted, tickled by their banter. "Sounds like she's got you pegged, Ava." Reviewing her mental calendar, she tried to calculate how long it had taken Ava and Katrina to establish such a lighthearted, borderline flirtatious connection. Had they known each other even a week? To watch them interact, one might assume they'd been together for months. "I'm thrilled Jude managed to find someone capable of going toe-to-toe with you—*and* your attitude."

Ava frowned, seemingly less amused by that sort of remark when it wasn't delivered by the attractive young blonde who helped her in and out of shower stalls. "I don't have an *attitude*."

"Sure you do." Katrina's breeziness immediately melted away Ava's outward discontent. "Luckily, I'm well-equipped to handle even the mouthiest clients...something about having charm and a pretty face."

Having known Ava intimately for close to twenty years, Diana didn't miss the flicker of sexual excitement in her eyes at Katrina's mild entendre. "I'll say."

Katrina edged toward the door, giving them a friendly wave. "See you tomorrow, *Ava*. You did good today."

"So did you." Winking, Ava waved back. "Be safe out there."

Katrina smiled so brightly Diana had to look away. It felt intrusive not to. "I promise not to accept any rides from strange men."

"Or strange women," Ava called out, in a deceptively humorous tone. "Be sure to watch out for them, too."

Katrina paused with her hand on the doorknob, glancing over her shoulder to shoot Ava another sweet grin. "I always do." She slipped out the door, then engaged the lock behind her.

Diana turned to Ava, eyebrows raised. "Down, girl. She's a *child*."

Ava clicked her tongue. "She's *thirty-one*, Di. Hardly a child." Glancing at the door, she said, "On the contrary, Katrina Monaco is a full-grown, highly capable, downright *gorgeous* adult woman. One I really must thank you for finding."

"You're welcome." Diana sat on the edge of the bed, craning to catch Ava's distracted gaze. "She does seem to have lifted your spirits."

Ava sheepishly refocused on Diana's face. "She really has. Yes. Thank you."

"Despite making you do painful things?"

Ava grimaced and shifted her weight. "You'll be shocked to hear this, but I was a stone-cold bitch to Kat the first time we met. To be fair, she *did* attempt to force me out of bed immediately after barging through my door. About twenty minutes in, I threatened to fire her for being so goddamn pushy, but she told me you'd explicitly instructed her to ignore me if I tried."

Diana chuckled. "Can you blame me? I know how you are as a patient. That's why Katrina and I discussed a few different contingency plans during our first phone conversation...in case you were difficult."

"Yeah, she mentioned that, too. She said...a lot, actually." Ava stared at her hands as they twisted nervously in her lap. "That I was being selfish, that you clearly cared for me a great deal, that my life was over only if I let it be. She told me I wasn't dead yet, that she's had clients twenty years older than me come back from worse." Her cheeks glowed pink, an uncharacteristic hue for a woman who'd always been the antithesis of bashful. "Also, that I'm too attractive to waste away in bed, alone. While I'm fairly certain that last part was her catering to an openly receptive audience, it was exactly what I needed to hear. *She's* exactly what I need, at least right now—an objective third party to help pry my head from my ass, as necessary."

"Sign me up for the Katrina fan club, because that's the best news I've heard all day." It was a good thing Jude wasn't there, or else Diana would've hugged her out of sheer relief. "I'm elated she was able to get through to you. I've missed my favorite badass warrior woman."

"So did I." Ava held Diana's gaze, eyes bright with unshed tears. "Anyway, Kat promised me ten minutes a day to wallow in self-pity, on the condition I spend the rest of my time doing everything I can to get stronger. I told her okay." Her smile returned. "She *is* right, after all. And hot. You know I have a hard time saying no to hot."

"I do know that, but please be mindful of the eighteen-year age gap between you." Diana reiterated the inappropriateness of Ava's crush as tactfully as possible, choosing her words so as not to dampen the mood. "Just...be careful. You don't want to spoil a solid working relationship by crossing the line with someone who isn't a serious romantic prospect. Not with your health at stake."

Ava shot her a foul look. "Why isn't she a serious romantic prospect? Setting aside the sad reality that I can barely wipe my own ass at the moment, let alone fuck anyone—" She paused, apparently to let that fact register. "A romantic relationship between a forty-nine-year-old woman and a thirty-one-year-old *adult woman* is hardly unprecedented, let alone out of the realm of possibility. Shit. She's not that much younger than you."

"Eight years! She's *eight years* younger than me."

Scoffing, Ava groused, "Since when are you so fucking uptight about age, Di? Certainly not when you let a woman ten years your senior lick that soft, yummy pussy the night after college graduation."

Diana sighed at the memory of her first time. She supposed Ava had a point—a measly ten years hadn't seemed like a big deal when she was the less-experienced party. Did that make her a hypocrite now that she was the older woman? Recognizing that she was at least partially projecting her own fears of intimacy onto Ava, Diana offered an apologetic shrug. "You're right. I'm sorry. I didn't come here to torpedo your high spirits."

"Could've fooled me."

Sighing, Diana stretched out to lie on her side across the foot of Ava's bed. "Listen, I'm glad you're having fun with Katrina. I have no idea whether she's even into women, but if she's making you happy, then I'm happy. Especially as she's the one helping get you back on your feet."

Ava scrutinized her face. "How was the yoni massage with Jude?"

"Fine." Diana both did and didn't want to talk about it, simultaneously. *Schrödinger's conversation.*

"Did she come?" Ava wore a knowing smile.

"Repeatedly."

"And you?"

Diana averted her gaze to study the pattern on Ava's comforter. "We ran out of time."

"Uh-huh." Ava poked Diana's thigh with her foot. "On purpose?"

"I was focused on teaching." A weak justification, and Diana knew it. "My job is to show the class how to perform a thorough, pleasurable vaginal massage—not get off for their amusement."

"What about your own amusement?"

Diana gave Ava a dirty look. "It seemed unwise to indulge my desires with the hired help. Not to mention unethical."

"You're fucking Jude for money, love. Yet you draw the line at letting her fuck *you*?" Ava appeared legitimately disgusted by her supposed honorability. "As far as you're concerned, *that's* where the situation becomes problematic?"

Rolling onto her back, Diana studied the ceiling to avoid the spectacle of Ava overreacting to her excuses. "I don't expect you to understand."

"Of course not. I'm just a dirty old lady who gets off on seducing innocent young maidens." Ava knocked Diana's hip with her foot. "Did Jude offer to reciprocate? I would've expected her to be interested in the free massage lesson, if nothing else."

"She offered." Diana made the admission only because she knew Ava would see through a denial. "I turned her down."

"Speaking of selfish." Ava kicked Diana even harder—then groaned at the exertion. "If Jude wants to learn, teach her. If you happen to come while doing your damn *job*, I promise the safe existence you've built for yourself won't instantly crumble. All it'll do is make you more pleasant to be around. Ideally."

Unprepared to admit why she was so hesitant to interact with Jude any more than necessary, Diana brought the subject to a close. "In any event, this debate is currently moot. I'm flying solo for this upcoming class, remember?"

"Mmm. That's right." Ava's throaty moan made Diana instantly wet. The telltale sound of Ava's arousal rocketed her own sex drive into the stratosphere, emboldening her to reach over and stroke Ava's inner thigh suggestively. Ava placed her hand on Diana's to still its motion. "Masturbation 101. One of my personal favorites." She peeled away the fingers creeping up her thigh, then gestured at Diana's lower body. "How about giving me a sneak peek? Since I won't be there for the main event."

Diana's inner horndog urged her to leap at the chance for any kind of sexual interaction with the woman she trusted above all others, even a one-sided, exhibitionistic display. Yet the nagging thought that Ava's suggestion had arisen from a place of pity, rather than legitimate interest, cooled her rising ardor. "Thanks, but I'm fine."

"I know you're fine." Ava drew her toes up the inside of Diana's thigh. "Why do you think I want to watch you touch yourself?"

"Because you're feeling sorry for me now that my sole sexual outlet is broken." Diana pursed her lips, stubbornly ignoring the sensual nature of Ava's caress. "I'm a big girl, Ava. One who can take care of herself."

"Oh, I know you can. You literally teach a class on the subject." Ava delved between Diana's denim-clad thighs with her foot, applying light pressure to reignite the fire inside. "But I also know you're dying to share your pleasure with an interested party. Aren't you?"

Diana gritted her teeth as Ava pushed more firmly against her clit. "Not if you're too injured to enjoy it."

"Who says I won't enjoy it?"

Struggling to clear her head, Diana said, "I can wait until you're better. Honestly." She hissed at the slow removal of Ava's foot from the juncture of her tense thighs. "I don't want you to overextend yourself."

"Don't worry about me." Ava wore a brave face, but Diana could hear her underlying sadness. "My body may not be up for this, but my eyes sure as hell are. Please, Di. Now that my depression has lifted, I'm super fucking horny—and helpless to do anything about it."

"I think you mean now that you're spending your days flirting with a woman who was born right around the time you started college." Despite the comeback, Diana's resistance softened. "Sweetie, if you need to come, I can use the vibrator on you. Or rub your clit with my fingers. Whatever's easiest on your spine."

Ava thrust out her lower lip in a dramatic pout. "I love that idea in theory, but…" She heaved a sigh, causing her delicate features to momentarily tighten with discomfort. "I suspect I'm still a couple weeks away from that level of physical exertion. Unfortunately."

Diana's libido cooled once more. "I can wait, Ava. I don't want to torture you like that."

"Please," Ava whined. "I'm tortured already. Do me the small favor of letting me live vicariously through the orgasm you're about to give yourself." She prodded Diana's stomach with her toes. "Unless you're saving it for Jude…"

Annoyed by the implication, Diana leapt to her feet and opened the top button on her jeans. "Fine. You're on. Just promise you won't cry to me later about your aching clit."

"You're a real bitch when you're undersexed." Ava's wry grin took most of the sting out of her pointed remark. "Even more reason to endear yourself to your dear, bedridden friend with a dirty peep show."

Diana stripped off her jeans and climbed back onto the mattress. Stretching out on her back, she shifted so her head was at Ava's feet, then let her legs fall open to offer the most generous view possible for her friend's limited range of motion. "You're the dirty one. Begging me to touch my pussy." She snuck a hand under the waistband of her panties, exaggeratedly rubbing her index and middle fingers along her labia. Already slippery with arousal, Diana laughed breathlessly at Ava's high-pitched, needy whimper at her blatant teasing. "Can you see?"

"Yes." Ava laid her palm on Diana's left thigh, fingers curled to hold on loosely. "Why don't you take off your shirt? Let me savor the whole, delectable package."

Diana removed her hand from her panties, sitting up to tug her shirt and bra over her head in a single, semi-seamless motion. She dropped them over the side of the bed before resuming her supine position, ready to comply with whatever order she was given. Her best friend's dark eyes tracked her at every step, scanning her half-nude body from tits to pussy with all the subtlety of a brass band. "Like what you see?"

Ava shuddered, then winced, then stopped moving altogether. A look of fierce concentration swept over her pain-etched face, and she licked her lips, tearing her gaze from the visual feast she'd ordered. "You know I love your body." She jutted her chin. "Touch it for me."

Purposefully misunderstanding, Diana cupped a breast in each hand, pushing them together, then pinching the hard nipples between her fingertips. "Oh," she moaned, leaning in to her vocal delight. It was a thrill to watch Ava fight to remain unmoving, to resist pushing her body beyond its limits. Drunk from the power she still held over her first and oldest lover, Diana plunged her right hand into her panties to investigate her labia once more. "I'm so wet," she whispered, spreading her legs. "Fuck, I want to come."

"Then do it. For me, sweetheart. Rub that wet pussy for me."

No longer interested in extending their mutual torment, Diana dragged the crotch of her panties aside to reveal the practiced dance of her fingertips around and atop the hood of her swollen clit. "This won't take long."

"Probably for the best." Ava managed a strained chuckle. "Because you're killing me, Diana. Do you have any idea what I want to do to you? All the awful, nasty desires running through my mind? Consider yourself lucky I can't fuck you right now, Di, because I'd fuck you *hard*. Too hard." She swallowed, then briefly closed her eyes as though composing herself through meditation. When she reopened them in a moment, she appeared markedly calmer. "Stick two fingers in. Fuck yourself with them." She waited a beat. "Please."

Ava's politeness made Diana laugh, adding yet more pleasure to the already exciting encounter. "Only because you asked so nicely." She positioned her index and middle finger at her opening, then slowly eased both digits into her vagina until they were fully embedded. Her right hand kept circling the engorged head of her clitoris, keeping her wet enough for the penetration while also propelling her dangerously close to the edge. "*Shit,* that feels nice."

"Looks nice, too." Ava licked her lips. "I swear I'm about to get off without even being touched."

"Much like a May-December romance, that's not outside the realm of possibility," Diana pointed out. "But you already knew that. Didn't you?"

Ava's nostrils flared as she very cautiously allowed her free hand to rest between her own outstretched legs. "Indeed."

Rapidly approaching her peak, Diana uttered her next request more out of habit than anything. "May I come for you, Ava? Please. I'm so *close*."

"Go ahead, come." Ava tightened her grip on Diana's quivering thigh. "Don't hold back. Let me hear how fantastic those naughty fingers feel in that greedy hole you call a cunt."

Diana arched her back, gasping at Ava's masterful way with the filthiest of words. "*Fuck*," she cried out, doing exactly that. She worked both hands tirelessly, stroking and pumping and rubbing until she eventually contracted around her fingers in a transcendent explosion of incoherent sound and hot, liquid satisfaction. Body quaking, Diana rolled onto her side and pressed her lips against Ava's warm ankle while she rode out the staggering climax. "Fuck," she repeated in a whisper, finally slowing her hands. "*Yes.*"

Ava caressed her hip lovingly. "Feel better?"

Diana mustered a hoarse chuckle. "Yeah. Thanks for that."

"Ditto." Ava gave her bottom a tender pat. "By the way, you have a real talent for diddling. Ever consider going pro?"

Resuming her supine position, Diana prepared for the herculean task of sitting up. "All the time."

"I'd pay to watch that show." Ava ran her longer-than-normal fingernails along the inside of Diana's thigh, making her shiver. "Assuming I didn't already have a free, all-access pass."

Diana produced her most entreating smile. "Is that your way of offering to pay for the pizza I was about to suggest we order?"

Ava laughed and shook her head fondly. "I'll buy the pizza, but only if you promise to ask Jude for the scoop on her cousin next time you see her. Nothing crazy, just a basic bio…and her full dating history, if possible."

"Is that all?" Diana couldn't fathom acting as a go-between, or really doing anything to facilitate a dalliance that seemed misguided at best. "What about her favorite sexual positions? Or whether she's willing to bang a woman who's technically old enough to be her mother?"

That earned her a sharp slap on the thigh and a scowl. "Even after an orgasm like that, you're *still* a brat."

"But you love me," Diana pointed out.

Ava sighed. "I do." Her stern countenance dissolved into a toothy grin. "Anyway, if you *did* somehow manage to deftly extract that level of intimate detail from Jude…I wouldn't close my ears to a discreet retelling." She reclined against the headboard, transforming her mischievous laughter into an agonized hiss. "And it's time to lie down again. Have you recovered enough to help me onto my back?"

Diana surged upright without hesitation, anxiously awaiting a battle plan to alleviate Ava's pain. "Just tell me what to do." She mirrored Ava's amused look with a smirk of her own. "Like usual."

CHAPTER NINE

Striding into the building's sole laundry room at nine o'clock on Friday night, the last thing Jude expected was to encounter another anti-socialite who'd chosen to prioritize dirty clothes over basic human interaction. She was therefore rather proud of herself for managing not to freak out and die when, upon her entrance, Diana Kelley glanced up from the thick paperback book she was reading while perched atop a quietly humming dryer on the far side of the room. Jude came to a stop just inside the door, unsure whether the sharing of appliances violated her new boss's rules about fraternization. She hefted the basket of clothes in her arms, then lifted her chin to gesture at the hallway behind her. "I can come back later."

Diana lowered her book to her lap. "Why?"

"Because..." Jude stepped farther inside to ensure they were alone before she finished the thought. "I don't want to make you uncomfortable. I wasn't sure...if this was awkward, or what."

Diana raised an eyebrow, delivering a spot-on impression of someone with no clue what Jude was talking about. "Doing our laundry at the same time?"

The question amplified Jude's growing feeling of silliness by a factor of one million. Frustrated, she said, "To be honest, Diana, I have no idea *what* you might find awkward. I only know you've repeatedly expressed worries about how this new working relationship will affect our neighborly rapport."

"Like chasing you away from a hot date with your dirty socks, for example?" Diana marked her page, then closed the book and met Jude's wary gaze. "Do you still believe my concern is unfounded?"

Weary from their precarious dance around the elephant in the room, Jude trudged to the nearest washing machine and dropped the heavy basket in her arms onto the floor. "I don't even know anymore." It was the truest answer she had. "It's not as though we see very much of each other outside class. And I'd like to think I've done a sufficient job of demonstrating my total lack of interest in hounding you for any sort of extracurricular activity. So in that sense, yeah, I do think your concern is unfounded." That she was fudging the truth—just a bit—triggered a guilty pang in Jude's gut. Fearful that Diana had already gleaned her innermost desires simply by looking at her, Jude threw open the lid of her washing machine with a little too much force, then overcompensated by grumbling her concluding remark in a vaguely shitty mutter. "And hurtful, frankly. How fucking pathetic do you think I am?"

Diana exhaled behind Jude. After a beat, she said, "I'm the pathetic one."

Still smarting from the close brush with being called out for her stupid, unstoppable infatuation, Jude shoved one last handful of clothing into the washer and closed the door. Then she swiveled to face Diana, arms folded over her chest to protect herself from whatever happened next. "I hope you aren't waiting for me to disagree."

Diana winced, holding a hand over her heart. "Ouch. Though I suppose I deserve that. For having offended you, if nothing else."

Not about to volunteer her opinion on the matter, Jude busied herself doling out detergent and fabric softener, then initiating an extended cycle for the hefty load. She mulled over what to say next and how to move beyond the undeniably tense moment, but Diana saved her the trouble.

"I don't think you're pathetic, Jude. In the least. On the contrary, you're a smart, beautiful, seemingly capable—and very sexy—young woman who has a bright future ahead of her. A future chock full of more sex and romance than you'll know what to do with, no doubt." Diana set her book aside and scooted forward to the very edge of the dryer. She waited for Jude to make eye contact, then continued. "I apologize if I've implied you might be desperate for a middle-aged girlfriend, or even another playmate for your already bustling stable of sex partners. To be clear, my paranoia has everything to do with me and virtually nothing with you. I don't *actually* imagine that a few paid fucks in a classroom setting will inevitably cause you to fall in love. Or leave you yearning for some kind of deeper entanglement." She scoffed and glanced down at her hands. "In no way am I that full of myself, despite how I may come across sometimes."

Sighing, Jude hopped up to sit on the edge of her steadily churning washing machine. She turned her body to face Diana's, all while struggling internally with the reality that, in fact, she *was* falling in love. She *did* yearn for a "deeper entanglement," whatever form that might take. She craved everything, *anything*, Diana could give her, like an addict craves her next hit. Whenever Jude closed her eyes at night or otherwise dreamed about what lay ahead, especially lately, Diana always featured prominently in the fantasies her heart refused to abandon. Perhaps *desperate* wasn't the most accurate way to describe how she felt, but Diana's concerns weren't even close to unfounded.

Wracked with guilt, Jude shifted some of the blame for their interpersonal challenges back onto herself. "I know I can be forward sometimes. I get why you feel the need to set firm boundaries with me. You're depending on Ava's replacement to show up at work, smiling, for no fewer than six weeks. If we wound up in some kind of sexual or romantic drama before the end, that could seriously fuck you over, financially." Wishing she knew how to better negotiate the treacherous chasm between her forbidden crush and Diana's comfort level, she added, "Also, you've never come across as conceited to me. Just scared."

Saddened by the shame that passed across Diana's face, then the numb resignation that followed, Jude had to restrain herself from dashing across the room to offer comfort. At a loss about what to do instead, she kept talking. "I don't know what happened in your past to create that fear, but I wish you hadn't gone through it. If someone hurt you…I hope they haven't found their happily-ever-after either. And that one day you'll be able to find yours. Because in all seriousness, Diana, you are hands-down the most desirable woman I've ever met." Jude's heart catapulted into her throat the instant the admission escaped her mouth. Despite her fear of blowing everything for real, she soldiered ahead with the potentially ill-fated bout of truth-telling. "I hope it's all right to say that out loud. I'll shut up if I'm freaking you out, but only if you stop trying to convince yourself that someone like me couldn't possibly be interested in someone like you. I could. Believe me, I absolutely could."

Diana held her gaze. "I'm not freaked out."

"Phew." Jude grinned, playacting a lightheartedness she wished she actually felt. "Glad to hear that." Afraid to let Diana interject, she babbled onward. "It's not like I've ever denied my attraction. Given the nature of our workplace collaboration, how could I? My body makes it obvious… wouldn't you agree? I couldn't hide *that* if I tried."

"Not with my finger inside you, certainly."

Startled by the directness of Diana's murmured rejoinder, Jude gripped the edge of the washing machine to maintain not only her balance but, more crucially, her self-control. With effort, she summarized her point in an equally hushed tone. "I may find you eminently fuckable, Diana Kelley, but that doesn't mean I'm going to betray your trust. Because I won't. I *wouldn't*. Not intentionally."

Tears gathered in Diana's vibrant blue eyes, rapidly spilling over in a show of emotion that stunned Jude silent. "While I appreciate the sentiment..." Diana shook her head, laughing as she self-consciously dabbed at her wet eyes with the hem of her well-worn, V-necked T-shirt. The action exposed a narrow swath of bare stomach, testing Jude's sense of decency until she opted not to linger on the captivating sight. "I *have* heard that one before. When you're falling for someone new, it's far too easy to believe all kinds of promises." She rearranged her shirt, then briefly pressed the heels of her hands over her eyes. "I'm sure my ex even believed her own bullshit in the beginning. It *did* take over a year for her to show her true self."

Jude leaned forward, hungry for the insight into Diana's psyche. "This is the woman who broke you?"

Diana blew out a tired sigh. "Her name was Janine." She narrowed her gaze, pointedly. "And I wouldn't say she *broke* me. More like cured me of any desire to share my life with another person."

Jude couldn't hide how unbearably tragic she found that. "Fuck Janine. You're really going to let her keep you alone and miserable for the rest of your life?"

Diana bristled, throwing back her shoulders with a defiant look. "Fuck *you*, Jude. Who says I'm miserable?"

Humbled, Jude bowed her head and closed her eyes. She shouldn't make assumptions like that. "You're right. I was out of line. Please accept my apology. I...misspoke." Trembling everywhere as she awaited Diana's response, she muttered, "I was angry—at Janine."

After a protracted silence, Diana said, "I forgive you."

On the verge of tears herself, Jude lifted her face to stare into Diana's shining eyes. "It was wrong to assume we want the same things out of life. Some people just aren't interested in love and romance. I can respect that."

"Good." Diana's cool facade wavered slightly, yet she seemed determined to hold their stare. "No offense, but I wouldn't expect a young lady with your active and varied sex life to stumble over the concept of no-strings-attached. You must meet plenty of women who are only interested in one night with you."

"Some, yes." Jude wanted to point out that most were young, and none hosted sex and intimacy workshops for couples, but in the interest of avoiding another argument, she moved on. "I know where you stand, and you know where I stand. I have a great time working for you. The pay is fantastic and the job itself..." She couldn't suppress a smile as images from their first two workshops filled her mind's eye. "Is *satisfying*."

Diana's breathing hitched, no doubt due to the emphasis she'd placed on that last word. "I'm glad you feel like things are going well. So do I. You're confident, responsive, and *finally* taking direction without offering snark in return." She winked, snatching up her book to worry the pages with her fingertips. "A *little* snark is acceptable, mind you. Keeps me on my toes."

"Yes, ma'am." Hearing the unintended sultriness of her reply, Jude twisted at the waist to check the empty doorway behind her. Reassured they were still alone, she turned to discover Diana openly admiring her chest. Her first instinct was to call Diana out, humorously, in an effort to ratchet up the sexual tension—but instead she chose the high road and allowed the transgression to pass without comment. "Back to what I was saying..." She swallowed, unable to believe how intimate Friday-night laundry had become. "I only want you to be happy, and I don't intend to screw up this job. Even if Janine was a horror show, *I'm* making a promise to never give you any reason to fear me. Or my presence in your life... whatever that amounts to."

The dryer under Diana chose that moment to signal the end of its cycle with a loud beep that startled them both, but Diana most of all. Jude guffawed at Diana's sharp yelp and the short-lived flailing of her arms as she fought off some imaginary threat. Recovering impressively fast for a woman who'd seemed momentarily convinced of her imminent death, Diana settled into a glowering scowl that only furthered Jude's amusement.

Tittering, Jude finally managed to say, "I can't make any promises for that dryer, however."

"Shut up." Diana's frown morphed into a begrudging smile. "Brat."

"You like that about me." Jude's confidence grew alongside Diana's grin. "Maybe a little?"

"Maybe." Diana glanced toward the ceiling, then hopped off the dryer to wait out the last couple of rotations of the drum. Facing away, she posed a question Jude couldn't help reading something into. "If you don't mind me asking, why are you spending Friday night alone, doing laundry? Surely you had better options."

"My clothes needed washing." Jude shrugged even though Diana's back was turned, unsure how to explain her general malaise for casual sex without sparking the fear she'd just promised never to create. "Who wants to pick up a one-night stand in dirty panties?"

"I didn't take you for a woman who'd let panties come between her and a night of fun." Diana faced her without opening the now-silent dryer, cocking an eyebrow at Jude's lavender sweatpants. "What're you wearing under those?"

Jude swallowed, electrified by the excuse to reveal such a thrilling detail. "I'm not."

"So you can go commando in front of me, but not the women you're trying to bed?"

"To be fair, I didn't expect to run into anyone down here." She waited until Diana had turned to unload the dryer, then added, "Least of all you."

Diana chuckled. "Thanks, I think?"

"I assumed you were at Ava's. Keeping her company or whatever."

"Nope." Diana folded a shirt. "I hate to upset your expectations, but I always insist on spending my Friday nights alone. I have a whole routine. First, takeout while I catch up on my shows. Then laundry, accompanied by a romance novel. After this I'll feed Karen, then soak in a hot bath… and most likely read an erotic short story before bed." Dropping a lacy undergarment into her basket, Diana glanced over her shoulder at Jude. "What's not to look forward to?"

Not about to disagree, Jude questioned the one ingredient in Diana's recipe for perfect solitude that hadn't made sense. "I don't mean to pry, but who's Karen?"

Diana hesitated, then turned to reveal unexpectedly pink cheeks. "Uh…my girlfriend, I suppose. At least that's what Ava calls her."

Stabbed by jealousy she prayed Diana wouldn't detect, Jude pretended not to give a shit about who Karen was or why Ava would award her the title of girlfriend. "Oh?" Affecting nonchalance—poorly, she suspected—she asked, "Do tell."

"Karen is an Avicularia avicularia." Diana responded to Jude's bewilderment with an almost equally baffling clarification. "A common pinktoe tarantula. My pet tarantula."

Jude's jealousy vanished, replaced by an equal mix of horror and amusement. "Your *pet*? You've allowed a fucking *tarantula* to set up residence next door to me?" She had no idea how to feel, except captivated. And creeped out. "Fuck...and you named this giant pet spider *Karen?*"

Diana burst into laughter so infectious that Jude had to join in. "What, you don't approve?"

"I mean..." Jude considered a handful of other monikers, then said, "I suppose Karen is as good a name as any for a terrarium-dwelling nightmare."

Diana folded her arms over her chest and tilted her head in challenge. "She's actually rather cute, in her own way. Certainly not as horrific as whatever you're imagining."

"I'll have to take your word for that." Jude lifted a skeptical eyebrow, trying to fit this new data into her understanding of the woman who occupied her every thought. "Why in the *world* do you own a tarantula? You're not..." She shuddered. "You're not, like, super into creepy-crawly things, are you?"

Diana smiled. "The opposite, actually. I acquired Karen after attending a seminar on the benefits of exposure therapy. In essence, by exposing yourself to the things you fear and avoid, you can eventually reduce fear and decrease avoidance."

Jude swallowed the first, facetious question to pop into her head— *Can that same technique reduce your fear and avoidance of intimacy? Because if so, I'll volunteer to be your exposure object*—and asked, "You're an arachnophobe?"

"From way back. One of my first memories is of a big, black spider crawling into my crib when I was a toddler." Gazing into the distance, Diana reminisced. "I flipped out, screaming, crying...it took my parents forever to come check on me. Or at least long enough to solidify a lifelong phobia."

Jude ached for tiny, frightened Diana. "What a truly awful formative experience. Did Karen help you get past that?"

Diana refocused on Jude, offering a sheepish shrug. "Yes and no? I'm definitely less intimidated by her, and other tarantulas, than I used to be. Watching Karen proved to be so fascinating—once I worked up the courage to look at her for more than a second or two—that I ended up doing a lot of reading about the various species and their habits. Tarantulas are usually quite docile creatures. Relatively harmless, too, especially in the Americas. Karen's species hails from the region that stretches from

Costa Rica to Brazil, as well as the southern Caribbean. Old World species possess more potent, medically significant venom and are often quicker to exhibit defensive behaviors, but a spider like Karen is more inclined to flick itchy, urticating hairs at you than bite. But no tarantula is capable of *killing* you, which I find extremely reassuring." Diana's mouth twisted wryly. "On the other hand, tarantulas aren't like house spiders. House spiders are the *worst.*"

Jude snorted. "So tarantula therapy goes only so far?"

"Given that the last time I found a spider in my bedroom, I slept on the couch for a week…yeah, Karen's no miracle worker." Diana grabbed another shirt to fold. "But she is a terrific companion. Always lets me control the remote, rarely nags, is indifferent about me doing my own thing…"

Laughing, Jude regarded Diana warmly. "She sounds wonderful. You know, except for being a big, scary tarantula."

"Ava thinks having a pet is good for me. I can't disagree." Surprisingly, Diana abandoned the task of folding her clothes to address Jude face-to-face, rife with sincerity. "Speaking of my fine, injured friend…thanks for putting me in touch with Katrina. Ava likes her a lot."

Jude snickered. "So I heard."

Diana paled noticeably, as though Jude had delivered the worst of news. "You…Ava isn't too much for your cousin, is she? She has a tendency to flirt, which I should've warned Katrina about from the beginning. I mentioned the grumpiness and that Ava would test her patience, but I guess I didn't anticipate…" She reached behind her hips to brace herself against the dryer, sighing. "I just…didn't anticipate."

"Ava's fine." Regretting that she'd caused so much worry, Jude tried to reassure Diana. "Katrina's very open-minded. Hardly the type to panic when women flirt with her."

"Even old women?"

"Wow." Offended on Ava's behalf, Jude snorted in disbelief. "Some friend. She's not even here to defend herself."

"You know what I mean." Diana leveled her with a piercing look. "Ava's forty-nine. Eighteen years isn't an insignificant age difference."

Jude read the subtext of her statement. *Neither is thirteen years.* Pushing back, she said, "It's not like Ava has asked for her hand in marriage. They get along well, and they have good chemistry. As long as they're both comfortable with the dynamic they're establishing, who are we to judge?"

Diana stared without blinking, then tipped her head in concession. "Touché."

"Don't worry about my cousin. She's a big girl. If Ava pushes too hard, Kat won't hesitate to let her know. And smack her down, if necessary." Jude didn't mention the clients Katrina had needed to correct in the past, all men, after they'd crossed lines she refused to endure. Given the stories she'd heard, she wasn't concerned about Ava—or Katrina—in the slightest. "Until then, let them have their fun. If flirting with Katrina motivates Ava to heal, doesn't that make all our lives better?" Chest tight, she pointed out, "The sooner Ava's back on her feet, the less time we'll have to spend feeling awkward around each other. Right?"

"I don't feel awkward with you," Diana said, unconvincingly.

Jude wished she could claim the same. "I don't *want* to, but...it's obvious you don't trust me. I know you don't, and that..." She blew out a shaky breath. "Adds a lot of pressure to every encounter."

"Maybe in time, I will." Diana's eyes entreated her to empathize. "Trust doesn't come easily for me."

"I understand." Or at least she wanted like hell to. "Maybe in time," she echoed, and fell silent to watch Diana finish folding her laundry. Sensing her imminent exit, and missing her already, Jude attempted to keep the conversation going. "Good luck with your solo class tomorrow. I'm sure it'll be amazing."

"Much appreciated." Diana tucked the last of her clothing away and hefted the basket into her arms. She didn't attempt to leave, but instead stood in place holding her laundry like a shield. "It should be fun, despite the two last-minute cancellations I got this morning."

Jude downplayed her incredulity that anyone would miss the chance to watch Diana rub one out. "That sucks. It's their loss."

"Mine too, unfortunately. I refunded their enrollment fees, less the deposit." Diana shifted her weight to the other foot. "At least the next two workshops are full. Everyone loves role-play. And let me tell you, there's no shortage of lesbian couples interested in spanking and discipline."

Jude nodded, careful not to dwell too long on thoughts of what would be required of her for that workshop. With Diana in the submissive role, she shouldn't have any reason to stress. Hopefully. Shaking her head, Jude focused on a more immediate concern: securing her ticket inside Diana's self-pleasuring seminar. "If it wouldn't be too weird, I'd love to sign up for your workshop. Help lessen the financial impact of those no-shows."

Diana frowned at her dubiously. "Pardon the assumption, but don't you already know how to masturbate?"

"Are you kidding?" Jude laced her hands in front of her, flexing the digits cockily. "I'm near professional level myself."

The fondness in Diana's smile made Jude warm all over. "I figured."

"I don't need instruction. I've just always had this fantasy about masturbating in a group setting."

"You don't already have plans?" Diana narrowed her scrutinizing gaze. "We *are* talking about your only free Saturday night for the next month and a half."

"My date bailed on me a couple of hours ago, over text," Jude lied. She hadn't attempted to make plans, having decided to spend the evening immersed in video games unless Diana agreed to indulge her exhibitionistic slash voyeuristic streak. "You're not the only one smarting over a last-minute cancellation."

"Thanks for the offer, but I can't take your money. I know you don't have it to spend."

Answering under the presumption that actual negotiations were underway, Jude countered. "Likewise, I wouldn't feel right attending for free. You also need the cash."

Diana searched her face for a dozen heartbeats, then said, "Would you accept a deep discount? I'll withhold a hundred bucks from your next paycheck."

"Withhold half and you've got a deal."

Diana frowned at her. "Having you in the audience will give my students top-notch fodder for their imaginations. You'd be doing me a service. Hence the reduced fee."

Disinclined to push, Jude nodded. "You talked me into it." How she'd finagled her way into precisely the scenario she'd most desired without repelling Diana, she had no clue, but she would embrace her good fortune—after checking in one last time. "It won't be too weird? Having me watch?"

If Diana had any misgivings, she hid them masterfully. "Considering what we've already seen of each other—" Her gaze flicked to the door before zeroing in on Jude's. "With all we've felt, and tasted…why should tomorrow be any weirder than the other Saturday nights we've spent together?"

Diana seemed committed to proving her lack of hesitation, and it wasn't like Jude had the stomach to back out, anyway. Jude saluted. "Then I'll be there."

"Should we ride together again?" Diana edged toward the door, openly self-conscious about her proposal. "Save money, help the planet."

"I'm down for that." Yearning for the day when their interactions became comfortable, Jude offered a shy wave as Diana retreated to the exit. "Enjoy your night. Consider practicing for tomorrow, maybe." Wolfishly, she called after Diana's retreating form. "Loudly, if you wouldn't mind. Right up against our bedroom wall." Guessing that Diana would greet the request as a playful lark, she explained, "Your students aren't the only ones in need of inspiration."

Diana paused in the doorway, then executed a crisp about-face to pin Jude with an intense stare. "See, I have this policy about avoiding orgasm for at least twenty-four hours prior to a workshop. Especially if I intend to come for my students."

Unbearably aware of the soaked crotch of her sweatpants, Jude said, "Bummer." Under her breath, she added, "For you."

"I'd love for you to follow the same rule. Please." Diana's gentle smile softened the cruelty of her request. "For me."

Jude knew she could refuse, or just lie and get herself off anyway, but for some reason she felt an inexplicable eagerness to comply. "Okay. Bummer for *us*, then."

"It'll be worth the wait." Diana wetted her lips with her tongue, unspooling a dozen concurrent fantasies in Jude's fevered brain. "You'll see."

Watching Diana's miraculous ass disappear around the corner, Jude didn't doubt it.

Jude arranged her blanket along the outermost edge of the semicircle of women around Diana, convinced that they'd massively underestimated the inherent oddness of this situation in the race to demonstrate their mutual chill. Despite agreeing to serve as eye candy for her fellow classmates, the mostly silent shared car ride with Diana had stripped Jude of the confidence to put herself front and center. Plus, she wouldn't have anywhere to look except into Diana's seductive blue eyes.

Jude's inner voice whispered forebodingly. *If you make eye contact, what will she see?*

Head bowed, Jude took deep, even breaths to calm her nerves. Diana had already eaten her out and vaginally massaged her to within an inch of her sanity. What was a little mutual masturbation between platonic neighbors who fucked for cash? She kept her eyes lowered until Diana called everyone to attention, then decided she needed to pull her shit together and act normal to avoid screwing the night up completely. Only half-listening to Diana's speech about the physical and mental benefits of masturbation, and the optional use of toys to enhance enjoyment, Jude cast a furtive look around. This was her first time watching Diana work from the perspective of a student—an impressive sight to behold.

Her classmates devoured their instructor's every syllable. While most appeared nervous to some degree, Jude could see their tension ease as Diana established a friendly, nonjudgmental atmosphere with her openness and unforced confidence. It blew Jude's mind that this was the same Diana who'd dissolved into tears while doing her laundry on a Friday night. Diana the educator was powerful and in control. She exuded self-assurance, and compassion, and strength beyond measure. She was *hot as fuck.*

Diana stood to undo the top button of her shirt. "I know it's intimidating to share an act this private with a room full of strangers, even lovely ones, so how about I break the ice?" She unbuttoned her shirt casually, letting it fall to the floor before she reached behind her back to unclasp her bra. "You can decide how much to disrobe, if at all. I will so everyone can see what I'm doing, but if you're more comfortable keeping your clothes on, that's a perfectly valid choice."

Nodding along with her classmates' murmured assent, Jude slowly exhaled—then stood. With the still-seated women between them no longer acting as a buffer, she had no choice but to meet Diana's inquisitive stare. Throat dry, Jude said, "You shouldn't have to get naked alone."

"I won't complain if you want to join me." Diana winked gratefully, unfastening her skirt to reveal sheer black panties attached to the stockings with matching garters. "Full disclosure, Jude is temporarily assisting at my couples' workshops while my usual partner in crime recovers from a serious back injury. I asked her to join us tonight because I figured her presence might fuel some imaginations—including my own." She paused for a long, drawn-out moment—topless and channeling a Victoria's Secret ad from the waist down—then tapped her toe comically. "What do you say, you gorgeous girl? Ready to show off that delicious body?"

Thankfully, Jude's libido assumed control of both her brain and her bodily functions, allowing her to shed her shirt and jeans with minimal clumsiness. She shrugged out of her bra next, then, going one step farther than Diana, stripped off her panties and kicked them aside. Total nudity achieved, she sank down to lounge—gracefully, in theory—on the blanket once more. Diana beamed and did the same, arranging her body with her thighs open and her back against the plush reading pillow she'd carried in from the trunk of her car. Jude heard the other students rustling around—some undressing, others merely loosening their clothes—before the lesson resumed.

If Diana possessed any groundbreaking wisdom about the art of jacking off, Jude would never know. Her brain shorted out the instant Diana launched into a detailed description of her favorite method for slowly building to climax—step one, using the tips of her index and middle fingers to tease herself through her panties—while simultaneously demonstrating in real time. Convinced her insatiable lust had to be plain enough for every living soul to behold, Jude turned her face so Diana wouldn't perceive the depth of her all-consuming desire. She locked eyes with the woman next to her, a silver-haired butch whose gaze instinctively lowered to skitter nervously over Jude's bare breasts.

"Hi," Jude whispered, glad for a distraction from Diana. The butch forced her eyes up to Jude's, clearly mortified about her indiscretion. Jude soothed her with a warm smile and the same seductive tone that always worked magic for her at the club. "Don't be shy. Go ahead. Look all you want. I promise I don't mind."

The butch's cheeks reddened. Her previously flexing arm had gone still, along with the hand in her pants. In a hushed undertone, she murmured an apology beneath Diana's continued narration. "I swear I'm not a creep...or some perverted old butch letch..." She removed her hand from her jeans, blushing harder. "Maybe this was a bad idea."

"Hey, wait." Jude leaned toward the woman as though physically preparing to stop her from leaving. She instinctively softened her pose, not wanting to further intimidate, and extended her hand in a plea for her classmate to stick around. "Don't go, please. Stay." Unsure whether it was the right move, Jude lowered the same hand between her legs to graze the well-lubricated labia peeking out from between her outer lips. "You're not the only one in need of imagination fuel."

The butch managed an uneasy smile. "Uh, thanks...but...why me?" She conducted a rapid visual scan of the room, ending at Jude's face. "That is...well, you know."

Jude was honest. "I like older women. They turn me on." She dragged her index finger up to circle her clit, shuddering. "Do I turn you on?"

The butch groaned, lowering her gaze to watch Jude stroke herself. Despite her steely determination to focus on her own performance, it wasn't long before Jude succumbed to temptation and glanced at the front of the room—just in time to witness Diana unsnap her garters, then slide her panties down the length of her long legs. Rubbing her clit faster, Jude forced her attention back to her hesitant neighbor and discovered that the butch's previously errant hand had made its way back inside her jeans.

Sheepishly, she said, "I'm Beth." The movement of her hand slowed to a crawl. "Seems like you should know if I'm going to…" She nodded at Jude's continued self-pleasuring, face beet red. "You know, watch."

Taking pity on poor Beth, Jude asked, "Would this be easier if I didn't look at you?"

Beth frowned apologetically. "I'm so sorry, but…I think maybe yes."

"No worries." Drawing renewed confidence from the flustered responses, Jude faced the opposite way with a flourish. She bent at the waist, set her knees apart, and ran her fingers over the slick, exposed folds in an intentionally provocative display. The woman on Jude's other side—around Diana's age, curvy, intellectual in appearance—grinned, then tugged the crotch of her own panties aside to penetrate her vagina with the slim vibrator she'd retrieved from her purse at the beginning of class. Jude returned her smile, inserting a finger into her own eager opening for her audience of one. "That's a beautiful pussy," she said amidst her new neighbor's escalating moans. "And you seem to know exactly what to do with it."

Her neighbor nodded proudly, then closed her eyes in what appeared to be deep concentration. Cut off from that line of interaction, Jude hung her head to focus on her own pleasure. Was Diana watching her perform for Beth, a woman at least twenty years her senior, and if so, what did she think? Did her exhibitionism arouse Diana? Was she jealous?

A familiar groan from the front of the room beckoned Jude to investigate. Raising her head, she drank in the stunning vision of a stocking-clad Diana furiously stroking her clit and staring directly into her eyes. Jude's inner muscles contracted to send even more wetness gushing onto her fingertips. The knowledge that Beth had seen the molten flash flood only intensified Jude's excitement. Abandoning her clit, she pushed her finger back into her vagina to fuck herself. Beth's audibly labored breathing heightened Jude's arousal until she could no longer think.

Acting instinctively, she withdrew her finger and rearranged herself over the pillow she'd borrowed from Diana, resting her upper body on the blanket to free up a second hand. Without breaking eye contact, she lodged her wet digits back into her opening, then thrust her butt into the air so her other hand could sneak under her stomach and massage her throbbing clit.

Nostrils flaring, Diana addressed the room in a noticeably strained tone. "If you're the multi-orgasmic type, or suspect you might be, climax however quickly you'd like. One of the greatest benefits to womanhood—beyond the obvious—is that..." She inhaled, thighs quivering. "For many of us, each additional orgasm after the first will...take significantly less time and stimulation." Her stomach muscles rippled, hinting at the real reason for her new directive. Gasping, she said, "I'll go first," then went rigid with a full-throated shout.

In awe of the dazzling crescendo, Jude hastened the fingers on her clit, letting her other hand slip out of her vagina so she could concentrate on the primary target. She rocked against her fingertips, hungry for the climax hovering just beyond her reach. It kept threatening to crash over her—as Diana came down from her orgasm, as she twisted her nipple between those perfectly manicured nails to trigger another round of aftershocks, then as she sighed in contentment once she'd finally recovered—yet somehow, Jude couldn't achieve release. Cursing, she used her free hand to spread her buttocks and offer Beth a more explicit view. But even Beth's ecstatic moans failed to push her over the edge.

"Fuck." Jude clenched her jaw. "Come on." She coached herself under her breath. "*Come on.*" Stymied, Jude blinked away tears of frustration. "*Please.*"

Coming to her aid, Diana lunged forward, looked into Jude's eyes, and ordered her, "Come for me, you gorgeous girl."

After that, Jude wasn't sure she'd ever return to earth.

CHAPTER TEN

A wake in bed four nights later, Diana fought to shut off her brain and sleep. This was her new nighttime ritual: struggling to forget the noises Jude made when she climaxed, or how she'd fucked herself for Beth Watkins's (initially reluctant) entertainment, or the way she'd spent last Saturday seemingly determined to avoid eye contact, yet unable to look away. But forgetting was impossible. Especially when Diana's brain insisted on obsessively replaying her favorite mental movie on a frenetic loop: Jude orgasming at her command—not just once, but three times.

How could she *possibly* sleep with that delicious food for thought rattling around in her head?

Sighing, Diana slipped her hand beneath the comforter, then between her thighs. She lacked the energy for a big effort—too cozy under the covers to go grab her favorite toy, too tired for very much buildup. But if there was any chance that getting off would sate her fevered mind, she was more than willing to try. She reached beneath the waistband of her nighttime shorts to stroke her labia, testing her readiness.

"Already wet," she whispered aloud, delighted by the copious juices at her opening. "That a girl, Jude." Diana petted herself, closing her eyes to pretend she was feeling Jude's diligent tongue. "Get that pussy nice and juicy for me." Pleasure shot through her lower body. "Lick it up, baby. Just like I taught you."

A muffled thump from the wall behind her head—Jude's bedroom wall—startled Diana wide awake. She tore her hand from her shorts, guilty as a teenager without a lock on her bedroom door. Another thump reverberated through the wall, followed by muffled laughter. Frowning,

Diana realized what was happening. For the first time in over three weeks, Jude had brought home an overnight guest. They were about to fuck while Diana lay in bed only feet away, horny and alone. She would have to listen.

"You don't *have* to," she mumbled, mostly to convince herself. "You *could* sleep on the couch. Or listen to music." The languorous moan of a woman who most definitely *wasn't* Jude nearly convinced her to do just that. "Through headphones."

The quality of the moans changed abruptly, hinting that Jude had started to work her special brand of sexual sorcery. Diana's reticence melted as she lost herself in thoughts of Jude's soft, wet tongue, of hovering above her open, eager mouth, of how it made her feel to receive oral worship from such a beautiful young thing. Without making a conscious choice, she returned her fingers to her clit.

Their loud fucking lasted well over an hour, enough time for Diana to enjoy a trio of orgasms. After recovering from the last one, as the ruckus from Jude's bedroom resumed for an apparent third round, Diana tore her hand from her shorts and rolled onto her side. The hot bitterness of the tears streaming down her cheeks shocked her, as did their swift transformation into silent, racking sobs. She attempted to shut off her brain for a countless time that night, but all she could do was think.

She thought about how exciting it was to flirt with Jude, and how elated she felt when Jude flirted back. She imagined touching Jude in private, with nobody watching. Or even better, kissing her, the kind of kiss she hadn't experienced in a decade—long, passionate, and deep.

Then she remembered how Janine had provided similar thrills, in the beginning. For the first thirteen months of their nearly six-year relationship, Diana had been certain they would grow old together. With Janine, laughter came easily, and their chemistry was incendiary—in every way, as it turned out. Early in their second year, the insults started. Janine always had something to say about her outfit, her behavior, the way she smiled at the waitress, or most viciously, her active and varied sexual past. Diana still couldn't understand the shift in Janine's attitude, except as the natural consequence of settling into a long-term relationship with a bona fide jerk. Once the frequency of their lovemaking inevitably slowed from its initially breakneck pace, Janine had turned jealous and cruel, disapproving of her in seemingly every way.

Being young and stupid, Diana had rationalized the souring of their relationship as at least partially her fault. She hadn't made Janine feel appreciated or curbed her naturally flirtatious tendencies enough for their monogamous lifestyle. It had taken almost five more years for Diana to accept that she didn't deserve the abuse Janine dished out on an almost daily basis. Despite her adventurous youth, she'd never been unfaithful. And while her outfits occasionally revealed a hint of cleavage or bare skin, they were never inappropriate. She'd never given Janine any reason to doubt her fidelity, and it wasn't her job to fall in line to assuage her partner's insecurities.

Leaving Janine hadn't ended her misery. It took another two years for Janine to lose interest in the stalking and harassment campaign she'd launched after their separation. If her ex hadn't met her current girlfriend, Trish—bless her soul—Diana assumed she'd still be deleting vicious texts and voice mails.

Flirting with Jude might be exciting, but it was also pointless, and stupid. It was the very definition of selfish, a dead-end action that risked blurring the boundaries Diana had worked hard to establish.

That's what she kept telling herself, over and over, as she ached to be the one in Jude's bed and to wake up beside her the morning after, entangled and exhausted. Diana's craving went beyond sex, and that's where the real problem lay. She wanted to take Jude out to a nice restaurant, somewhere fancy, so they could dress up. She envisioned zipping up the back of Jude's dress—and sobbed even harder.

Who was she kidding? Even if she could overcome the foul aftertaste of life with Janine, poor Jude deserved more than she had to give. She was damaged goods, one of the biggest reasons she refused to date. No one deserved the baggage she'd bring to a relationship, an earnest twenty-six-year-old least of all.

Sniffling at Jude's audible groan, Diana crawled out of bed, grabbed her pillow and blanket, and fled the room. Her sanity demanded she sleep on the couch tonight.

If only her brain let her rest.

An hour later, Diana ventured back into her bedroom on a mission to find her phone. Thankfully, Jude and her lover had fallen silent. Even so, Diana grabbed what she needed and reclaimed her spot on the couch. She wasn't ready to return to the scene of the crime. Counting on Ava's night-owl tendencies to hold true despite her injury, Diana typed a brief text message—driven by loneliness as much as concern.

How are you feeling?

Ava replied almost immediately. *Better. Having Katrina here helps…but I'm still a long way from taking a dildo in the ass or being spanked.*

Diana winced at Ava's assumption that her query was at least partially self-serving. Mainly since she wasn't wrong. Rather than add to Ava's burden, Diana lied.

Take your time. Things are going well with Jude. Our arrangement seems to be working out.

How well, exactly?

Rolling her eyes at Ava's winky-face emoticon, she tapped out a hasty response.

She respects my boundaries, and her pussy is wetter than the ocean. So…quite well.

Fallen for her yet?

Diana closed her eyes, stunned by how the good-humored question left her feeling so agonizingly alone. She didn't wallow for long, however, so as not to appear shaken.

Decisively, Diana typed, *Nope. She's too young for me, and I'm too old for that shit. By "shit," I obviously mean sex and romance.*

Ava spent a long time penning her reply. When the text finally arrived, it started with a bang.

Fuck you, too old. I'll have you know that this much-older lady isn't close to done with sex and romance yet…even with *a broken spine.* She punctuated that declaration with a string of emoji to convey her displeasure. *Too old, my ass. You're not old. You're a chicken.*

Anger flaring, Diana muted her phone and dropped it onto the coffee table. After a beat, she slid it across the smooth wooden surface until it came to rest a few inches beyond her reach. That way, she was less likely to do something stupid, like reply.

"Serves me right, reaching out to Ava in the middle of the night," Diana muttered, rolling onto her side to face the back of the couch. "Should've known." Though she loved Ava like family, her perceptiveness was a giant pain in the ass. Sometimes it sucked to be known so well.

Yet Diana wouldn't trade Ava for anything. *Does that mean I'm still capable of loving? Of being loved?*

She drifted off to sleep without finding an answer that didn't scare her to death.

Jude lay unmoving beneath the heavy, slumbering body of Geri, the cute, curvy chick she'd invited home to prove she wasn't hung up on someone unobtainable—both to herself and Diana—and wondered how three orgasms apiece could leave her so unfulfilled. Geri had shown up for drinks looking red-hot in a cleavage-baring little black dress, their conversation stayed lively throughout the evening, and the sex hadn't sucked by any measure. Still, the woman in her bed didn't excite her like Diana did. Jude acknowledged that this wasn't Geri's fault, exactly. The woman was funny, flirty, and passionate about working with children. She was *great*.

She just wasn't Diana.

Eyes closed, Jude listened for any sign of life in the bedroom next door. Had Diana heard that entire show? She'd intended for her to. Alone with her thoughts, Jude couldn't stop running through the various ways her gambit might've been received. She hoped Diana had been reassured. Amused, even. Or better yet, aroused. What if she'd gotten herself off alongside them? The idea made Jude tingle in places she was too tired to contemplate even without a sleeping human blocking access to her clit.

But what if Diana *hadn't* enjoyed the display? They'd been loud—louder than Jude wanted. Geri hadn't been shy about voicing her approval, that was for sure. If they'd kept Diana awake past her bedtime…or caused her to feel jealous in some way—perhaps because her own lover was out of commission—well, then Jude would feel like absolute shit. She'd fucked Geri to demonstrate that she hadn't become overly attached, that their recent encounters hadn't ended her non-monogamous lifestyle.

And how did that work out for you?

Jude sneered back at her inner critic, but she knew the answer. All tonight had proved was her own lack of interest in sleeping with anyone else. She didn't want to do it again until Diana was through with her for good.

Wishing it wouldn't be rude to shake Geri awake and ask her to leave, Jude stewed in her worry and regret until she finally drifted into an uneasy sleep.

CHAPTER ELEVEN

Standing with Jude in front of the ten couples who'd gathered to watch them role-play, Diana hoped like hell that whatever fantasy they enacted wouldn't get her into too much trouble. She was so hungry for her young neighbor she could barely think, let alone act rationally. And she was jealous. Stupidly, illogically jealous of the hussy Jude had fucked Wednesday night, to the point of wishing for some way to mark Jude as her own. She craved to lay claim to her, just until Ava recovered, so she would never again have to imagine—or worse yet, *hear*—what pleasure another woman was giving her.

Only while they worked together, of course. After that, Jude's personal life was her own business.

Impatient to get started, Diana cleared her throat. "Good evening, ladies, and welcome to a truly fun night. This is Intro to Role-Playing, also known as Dirty Make-Believe 101." She paused to return the smiles she received. "This workshop is a bit different from most of the others I teach. While I usually encourage audience participation, this topic doesn't easily lend itself to watching, listening, *and* performing on your own, all at the same time. So tonight, my lovely assistant Jude and I will improvise a role-playing scene for your viewing pleasure. Introducing the elements of make-believe and fantasy fulfillment into your sex life can be a powerful way to reinvigorate your passion for one another. It'll help keep your lovemaking fresh, keep you from falling into those standard routines that inevitably begin to feel, I'm sorry to say, a little boring."

For the skeptical audience member—because there was always one—Diana addressed the most common concern she usually heard head-on. "Never hesitate to invite your lover to enjoy a stranger in bed when that stranger is *you*. As lesbians, we tend to be drawn to nest, to settle down. But as humans, it's only natural to be turned on by novelty. When the person you love is willing and able to provide that novelty, you've truly found a gift to be treasured."

Shifting gears, Diana glanced at Jude's inscrutable expression, then returned her attention to the crowd. "All right. We'll save any questions you may have for after the show. Right now, Jude and I have a question for all of *you*." On impulse, she wrapped her arm around Jude's waist and tugged her closer. "We don't have anything rehearsed, so this role-play is in your collective hands. Would you ladies be so kind as to toss out a few ideas? Inspire us."

"Cougar and cub!" Liz, whom Diana had last seen at the vaginal massage workshop, had a shit-eating grin plastered across her face.

Diana demurred. "I'm afraid I have to pass on that one. Hits a little too close to reality, I'd say."

"Yeah," Jude chimed in, a bit timidly. "This is your chance to be creative. Give us roles we can sink our teeth into."

"Vampire/victim!" a first-time student shouted, eagerly seizing upon Jude's unintended imagery.

Having never been a big fan of vampires, Diana gestured for more. "Keep 'em coming."

"How about slave and master?"

Diana tried not to immediately glom on to that concept, much as she wanted to, if only because her next workshop—spanking and discipline— was bound to touch on similar themes. "Good. Let's hear some more."

"A queen and her loyal servant!" That woman's partner shouted, clearly angling for the same dynamic.

Liz piped up with another on-the-nose suggestion. "Teacher and student?"

Her partner tossed a contender into the ring. "Repairwoman and bored housewife?"

"*That* could be fun," Jude said. She shot Diana a sidelong grin. "You would play the bored housewife, of course."

Diana knew her lack of enthusiasm for that scenario arose from the worst reason imaginable. She couldn't lay claim to Jude as the bored housewife. She couldn't *take* her, or punish her, or torment her with any real authority in the guise of a horny middle-aged homemaker bent on seducing a sexy repairwoman. Naturally, it was the safest choice they'd yet been given, even if the concept didn't exactly soak her pussy. She opened her mouth to accept the role, but Liz cut her off to blurt out a real gem.

"Ooh! Or a dangerous prisoner and the cold bitch sent to interrogate her!" Liz clapped her hands three times in quick succession. "Please, please, *please*."

Digging her nails into her palms, Diana forced her mind away from the dark places she could take such a fantasy. What the hell was wrong with her, anyway? If she wanted Jude, she could have her. Jude couldn't have been any clearer about that. But Diana *didn't* want her—or rather, didn't want to fall in love with her. The idea of getting that close to Jude, of trusting *anyone* like she'd trusted Janine, twisted her insides into a Gordian knot. And that…that made Diana sad, and lonely, and angry. Angry at Jude for coming into her life at all, for living next door, and especially for bringing women far hotter than Diana home to fuck, loudly, on the other side of her bedroom wall.

She hadn't cared before being inside Jude for herself, but now that she had, she wasn't keen to share. Though she had no right to harbor possessive feelings for a woman she refused to fuck on her own time, Diana couldn't change her stubborn heart. She wanted Jude to belong to her, but only if she didn't have to become vulnerable in the process. She wanted exclusive access to Jude's body, but without having to offer anything in return.

What she wanted was impossible. Impossible, selfish, and far more than she deserved.

Guilty for feeling upset when Jude had done nothing wrong, Diana tightened the arm around her waist and gave her a patient nod. "Your choice, sweetheart. Would you like to come fix this bored housewife's refrigerator?" She grinned. "Or be interrogated about your crimes?"

Jude looked uneasy about being tasked with the decision. "Which do you prefer?"

Diana slipped her thumb under the hem of Jude's shirt to stroke the silky skin above her hip. "Nope. You pick. One of those scenarios is fairly edgy, so I want you to set the tone."

Searching Diana's eyes, Jude emanated a distinct vibe of yearning to please. "I can do edgy."

Diana studied Jude's face, hoping to determine her true desire. "But do you *want* to?"

Jude's drawn-out hesitation contradicted her eventual answer. "Sure."

Diana despised that she briefly considered accepting Jude's less than wholehearted consent simply because she longed for tonight's encounter to be dirty and rough. She wanted to reprimand Jude for bringing home that stranger with a hard, demanding fuck, with sex so raw and unrestrained it would ruin her young assistant for anyone else—for the next month and a half, anyway.

Thankfully, Diana's better nature kicked in before her own hesitation became awkward. "Let's do repairwoman and bored housewife."

The mild relief in Jude's eyes confirmed that she'd chosen wisely. "You sure?" Jude smirked, an attempt at cockiness that didn't quite succeed. "Because I don't mind being dominated by you. In the least."

"Bored, *dominant* housewife seduces surprised but compliant repairwoman, then." Diana asked the class. "What do you think? Is that a role-play you'd like to see?" She half-bowed at the resulting cheers and scattered applause. "All right. The people have spoken."

"Great." Jude practically vibrated, no doubt from anticipation. "So…where should we start?"

"First, with a safe word. What'll it be?"

Jude didn't even think. "Laundry."

"Laundry, it is." Releasing Jude, Diana dragged the oversized beanbag she'd brought as an all-purpose prop into the center of the room. "Next, we define our characters, our props, and the situation." She poked the beanbag with her foot. "Let's say…soon after this sexy repairwoman arrived to fix my broken fridge, I decided—in a fit of boredom, probably brought on by my housewifery—to strip down to my camisole and panties…" Acting out the impromptu narrative, Diana unbuttoned her blouse, then her pants. "And self-entertain while I wait for her to finish the job and come collect her payment." Clad in lacy red tanga panties and a sheer white camisole, Diana arranged herself atop the beanbag, striking the most provocative pose she could muster. Gazing up at Jude, she lowered her hand between her thighs and stroked her clothed vulva teasingly. "Excuse yourself to the 'other room,' my dear, and get into character. Our scene begins when you return to discover what I've been doing while you were hard at work."

Jude gawped dumbly, then hurriedly stumbled backward a step. "Sure. Yes, ma'am." When she swiveled to retreat into the far corner of the room, Diana saw her cringe. Jude was embarrassed, and Diana adored the sight.

After standing in the corner for a full thirty seconds, Jude strode back to the center of the room. As she approached the beanbag, she pantomimed stepping through a doorway, then flinched and shielded her eyes. "Ma'am, I...I'm extremely sorry to disturb you, ma'am, but I've finished your repair. And I, uh...have some paperwork for you to sign before I go."

"What sort of paperwork?" Diana patted her concealed labia with her fingertips, sighing at the pleasant reverberations throughout her lower body. "Can it wait?"

"Uh...well...I guess I could..."

Impressed by the flustered performance, Diana murmured, "Are you in a rush to leave? Do you have another appointment?" She assumed the vampish role with ease, massaging her labia through the damp fabric, then slipping her pinkie finger under the elastic band to graze her wetness. "Because perhaps you didn't notice, but I'm currently right in the middle of something here—"

Jude looked up at the ceiling and away from Diana. "Should I come back later? I can go grab some lunch, give you time...to finish. What you're doing." Another cringe, this time in character. "If you want."

"What *I* want...is for you to stay." Diana released a quiet moan, further exploring her state of arousal. "And help."

Jude's shoulders tensed, as though she were genuinely taken aback. "Ma'am?"

"Do you know...I can't even *remember* the last time anyone made me orgasm? My husband—he and I are separated, soon to be divorced— well, he would try and try, but..." Diana eased her entire hand down the front of her panties, positioning the index and middle fingers on either side of her fantastically swollen clit. "Bless his heart."

Jude chuckled, along with the rest of the class, at the distinctly Southern twang with which Diana delivered the line. At long last, Jude lowered her gaze. Openly reluctant to let her attention drift below Diana's neck for more than a second or two, she cleared her throat and asked, "Help *how*, ma'am?"

As she traced slow circles around her clit with her right hand, Diana gathered the crotch of her panties in her left, pulling the material aside to expose her slippery labia to Jude's ravenous eyes. "Don't be coy with me, young lady. You look like the sort of girl who knows *exactly* what to do with a wet pussy."

Jude licked her lips, lashes fluttering. "Yes, ma'am. I do know my way around the female anatomy." Inching closer to the beanbag, she sank to her knees and shyly met Diana's eyes. "I'm also great with my hands."

"Perfect." Diana moved out of the way, raising both arms above her head to allow Jude room to work. After a beat, she lowered one to caress Jude's flushed cheek. "Go on, darling. Show me what those pretty fingers can do."

A noticeable tremor ran through the hand Jude brought down to rest on her panty-covered vulva. She kneaded Diana lightly, then carefully delved between her outer labia to fondle the sensitive inner folds concealed by the sodden material. Sighing in appreciation, Diana yanked her camisole up around her neck and gave her painfully stiff nipples a sharp, sobering twist. Her hips canted off the beanbag sharply, a movement Jude used to her advantage. Without hesitating, she grasped the waistband of Diana's panties and dragged the lacy material down to bunch around her knees. Leaving her tangled—trapped, even—in her own underwear, Jude sought out Diana's vulva once more, cupping the heated flesh in her soft hand. She lingered there only momentarily, then shifted to spread Diana's labia open with her left hand so she could explore the slick, engorged flesh with the right.

"How's this?" Jude trapped the hood of Diana's clit between her fingertips, jerking her tenderly. "Does this help?"

Diana gasped at the deliberate tightening of her grip. "Very much."

"Glad to hear it." Jude continued to manipulate that most responsive ridge of flesh, stopping only when Diana's thighs quivered beyond her control. Unhanding her completely, Jude asked, "What about penetration? Do you want my fingers inside your poor, neglected hole?"

Simultaneously turned on and challenged by her assistant's growing confidence, Diana clamped onto Jude's slim wrist and guided her index and middle fingertips to her entrance. "Careful. Don't forget who's in charge." She pushed Jude inside her body with a lusty growl. "And who's serving *whom*."

Jude dropped her head, seemingly taking the warning to heart. "Yes, ma'am." Her lips twitched as she plunged all the way inside Diana for the second time. "As they say, the customer's always right."

"You'd do well to remember that." Diana groaned at the thorough vaginal massage Jude had begun to perform, only two weeks overdue. Afraid she might finish before they'd even started, Diana slammed her legs closed on Jude's flexing arm. "On a related note..." She grasped

Jude's wrist, cautiously extracting the prodigious digits embedded within her depths. "Time for you to suck my pussy. It's been *ages* since I was last eaten."

Jude sat back on her heels. "Happily."

"That's the spirit." Diana slipped her panties the rest of the way off, then faced the other direction, draping herself over the beanbag with her ass thrust into the air. "Get to it, girl. Lick me." She instinctively held her breath while Jude crawled into position behind her, then cursed at the tentative, exploratory slide of her imaginary repairwoman's hot tongue along the exposed labia. Reaching backward, Diana grabbed hold of Jude's hair and yanked her closer, trapping her between her cheeks until she flailed for air. She granted Jude a few seconds of reprieve to catch her breath, then promptly hauled her back in. "Stick your tongue inside my cunt. Fuck me like you mean it."

Jude surged into her ardently, following the command with gusto. Diana's mouth dropped open in ecstasy, the impassioned, worshipful touch electrifying her from head to foot. She kept Jude trapped against her for as long as humanely possible before letting go. Shaking from the steamy, parting kiss Jude planted directly atop her anus, Diana had to fight the urge to force her head back down.

Catching her breath, Jude quipped, "On a scale of one to ten, how satisfied *are* you with my customer service? That happens to be the very first question on the customer survey I'm supposed to have you fill out. Enough positive evaluations, and I'll get a quarterly bonus."

Diana chuckled at Jude's innocuous stab at humor. Flipping over, she settled onto her back in a semi-seated position and parted her legs—for Jude *and* their spellbound audience. "Sounds like you should be working extra hard to please me, then. Hope you're ready to do whatever it takes."

Jude stretched to retrieve the topmost blanket from a nearby pile, spreading it out at Diana's feet with her eyes averted. "Your satisfaction is my highest priority, ma'am. And I *do* take a tremendous amount of pride in my work. Always have."

"Lucky me." Diana toyed lazily with her clit as she watched Jude lower herself onto her belly, awaiting the welcome return of her assistant's dutiful tongue. "To have such a willing, *nasty* slut sent to kneel at my feet."

Jude blinked a couple times before maneuvering her shoulders between Diana's thighs. After the tiniest of pauses, she bent, open-mouthed, to hover mere inches from Diana's shiny, pink folds. "May I?"

Diana caught her by the neck and urged her downward. "Only if you want that positive evaluation…"

"Mmm." Jude feasted enthusiastically, slurping Diana's labia without any hint of self-consciousness. She came up for air long enough to breathe "Yes, ma'am," then got back to it.

Diana whimpered against her will, unable to remain cool and controlled with Jude tending to her so thoroughly. The sight of her neighbor's exquisite face buried in her pussy, the bliss of that tenacious suction—it was little wonder Diana couldn't prevent the involuntary quaking of her body as Jude steadily drove her toward release. Taking control of the bobbing head between her legs, Diana rolled her hips to fuck the tongue that undulated against her with expert precision. Unbidden, a question bubbled up to distract her from the wholly indulgent head she was receiving.

Is this what Jude does for everyone she takes to bed? It would explain the noise level.

Soured by a stab of envy for those women—women who could just *be* with Jude, free of fear—Diana wound her hand in Jude's hair and yanked. "I bet you do this all the time, don't you?"

Unable to offer a verbal response with her face in Diana's pussy, Jude shook her head and kept on licking.

Incensed at the blatant lie, Diana growled. "Yeah, right." She grunted when Jude increased her suction, then the speed of her tongue. "I'm sure you don't have any trouble remembering the last time *you* ate pussy. Do you?"

Jude faltered just long enough to confirm that the not entirely unsubtle dig had hit home. When Diana dragged her away from her clit for another necessary break, Jude shook her head and closed her eyes in shame. "No, ma'am."

To ensure Jude knew precisely what she was talking about, Diana grew snarky. "It hasn't even been a week. Has it?"

Tensing, Jude whispered, "No, ma'am."

"See? Fucking *slut*," Diana hissed, then forced Jude's face into her pussy for more. "I knew you'd do anything I told you to." Placing a hand on either side of Jude's head, Diana raised her hips to force her clit even farther into Jude's open mouth. "Even miss your next appointment to be my obedient little fuck-toy. Isn't that right?"

With her mouth full and movement restricted, Jude could only whimper.

Not too far gone to remember the importance of checking in, Diana let go of Jude entirely. After giving her a chance to recover, Diana caught Jude's cum-slicked chin in her firm grip and craned to stare into her unfocused eyes. "Should we keep going?"

In an Oscar-worthy performance, Jude nodded tearily, whispering, "Please, ma'am. Let me finish this job."

Thrilled by Jude's vulnerability, feigned or not, Diana smiled. "Only if you let me fuck you after I come. Any way I want."

"Yes, ma'am." Jude tried to downplay her emotion, but Diana detected the sheer joy in the simple response. "Anything to please you."

Then stop fucking other women. But Diana could never say that aloud. Instead, she issued a terse command. "Stick two fingers in my pussy and finish sucking me off. Once you're done, I'll show you exactly what it takes to please me."

"Thank you, ma'am." Jude readied her fingers against Diana's opening, then stopped to search her eyes. Shyly, she murmured, "Do I have your permission?"

Luxuriating in the expertly delivered submission, Diana answered with a lackadaisical wave. "Fine. Go ahead." She gasped, back arching, at the glorious friction of Jude's fingers forging a path to her core. Within seconds she was gasping again—gasping and writhing—when the heat of Jude's mouth enveloped her and the persistently fluttering tongue Diana had missed so desperately resumed its mission to conquer her clit. "*Shit.*" Diana groaned, fucking back with her hips. "Keep that up and I'll come all over your face."

Jude licked her even more vigorously, fingers pumping in and out at a steadily increasing rate of speed. Her sloppy, sucking noises provided a lewd soundtrack for their audience, most of whom—Diana noted with pride—appeared fully invested in their performance. Spotting at least three distinct cases of poorly concealed self-pleasuring in the front row of seats, Diana threw herself into the role-playing Jude was too busy to perform.

"I can't wait to get inside you." Diana leaned forward to grab Jude's clothed ass for a crude squeeze. "Find out how tight that cunt is. You never know, right? Easy girl like you."

Jude clamped her lips around Diana's clit and sucked, pistoning her arm in a sudden sprint to the finish. Falling backward onto their make-believe couch, Diana clung tight to Jude's shoulder with one hand and jammed the other into her mouth to muffle a climactic scream. Her vagina contracted around Jude's still-moving fingers with a strength she could scarcely believe, especially when she considered how long it had been since she'd last given her mind and body to a relative stranger. Emotion—a confused, overwhelming tangle of far too many feelings, none of which she wanted—swelled in Diana's chest, forcing out a choked sob she instinctively squashed by retreating into the stone-cold-bitch version of her "bored housewife" persona. Though she wanted nothing more than to ride out her orgasm to its teary conclusion, Diana shoved Jude away, then sat up and captured her forearm in an iron grip.

"That was adequate," she lied, worried that Jude had already heard and felt the truth. "Now it's my turn." Without waiting for the agreement she knew would come, Diana drew Jude forward, then bent her over the massive beanbag until only her tiptoes touched the floor. She stopped to admire the shapely bottom on display, then beamed at her rapt students and gestured for them to do the same. "Beautiful," she murmured. She very nearly punctuated the compliment with a disciplinary slap, before remembering that Jude didn't want to be spanked. In search of an alternative outlet for her conflicted feelings about the perplexing, far-too-young girl next door, Diana unfastened Jude's pants and lowered them around her ankles. She planted her left hand between Jude's shoulders, then bent to murmur into her ear while fondling the drenched folds she'd just revealed to the class. "Do you like being taken from behind?"

"Yes, ma'am," Jude breathed. As though realizing nobody else would've heard her, she repeated, "*Yes,* ma'am. Take me, please." She wiggled her luscious butt, covering Diana's wrist with her juices. "I want you to fuck me."

Diana wrapped her free hand around Jude's throat, holding her steady, and swiftly entered her with two fingers. She used her thumb to tease the tight pucker of muscle exposed by Jude's subservient pose and savored the resulting moan. Almost immediately, she remembered the last time she'd heard Jude's vocal pleasure—and her resentment swelled. Bent over Jude, Diana lobbed another taunt for everyone to hear. "Ordered a repairwoman, got myself a whore. I need to break my appliances more often."

Jude's hips slowed. "Don't call me that. Please."

"What, '*whore*'?" Immersed in her performance—and blinded by the bitterness driving it—Diana failed to question Jude's unusually strained tone. Painting a wet circle around Jude's anus with her thumb, she sniped, "If the tool belt fits, honey…"

"Laundry." Jude breathed the safe word so faintly Diana almost missed it. *"Please."*

Her whispered plea sliced through Diana like a monstrously sharp blade, eviscerating her within the span of a single heartbeat. She let go of Jude's throat, then removed the fingers from inside her vagina. As calmly as she could, Diana said, "Do you want to stop? It's perfectly all right if you do."

Eyes glistening, Jude glanced over her shoulder with an empathic shake of her head. "I want to keep going. Just...stop using that word." She swallowed, then whispered, *"Whore.* I can handle 'slut,' but not...not that one, okay? It..." She hung her head, but not before Diana spotted the color rising in her cheeks. "Doesn't make me feel sexy."

Rattled to have mindlessly crossed a line she'd never intended, Diana straightened so as not to loom over Jude anymore. Then, woefully aware of the teaching opportunity created by her faux pas, she took Jude by the shoulders and carefully rolled her over. Though it was difficult to meet her eyes, Diana did so while choking out an apology. "I'm truly sorry, Jude. I didn't mean to make you feel unsexy, or bad in any way." Internally, however, she chided herself. *Didn't you, though?* While she certainly hadn't meant to goad Jude into using her safe word, she'd injected real venom into her dialogue. Feeling lower than she had in years, Diana said, "I'll never use that term with you again. I promise."

Jude raised her hands to cover her face. Bright pink and obviously mortified by Diana's contrition, she bit her lower lip, chin quavering as though she might burst into tears. "No, *I'm* sorry...for fucking up our scene."

"You didn't." Diana struggled to keep smiling despite her evidently fathomless capacity for remorse. "Sweetheart, you *didn't.* Not even a little." Before she could quell the impulse, Diana gathered Jude into a heartfelt embrace. She pressed multiple, feather-soft kisses across Jude's knuckles, then peeled the hands away from her face to place a desperate kiss on the vaguely salty lips hidden beneath.

Sighing, Jude slipped her tongue into Diana's mouth to join her for a heated dance that obliterated any regret she might've felt about literally stopping to make out. Temporary amnesia set in at once, erasing Diana's awareness of her students, their time limit, and her self-imposed boundaries. She savored the sweetness on her lips and tongue far too briefly, until the urgent need for oxygen forced her away. Given the opportunity to recover not only her breath, but also her senses, Diana narrowly resisted the urge to return for more. Instead—not quite sorry for that lapse in judgment, yet worried about the implications—she angled to look at the women who still watched in rapt and silent fascination.

To cover her loss of control, Diana reverted to teaching mode. "Don't be afraid to change tone, or even the characters and scenario, right in the middle of your role-play. Sometimes what one or both of you wants or needs from the other will change—and that's okay." Glancing down at the half-naked young woman who awaited her next command, Diana brushed the hair off Jude's face, then stroked her forehead, followed by her cheek. "A queen and her loyal servant. How about we try that one next?"

The woman who'd originally suggested those characters let loose an excited whoop. "*Yes!*"

Jude's laughter filled Diana with unadulterated relief. Sitting up, Jude performed a jaunty bow. "Sounds lovely, your highness."

"Not so fast." Diana planted her hand on Jude's chest and gently encouraged her to lie back. "I'm here to serve *you*." She grabbed hold of the pants still bunched around Jude's ankles, freeing each foot with a reverence befitting their new roles. "My Queen."

Jude's throat jumped, and the rise and fall of her chest quickened. "All right." Nostrils flaring, she spread her legs wider. "If you insist."

"I do, my Queen." Lying on her belly, Diana maneuvered between the trembling thighs and hooked Jude's legs over her shoulders. She kissed the velvety juncture of hip and thigh—to the left of Jude's pussy, then the right—before dipping to run her tongue through the delectable wetness coating her labia. Prepared for a long and gratifying journey to redemption, Diana lifted her head to deliver one final line of dialogue. "Whatever it takes to make you feel good."

CHAPTER TWELVE

Only fifteen minutes out of bed and therefore still in her pajamas, Jude suffered what felt like a minor heart attack at a firm knock on her apartment door. She checked the time as she tiptoed suspiciously to the peephole. *Who the hell drops by unannounced at nine o'clock on Sunday morning?*

Her question answered itself. Before she could take a peek at her mystery visitor, Diana's voice filtered through the door. "It occurs to me that I should've texted first. If you're busy, or don't want company, you can tell me to leave. Or to come back later." Through the peephole, Jude watched Diana fidget uncomfortably. "But if you're up for a short visit and another sincere apology...well, I brought breakfast."

Jude closed her eyes, wishing once more that she'd kept her mouth shut and their safe word unspoken. "Diana..." Unwilling to have this conversation within earshot of a public hallway, she disengaged the deadbolt and swung open the door. She was stunned by the redness of Diana's eyes and her somber, exhausted expression—neither of which hindered the polite smile she mustered when their gazes met. With her own, reassuring smile, Jude said, "I don't need another apology. You didn't know, okay? Now you do." She worked up a broad grin she doubted would convince Diana of anything, straining her facial muscles. "However, I *do* have a rule about never turning down breakfast. Especially after a busy night."

Diana hoisted three large canvas bags. "I brought a little of everything. I wasn't sure what you liked."

"Waffles?"

Diana's face lit up. "Yes! I have Belgian waffles. Pancakes, too. And a few slices of French toast."

Unsure whether to be impressed by her thorough effort or horrified by all the calories on offer, Jude ushered Diana into her apartment. "It's clear you left nothing to chance." She took all three bags from Diana once they reached the kitchen, depositing them on the counter to unpack container after container of breakfast fare. "I hope you're hungry, because we're about to *eat*."

"Not very, I'm afraid." Diana's tone hinted at the guilt behind this visit—and no doubt her weary countenance as well. "I know you don't want another apology, but if you don't mind, I'd really like to give one anyway."

Jude folded her arms over her chest, then nodded for Diana to proceed. "But only if you think you'll actually feel better afterward. Otherwise, I say we both move on." She arched a gently reproachful eyebrow. "Like I already have."

Diana took a breath before launching into a seemingly prepared speech. "Jude, I feel terrible about what happened last night. I should have read your body language, and listened to what you were telling me, long before you had to resort to using your safe word. You asked me to stop doing something, but I kept going. I repeated the word, even, just to see you squirm." She wetted her lips and swallowed. "I…I let my personal feelings cloud my judgment. By which I mean…" She shrank under what Jude suspected was a wave of brutal self-recrimination. "Despite having absolutely zero right…I was jealous. Or I guess…I was resenting the sex I slept on my couch last Wednesday night to avoid overhearing. The sex, along with whoever it was that showed you such a nice time."

Not sure what to say about that, Jude carried plates, utensils, and a stack of random food containers to the table and sank into her chair to process. After a lengthy silence, Diana claimed the seat opposite hers. Cracking open two cardboard boxes, she served Jude a golden-brown waffle from the second without meeting her gaze. Painfully aware that Diana was awaiting her response, yet clueless about how she was supposed to react, Jude pooled syrup inside every individual flavor compartment in her waffle before offering a tentative reply. "I'm sorry about the noise. I never wanted to upset you."

"Listen, you're allowed to fuck whomever you want, *whenever* you want." Diana flashed her a joyless smile. "Like I said, I'm not entitled to an opinion about your sex life. Not as your next-door neighbor, and certainly not as your employer."

Jude stifled the urge to point out that she would forever be ready, willing, and borderline desperate to change their status *and* Diana's entitlements. Why bother? Diana already knew she was interested and would presumably speak up if and when their hearts ever came into alignment. Until that happened, Jude would do her part to make sure their relationship remained strictly professional—even if her desire for meaningless sex with strangers had vanished for good at the discovery that the woman of her dreams actually *cared*.

"As someone who shares my bedroom wall, I'd say you're entirely justified in getting frustrated about being kept awake. Especially on a weeknight. For that, I apologize. Sincerely." Jude ducked her head, ashamed of her intentionally provocative behavior. "It was extremely rude of us...of *me*...to force you into listening."

Diana served a pancake onto her plate, then some home fries. She took a nervous, bird-like nibble of potato, chewing in silence while she engaged in a stubborn appraisal of the tabletop. Jude stayed patient, waiting for Diana to acknowledge their shared responsibility for the ill-fated turn their role-play had taken. But when Diana finally met her eyes, it was to reject the attempt to distribute blame with a fierce shake of her head. "No. You've always had loud sex, and it's never bothered me before. I hate to give you mixed signals by confessing my sudden distaste for hearing you with other women, but after the way I behaved last night..." She paused, swallowing with visible effort. "My honesty is the least you deserve."

Appetite lost to Diana's heartbreaking angst, Jude set aside her sense of caution, transferring her fork to the other hand so she could reach across the table and squeeze Diana's bare forearm. "Stop beating yourself up. How could you have known what that particular word would make me feel? *I* had no idea. I never told you that was a hard limit, but only because I didn't realize it. Not until you said it."

Horrified by the sight of Diana's troubled blue eyes brimming with unshed tears, Jude rushed to mitigate any additional damage she'd just inflicted. "It seriously wasn't that big a deal. I said my safe word, you stopped—and then spent the next forty-five minutes delivering the three most mind-blowing orgasms anyone has ever given me." She summoned a coy smile, desperate to assuage the guilt etched into Diana's grim countenance. "Even if I *had* been angry with you about the name-calling, all that queen/servant stuff afterward would've more than earned my forgiveness. So forget about it. I plan to."

Diana balanced her fork on her plate, then hesitantly covered Jude's fingers with her own. "Sweetheart," she murmured, and Jude's heart swelled until she heard what followed. "That I let my anger dictate not only what I said, but how I treated you…that *is* a big deal. You can pretend what happened didn't hurt you, but…I was there, too. Jude, I saw your face. Your eyes…" Sighing, she raised Jude's hand to her lips and kissed her knuckles softly. "If my careless words triggered anything unpleasant for you, or came across as intentionally cruel…" She hung her head, shoulders curled inward from shame she couldn't seem to overcome. With Jude's hand still cradled in hers, she murmured, "All I can do is tell you it wasn't your fault. You didn't deserve to be treated with disrespect—or to feel anything *but* sexy while performing nude for twenty strangers."

Jude abandoned her meal to try to get Diana past what was, in the pantheon of traumatic moments comprising her relatively short life, barely a blip on her radar. If Diana needed to talk through this situation to feel better, she would oblige. "Really, at this point it's silly to be bothered by that word. *Whore.*" She crinkled her nose, disgusted by the bitter taste it left in her mouth. "Except…that was one of my stepfather's favorite names to call me, usually deployed alongside a physical beating, but not always. Bastard loved to accuse me of fucking every boy at my school, of being a trashy *whore* who probably got on my knees anytime someone offered their cock to suck. Shows how much he knew about his wife's kid, fucking *genius.*"

She scoffed, hoping to keep the shame that miserable bastard had worked so hard to instill at bay. "Prick spent the five years I lived with him reacting like a jealous, violent boyfriend to any hint of my sexuality. He basically made it his mission to inform me how dirty and wrong I was, whenever and however he could. My natural adolescent response was to go out and try everything he warned me against. Which is how I figured out that sex feels wonderful, and also…" Jude hesitated, unsure whether to reveal more about her inner life.

"Also?" Diana prompted, without judgment.

Putting her faith in Diana's inherent kindness, Jude completed the thought. "Also how it made me a little less lonely, at least temporarily." She cleared her throat, sheepish to have vocalized such a pathetic notion. "At any rate, despite figuring out that my stepfather was full of shit long before I turned seventeen and filed for emancipation…apparently I still can't handle being called a whore. I wish I could. Feels like letting him win."

Diana's expression remained steady even as an errant tear escaped her left eye, then the right. "Thank you."

Uncomfortable with the intensity of Diana's stare—and the fact that they were still holding hands—Jude barely managed a nervous shrug. "For what?"

"Telling me about your stepfather. I know that can't be easy to talk about, but it helps. Or rather, *will* help...in the future." She bowed her head with a deference Jude struggled to comprehend. "Assuming you're still comfortable working together."

"Diana." Jude gripped the fingers tangled loosely in her own. "Don't be silly, and please...*listen* to me. *Trust* me. You didn't do anything wrong. Got it? If I'd asked you not to call me a whore and you did anyway, *then* we'd have a problem. But despite our multiple conversations about limits, you and I both know that one never came up. I said no spanking, no hair-pulling—boundaries you've respected—but never mentioned any forbidden words. I wish I had, that I'd known how a single line of dialogue could stir up shit I'd rather leave in the past, but I didn't...so last night was as much my fault as yours. More, even."

Diana shook her head, more miserable-looking than ever. "Jude—"

"Please." Jude couldn't keep doing this. "Let this go...unless you *want* me to feel even shittier about using my safe word."

A pregnant silence stretched out between them, until finally Diana tipped her head in acquiescence. "*Never* hesitate to use your safe word. With anyone, but *especially* me. I'd rather give up sex forever than cause you any more distress."

"Message received." Jude released Diana's hand, then gave her a teasing slap on the wrist. "Now for the millionth time, I'm *fine*." She picked up her fork, stabbing a fresh pancake to demonstrate the resurrection of her hunger. "Mind if we talk about something else?"

"Fair enough." Diana cleared her throat, then grabbed her own fork to gamely spear another bite of syrup-soaked pancake. "If you wouldn't mind, I'd love to hear more about you. Emancipated at seventeen..." She looked at Jude as though truly seeing her for the first time. "That's an awful lot of responsibility for a young kid. How'd it work out for you?"

Chewing slowly, Jude questioned how much she wanted Diana to know. *Everything,* her heart insisted, but her head wasn't as certain. How much *did* she trust Diana? Enough to lay herself bare? Enough to grant this woman the power to destroy her completely? Swallowing, Jude spoke from her gut. "Well, I've got my own apartment, enough money saved to write for two years—two years *plus*, thanks to you—and a cousin living nearby who happens to double as my best friend. So I'd say my life has worked out pretty damn well."

"I'd say you're right." Diana rose to retrieve an orange juice from one of the bags they'd left on the counter, then opened three cabinets before locating the cups she sought. After she'd poured the beverages Jude had neglected to offer, she retook her seat and passed one over. "You're a genuinely impressive woman, Jude Monaco." Diana tapped the rims of their cups together before draining hers in a few hearty swallows. She placed the empty cup back on the table to refill it halfway. "I mean that, from the bottom of my heart."

Blushing, Jude conducted a hasty mental review of all the details she'd omitted. She doubted the real story of her emancipation was as inspiring as whatever hard-luck story Diana's imagination had conjured up to explain her success. "I don't know. Most of the credit belongs to Katrina. She let me move in with her to finish high school, then crash at her place for another year after I graduated. If she hadn't given me a roof over my head and food in my stomach, I'm sure I would've ended up on the streets. Or worse."

"Katrina may have given you a fresh start, but *you're* the one who overcame a traumatic beginning to become financially able to chase your passion for a couple years—all by age twenty-six." Diana relinquished her utensils for a second time, pushing her plate aside to lean farther across the table. "My parents paid for one-hundred percent of my undergraduate studies. Then offered me a no-interest loan for my master's degree. I always knew how incredibly fortunate I was to have them, but that meant I didn't become a responsible, full-fledged adult until I was about twenty-three years old. I'm not sure what would've become of me if I'd grown up in your stepfather's house. I want to believe I'd have turned out as well as you, but…I'm skeptical."

"I'm glad you'll never have to find out." Giving up on the idea of finishing a single item from their over-the-top buffet, Jude slid her plate next to Diana's and rested her palms on the tabletop between them. In the span of a single heartbeat, she disregarded her emotional safety and pushed her chair back to stand and offer Diana a hand. "Would you be willing to finish this conversation on the couch? We'll be way more comfortable, and we won't feel this pressure to keep eating."

"We also won't have food to distract us." Diana's tone made it clear she considered that a negative. "From each other."

"And if I promise not to seduce you?" Jude wiggled her fingers enticingly.

A series of faintly shifting facial expressions gave away Diana's internal conflict. "I don't want to monopolize your Sunday morning. If you have other plans, I *can* go."

"If you'd rather not stay, I get it." Jude lowered her hand and stepped aside to clear a path for Diana to escape. "No hard feelings, just gratitude for a yummy breakfast. It was very thoughtful, as was the apology." Heartened by Diana's conflicted frown, she went on. "Otherwise, I'm happy to tell you more about my emancipation—about what I ended up doing to get by. Thing is, that's not a conversation I can have with you staring at me from across the table. I've never told anyone except Katrina about my past, but even her...not everything."

Diana blinked, staring up at her searchingly. "You know you don't have to tell me anything, right? If you'd rather keep your history private, I understand."

Given how little she knew about Diana, Jude suspected that was true. But, aiming to lead by example, she declined the offer of secrecy. "I *want* to tell you. You asked, you're interested, we're fucking...maybe you could even consider us friends?"

"Yes. We're friends." The easy admission surprised Jude, but Diana shrugged halfheartedly. "Doesn't mean I'm owed any secrets."

"If it'll prevent another incident like last night's, I'm open to sharing a few." Jude offered her hand once more. "But on the couch. If you don't mind."

Diana was silent a moment, then said, "All right." She let Jude help her stand but released her hand for the walk to the couch. "Whatever you want."

You, in my bed, Jude's shadow pervert supplied. *In my mouth, around my fingers...* She dropped onto the couch, unsurprised when Diana plastered herself against the opposite arm. Fine with her. Any closer and she might lose the courage to launch into a full-fledged confession. She suspected she'd built this conversation up too much already. Maybe Diana would find her embarrassment precious. The woman *was* a sex worker, after all—of a sort. *But what if she decides I really* am *a whore? Even if she's too polite to ever say it to my face again.*

"Jude, honey..." Diana cast her a warm smile. "Truly, you *don't* have to do this."

"I know." Jude exhaled, steadying her nerves. "But you're so impressed by the money I've saved, and by my being able to thrive with only a high school diploma…" She shot Diana a fleeting, sidelong glance. "I don't want to lie to you. Or let you believe something that isn't true."

Diana peeled herself away from the arm of the sofa to edge slightly closer, her interest visibly piqued. "Like I said…whatever you want." She chuckled, then paraphrased Jude's earlier condition. "But only if you think you'll actually feel better afterward."

Jude snorted, gazing down at the anxiously twisting hands in her lap. "Eighteen years old with only a high school education and no real work experience…there weren't a whole lot of options for me at that time. Not that would've gotten me out of Katrina's apartment and into a place of my own in a halfway decent amount of time, anyway." Reminding herself of Diana's line of work and everything else she knew about the woman, Jude tried to forget how deeply it had cut to hear Diana echo her stepfather's accusations. "Katrina was so young herself. Going to school, paying the lion's share of our rent and utilities…I spent four months feeling like dog shit about giving her another mouth to feed, let alone a fucking *teenager* to worry about. As soon as I turned eighteen, I went out and found the most lucrative work available for someone with my skill set."

"Sex work?" Diana asked, gingerly. "If that's what you're worried about telling me, don't be. It's all right. As long as you were safe about it."

"I was." Encouraged, Jude raised her face to meet Diana's eyes. "I got lucky. Fucked an older lady a few times—for fun, actually—who wound up landing me a gig at an escort service she'd once frequented. I mostly accompanied wealthy older men, but occasionally women, to events. Sometimes sex was involved. Usually not, but…sometimes. With male clients, as well." This was the admission she'd most dreaded making, yet Diana didn't flinch. Jude's entire body unclenched. "Katrina hated it. Escorting got me into my own apartment, even paid for an undergraduate marketing degree, but…" She delivered her impression of a carefree shrug. "My cousin had a childhood like yours. She's always had parents to fall back on, so she…didn't understand my choices, at times. But she loved me." Jude's smile softened into something more genuine. "*Loves* me."

"Jude, sweetheart…" Diana's throat worked, drawing Jude's focus to the graceful column of her neck. "There's no shame in survival. However you chose to get by after leaving your parents' house…it was your body, and your decision. I only hope that no one hurt you, and that you enjoyed the work to some extent."

"I suffered through some pretty terrible sex, but nobody hurt me." Jude smirked. "Plus, the experience helped prep me for my newest foray into fucking for money. Thank goodness, too, 'cause the pay is generous as hell, and the benefits...out of this world."

Diana paled. "Shit. What did Katrina think about me hiring you? She's seemed friendly enough the times we've spoken, but..." She steeled herself. "Does she hate me?"

"No. She thought it was fantastic. At first she assumed you were an art teacher who'd hired me to model nude, which she thought was wonderful and also a far cry from 'what I used to be into.' When I explained about the workshops, she was still enthusiastic. She actually said it sounded like an ideal gig."

"I'm relieved to hear that." Diana's posture relaxed by a degree. "I'd hate for anyone to make you embarrassed or ashamed of the sex you've had. Including me."

"Thanks." Stirred by the unmistakable self-reproach in Diana's voice, Jude inched onto the middle couch cushion. "I forgave you already, remember?"

"I remember. Unfortunately, I haven't quite forgiven myself." Diana's eyelashes fluttered rapidly, and then when a tear escaped, she closed her eyes. "I'll get there. Granted, now that I know..." She exhaled, then restarted. "I appreciate you sharing so many intimate details about your life. It *does* help. I hope...I hope this conversation helps you, too." She blinked to reveal the breathtaking blue eyes Jude adored and a smile that cracked her heart open. "You told me about your past, and nothing catastrophic happened as a result. On the contrary, I feel like I know you on a deeper level now. *And* I have a more complete picture of what words and actions aren't likely to arouse you sexually. That'll be huge, going forward." Diana's smile widened anxiously. "The next few workshops will likely be intense. Communication is everything."

"Right. I agree." Jude sat up straighter, wondering whether Diana might choose to reveal any intimate details of her own. It was obvious her past hadn't been all happy times and financially supportive parents. Some kind of trauma or tragedy was buried in Diana's history, some person or event who'd soured her on the idea of dating. Most likely the ex-girlfriend she'd mentioned—Janine. Jude yearned to know what had gone down between them, exactly, to make Diana swear off love and romance forever. Understanding the source of those scars would help Jude every bit as much as her own sordid tale had enlightened Diana. Dropping a hint, she reiterated, "Going forward, communication is key. I'm thrilled we're finally at a point where we can be open with each other."

"Next weekend's workshop covers spanking, discipline, and power dynamics." Diana scooted another inch closer, hastening Jude's heart rate. "Even if you're not on the receiving end, I imagine your memories of being hit in anger could impact your ability to have fun with what we're doing, even if it is consensual. Are you certain you'll be comfortable hitting me?"

"*Spanking* you. There's a difference."

"You're right. There is." Diana paused to study Jude's face. "My goal is for you to never have to use your safe word with me again. Also, for you to feel safe enough to opt out of any act you aren't excited to try. I won't let you suffer through any terrible sex on my account."

Realistically, Jude was excited to do just about everything with Diana. Even being taken over her knee didn't seem entirely out of the question. Because of the time limit on their sexual relationship, a part of Jude felt eager to take anything and everything she could get. But out of respect for Diana, she thoroughly considered the question before answering.

"I've smacked my fair share of asses, you know. Mostly while being ridden or fucking a woman from behind…and it's hot, no doubt. More than a few women have asked me to spank them. I've never actually 'administered discipline'…like, spanked someone for the sole purpose of enforcing a power dynamic." Taking a deep breath, she admitted, "Here's the thing. I've thought about spanking you more than once since you told me what topics we'd be covering. Thought about it *hard*, you know, during my extra-special alone time…" She grinned at Diana's amused snort. "And I swear to you…those fantasies make me very, *very* wet."

"In my experience, sweetheart, *everything* makes you very, very wet."

Jude opened her mouth to spit out an unthinking retort but stopped just in time. *Probably shouldn't admit I've never gotten that wet for anyone else.* "What can I say? I love sex."

"Still, there's a distinct difference between fantasy and reality. It's not uncommon for some women to entertain fantasies about losing control to a powerful or even violent lover, but that doesn't mean they actually *want* to be violated or harmed in real life." Diana studied her face in earnest. "In any event, I'd rather we not discover your aversion to this particular activity during class."

"What do you suggest?" Jude's stomach fluttered. "I'm not in the mood for another one-night stand this week. Honestly, I started my period this morning, so I'm a bit antisocial."

"Impeccable timing. Well done."

"Aw, shucks." Jude rubbed her abdomen, wincing. "I'm glad someone's happy."

"If your cramps aren't too painful…" Coughing, Diana shuffled yet closer. "We could review the basic lesson plan. You know, since you'll have to demonstrate my suggested techniques. Given your lack of history with this sort of play, I'm thinking this workshop will require more preparation on our parts than previous ones."

"What are you thinking?" Jude licked her lips, cursing her ovaries for hindering an otherwise ideal setup to potentially transition their work-oriented partnership into something—*anything*—more. "That I should actually *spank* you, right here on my couch, to practice?"

Diana flushed, turning deep pink from her forehead to the enticing slice of chest revealed by her V-necked T-shirt. "It would let us know ahead of time whether you should sit this one out." Her skin practically glowed, rosy with apparent mortification. "If you're open to a brief, fully clothed lesson, I'll feel *much* better about next Saturday once I'm confident you'll also have a great time."

Jude wanted to tell Diana she always had a great time when they were together, which was true, but Diana would surely counter by arguing that last night proved otherwise—technically, also true. However, Jude wasn't inclined to refuse an opportunity to touch Diana anywhere, let alone her luscious butt. "Sure. We can do that, if you want."

"I want." Diana shot her a sidelong glance. "It doesn't hurt that I already feel bad about my behavior, and ashamed, and like I deserve to be punished."

Jude frowned. "I'm not *hitting* you, remember? Even if you ask me to."

Diana nodded, then stood. "Of course. But I will ask you to be firm. It's part of the lesson plan, so if that makes you uneasy—"

"Diana, I'm not bailing on you. Do you even *have* another assistant available this weekend?"

"I can find one if I need to." Diana's blue eyes didn't betray any emotion as she loomed over Jude, ostensibly waiting for an invitation across her lap. "Remember, no hard feelings. We'll just reconvene at the next workshop. Strap-on sex…I imagine you won't have any trouble on either end of that equation."

"Damn right, I won't." Though Jude wished they could simply skip ahead a week, she'd be damned if she wouldn't fulfill their original contract. Patting her thighs, Jude gestured Diana closer with a jerk of her chin. "I'm not convinced I'll have any trouble with this lesson, either. Why don't you get your sexy butt down here so we can find out?"

Diana's hand drifted to Jude's cheek, caressing tenderly. "We'll start the lesson with spanking in the classic, over-the-knee position. Scootch onto the center cushion, darling. Give yourself room to work."

"Yes, ma'am," Jude chirped instinctively. She grimaced as she moved to the spot Diana had indicated. "Sorry, old habits. What I meant to say was 'yeah, no problem.'"

"Relax." Diana was clearly trying to soothe her, despite looking far from calm herself. "During class, I'll have you order me to remove my pants before getting into position—but we'll leave them on for this demonstration."

"Understood," Jude murmured, then sucked in a startled mouthful of air when Diana crawled across her lap to assume a facedown pose over her tense thighs. Her round, denim-clad butt came to rest within perfect striking distance from Jude's hand, causing her fingers to twitch in anticipation of the first, experimental slap. "Am I disciplining you for any particular reason? Just because it makes your pussy wet?" Jude clarified her question. "In class, I mean. I know why you're being spanked today."

Diana inhaled audibly. "Up to you. We don't necessarily have to give a reason, though it could help inspire whatever dirty talking you might want to do. Personally, I'll be telling myself it's for letting my emotional inaccessibility damage the people around me…but I'd prefer not to share that backstory with the students."

"Tell you what, I'll spend the week thinking on it. I'm leaning toward punishing your shitty attitude about turning forty, alongside a huge helping of 'stop treating me like a kid.'" Jude hovered her hand above Diana's tempting derriere but didn't make contact. "May I touch your bottom? Put my hand on it, that's all."

"Sure." Despite giving permission, Diana jolted slightly at the bare pressure of Jude's palm. "We'll start slow and not terribly hard. Make sure to keep the arc of travel between your hand and my butt cheek neat, tight, and a true arc. By that I mean your movement should be oval or circular in direction. Aim for your hand to arrive with a bit of an up-swing when it connects with my buttock. Use your other hand—and arm—to keep my body under your tight control. If I squirm, hold me still. *Tell me* to remain still." She glanced over her shoulder, catching Jude's gaze with an encouraging smile. "That's where the power dynamic comes into play. The spanking should increase in intensity until you've turned the skin red. Don't stop until I beg you to. Still think you can handle this?"

Rather than answer, Jude drew back her hand and, concentrating on her arc of travel, landed a sharp slap against the underside of Diana's right buttock. "Definitely. Can you?" She followed up with a hard smack across the other cheek. "Too much, or just right?"

Diana gasped. "Not too much, but…a little softer to start when we're in class. Some of these women may need to be eased into the concept gradually." She jumped at the next blow, despite it being half the strength of the last. "Excellent. That works."

Alternating cheeks, Jude delivered slap after slap to Diana's increasingly sensitive rear end. Her left arm naturally came to rest between Diana's narrow shoulders, allowing her to pin down the writhing body atop her lap. "Does that hurt? Huh?" Jude slowed, faking the cessation of Diana's punishment. "Like you hurt me?"

"*Yes*," Diana choked out.

Jude paused to confirm. "Really? Do you want me to stop?"

"*No*." Diana had never sounded so desperate. "I mean, you're doing well. How is it for you?"

"Wonderful." She struck Diana one final time, the most vicious blow of all. Then Jude sat, listening as Diana heaved to catch her breath and noting the insistent backward press of the undoubtedly sore butt against her tingling hand. She wanted more than anything to slip her fingers into the steamy crevice between Diana's closed thighs and check the reaction to her performance, yet managed to resist. But still, she needed to know. "Are you wet?"

"During the workshop, I'll let you check for yourself. For now, I can assure you that *yes*…I'm positively dripping."

"So am I." Jude squirmed beneath Diana's trembling weight. "Don't worry about me and spanking, okay? I'm fairly certain I enjoyed this a little *too* much."

"No such thing." Diana sounded relieved by the positive review. "If it's all right, I think I'll sit up now."

Tickled that she'd even bothered to ask, Jude said, "Of course." She raised the arm she'd laid across Diana's shoulders, then the hand still resting on her butt. "Sorry."

"Why?" Diana eased off her lap, retreating to sit beside her once more—much closer this time. "You were fantastic."

"Glad you think so. I'm looking forward to playing like that for real."

"'For real' as in when you can also finger me?" Diana gave her a knowing smirk. "If so, that makes two of us."

Jude exhaled, overwhelmed by her unrelenting desire for the woman on her couch. Afraid to further erode their slowly crumbling boundaries—and terrified by her impulse to swing a sledge hammer and dive on in—Jude stared at the carpet to protect what she'd been trying so hard to respect. "So, uh...you have any plans for the rest of the day? Going to see Ava?"

"Going to see Ava, yes, for dinner. Until then..." Diana's sultry delivery coaxed Jude's attention up to her face. "I might head home for some extra-special alone time."

"Oh, yeah?" Unable to hold her gaze, Jude glanced at the most stubborn stain her carpet had suffered—red wine spilled by a tipsy overnight guest whose name she couldn't remember. "What a coincidence."

"Indeed." Diana rubbed her hands together, then rocked her weight forward to signal her imminent departure. "Not that you need my permission, but please feel free to imagine what I might be doing on my side of our bedroom wall. Just knowing that you're thinking about me, thinking about..." She stuttered, cheeks flooding with color. "About you...well, shit. I'm legitimately the worst at this whole not-sending-mixed-signals thing. Aren't I?"

"You're fine," Jude said as blithely as possible with her heart doing its impression of a Buddy Rich drum solo. "We're okay, and you're fine." She threw herself off a metaphorical cliff, leaping even without faith. "Would you like to stay? We could masturbate together. Mutually. As *individuals,* of course...who happen to be in the same room." Answering the argument Diana hadn't yet made, Jude put together the strongest case she could while horny and under pressure. "We've already tiptoed past one line today. Why not another?"

For half a millisecond, Diana actually seemed tempted by the offer. But she rather swiftly shook her head and stood. "Because we might not stop. We might lose track of those lines altogether."

"You're still convinced that would be so bad?"

"It wouldn't be good." Diana gave her a sad smile and stepped away from the couch, toward the door. "Particularly for you. So...enjoy those leftovers. And your alone time, if you decide to have it."

"Oh, I'm having it." Disappointed by the fast retreat, Jude didn't censor herself. "As soon as you're gone, I'm going into my bedroom, taking off my pajamas, and getting out my favorite dildo. I plan to rub my clit and fuck myself for at least an hour, minimum. That's more or less how long it usually takes for me to build toward a slow climax when I have time to let my fantasies run wild."

"From the bottom of my cold, black heart, I thank you for the delightful parting image," Diana said. When Jude rose to walk her out, she implored her to stay put with a raised hand and a pleading look. "You don't need to see me out. I'll just..." She hiked her thumb over her shoulder, nearly hitting the doorframe she was about to back into. "Go." She swiveled around, then wrestled clumsily with the door before eventually flinging it open with palpable exasperation. "Thanks for the hospitality, Jude. See you around?"

She was gone before Jude could draw the breath to answer.

CHAPTER THIRTEEN

Jude sought out Katrina's advice the following evening, a sure sign that breakfast with her favorite sex therapist had disrupted not only her emotional state, but also her usual distaste for admitting that she didn't know what to do. As her and Diana's relationship was so tied up in paid sex, she'd been hesitant to keep raising the subject with her cousin. It wasn't that she didn't value Katrina's opinions, because ninety percent of the time, they were gold.

Yet for as compassionate and well-intentioned as she usually tried to be, especially lately, Katrina did harbor an occasionally judgmental nature. That shadow self most often came out during discussions of Jude's sex life or early work history, and always made her feel lower than low. It was always possible she might not like whatever Katrina had to say, and any conversation they had could leave her even more twisted up inside.

But this thing with Diana, whatever it was, went so much deeper than sex. Their connection, however tenuous, already felt far richer than any Jude had forged with past lovers—including the two she'd dated at length. She'd never fallen this hard before, and never for someone so utterly determined not to return her feelings. The sensation exhilarated and terrified her in equal measure, and all Jude knew for sure was that she'd never untangle the mess she'd made of her love life without seeking an outsider's take.

Praying for Katrina to understand that this wasn't another of her sex-crazed escapades, Jude served her cousin a slice of pizza from the box she'd dropped onto the coffee table in front of them, then launched straight into the reason for her impromptu visit. "I'm in big trouble, Kat. I don't know what to do."

"What kind of trouble?" Katrina took a hearty bite of her veggie pizza, folding her legs beneath her. "Girl or money?"

Jude scowled as she nibbled on her own slice. Tempted as she was to object to Katrina's assumptions, they both knew damn well the question was rooted in reality. "*Woman.*"

"Ah." Katrina gave her a knowing grin. "You mean Diana."

Unimpressed by the deduction, Jude rolled her eyes. "Of course Diana."

"Still crazy about her?"

"You have no idea." Jude expelled a sigh, then tossed her pizza slice into the open box and sagged against the couch. "She brought me breakfast on Sunday. At my apartment."

Katrina arched an eyebrow. "Oh, *really?*"

"To apologize, *again*, that I had to use my safe word with her on Saturday night. She'd been feeling super guilty about the whole thing, even though it totally wasn't her fault. Like…guilty enough that she had me spank her right then and there. On my couch."

Katrina's eyes widened and her mouth dropped open. "She…*what?*"

Aware of how that bombshell had landed without any context, Jude said, "Next weekend's workshop is about spanking, discipline, and power dynamics. She was worried I might have a problem with the subject matter, even though I'd told her from the beginning that while I'm not comfortable being spanked myself, I'd be fine in the role of disciplinarian. Anyway, she suggested we practice ahead of time. It was the most sexual contact we've had outside the classroom. She'd forbidden it before, emphatically."

"What did she do, exactly?"

Jude's face heated at the memory. "Well, first she lay facedown across my lap, and then—"

"To have you use your safe word." Katrina halted Jude's retelling with a raised hand. "That's what I meant."

"Oh." Flushing hotter, Jude shrugged in a weak impression of nonchalance. "Called me a whore. As part of this role-play we were doing, but still…too many shades of Travis. That asshole loved calling me whore, usually whenever he felt the urge to hit me. I hated the word even before I knew what it meant. Hated how it made me feel."

"Jesus." Katrina ditched her plate to put a hand on Jude's knee. "You have no idea how badly I wish I could've spared you from your mother's psychotic husband. If I'd known…we'd have gotten you out of that house a lot sooner."

"I'm not sure you could've handled the care and feeding of a fucked-up teenager any sooner than age twenty-two." Jude winked to assure Katrina she didn't hold any grudges about the timing of her rescue. "Honestly, it's fine. I mean, it sucked, but *I'm* fine. Except on rare occasions, I suppose…like that particular exchange with Diana."

"Sorry, Jude. Sucks for something like that to come up during sex. I'm sure it felt even worse because you had spectators."

"You're telling me." Jude glanced at her pizza, stomach twisting uneasily. "The weirdest part about Diana's apology—"

"Weirder than asking to be spanked?"

Jude chuckled. "She admitted to being jealous of this woman I brought home last week and said that partially drove her dialogue during our role-play. Hence why she felt so awful about the whole thing."

When Katrina merely raised an eyebrow, waiting for more, Jude went on. "She keeps saying she doesn't want to send mixed signals, but that's literally all she does. She told me she hated hearing me fuck another woman, and brought me breakfast, and let me put her over my knees and spank her…on my couch, *in my apartment*—after insisting, repeatedly, that we must never touch outside of class." She slumped lower in her seat, sighing. "I don't understand. Why do that?"

"Maybe you're getting to her." Katrina tilted her head thoughtfully. "Has Diana indicated that her stance on dating might be evolving?"

"She doesn't want to date me." Jude poked out her bottom lip. "She didn't even want to masturbate in the same room as me."

"You asked her to?" Katrina's eyebrows popped. "This was one hell of a breakfast date."

"Only after she announced her plan to go home and get herself off—then invited me to think about her if I chose to follow suit." Jude threw up her hands, helpless to explain the impact of Diana's inscrutable behavior. "How am I supposed to feel about any of this?"

"I don't know. How *do* you feel?"

"Afraid." Jude surprised herself with the instantaneous answer, then with the tears that gathered at Katrina's sympathetic frown. "Excited, nervous, horny…even optimistic, on occasion. Like when she apologized…that she so clearly recognized my feelings, then took responsibility for her part in hurting them…" Her breathing hitched. "I felt listened to, and seen, and *respected* in a way I never had before."

"That's wonderful." Katrina gave her a sunny smile. "Right?"

"It would be if I wasn't convinced Diana's going to break my heart someday. Accepting this job with her was the most brain-dead stunt I've ever pulled."

"Maybe, but who's to say everything won't turn out exactly the way you want it to, in the end?" Katrina patted her knee supportively. "Somehow."

"I can't let myself think that way anymore." Jude stared at the ceiling, a futile attempt to recall the tears clinging to her lower lids. "For my own sanity, I have to take Diana at her word. She wants zero to do with me romantically, regardless of what she says when she's jealous or turned on."

"Agreed. Don't get your hopes up." Katrina rubbed Jude's arm, then picked up her uneaten pizza crust and bit off a chunk. "All I'm saying is I don't think it's *impossible* Diana will decide you're worth the risk. If she's already started bending her own rules less than a month in, she's likely every bit as conflicted about her feelings as you are about yours."

"Doubtful," Jude said, but without conviction. What did it mean for Diana to struggle with sex Jude had on her own time? Potentially nothing. It was possible to feel jealousy over someone you didn't actually want… wasn't it? "I'll never get through the rest of those workshops if I allow myself to think like that." She fell silent, closing her eyes to chase away the headache threatening to erupt. "You know, I'm actually tempted to quit. I don't want to screw her over or anything, but…I don't want to screw myself over, either."

"Maybe you should, if that's how you feel." Katrina's hand returned to its spot on Jude's knee. "Unless, of course, you think *she's* worth the risk. If so…maybe keep going. Maintain a healthy dose of pessimism, but see what happens."

Was Diana worth the risk? Even when the odds of their becoming an actual couple hovered somewhere close to zero? "Obviously I'm full of shit. You know I can't quit. If there's even the slightest chance…" Jude didn't let herself complete the misguided thought. "I don't want to stop. How can I, when the sex is even better than the money?"

"Do you think Diana has any idea how you feel?"

"I believe she does. I haven't exactly kept my attraction a secret." Opening her eyes, Jude rolled her head to the side to meet Katrina's concerned gaze. "She may not realize I'm *in love* with her, but that I'm attracted and basically infatuated? Yeah, she knows."

"Ava tells me her best friend is a humane, compassionate, kindhearted woman—albeit one haunted by some heinous past relationship—so why not give Diana the benefit of the doubt and assume that the next time you see her, she'll either apologize for the mixed signals or else cop to wanting more from you than she initially thought?" Katrina extracted a chuckle from Jude with her silly, disarming smirk. "Either way, you deserve to know whether the boundaries she laid down for the two of you still stand. Make sure and call her on it if she doesn't address the blurring of lines in your apartment. Be clear about your own boundaries. She may be paying you, but that doesn't mean she gets to write all the rules."

Jude nodded, impressed by the strength of that advice. "You're right. Thanks." Not for the first time, she regarded Katrina's unwavering sense of self with respect bordering on awe. "Deadly serious, Kat...one day I hope I grow up to be like you. How do you always have your shit so together? No wonder you think I'm fucked up."

"*Jude.*" Katrina poked her in the gut. "I don't think you're fucked up. I never did." Her expression softened with apparent remorse. "I'm sorry if the stupid shit I've said over the years has made you feel otherwise."

"I appreciate that." Too drained to be anything but unfiltered, Jude admitted, "Because, yeah, some of that stupid shit *was* hurtful. Unfair, too, when you consider the life I've been able to build for myself—even if it's mediocre, at best."

"Stop." Katrina appeared increasingly distraught about her unrelenting self-deprecation. "If it helps, my shit isn't anywhere near together these days." She paused, unwittingly building suspense for whatever revelation she seemed reluctant to make. "Like how a few days ago I engaged in some blatantly unprofessional behavior...with a client." After a beat, she groaned. "With Ava."

"Oh, fuck," Jude muttered, caught somewhere between shock, amusement, and pride. "You kissed her?"

"Yes." Katrina stared into the distance, presumably transported by the memory of her transgression. "And—"

"*And?*"

The only thing brighter than Katrina's fiery cheeks was her beaming countenance. "And...I masturbated her. With my hand."

As that was quite literally the last thing she'd expected to hear from her bi-curious but straight-leaning, vaguely conservative cousin, Jude had to shake her head to process the disclosure with some measure of coherence. "You...gave Ava a *hand job?*"

Katrina flinched, chastened by either her incredulity or her blunt naming of the act. "I didn't mean to. It just...happened."

"Clit rubbing doesn't just *happen*." Jude scoffed, overjoyed to finally be on the other end of this conversation. "Tell me everything. Don't spare any details. I demand to know how Ava coaxed you over to our side. I thought you'd sworn off dating women forever."

"I did…unless the right one came along."

Jude straightened at the implication. "Are you saying Ava's the *one*?"

"I think she's too charming by half, but…I can't deny that the time I spend in Ava's company is the highlight of my day. Consistently, day after day." Katrina dissolved into a gooey smile. "Despite her stubborn obstinance."

Jude blinked, unaccustomed to hearing Katrina talk about a love interest with such unabashed affection. "You seriously like this woman."

"I shouldn't." Katrina made the declaration as though to convince herself. "But…I think I seriously do."

"How does Ava feel?"

"The same." Katrina transitioned from dreamy-eyed to remorseful as though a switch had been flipped. "I'm sorry. This is incredibly insensitive, isn't it? I should have waited to tell you, but I'm freaking out about the ethical implications. Still…you don't want to hear me talk about falling for an older woman. Not tonight."

Jude denied her envy with a brusque wave. "Don't be ridiculous. I would've been pissed if you *hadn't* told me." She plastered on a grin she wished she could feel. "Now stop dodging my question. How did your hand find its way between Ava's legs?"

Katrina muttered under her breath but didn't duck the interrogation. "I arrived for our Monday appointment twenty minutes ahead of schedule. It was the first time I'd ever shown up anywhere close to that early, so it makes sense that she didn't expect me to walk in."

"Sounds like the premise of a fairly stellar porn movie to me."

"That's exactly how it felt, too. Except…more intimate. And without the fake tits." Katrina wet her lips with the tip of her tongue, Jude assumed unconsciously. "I texted her on my way upstairs, then let myself in using the key she'd given me…and there she was, just lying in bed…pajama pants around her upper thighs, fingers working her clit…" She shivered. "She never heard me come in, and once I was close enough to see what I was interrupting…" Katrina licked her lips and whispered, "I froze. Just stood there, watching."

"How long did it take her to notice?" Resentful or not, Jude needed this cliffhanger resolved. "And what was the reaction when she did?"

"Her eyes were closed, so…" Katrina hid her own eyes behind her hand. "It was completely, *unforgivably* wrong, but…I must have watched for over a minute, maybe close to two, before I decided I had to say something."

"What did you say?" Jude couldn't believe that Katrina had inadvertently stumbled into the fantasy of her dreams. "Lucky bitch."

"I said I was so sorry."

Jude rolled her eyes. "*That's* your big, seductive opening line? 'I'm so sorry'?"

"Of course! I just *knew* Ava was about to open her eyes and discover me at the foot of her bed, leering like a creep. So I was rehearsing an apology in my head the entire time, convinced I'd need a real doozy." Katrina bit her lower lip, then uncovered her face to meet Jude's inquisitive stare. "The suspense was unbearable. After a while, I couldn't stand it anymore. All of a sudden I was babbling about how sorry I was—and she was screaming. Just a bit."

"She *screamed?*" Jude retrieved the slice she'd abandoned, finally distracted enough from her own issues to tend to her stomach. "Damn. Hope the neighbors didn't hear."

"Her alarm was fairly short-lived." Katrina chuckled. "Thank goodness."

Jude gestured for her to keep going. "And *then?*"

"Unfortunately, she startled rather violently at the sound of my voice. Tweaked her back so bad her eyes teared up and she couldn't move, even to pull up her pants…or really to preserve her modesty in any way." Katrina looked down, undoubtedly ashamed of that particular consequence from her voyeurism. "I felt so awful about the whole thing, I didn't even think…just rushed to her side. She was beyond mortified, as I'm sure you can imagine. When I asked for permission to get her pants back on, she told me she'd need a minute before she could move. So we sat there together, on the bed—Ava nude below the waist, both of us mortified—while we waited for her to recover. When she finally spoke again, it was to apologize…to *me*. Profusely. She was terrified I would feel uncomfortable around her or decide to leave."

"Like quit?" Picturing the scene, Jude experienced a wave of sympathy for Diana's best friend. "Poor Ava. From the highest of highs to the lowest low—all within one minute, or maybe close to two, flat."

Katrina reacted to the teasing comment by poking Jude's thigh with her socked foot. "I know, right?" Her mouth quirked, signaling her arrival at the turning point of their story. "To sum up, somewhere between reassuring Ava that I had no problem whatsoever with the sight of her naked vagina and realizing I'd grabbed her hand at some point and was holding it…I kissed her. Mainly to stop both of us from apologizing anymore."

"I assume she kissed you back?" Jude folded her arms over her chest, protecting her heart from its foolish desire to share a moment that sweet with Diana.

"She did."

"With tongue?" Tickled by Katrina's sheepish nod, Jude punched her bicep jokingly. "Lady killer."

Katrina barked laughter. "Very nearly!" Once their giggles subsided, she reclined against the arm of the couch with a heavy sigh. "So we did that for a while. I can't honestly say how long. And…" She winced, smiling contritely. "It was *incredible*. By far the best make-out session I've had in…ever."

Despite her own impending heartbreak, Jude couldn't *not* celebrate Katrina's revelatory impropriety. "That's amazing, Kat. I couldn't be happier for you." Lest Katrina think she'd forgotten, Jude elbowed her gently in the side. "Now, to the literal climax of your damn story…Did you offer to finish her off? Or was that Ava's idea?"

Katrina's coy grin widened exponentially. "Well…I offered. But only after…" She buried her face in her hands, vibrating from embarrassed mirth. "She made this comment about how close she'd been, but how it might be a couple days before she'd be physically able to finish what she'd started. Since it was all my fault to begin with…I told her I could help her, if she wanted."

"And Ava just…agreed?" Jude wished Diana possessed even a fraction of her dearest friend's adventurous spirit. "Way to fall for the easy one."

Katrina snorted, lifting one shoulder in an aw-shucks shrug. "I wouldn't have it any other way."

Even if Diana drove her crazy and their arrangement seemed destined to end in bitter disappointment—at least for her—Jude was surprised to discover she felt exactly the same.

CHAPTER FOURTEEN

Diana gritted her teeth at the sharp upswing of Jude's hand against her bare buttocks, glad for the sting from the harsh smack. "Harder," she said, then winced when Jude obeyed. "Excellent." Draped across her assistant's tense thighs, Diana absorbed another blow through clenched teeth, then turned her head to address the class.

"Some of you will undoubtedly prefer a milder touch, but for others, the endorphin rush triggered by reasonably inflicted pain may prove too tempting to resist. Either way, keep in mind that the psychological aspect of spanking cannot be understated. Make sure you're ready for the emotional catharsis that can arise from this level of submission." She paused to allow Jude another slap, smiling when it connected. "I've had more than one client tell me that corporal punishment had proved deeply beneficial for their mental health."

For Diana, too. Twisted as it felt to ask Jude to punish her stupidly complex emotions and the misplaced desire they created, she relished the admonishing drumbeat of Jude's well-trained hand. While she suspected her pussy was literally dripping with arousal, Jude hadn't yet bothered to check. Thank goodness. Diana didn't want pleasure when she deserved to suffer.

Switching cheeks yet again, Jude delivered a somewhat less intense smack to the fleshiest part of Diana's butt. "Do you like this?" Her next slap landed lighter still, more tease than reprimand. "You like being bad for me?"

"Yes, mistress," Diana murmured, determined not to succumb to the attempted de-escalation. "*Harder*, please." She wiggled her ass to and fro, presumably right under Jude's face. "*Harder.*"

The next swat nearly took her breath away, and the blow after that succeeded. She gasped when Jude spanked her a third time, albeit less forcefully than before. Rather than continue, Jude placed her hand on Diana's tender ass and rubbed the skin to ease its fiery ache. "Your bottom is a lovely, bright-red color. Any more and it'll turn purple."

Bring it on. "Keep going," Diana said. "Even harder."

Jude hesitated, then drew her arm back to land a teeth-rattling smack across both cheeks. Unable to stop herself, Diana let out a tortured squeak that brought the spanking to a swift halt. "All right," Jude said, noticeably shaken by her vocalization. "Time for a break." She resumed her calm rubdown of the enflamed flesh. "You bad, *naughty* girl."

"Yes, mistress." Diana opened her mouth, about to beg for the punishment to recommence—then promptly snapped it shut. *Hold up, genius. Remember what happened last time you failed to heed her cues? Yeah...*this. Diana exhaled, allowing the comfort of Jude's touch to wash over her. To be sure, Jude's reluctance to impart any serious discomfort deserved her respect. Exhaling, Diana murmured, "Thank you, mistress."

"About time you stopped telling me what to do." She heard Jude's smirking tone and immediately pictured how adorable she must look with those full, pink lips curled into a bratty grin. "If I didn't know better, I'd think you were enjoying this a little *too* much."

"Yes, mistress." Diana kept her gaze locked on the cushion upon which her upper body rested, taut with anticipation over where Jude's wayward caresses would take her hand next. Seconds passed—seconds that stretched into days—before Jude eventually snuck lower to graze the slippery heat of Diana's labia with an exploratory fingertip. "*Yes, mistress,*" Diana repeated, far too eager to disguise her need. "Please."

"Please, what?" Jude swirled a finger around her opening to collect the copious juices, then painted a sensual line up to circle the tiny, puckered hole between Diana's sore cheeks. "Please feel how wet your cunt has gotten? Please stick my finger inside that tight hole and fuck it already, for fuck's sake?"

Diana wouldn't have predicted this self-assured dominance from her young friend, or her own desire to submit to Jude's will entirely, without hesitation. "Both, mistress."

Jude curled her fingers against Diana's exposed labia, then angled their bodies to show off the lewd grip she'd established. "You honestly think you've earned the privilege to come while I'm inside you?"

Shuddering at the unspoken threat of *not* being allowed to come, Diana murmured, "I hope so."

"How, by saying you were *sorry?*" Jude unleashed another medium-strength slap, followed by a rough pinch to Diana's throbbing butt cheek. "By allowing me to discipline you in front of these nice women?"

"Yes, ma'am. And also by—" Diana moaned at a lazy swat that ended in a moment of fleeting contact between Jude's hand and her sensitized labia. "By taking my punishment with the correct attitude."

"Indeed. Maybe you *have* earned a deep, thorough fingering." Jude slipped her thumb between Diana's labia, delving into her heat. "But first I need you to beg."

Disappointed in herself for wanting with such ferocity, Diana pleaded, "Mistress, *please* put your fingers inside my cunt and fuck me with them. I'm begging you...*please*. I need to come so bad, mistress. So bad I might die if you don't help me."

Chuckling, Jude slowly maneuvered two fingers past Diana's snug entrance. "Can't let that happen, can we? Poor thing."

Diana sobbed ecstatically when Jude sank into her the rest of the way. "Oh, *fuck*."

"Patience, darling. I'll get there." Jude curled her fingers, intuitively locating her G-spot without any need to hunt. "Once I've had my fun."

"Of course, mistress." Powerless to resist Jude's will, Diana abandoned any pretense of caution, balling her fists to prepare for another wild ride. "Take anything you want from me."

Except my heart.

CHAPTER FIFTEEN

In bed with Ava the day after her public spanking, Diana uttered a dejected sigh and snuggled into the motionless body at her side. Lacking the courage to fully confess the inner turmoil currently keeping her up at night, she murmured, simply, "I miss you." She kissed Ava's shoulder, then the slope of her breast. "Can't wait till you're healed."

"Likewise." Ava snorted, guiding Diana's head onto her shoulder. "Easy there, tiger. Let's keep this cuddle session G-rated."

Diana groaned and trailed her fingers along the stripe of bare stomach exposed by Ava's skimpy camisole. "You sure? I'm willing to do anything you think might feel pleasant. *Anything*, literally." She drew her fingernail around Ava's belly button, eliciting a nearly imperceptible shiver. "Just ask."

"Here's a question. How's business?" Ava didn't hide her relief when Diana rolled onto her back, away from the suspiciously unresponsive body she'd failed to rouse. "Specifically, working with Jude?"

Annoyed by the abrupt subject change, Diana took care not to let her frustration show. "Business is great. The workshops are going well. At least as well as can be expected without you there." She answered Ava's dubiously raised eyebrow with a solemn nod. "I mean it. I really miss you."

"And I miss you, but it's not like my replacement isn't twenty years younger and the perfect physical embodiment of young, healthy femininity." Ava gave her a pointed look. "It's hard to believe that Jude hasn't more than filled the void my absence left."

"Sure. Jude may be young and hot, she may have a perpetually wet pussy and an absolutely mind-blowing desire to please…but she isn't *you*.

I don't know her the way I know you." Afraid to get called out, Diana conceded the basic facts. "Look, you're right. Jude's a great girl, and not at all what I initially thought she'd be. In a good way. She's respectful of my boundaries—" Far more respectful than Diana herself, especially lately. "And way more mature than I'd anticipated." Debating what to disclose, she settled on saying, "She had a rough home life as a teenager—abused by her stepfather and, from what I gather, neglected by her mother. The courts emancipated her at seventeen."

Ava whistled quietly. "Poor girl."

"I know. She's been through a lot. A lot more than me, particularly by that age." Merely thinking of Jude's formative years sparked a visceral desire to hug the young woman and never let go. "I'm blown away by how well-adjusted she is, considering."

"Sounds like you two have something in common, after all." Ava quirked a lopsided smile at Diana's skeptical eyebrow. "Granted, your rough home life didn't begin until your late twenties, but even so...you know how it feels to be mistreated by someone who's supposed to care about you. Don't you?"

Diana attempted to shut down the psychoanalysis with a withering glare. "Those situations aren't even close to the same."

Ava caressed Diana's cheek like she felt sorry for her. "Sweetheart, what Janine did to you—"

"*Sucked*. Yeah, I get it." She wasn't in the mood to hear Ava elucidate the worst years of her life. "Janine was an asshole, no argument there. But it's not like she beat me."

"Diana, please. You and I both know the emotional wounds often linger the longest." Ava's face was awash with sadness. "Besides, I know she hit you. Remember?"

"Right, but like two, *maybe* three times." Shame, the stubborn companion Janine had first introduced into her life, urged her to sit up and turn from the sight of Ava's pity. "A rare slap across the face is nothing compared to the frequent, sustained beatings Jude's stepfather subjected her to—when she was a *child*, mind you. We're talking about a young teenager going up against a full-grown adult man, not two women of approximately the same height and weight." Annoyance sharpened Diana's tone. "*No* comparison."

"Fine." Ava ghosted her fingers over Diana's lower back, a conciliatory touch she didn't acknowledge. "I wasn't saying that to offend you. I was only saying..." Her hand fell away, leaving Diana cold in its absence. "Both you and Jude fell victim to another person's shortcomings yet persevered."

"She's a strong woman," Diana said, staring at the far wall. Jude truly *had* persevered, but she couldn't claim the same about herself. "A woman who overcame a lot of hardship to get where she is today. The very last thing she needs, or deserves, is a forty-year-old girlfriend with serious trust issues."

"Still, I suspect Jude would appreciate the mark Janine left on your life. If you ever chose to tell her, that is."

Diana exhaled. "The lines are blurry enough already. Spilling my guts would send the wrong message."

"What, that you trust her enough to share private details about your life? Like she's trusted you?" She didn't need to see Ava's face to hear her disapproval. "Does this mean you've taken the idea of friendship off the table, as well?"

"We can't be friends."

"Oh. Great, so I'm the only person you plan to have any sort of relationship with for the rest of your life?" Ava didn't bother to hide her irritation. "Marvelous. No pressure there."

Wanting to relieve Ava of any burden created by her own social isolation, Diana sought to allay her concern. "No, but Jude is attracted to me. And frankly, I'm attracted to her. We've already had a bunch of sex—*incredible* sex—and she's never hidden that she'd be open to more. Surely you can understand my doubts about whether we can set all that aside for the sake of a platonic friendship."

Ava pressed a hand against Diana's spine, waiting for her to turn and look. When she did, Ava smiled. "I get it."

"Hooray." Diana huffed, lying back against the pillows to stare at her favorite section of ceiling.

"It's just a real shame." Ava's wistfulness dumped a tall glass of ice-cold guilt over Diana's head. "You obviously like this woman. More than you've liked anyone since…oh, hell, let's say me." Ava's amusement was infectious, drawing out a begrudging snort from Diana despite her efforts to keep her expression grim. "Even if you don't want to *date her*, date her, why not have a little fun on the side? You said she respects boundaries. Do you really think she can't handle casual sex with you?"

"Maybe she can, but I'd rather not take the chance." Besides, it wasn't Jude's ability to stay casual that most worried her. "She lives next door to me, Ava. We share a bedroom wall. It's one thing to hear her fuck other women as my neighbor. I'm not sure I want to put myself through listening as her lover, however casual."

"You don't think it could be kind of hot?" Ava fingered a lock of Diana's hair, teasingly. "If you don't have any feelings for her—"

"I never said I didn't have feelings." Diana's chest felt like it might crack open, like she might bleed out right there next to her best friend. She didn't want to admit that she sometimes yearned far more than she let on, and she sure as hell didn't need Ava urging her to rescind her policy on dating and chase more heartbreak. "I'd like to stop talking about Jude now. Please."

"Diana—"

"*Please.*" She slammed her eyes shut, dangerously close to jumping up and storming out of Ava's apartment. "I can't go down this road. Not yet. If and when I finally do, I swear I'll come to you for advice. All right?"

"All right." Seemingly chastened by the heartfelt plea, Ava stroked her hip. "I'm sorry you're having a rough time. I wish I could fix it for you."

Diana laugh-sobbed. "I'm too busted to fix."

"No, you're not." Gingerly, Ava wrapped her arm around Diana and gathered her into a loose embrace. "Listen to the lady with the broken spine. If I can heal, so can you." She kissed Diana's hair, then whispered, "Our lives aren't over yet. We still have so much left to do—both of us."

Stirred by Ava's passion, Diana craned to capture her lips for a healing kiss. When Ava almost immediately broke away, pressing her mouth against Diana's forehead with a gentle, murmured endearment, Diana could no longer ignore the blisteringly obvious. "You won't even let me kiss you?" She pulled back from Ava, then helped guide her friend into a comfortable position on the mattress. "Don't tell me this is about your broken spine. I understand being too sore for sex, but a kiss? It feels more like you're forcing yourself not to recoil at my touch. Have I done something to piss you off, or are you not attracted to me anymore?"

Ava's freely flowing tears simultaneously tugged at Diana's heartstrings and confirmed her worst fears. "Of course I'm attracted to you. You're a wonderful lover, and my closest friend."

"But?" Diana despised the pain in her gut, an all-consuming ache she remembered from her days of chasing sex and romance. Searching for an explanation she could live with, she asked, "You're not giving up on sex altogether, are you? Because you know I'm still very attracted to you, too. Busted spine and all."

"I know you are." Ava gave her a doleful smile. "I'm not struggling with my self-esteem or suddenly blind to your many charms." She breathed out shakily, renewing Diana's panic. Something had changed. Ava's face said it all. "On the contrary, I'm…quite certainly falling in love. Or in love already, I don't know." She captured her lower lip between her teeth, a faint tell Diana easily recognized from their many years together. "With Katrina."

"Jude's cousin." Diana spoke flatly, careful to keep the anger out of her tone. "Are you fucking kidding me?"

"I know, I know. I'm too old for her. I don't care."

"I never said you were too old." Conscious of Ava's recent struggles around the issue of aging, Diana amended her previous stance. "Only that Katrina was too young. There's a subtle but distinct difference."

"Either way, I don't agree." Ava's lips curled into a poorly stifled grin. "Apparently, neither does Katrina."

Diana frowned at what Ava had left unspoken. "What does that mean?" She instantly landed on the worst-case scenario. "You fucked her?"

"Are you kidding *me?*" Ava waved a hand to showcase her stiffly held posture. "Do I look like I'm capable of fucking anything at present?"

Only the great thing we had going. Diana swallowed the uncharitable comeback and resumed her interrogation. "I'm not asking if you strapped on a dildo and pounded her doggy style. Have you touched Katrina sexually?"

Ava hesitated, then said, "No. We kissed."

Once again, Ava's face conveyed volumes. This transgression hadn't ended at a mere kiss. "Did Katrina touch *you* sexually?"

Ava's chin wobbled, betraying the truth ahead of her hesitant whisper. "Yes."

"Perfect." Diana laughed, but only so as not to cry. "Fucking excellent."

"I knew you'd be upset, which is why I've dreaded telling you." Ava clenched her jaw, then her fists. "But that's absurd, isn't it? You and me, we're not in a committed relationship. We've never been monogamous. If I meet someone I want to fuck—or, you know, let finger me—I shouldn't have to worry about how you'll react. We're best friends who occasionally sleep together for fun. I'm well within my rights to fall for someone else."

She wasn't wrong, but that hardly quelled Diana's sweeping rage. Upset was an understatement. She felt like she was drowning, like the room was closing in on her...like what little she had was just stolen away by a younger, less damaged temptress in scrub pants. Fighting through the emotional maelstrom created by Ava's tearful performance, Diana said, "You're right. You don't owe me anything. Except the courtesy of not making my life more complicated than it already is."

"Diana, sweetheart." Ava clasped her arm. "Actually, this isn't about you at all. It's about breaking my spine, deciding my life was over, then meeting the girl of my dreams."

"*Girl,*" Diana muttered in a nasty undertone, fueled by spite and self-loathing. "Precisely."

Sighing, Ava released her with a halfhearted squeeze. "I'm sorry I won't get physical with you right now. I don't intend to cause you pain— or complicate your life, for that matter. Because I love you. I'll *always* love you." She paused, but Diana stubbornly avoided her imploring gaze. Wearily, Ava said, "I'm not turning you down to hurt you. I'm saying no because I'm genuinely interested in Katrina. Now that she and I have crossed the line from flirting to third base, I need to figure out where her head is at before messing around with anyone else." She covered Diana's limp hand with her own. "Even my dearest friend in the world."

Diana mentally counted to five, then said, "I'm not entitled to sex from you. I hope my disapproval of Katrina's unprofessional behavior doesn't suggest I believe otherwise."

"Hey." Ava hardened her tone. "Don't. Katrina did nothing wrong. You know I'd been flirting with her for weeks. I practically begged her to."

"Whatever." Diana prepared to retake the high ground. "Of all the women you could fall for, you had to pick Jude's *cousin?* It's like you're *trying* to make me look bad."

"What are you talking about?" It looked like it was killing Ava to stay flat on her back. Ire roused, she went on the offensive. "How many times do I have to explain that my feelings for Katrina have nothing to do with you? Are you really this self-absorbed?" Her eyes narrowed. "What happened to being happy that I'm happy?"

"Nothing to do with me?" Laughing bitterly, Diana sat up and swung her legs over the side of the bed. "Let's see...I hired Katrina to watch after you, and I'm paying half her salary, so her professional conduct is most definitely my business. She's also related to Jude. That *absolutely* makes any relationship between you two very much my concern."

"Why?" Ava didn't reach for her this time. "You don't want to date Jude? Fine. Why should that stop me from seeing Katrina?"

Diana braced her palms against the mattress. "Because by doing so, you're poking a giant hole in my argument against intergenerational dating."

"I'm under no obligation to support your arguments or your stupid hang-ups." Ava didn't sound sorry in the slightest. "Particularly when I think they're dumb."

"*Eighteen years,* Ava. You were a freshman in college when Katrina was born."

Ava chuckled. "No wonder being with her makes me feel so young and alive."

Diana battled a ferocious surge of jealousy mixed with envy, a confusing whirlwind of emotion that hurtled her from one resentment to the next. Not only was she losing her sexual partner, but Ava had apparently found true love and contentment—two dreams Diana had long since discarded. She and Ava had been carrying on their pseudo-relationship for years, since shortly after she'd left Janine, and for the first time, Diana realized she'd never really pictured its ending. Despite her protestations against commitment and genuine disinterest in attempting another serious relationship with Ava, some part of her must've assumed they'd remain lovers into their senior years. True, things might not work out between Ava and Katrina…but now that she'd seen how easily she could be dropped, the entire foundation of her post-Janine existence was crumbling.

Shaken, Diana glanced over her shoulder to ensure Ava both heard and saw her disdain. "What could you two *possibly* have in common?"

Her baiting didn't seem to faze Ava. "All kinds of things. For one, we're both open to the possibilities. We enjoy each other's company, and we're not afraid to see where our attraction takes us. We *want* to be happy."

Whether or not Ava intended it to be, Diana couldn't help but take that as a personal slam. Filter disappearing with her patience, she leapt to her feet and snarled, "Fuck you, Ava."

"Oh, really. Fuck *me?*" Ava shouted as Diana stormed across the apartment to leave. "Fuck *you!*"

"Genius comeback," Diana snapped, knowing full well that hers hadn't been any cleverer. "Anyway, I should get home. I've got a busy evening of being willfully miserable ahead of me. You know, since I don't want to be happy."

"Diana—"

She threw out one last shitty, cutting remark, wanting Ava to feel miserable like she did. "Have fun exploiting your hired slut. Try not to be *too* disappointed when she eventually admits that she isn't *seriously* interested in an old lady like you. Make no mistake, any heartbreak that girl causes won't be her fault. You're the one with more than enough life experience to know better." With that, Diana threw open the door for a dramatic exit…only to discover Katrina mere inches from Ava's welcome mat.

Clutching two bags of Chinese food in her white-knuckled hands, Katrina sported a classic deer-in-headlights stare. Commendably, it didn't take long for her to break the awkward silence. "Hello," she said, polite but guarded. "Is this a bad time?"

Diana snorted, shouldering past Katrina en route to the elevator. "She's all yours."

"You're welcome to stay for dinner," Katrina called after her. "I brought plenty of food."

Pulling a face she was only sort of glad Katrina couldn't see, Diana kept on walking. "No thanks. Just lost my appetite."

CHAPTER SIXTEEN

Diana managed to avoid seeing Jude again until half past five on Thursday evening, when an unexpected knock at the door triggered her second mild freak-out that day. With Ava out of commission—and presumably too furious about their argument to visit even if she were able-bodied—Diana knew only one person bold enough to drop by unannounced. Naturally, that would be the woman to whom she'd first established surprise visits as acceptable. Setting her glass of red wine on the coffee table, Diana straightened her pajamas and went to answer.

Any irritation she might've felt about the imposition slipped away as soon as she laid eyes upon Jude's breathtaking face. Her tentative, hopeful smile made Diana feel warm and gooey all over, despite her fervent wish not to feel anything. The pizza boxes in Jude's arms hinted at the motive for her visit, as did the timing. Jude glanced at the pizza, then Diana, unable to hide her blatant anxiety. "Hey. You're dressed for bed."

"I suppose this makes us even." Diana folded her arms over her chest to hide her painfully erect nipples from Jude's roving gaze. "Don't worry. I'm not ready for sleep quite yet—just hoping to relax for the rest of the evening." Or try to, in between mourning the demoralizing loss of her sexual and social security blanket and wildly theorizing about how much Ava had told Katrina about their fight, and by extension, what Katrina might've told Jude. Concerned that some such megaton disclosure was behind this impromptu visit, Diana kept her expression neutral ahead of Jude's explanation. "What's up?"

Jude hefted the pizza boxes into the air. "I, uh...well, I wasn't sure what toppings you liked, so I ordered one plain cheese and one garden vegetable—mostly because that's *my* favorite."

"Duly noted." Unsettled by the silky timbre of her own low voice, Diana cleared her throat. She hadn't meant to *flirt*, for Pete's sake. "Both sound delicious."

"Great!" Visibly relieved, Jude stared awkwardly for half a beat, then shuffled her feet. "I guess I also wondered if you wanted to go over this weekend's workshop ahead of time, like we did the last one. That worked out pretty well, I thought. My regrettable, late-stage attempt at line-crossing aside."

Diana recalled the superhuman willpower she'd had to exercise in order to flee Jude's apartment rather than accept her invitation to mutually masturbate. That situation had been her own damn fault, however, not Jude's. By announcing her plans to finger herself on the other side of their shared bedroom wall, she'd emboldened Jude to propose getting naked outside of class. Taking responsibility, Diana said, "As I recall, I stuck my toe over that line first. I shouldn't have teased you the way I did."

Jude's nostrils flared. "What if I like being teased?"

Rather than answer directly, Diana said, "It won't happen again—outside of class, that is." Regretting Jude's clear disappointment, she lowered her guard, stepping aside to grant Jude passage into the intensely private sanctum she'd only ever shared with Ava. "Come in. Before our dinner gets cold."

Jude blinked, then carefully crossed the threshold. "Not as though cold pizza is *bad* pizza." She shot Diana a cautious smile. "Let's be clear. There's no such thing."

Closing the door behind Jude, Diana crinkled her nose in exaggerated disgust. "I beg to differ. Few things gross me out more than nasty, congealed cheese on soggy bread." She walked them to the kitchen, mindful to snag her wine from the coffee table along the way. "Hot and fresh, pizza is truly the food of the gods. But cold? Worse than garbage."

"*What?* You're nuts." Jude tossed the cardboard boxes onto the dining table, then slowly swiveled in place to survey the room. "I would gladly eat unheated, leftover pizza every day of the week. There's no yummier way to wake up than with a cool slice of garden vegetable."

Shuddering, Diana grabbed a second glass from the cupboard, then held up the bottle of wine. "Fair warning. I'm already on my second drink. Care to join me? I wouldn't mind being spared the temptation to finish this bottle on my own."

Jude hesitated long enough for Diana to notice. "A few sips. No more than half a glass, please."

"Being a good girl, are you?" Diana filled Jude's glass exactly halfway, then carried it to the table alongside her own. "Smart. I should probably follow your rather mature example and switch to water."

"Don't let me dissuade you from whatever you were doing before I ambushed you." Claiming the nearest chair, Jude flipped open the lid on the top pizza box to reveal a vegetable-laden pie whose savory aroma brought literal tears to Diana's eyes. "I won't stay long. I just figured... we should make sure we're on the same page for Saturday. You know, in case."

"Absolutely. You were right to come." Diana hadn't actually intended to initiate another lesson-planning session, given the near catastrophe she'd made of their last one, but it pleased her that Jude was asking anyway. Communication was vital for safe, sane, consensual sex, all of which she craved from Jude. "Have you ever played with a strap-on before?"

"Oh." Jude laughed, insistently avoiding eye contact until she'd swallowed a tiny sip of wine. "Uh, yes. On more than a few occasions."

Only half relieved to learn of Jude's proficiency, Diana said, "Great. Giving or receiving?"

Jude flashed a coy grin. "Both."

"Which role do you prefer?"

"Both," Jude repeated, downing another sip of wine. "Depends on my mood, and my partner."

Diana's heart thumped at the prospect of fucking Jude, and being fucked in return. "Would you like to choose a role for Saturday, or shall we plan on leaving ourselves time to switch?"

Jude fidgeted in her seat, seemingly just as aroused by the negotiation as Diana was. "Ideally, I'd love to each take a turn. That way I can get feedback about my technique from a real, live sexpert—without giving up the masterful drilling that sexpert will surely provide."

Draining her glass, Diana picked up the half-eaten slice of pizza she didn't particularly care to finish. Anything to keep her hands occupied. "Okay. Do you have a dildo you want me to use? If not, I'm happy to provide the toys."

"I do have a favorite." Jude twirled her wineglass by its stem, dancing the delicate vessel this way and that on the tabletop. "Would you...be willing to wear that one? You can pick one out for me to wear... whichever you want."

"Sure." Amused by how shy her wild young neighbor could be, Diana embraced her growing tipsiness and poured another drink. "I'll wear yours, and you can wear mine."

"Cool." Jude exhaled in a rush, eyeing the bottle next to Diana with apparent envy. "Should we talk dirty to each other while we're doing this, or—"

Diana shook her head. "I'm sure I'll tell you how sexy you are, how hot and wet your pussy is, how thrilled I am to be inside you…to have you wrapped around me…" Diana stopped to take a breath, then a quick sip. "Nothing *too* dirty, though. Not this time."

"How come?" Jude drained her empty glass for perhaps the third time, giving it a subtle shake to encourage the final, stubborn drops onto her tongue. "Because of that role-play?"

"No." Not completely. Daring to meet Jude's gaze—mostly to prove she could—Diana presented the calmest smile in her limited arsenal. "Strap-on sex is a fraught topic for some lesbians. I've had more than one client express the belief that penetrative intercourse using a strap-on dildo is akin to an admission of penis envy—and-or latent heterosexual desires on the part of the recipient." She smirked, relieved when Jude weighed in with an amused snort. "That's bullshit, of course, but we should assume not everyone shares our opinion yet…and keep the kink to a minimum. Easier to digest that way."

Jude gave her a lighthearted salute. "I can do that."

"I'm sure you can." Halfway through her third glass of wine, Diana was rapidly losing control of her inner flirt—and too intoxicated to care. *I really shouldn't be drinking.* "So far you've been exceedingly capable in absolutely *everything* I've asked you to do." Aiming for the compliment she assumed would delight Jude most, Diana added, sincerely, "You make me proud."

Jude tossed her pizza onto the plate and fanned her cheeks with a perceptibly trembling hand. "Maybe we should change the subject. Or…I could go."

Though she already knew the answer, Diana asked, "Go? Why?"

Jude didn't hesitate to tell the truth. "You're a little drunk, and I'm a lot horny. I don't want to do anything dumb…or otherwise fuck things up."

For reasons Diana couldn't explain, she hated for Jude to leave so soon. With Ava temporarily out of her life, the loneliness was downright unbearable. Her long-cherished solitude had become a prison of her own making, a pit of desolation and sorrow that left her frighteningly hungry for human interaction. Three measly days without Ava and she'd become a pathetic wreck. Grasping for some way to convince Jude to stick around, Diana said, "Okay, new subject. How's your writing? Making any progress on the novel?" Jude's deep sigh was all the answer she needed. "That good, huh?" Diana leaned back, crossing one leg over the other. "Sorry to hear that."

Jude shrugged, an unconvincing attempt at nonchalance. "I'll get past it. I always do."

"Are you blocked in general, or stuck on a particularly difficult chapter?"

"More of a general block, I guess." Jude pointed at Diana's plate. "You finished with that?" When Diana nodded, Jude snatched up the remnants of her abandoned slice. "The crust is the best part."

"Your writer's block...my workshops haven't become too much of a distraction, have they?" Diana didn't know what possessed her to suggest that she might be behind Jude's creative woes, and she definitely wasn't sure how she'd react if Jude agreed she was the problem. But if the workshops *were* disrupting Jude's sabbatical, Diana needed to set things right. Somehow. "Be honest. Your career is every bit as important as mine."

For some reason, Jude teared up. "I appreciate your concern more than you can imagine, but no...the workshops are fine. We're talking about sex for two hours every weekend. Even when you factor in these pre-workshop dinners, I'm spending maybe three hours of my work week being paid to orgasm. Four, tops. That's hardly overwhelming. Plus, I'm having fun."

Sadly, Jude didn't *appear* to be having fun. Not tonight, not with her. Afraid she'd really put her foot in it this time, Diana said, "I wish I could do something to help unblock you."

Jude smiled. "Thanks. Like I said, it happens sometimes. Writing-related crises of self-confidence are kind of my thing, though I keep hoping I'll grow out of them. The sad thing is, I honestly thought I'd worked through most of this bullshit the last time." The bravado in her voice belied her gloomy face. "Shows how smart I am."

"Too damn smart for your own good." Diana winked, sending Jude's self-conscious gaze to the tabletop. "That's my personal assessment."

"Maybe." Jude bit her lip, probably to hold back a smile, then glanced furtively over her shoulder...toward the exit. "On rare occasions."

Fearing that Jude was about to make her excuses and leave, Diana mentally scrambled for another question to ask. Her mind bounced wildly from one potential topic to the next, rejecting each in turn as too suggestive, or too intimate, or too perilous—until she finally landed on a subject she was certain Jude wanted to discuss. "Listen—"

Jude chose that moment to break her own silence. "I should—"

They both stopped, staring at one another expectantly until Jude broke their stalemate. "I'm sorry. You were saying?"

"I…" Momentum interrupted, Diana questioned the drunken impulse encouraging her to hemorrhage honesty. "Uh…don't remember."

"Then maybe I should go." Jude melted into a soft smile that made Diana's chest want to burst. "Before one of us says or does something she'll regret."

Diana blurted out the words that would keep Jude with her a little while longer. "Actually, I do remember. If you're still interested…I can tell you about Janine. The basics. I figure…you deserve to know. After you were so forthcoming about your own past and all."

As predicted, Jude stayed in her seat. When Diana noticed her gaze stray momentarily to the half-empty bottle, she spared her the decision by pouring a dash of the dark-red liquid into Jude's glass. She added an equal amount to her own, then took a long sip. Jude did the same, draining hers in one swallow. She exhaled, then made deliberate eye contact. "I didn't confide in you about Travis—my stepfather—to guilt you into spilling your guts in return. Of course I'm always interested to know you better, whatever you're willing to share. Just…you don't owe me anything, and I don't need to know any more than you're genuinely ready to tell." Swallowing, she murmured, "I don't want you to feel weird around me once you sober up."

That made sense. Honoring Jude's plainly articulated concern, Diana paused to consider the ramifications of allowing someone besides Ava into her circle of trust. Despite her youth and the crush she'd never denied, Jude had repeatedly demonstrated her willingness to observe boundaries—even while openly wanting more. At what point did Jude deserve her trust? With her and Ava on the rocks, a second friendship wasn't the *worst* idea in the world. Assuming Diana could stay out of her panties when they weren't in class, why not start with Jude what she'd built over the years with Ava? Intimacy without commitment.

Is this the wine talking? Diana searched for the truth inside her core self, putting aside her isolation and arousal and intoxication to focus on what her heart would want when the sun rose tomorrow and she awoke, sober, to face another solitary day.

Taking a leap she hoped she wouldn't regret, Diana said, "While I appreciate your concern—because you're right, I *am* slightly drunk, and most likely wouldn't bring up Janine if I weren't—I want to tell you because I think you should know. Not because I believe you're owed my secrets in exchange for yours. I'd just…like you to understand where I'm coming from. As my friend."

Jude's shoulders relaxed as she settled into her chair. "Okay. I'm listening."

"Right." Diana exhaled, wishing she were a *bit* drunker. She had no idea where to start, or how to explain the worst years of her life. "Um… so…"

"So when did you meet?" Jude nudged her in the right direction.

"I was around your age." Diana kept her expression stoic and her voice even, staving off the emotion triggered by her most vivid memories of life with Janine. "It was a couple of years after Ava and I decided we were better off as friends. A mutual acquaintance introduced me to Janine at his birthday party—at her request, apparently. She was five years older than me, smart as hell, tough, confident to a fault…" She cast her mind back to the beginning, long before she'd met Janine's true self, as she grasped to recall why she'd been so smitten. "Janine always knew exactly what she wanted and what she had to do to get it. And she was charismatic…" Diana laughed humorlessly. "In the beginning, she was *pure* charisma. That's why it was so shocking when, about a year later— shortly after we'd rented a place together, naturally—she finally dropped the act and showed me who she really was."

Jude fiddled with the corner of the pizza box, a nervous tic Diana tried to ignore. "What happened?"

Diana paused to sip her wine, reminding herself that Janine was a sociopathic loser who'd ruined her life with lies. That Diana had somehow deserved her cruelty was the biggest whopper of all. "I honestly can't remember an inciting incident. I believe it started with nasty comments about the way I dressed. Like the time I wore a V-necked T-shirt to a bonfire we attended at a private beach. Janine waited until we were at the party to pull me aside and call me a slut and accuse me of showing off my tits for attention. That became a regular thing. She also loved to bring up my sexual history from before we were together, specifically some of the wilder encounters I'd stupidly confided to her when we were first together. You know, when I was naive and trusted her not to use those details against me."

"She sounds like a real piece of work." Jude raised her eyes to Diana's, frowning. "I hope you weren't with her long."

"Almost six years." Ashamed, Diana took a few more sips of wine to let the admission fully register. Jude said nothing, only waited for her to go on. It took every last drop of Diana's courage to keep talking. Even with the self-protective layer of inebriation, the humiliation was excruciating. "I'm not sure what the hell was wrong with me. All I know is that I'll never put myself through that again."

"An abusive relationship?" Jude nodded. "Good call."

"*Any* relationship," Diana said. "It's not like you can always identify an asshole from the outset. At least I can't. I had zero awareness that Janine would eventually criticize every facet of my life, from my friends to my private sexual desires. Our first year together, Janine had me *convinced* that she was the love of my life. That she was special…that as a couple, *we* were special." Loose-lipped from the wine, she admitted, "Know what finally clued me in that she *wasn't* the one, that nothing I did, or didn't do, would bring back the woman I'd fallen for? When she hit me the second time." She chuckled at her own naïveté. "That's right, the *second* time. Somehow being slapped across the face and falsely accused of cheating—*again*—didn't make a big-enough impression the first time around. It took being smacked in the face, then shoved against the dresser, for me to accept that the Janine I thought I loved didn't exist. That I'd been duped. Like a dumbass."

Jude extended her hand across the table to rest mere inches from Diana's wrist—a silent offer of comfort for her to accept, or not, however she chose. "You don't seriously believe that, do you? That you were a dumbass for falling in love?"

Resisting the urge to hold Jude's hand, Diana instead resumed the journey to the bottom of her glass. The alcohol was doing its trick— dissociating her from the tragedy of losing so many years to Janine and numbing the impact of Jude's impassioned defense of her inaction. "The second time she hit me, we'd been together about three and a half years. I stayed for nearly two and a half more."

Jude shook her head, eyelashes fluttering as she blinked away tears. "Diana, you're a trained *therapist*, for fuck's sake. You must realize that plenty of very smart people end up in abusive relationships. I mean…"

She narrowed her gaze. "I hope you don't actually hold the opinion that only a dumbass ends up mistreated by her romantic partner."

Annoyed to have her personal assessment taken as a gross generalization, Diana admonished Jude with a frown. "Of course not. Sociopaths are often highly charming and difficult to spot, and people don't leave their abuser even after the mask has been taken off for plenty of reasons. I'm not casting judgment on anyone else's situation. Only my own." Her vision blurred as tears she could no longer hold off surged to the front. "I should've paid more attention to the red flags I did notice during our first year. And I shouldn't have been so foolishly optimistic— shouldn't have let myself think in terms of forever.

"I *definitely* shouldn't have run out and told everyone I knew how much I loved this woman I'd just met, how amazing our relationship was, how she'd already made me a better person...because that ended up making it feel even more impossible to leave. Breaking up meant admitting I'd been had. That I'd *failed.*" She stopped, swallowing the bitter pill of her regret. "I always assumed I'd be stronger. When I was young, with Ava—I knew what *I* wanted. I was never afraid to assert myself. I'd see or hear about women in toxic relationships and think...not me. *Never* me." She snorted. "Now it's *never again.*"

Exhaling, Jude rested her hand on Diana's wrist. "I'm sorry she put you through that. If there's any justice in the world, Janine will end up miserable and alone."

"I have no knowledge of where she is or what she's doing these days, and frankly, you couldn't pay me to find out." Diana swallowed, flustered by the warmth of Jude's fingers on her skin. "She basically stalked me for close to two years after I finally ended things. It took Ava going downright ballistic—and Janine meeting another woman shortly thereafter—for the harassment to stop."

"*Stalked* you?" Jude sounded genuinely horrified. "No wonder you swore off relationships."

"Right?" Pleased to have finally convinced *someone* of that logic, Diana beamed toothily, gratified by the fuzziness in her head and the rising heat between her thighs. "Nothing's worth another Janine."

"Still..." Jude stroked her thumb along Diana's forearm, perhaps unconsciously, and stared into her eyes. "You trust Ava, no? So you understand that not every woman wants to hurt you. Some of—" She stuttered. "Of them only want to love you, and care for you..." She broke their shared gaze to study their point of contact. "You shouldn't let Janine steal your chance to find happiness with someone who'll treat you right."

Instinctively affronted, Diana puffed out her chest in defiance. "I'm more than capable of finding happiness on my own, thanks." She snickered at the haughtiness of her vaguely slurred rejoinder, too silly from the wine to hold on to her fleeting outrage. "*You've* seen me masturbate." Her boldness intensified the rise and fall of Jude's lovely chest, hastening Diana's racing pulse. "Didn't I look and sound perfectly happy to you?"

"Happiness goes beyond orgasms, Diana. You know that."

Diana hardened her heart against the gentle lilt of Jude's voice. "Actually, I don't. Could be that your orgasms aren't as satisfying as mine."

"My body is perfectly tuned for mind-blowing ecstasy, thanks." Jude lowered her gaze to Diana's wrist, then sighed and withdrew her touch. "I appreciate you telling me about Janine. I know you don't like to talk about her—or yourself—so I realize it took a lot to confide in me about something that personal. And you're right. I *do* better understand your feelings about love now that I know what you endured. Of course I'm bummed out that an awful bitch like Janine has scared you away from giving some other poor schmuck the opportunity to love you right." Sheepishly, she folded her arms over her chest and reestablished cautious eye contact. "But I get it. Abuse isn't a thing you just get over. It can fuck you up for a long time. Maybe even forever."

Diana resisted the comparison of their pasts for a second time. "What Janine did to me is nothing compared to what your stepfather put you through. Of course, you're not the one who's fucked up forever now. Goes to show how strong *you* are...and I'm not."

Looking distressed, Jude said, "I don't buy that you're fucked up forever. Just scared, right now. But despite that fear you're living with..." She surprised Diana by giving her an affectionate smile she couldn't help but reciprocate. "You've decided to let me be your friend. I can't help but see that as proof your power to evolve remains intact." Her foot found Diana's under the table. "You escaped from Janine, what, only five years ago?"

"Roughly." Diana used her wine-soaked tongue to wet her parched lips, shocked by how strongly she felt the alcohol. Inhibitions close to vanquished, she battled the nearly overpowering impulse to stand up, haul Jude onto her feet, and kiss her senseless. *Don't be stupid, Di. Go easy.* "Sometimes it feels like yesterday."

"You're still recovering, then." Jude's toe brushed against her ankle, sending a shiver through Diana she neglected to disguise. "Just...don't write yourself off completely. Leave room in your heart for the possibility of further change."

Diana shrugged, sliding her socked foot up the length of Jude's denim-clad calf. "For the sake of that poor, hypothetical schmuck who wishes only to treat me the way she believes I ought to be treated?"

Lips parted, Jude studied her as though desperate to discern the hidden meaning behind Diana's flirtatious, mildly taunting words. Seconds passed before she responded, whispering a simple "Yes."

"I'll be sure to take your suggestions under advisement." Diana arched an eyebrow in warning. "So long as *you* promise not to mistake our friendship for anything more. Not if you want to keep it."

Jude thrust her hand across the table. "Deal."

Diana curled her fingers around Jude's, squeezing lustfully. Reluctant to let go, she prolonged the contact by tracing a lazy pattern along the inside of Jude's delicate wrist with her thumb. Jude's audible gasp went straight to her clit, triggering a moan that caused Jude's pulse point to thrum harder and faster under her touch. Before she could register what was about to happen, Diana's raging libido leapt into the driver's seat to eject her sense of caution and steer the evening toward imminent disaster. "Fantastic. It's *very* exciting, having a new friend to play with."

Jude froze, then lowered her gaze to watch Diana's roving thumb. "I'm excited to be your friend, as well." She withdrew her hand, leaving Diana hovering uselessly in the air. "It's wonderful to finally feel like I'm getting to know you."

"Oh, I'd say you already know me...more than almost anyone else on the planet, in fact." Equal parts unwilling and unable to self-censor after the half bottle of wine she'd downed, Diana slid lower in her chair and dragged her toes up the inside of Jude's calf. "Only Ava can claim a more intimate familiarity with my body. Granted, she and I have been friends for almost twenty years. We've had plenty of time to get acquainted." She snuck her foot between Jude's closed thighs. "And lots of practice."

Jude jolted upright, sitting rigid against her chair. Yet she didn't ask Diana to stop. Instead she whispered, "What are you doing?"

Intellectually, Diana hadn't forgotten why she shouldn't come on to Jude, or that she'd break a promise by carrying on further, but her dismay about Ava's poor judgment had the unfortunate side effect of perpetuating her own. "If you're serious about treating me nice, sweetheart, I'll teach you how. Show you all my favorite ways to be touched. Right here, right now. Would you like that?"

Blinking, Jude said, "You're inviting me to bed?"

"Not to my bed, no." Encouraged by the absence of a definitive *no*, Diana scooted her chair partway around the table to rest a hand on Jude's tense thigh. "Let's keep this casual, don't you think? I figure…what, we could trade oral? Maybe finger each other? Or I could get my harness and dildo…then we could call it work-related."

Jude dropped her gaze, still blinking. After a lengthy silence, she put her hand on Diana's to stop its ascent up the inside of her thigh. "We can't. You've had too much wine to make this kind of decision. *As your friend*, I can't in good conscience take advantage of your lowered inhibitions. I hope you understand, and that you'll forgive me if I've made this awkward. You must know how much I adore having sex with you." Fiddling with a lock of her lustrous hair, Jude shrugged, then whispered, "If I thought you could truly consent right now, I'd already be on my knees. Sadly, I don't, so…we can't."

Diana's gut reaction was to get angry, but the unjustifiable eruption flared out within milliseconds. In its place arose comprehension and deep, heartfelt gratitude. Once again, Jude had proven her trustworthiness. She'd honored the boundaries Diana had so painstakingly established—the same boundaries she was questioning more and more with each passing day. Inspired by the alcohol, Diana spoke from her heart. "Thank you, Jude. You're right, and I'm sorry. It's terrible to keep doing this to you, isn't it? There's no excuse, either. Not really. You're just…I'm just…" She took a deep breath. "Something about you, Jude Monaco, turns me into a damn fool. Every single time you're near."

Smiling, Jude scooted back from the table and stood. Before Diana could do the same, Jude walked behind her chair and wrapped her in an affectionate embrace. Warm lips brushed over her cheek, then pressed against the crown of her head, for the few, precious seconds prior to Jude's inevitable departure. "I'll see you soon. Be sure to drink lots of water."

Diana swallowed, hoping to sound reasonably unaffected by the brief, blissfully warm contact. "Will do. Thanks again for the pizza."

"My pleasure." Jude sounded like she'd nearly reached the door. "Enjoy the leftovers. FYI, cold pizza is the penultimate hangover cure."

Jude's callback to their earlier debate broke through her dejected mood, triggering helpless laughter, then an involuntary shudder. "You're disgusting." Diana had to grin.

"And yet you're still into me."

Afraid to do something else she'd regret, Diana kept her mouth shut, saying nothing in response. When the door opened behind her, she shut down the fantasy of begging Jude to stay—even if only to watch television together for an hour or two—by clamping her lips shut so tightly her jaw ached.

"Don't forget to lock up behind me."

Diana answered with a silent thumbs-up. Then, unable to watch Jude go, she stared at her empty hands, mourning the woman she'd become.

CHAPTER SEVENTEEN

Jude made a beeline for her bedroom on feet that barely grazed the floor. She didn't know how to feel about her pizza date with Diana, except *everything*. Elated, touched, frustrated, sad, furious, confused, hopeful, horny, and exhausted topped the list of easily identifiable emotions, but more would almost certainly surface once she'd freed herself from the rampant arousal currently holding her rational mind hostage. Shedding her jeans and panties as she crossed the threshold, Jude flopped onto her bed and let out a tortured groan.

"Damn it, Di." She thrust her hand between her legs, then rolled onto her stomach to muffle a moan she couldn't stifle. "You...are...*killing* me."

Scrubbing at her clit, Jude buried her face in the sheets and unself-consciously humped her busy fingers. There were two more workshops, possibly three, before their arrangement reached its natural conclusion. For the first time, Jude longed for the wild ride they were on to stop, or maybe just slow down, before she lost herself completely. Wonderful as it had felt to be treated as a genuine confidante, Jude was no closer to understanding Diana's true intentions, nor what she expected from the friendship she'd grudgingly permitted them to have. It sure sounded like extra friendly benefits were suddenly on the table, contingent on Jude's steadfast adherence to the ever-shifting lines she'd so far refused to cross—assuming Diana didn't change her mind upon sobering up.

Wasn't this a major step in the right direction? Shouldn't she be geeked?

Though Jude yearned to luxuriate in the joy of having swayed Diana's opinion on extracurricular activities, she hadn't the faintest clue how much longer she could keep up the delicate dance of fucking

Diana, or even being her friend, without confessing the staggering depth of her love. She was already beyond weary from the endless charade of downplaying her interest, and nights like this did nothing to ease her mental burden.

Why did Diana keep tiptoeing over her own stupid boundaries? Why repeatedly test Jude's integrity and willpower with the prospect of forbidden sex? Did the woman get off on toying with her, or was she legitimately *that* conflicted about her own desires?

Jude slowed her hand, painting slow, sensual circles around her stiffening clit to halt her rumination before the frustration it sparked could torpedo her climax. Did it really matter why Diana tortured her? She wasn't going to renounce her substitute-assistant role, much less cut off contact altogether. The pain of being near Diana couldn't possibly be worse than the agony of separation. Without any avenue of escape, Jude was stuck. All she could do was to embrace the sweetness of this suffering.

Thrusting into her hand, Jude imagined Diana standing behind her, a slightly-too-large dildo strapped to her hips. Jude arched provocatively, displaying her arousal to the imaginary spectator she'd placed at the foot of the bed. "Diana," she breathed. "Stick your cock inside me. *Fuck* me with it."

Unsurprisingly, fantasy Diana turned out to be every inch the tease her real-life counterpart was proving to be. *Not until you earn it. You can start by showing me that tight little asshole you promised to let me fuck next weekend.*

Jude whimpered, heart thumping as though Diana had issued the crude command herself. "Yes, ma'am," she whispered, reaching back to spread her left butt cheek open and expose her anus to Diana's heated stare. "Like this?"

Exactly like that. Now rub that clit for me, you clever girl. Move those hips like you're getting fucked.

Jude writhed against the mattress, executing fantasy Diana's instructions with an enthusiasm usually reserved for her partnered encounters. Though she'd stopped well short of imbibing to the point of tipsiness, she had no trouble channeling the spirit of the raunchiest porn actress alive to perform for her imaginary girlfriend. Working her clit vigorously, Jude yanked her left buttock even farther to the side, showing off for the pretend love of her life. "Please…" she murmured. "Stick it in my ass, anything you—"

A sing-song chime from somewhere near the bedroom door ripped Jude out of her fantasy and, in a stroke of irony she only appreciated after her heart rate slowed, sent her scrambling under the comforter to hide her nudity from prying eyes. When the chime resounded a few seconds later, she heaved a sigh of relief. She'd been texted, not busted.

"Thanks, universe." Jude kicked the comforter away from her lower body and reluctantly sat up. Though she had no reason to suspect Diana was the one behind those notifications, she decided to check her phone before resuming her one-woman show. Rolling out of bed, she knelt to search through the clothing piled in the doorway while telling herself—over and over—that it was *just* like Katrina to check in at such an inopportune moment.

But the messages weren't from Katrina. Incredibly, Diana's name sat atop her list of unread texts. Fingers trembling, Jude managed to open the new thread after a few, fumbling seconds of misplaced thumb presses. It took some time for Diana's words to stop swimming in front of her eyes, row after row of them, every one of them blurred and twisted and incomprehensible to her sex-addled brain. Eventually, though, comprehension returned and Jude began to read.

Are you as sick of my apologies as I am of screwing up? I should've let you go when you tried to leave the first time. You obviously knew I was about to make an ass of myself. Next time, please remind me that I may be older, but you're most definitely wiser.

Jude chuckled, sinking down onto the bed to answer.

You must've forgotten that time I invited you to rub one out with me after our most recent shared meal. I think it's fair to say that we're both more horny than wise sometimes.

True. An intermittently flickering ellipsis hinted at the multiple revisions Diana's response underwent before finally arriving at her phone. *Even so, you were the mature one between us tonight. Thank you so much for respecting my boundaries…even though I can't seem to.*

Jude spent at least three minutes composing her own meticulously worded reply. *You're my friend, Diana. I'll always treat you with respect, and I'll never, ever do anything I think might hurt you. After what you told me about Janine...I really do want you to be happy. Even if that means you're alone.*

It took almost six minutes for Diana to author a shockingly intimate confession.

It's not like I'm in love with being alone, *alone. Which is why I came on so strong tonight, I guess (the wine also played a role, naturally, as did the fact that you're beautiful and an excellent lover). And also...Ava and I had a somewhat major argument a few days ago. I'm sure we'll mend fences soon, but...I don't think we're sleeping together anymore, indefinitely.*

Multiple pieces clicked into place, shedding new light on Diana's mood and behavior. Debating, Jude ultimately decided she didn't feel right playing dumb. She typed.

Because she and Katrina are sorta kinda together now?

When did you find out? Diana continued texting as Jude crafted a hasty response. *Did Katrina tell you she gave Ava a hand job?!? I asked you to recommend a caregiver/physical therapist, not hook my BFFWB up with an ethically questionable orgasm dispenser.*

Jude frowned, irritated by the suggestion that Katrina was anything less than professional. Choosing her words with care, she shot back a pointed defense of her own best friend.

Ava had been hitting on Kat since their first meeting. She's never slept with a client before...and only one other woman, in her whole life. I'll cut you some slack because I know you're sad and most likely still drunk, but Ava's a big girl, and Katrina doesn't get sexual with anyone *unless she has real feelings for them. I am sorry you're lonely. Once you've sobered up, we can revisit the question of whether you sincerely want my help with that.*

She sent the wall of text, waited a beat, then followed up with a hasty disclaimer.

Unless you've already decided it's a terrible idea. If so, I wholeheartedly agree.

After another brief pause, she fired off one last note—to cover every base.

If not, I also wholeheartedly agree.

A few minutes passed before Jude's willpower evaporated and her hand drifted back between her legs. She massaged her vulva tenderly, using her palm to apply indirect pressure just north of her swollen clit. It would take her only another minute or two to climax, tops, but she hesitated to resume without reading what Diana had to say. Why, she didn't know. Rejection seemed the most likely outcome, second only to an ambiguously lukewarm one-liner. In the unlikely event of positive response, however, Jude's orgasm would all but take care of itself.

Approximately a million years passed before Diana finally answered.

I'm not convinced it's a terrible idea. Maybe a dangerous one. You're right. Best to be sober before making any decisions. But I want you to know...I do trust you, Jude. Far more than I would've ever believed was possible at this point in my life.

Touched by the sentiment—and grateful for the inebriated state enabling its unfiltered delivery—Jude took a break from idly stroking her labia to punch out a zippy comeback.

Because I'm a very good girl?

Within seconds, Diana sent a tears-of-joy emoji that had Jude grinning so hard her cheeks ached. The text that followed pulled a whimper from Jude's suddenly dry throat.

A very, very good girl. Sweet, too.

Jude inhaled, hyper-aware of how fast they'd veered into decidedly naughty territory. As she paused to weigh the consequences of continuing this jaunt down sexting avenue, Diana barreled forward at full speed.

Is your pussy wet?

Before Jude could begin to think of a response, Diana supplied an easy out.

You don't have to answer that.

After briefly wrestling with the pros and cons, Jude realized she didn't care if this was another test. If Diana was inviting her to sext, she would enthusiastically oblige.

Fairly certain I don't need to. How about asking something you don't already know?

Diana didn't hesitate. *Are you in bed?*

I am.

Touching your clit?

Jude grinned, wiggling in excitement. *I was...before someone interrupted me.*

Shame on them. The sporadic blinking of Diana's ellipsis kept Jude on the edge of her seat. *Well, don't let me stop you.*

Chewing her lip, Jude typed a question of her own. *First tell me if you're in bed, too.*

I am.

Jude's heart rate accelerated, the fine hairs on the base of her neck rising in awareness of Diana's close proximity.

In that case, this shouldn't take more than another minute or two. Thanks for the inspiration.

You're quite welcome. Who was providing inspiration before my very rude interruption?

Chest tight, Jude couldn't come up with any more reasons not to state the obvious.

Pretty sure you know the answer to that one, too.

This time she waited longer for Diana's response.

Well...I'm flattered.

The telltale ellipsis gave away a massive bout of indecision, as Diana appeared to compose, erase, compose, erase for minutes on end. Jude fingered her clit gingerly, eager to come, but even more eager to know what Diana found so challenging to articulate. When her concise, eight-word missive finally appeared, Jude let out a whimper.

I've thought about you, too. More than once.

Unable to stop herself, Jude typed, *Will you think about me tonight?*

I'm thinking about you as we type. Jude snorted at Diana's grinning, sweating emoji. *Have fun, sweetheart. Text me once you come...I'll feel better knowing you were able to take care of that ache between your pretty thighs.*

Every part of Jude cried out for her to reconsider Diana's offer of a work-related hookup, yet she managed to hold fast to the stance she'd taken only an hour ago. Giving up her fantasy of asking Diana if she'd fancy a fuck after all, Jude compromised by fueling her arousal via a blatantly saucy sign-off.

You'll know when I come. Promise.

Just under three minutes later, Jude raised her head from the pillow to release a full-throated moan, climaxing loudly enough to be heard through the wall. She pictured Diana straining to listen with her hand buried deep in her own pussy and promptly came again. Near the tail end of her second noisy finish, Jude fell silent—going so far as to hold her breath—at the glorious sound of Diana quietly erupting in pleasure one room away. Jude kept rubbing her clit throughout the modest vocal display, inducing a third orgasm, hardly trying. Upping her volume to make sure Diana heard, Jude rode the ecstatic waves until she collapsed on the mattress, sated at last.

Her phone beeped soon after Jude's hips stilled. She picked it up, checking the screen with hope in her heart. Thankfully, Diana didn't disappoint.

Thanks, my friend. I needed that.

My pleasure. Jude snickered. *Literally.*

Cute.

Surprised to see Diana still typing, Jude rested the phone on her chest while she waited for whatever came next. She smiled when the message arrived.

Get some sleep, darling. I want you well-rested for Saturday…and full of sexual energy.

Always. Jude rolled her eyes at the understatement. *Sweet dreams, Di. I'm glad we're friends.*

She cringed upon rereading her final sentence after she'd clicked send. "'I'm glad we're friends'? That's perfect. Fucking smooth."

Diana's fast reply soothed Jude's frazzled nerves.

Me too. Now go to bed, young lady. I don't want to hear another peep out of you tonight.

Unable to resist, Jude crawled up to place her mouth against the wall above her headboard. "Peep!"

Faint laughter, then one final text—*Brat,* accompanied by a rolling-on-the-floor emoji—confirmed that her humor was well-received. After tapping out her own parting message—*You know you love it*—Jude tossed her phone onto the nightstand and settled in for a well-deserved sleep.

CHAPTER EIGHTEEN

Blearily forcing her eyes open just shy of nine o'clock the next morning, Diana's first instinct was to pick up her phone. She ignored the disappointed clench of her belly when she discovered no new notifications, brought up Ava's cell number, and initiated a call before she could talk herself out of the apology she needed to give. Her teeth worried her lower lip nervously through two full rings, and she almost hung up midway through the third. It was possible Katrina had her occupied. That would explain the delay—that, or Diana was being ignored.

On the cusp of ending the call, Diana startled when Ava answered with a frantic, breathless, "Diana? Still there?"

Struck by her urgency, Diana put the phone back to her ear. "I'm here. Is everything okay? Am I interrupting, or…?"

"Everything is fine, and no, not interrupting. I accidentally left my phone on the bed before setting off on a long, arduous journey to take care of business in a real toilet. I'd only just embarked on the return trip when I heard your ringtone from across the room." Ava chuckled, panting from the exertion. "I've gotta say, I had no idea I was still capable of moving that fast."

Wincing, Diana scolded her. "Don't you dare risk life and limb to answer the phone, *especially* when you know it's me. I'll understand if you need to call back when it's more convenient."

"I know, I know. But I've…been hoping to hear from you." Ava hesitated. "And I didn't want you to think I was ignoring you on purpose because Katrina was here, or whatever."

Rather than deny that the thought had crossed her mind, Diana asked, "Is she there? Because we can always talk another time."

"Katrina's with another client this morning." Ava released an almost inaudible sigh. "She said she'll check in on me later tonight, but probably not until after dinner."

Diana experienced a sympathetic twinge at the powerful longing in Ava's voice. Relieved by the emergence of a more evolved, empathetic perspective, she relaxed into her pillow and reassumed the role of best friend. "Bummer. Sounds like you miss her."

"Terribly." After a beat, Ava added, "But not as much as I've been missing you."

Diana exhaled. "I was selfish the other night...a total bitch. You were right, of course. We aren't a couple, which means you're free to fall in love with anyone you want. I have no claim on your heart, even if I enjoy sharing your body sometimes." Horrified by the fit she'd pitched in reaction to Ava's big announcement, she cringed and retreated farther beneath the comforter. "You deserve a woman who loves and cares for you, free from any caveats. A woman who can give herself to you completely...who fits into your life better than I ever have or will."

"You fit into my life," Ava insisted. "Just...as my closest friend. She who knows me best."

Not for long, if this works out with Katrina. Diana silenced her cynical inner commentary, determined to focus on Ava's feelings first. "I love you, Ava, and I want you to be happy. I know I can't give you that. Not *true* happiness." Unsure how best to conclude her apology, Diana eventually settled on, "I was wrong to expect you to turn your back on the possibility of love just because I have. Please, forgive me." Ava said one word, but Diana slipped in another apology first—the one she considered most important of all. "Also, I never should've called you old. You're not, but I know you've felt insecure about your age since the accident, so it was extra shitty on my part to harangue you about the generation gap. In retrospect, that was unforgivably cruel."

"Even so, you're forgiven." Indeed, Ava's voice didn't carry any malice or resentment. "I understood why you reacted so harshly. It's not like I thought you'd be *happy* about me bedding Jude's cousin."

"Still, a real friend would've considered your feelings over her own." Diana paused, wishing she could take back the outburst that had led her down the dangerous path of befriending a younger woman she fervently desired. "My insecurities don't take precedence over your right to get it on with your naughty nursemaid."

"*Caregiver.*" Ava corrected her in a wry voice. "Katrina is a home *caregiver*. Nursemaids look after children."

"Exactly." Diana delivered the jibe lightly, optimistic it would be received as intended. "Don't forget, I've helped care for you on quite a few occasions since that nasty stomach flu hit you the morning after we slept together the second time. I woke up naked in your bed to the sound of retching, then spent the next week catering to your every whim while you plied me with promises of all the unbelievable sex we'd have once your diarrhea was under control."

Ava made a sound Diana couldn't easily categorize, an utterance halfway between hilarity and revulsion. "To this day, my most humiliating experience in front of a girl I wanted to impress."

"I was certainly impressed by your ability to even think about fucking me in that state."

"It's not that *I* was thinking about it." Ava chuckled. "More like worried that *you* were. That you'd get bored after too many days of me being physically repulsive and not putting out."

Guilt fell even heavier onto Diana's shoulders. "Our relationship has never been, and will never be, solely about sex. And you, my love, are incapable of physically repulsing me. Inexplicably, even when you're spewing out both ends."

Ava giggled, then moaned piteously. "Ow, stop. My back is killing me."

Diana frowned. "Maybe you should call Katrina. Or…I could come over. Roll you up a fatty and nursemaid you back to health."

"I'd love a visit, if you're up for it. Katrina actually rolled up a whole tray of fatties last night, so I won't even put you to work."

"Did she now?" That answered one question about their basic compatibility. "I'm not sure that's in her job description."

Ava laughed. "It isn't, but she's incredibly supportive of my desire to avoid opiates. Even offered to bake me medicated brownies if I gave her a recipe."

Diana had to grin. "Maybe you *have* found yourself a keeper."

"Maybe. I hope so." Ava trailed off, clearly hesitant to say more.

Aware that her former attitude was the roadblock, Diana said, "You can talk to me. No more judgment or high horses, I promise. Given that Jude and I ended last night with light sexting and mutual masturbation— in our own, separate bedrooms, mind you, but loud enough to overhear— it would be hypocritical to criticize you for being involved with a younger woman when I am, too. And now that I can't even pretend it's strictly professional."

"Wow." Ava sounded genuinely stunned. "That girl really *is* worming her way into your heart, isn't she?"

"Not my heart." Diana rolled her eyes at the lack of conviction in her weak protest. "Just…my panties. Apparently." She sighed. "Despite my best efforts."

"So…how was it? The mutual diddling?"

"Nice." Afraid to reveal the depth of her unwilling infatuation, Diana demurred. "It's always nice to share an orgasm with someone. Even in spirit."

"Amen to that." A muted hiss alerted Diana to Ava's otherwise stoic attempt to find a comfortable position for her spine. "I hope to talk Katrina into letting me finally return the favor. Tonight."

It was Diana's turn to be surprised. "You haven't touched her yet?"

"She says I need to take it easy. I think she's afraid I'll injure myself if she lets me do something my body's not ready for." After a lengthy pause, Ava added, tentatively, "But I *am* ready. Even if all I can do is hold a vibrator against her clit, I'm dying to give her even a fraction of the pleasure she's brought to my life."

Ava's wistful, affectionate tone made clear that her desire for Katrina went far beyond the purely sexual. Battling another jealous twinge, Diana marveled at how thoroughly Jude's cousin had won her over. "I don't think I've ever heard you this excited about a woman before."

"I don't think I've ever *been* this excited before." Ava exhaled in a rush. "It's scary as hell, to tell you the truth."

Heartened by the reminder that love was frightening for everyone, and not just her, Diana smirked. "Yup."

"But worth it," Ava hastened to add. "More than worth it."

We'll see if you still feel that way five years from now, whispered Diana's inner cynic. Aloud, she said, "Enjoy the ride. I do vaguely recollect how much fun it was to fall in love…before Janine permanently disabused me of the notion."

Ava sighed. "Janine is gone, honey. Remarried, moved to Santa Barbara, and out of your life for good. She can't hurt you anymore." Gently, she pointed out, "And Jude…she's not another Janine. Based on all Kat's told me, they're nothing alike. Jude sounds like a sweet girl…a smart, passionate young lady with a lot of talent and an impressive head on her shoulders. At the risk of upsetting our truce, I have to tell you that in my opinion, she seems like an ideal lover for you. One who could potentially restore your faith in women, given half a chance."

Already weary from the discussion, Diana tipped back her head to gaze at the wall separating her bedroom from Jude's. "Maybe that's what I'm afraid of. I don't want her to."

"Which makes zero sense." Ava huffed. "You just admitted how much fun falling in love used to be. What if you could feel that way again? Don't you *want* to? Please, Di…you can't let Janine ruin the rest of your life."

Diana prickled, on the defensive once more about everyone's favorite refrain. "She hasn't 'ruined' my life. Romantic love isn't everything, you know. It's not even the most important thing."

"Romantic love, no, but basic human connection…" Ava shut up, then sighed. "I'd argue that not being totally alone in the world is pretty damn important for most people on this planet. Including you." She cut off Diana's halfhearted protest with a succinct counterargument. "If you seriously didn't give a shit, you never would've gotten that upset about me and Katrina. But you did…you *do.*"

Diana opened her mouth to rebut, then snapped it shut. While more than simple jealousy had fueled her reaction, she couldn't deny Ava's basic argument. Lacking a comeback, she accepted defeat. "Touché."

"It's obvious you don't truly crave the solitude you always claim to want. Not sexual solitude, at least." When Diana declined to disagree, Ava continued building her case. "Tell me, have you even *attempted* celibacy for longer than a two- or three-month stretch?"

Diana couldn't lie. "I've never had to."

"Of course not. I've always been your safety net. Without the comfort of my casual, non-threatening sexual friendship, it wouldn't be nearly as easy to ignore the rest of womankind. We both know I'm the reason you've never felt moved to start dating again."

"You're right," Diana admitted. "I enjoyed what we had and didn't see a reason for anything to change. We work well together, our sex is on point, and I can fall asleep next to you without being afraid you'll wake me up an hour later to smack me across the face, call me an ugly, worthless piece of shit, and accuse me of screwing everyone I know."

Ava released a slow, shaky breath, hinting at the tearful rage Diana suspected she'd evoked with the pointed confession. "I'm so sorry Janine did that to you, sweetheart, and that I didn't see it sooner. It kills me to know you suffered for years without me ever realizing she was enough of a monster to actually *hit* you. Let alone berate you on a daily basis."

"Remember what I told you the last half-dozen times you apologized for failing to be my white knight? I put an incredible amount of effort into hiding everything wrong between me and Janine." Diana curled up on her side, fighting off the residual shame she feared she'd never shed. "I was far too embarrassed to let you believe my life with Janine was anything less than perfect. Admitting out loud that I'd managed to fuck up this perfect relationship I'd spent the past year convincing you was *it* for me... that the woman I loved was making me hate myself..." She choked down a sob. "What would you have thought?"

"That you needed help." Ava's compassion blanketed Diana beneath the warmth of unshakable friendship, bringing the uncontrolled chattering of her jaw to a temporary standstill. "And trusted me to provide it."

"I do trust you." Diana swallowed, once again lamenting the loss of their special bond. "Always have."

"I know." Ava waited, then asked, "What about Jude?"

Irritated by Ava's insistence on discussing her future prospects before she'd had time to mourn the demise of what they'd shared, Diana snapped, "What about her?"

"Don't take that tone with me." Ava admonished her, channeling the well-honed harsh-mistress persona that always left Diana slick and ready to be fucked after only a few sharp words. "Unless you want to send us right back where we started."

"I don't." Sighing, Diana opened her eyes to stare listlessly at the wall. "I shouldn't have barked at you. I know you're only trying to help... in your own misguided way."

"You're right, I am." A lengthy silence stretched out between them. Right as Diana started to relax, Ava interjected, "One last thought and I'm done."

Diana snorted. "You swear?"

"Yes." Ava paused for emphasis. "Now you swear something to me."

A lump formed in Diana's throat as she awaited whatever impossible request Ava was bound to make. "What?"

"I want you to consider—by which I mean contemplate in a direct, serious fashion—that if you were comfortable enough to both sext with Jude *and* play exhibitionist-meet-voyeur in your adjoining bedrooms on a Thursday night...you must trust her, too. At least somewhat."

"More than most, yes," Diana acknowledged. "But not nearly enough for whatever you think I ought to do next."

"Taking her out to a fancy restaurant?" With one breezy chuckle, Ava made Diana's most deep-seated fears seem silly, even small. "You've already fucked this girl, what, four or five times? Dinner and a movie is the easy part. I bet you'd even enjoy it. Your feelings for Jude are more than sexual, right? Going on a real date would help you decide how much more."

Diana bristled. "I never said my feelings for Jude were romantic."

"You didn't have to." She could envision exactly how smug Ava must've looked. "I'm your best friend. It's obvious."

"Fuck you, it's not."

"Fuck *you*. Jude has you hooked, and I'd have to be blind not to notice." Ava's smugness intensified. "Almost as blind as you."

"I'm not blind." And she wasn't. Diana recognized the undeniable sexual chemistry she and Jude shared. She knew her attraction wasn't just physical, that what she most desired from Jude was far more frightening than the potential folly of turning her next-door neighbor into a fuck buddy. "Just...pragmatic."

"You're scared, Di, and I get that. I really do."

"No, you *really* don't." Diana interrupted Ava's attempt at empathy with a snarl. Dating a loser or two didn't count. Ava had never suffered a betrayal of trust on the scale of Janine's rapid transformation into a relentlessly cruel bully. She had no idea how it felt to find yourself imprisoned within a relationship, too afraid to leave the captor who spends her days convincing you that her bad behavior is the result of your own irredeemable character flaws, and her nights sleeping beside you in bed. "And I'm glad—*thrilled*, even—that you're able to kiss Katrina without having to wonder if she'll turn mean one day, or stress about how to covertly boost her mood if she seems grumpy. I never want you to 'get' this...only to respect that you don't."

"That's fair. I *don't* know what it's like to be with an asshole of Janine's caliber, but that's because all the women I've dated were halfway-decent human beings—albeit not without their individual quirks." Ava spoke in a quiet, nonconfrontational murmur. "Most women are. You were extraordinarily unlucky to have met Janine. That doesn't mean you'll be unlucky a second time."

Diana said nothing. She wasn't sure what more to say, except, "Do you want me to come over now, or later? I'll bring food. Whatever you want, just ask."

In true best-friend fashion, Ava accepted the new topic without argument. "Doughnuts for now, tomato focaccia for later?"

"Sounds heavenly." Diana squeezed the back of her neck. "Ava?"

"Yes, my darling?"

"I appreciate you not giving up on me…even though I practically beg you to sometimes."

"Never." Ava's voice cracked, leading her to clear her throat. "Diana, I will *never* give up on you. Please don't give up on yourself, either. Deal? You're so close, sweetheart, *so close* to reclaiming what Janine stole from you. You just need to want it—want it, and be brave."

CHAPTER NINETEEN

Balanced on her hands and knees, Jude gazed into the watchful eyes of twelve strap-on-donning women and their anxious partners while everyone waited for Diana to hurry up and penetrate her already. She'd been teasing for well over five minutes by this point—minutes that felt like hours—drawing the tip of her attached dildo up and down Jude's labia, and on occasion around her swollen clit, to produce an obscene flood of juices that squelched wetly at her every move. Increasingly self-conscious about the vulgar sound of her arousal, Jude bit the inside of her cheek to stop herself from begging. She yearned for an end to the anticipation, yet didn't dare ask for mercy. She would wait however long Diana required. Anything to please her.

Jude gasped when strong hands gripped her hips and tugged her backward, then obediently lowered her chest to the blanket and raised her pussy into the air. Pressed even more firmly against the roving dildo, she shivered when Diana finally broke her silence to foreshadow the end of her interminable torture.

"Once she's wet enough..." Diana released her hip to graze over the soaked folds exposed by Jude's new position. Two fingers swirled through the hot juices gathered at her entrance for a few, tantalizing seconds before pulling away. "And lucky for me, my lovely assistant most assuredly is..." The head of the dildo replaced Diana's fingers to poke insistently against Jude's slick opening, poised to slide in with only the barest application of pressure. Jude held her breath, eager for what was coming.

"Hold the dildo in your dominant hand as you guide it into her vagina. Go slow and easy at first, making sure to check in regularly." Already half embedded inside her receptive cunt, Diana questioned Jude in a low drawl. "What do you think, sweetheart? Doesn't it feel *good* to have your tight pussy wrapped around something this thick and hard?"

Jude raised her face from the blanket to answer. "*Yes*…and fuck, you're *big*." In reality, Diana wasn't terrifically endowed—she was using Jude's favorite dildo, a decently sized yet hardly intimidating seven-and-a-half incher—but for Jude, the act of marveling at her lover's cock size was always half the thrill. "I love how you stretch me open."

"Can you take all of this?" Diana drew back, then drove forward slowly, advancing no more than a millimeter or two. "Ask nicely and I'll give it to you…but only if you say 'please.'"

"Please, Di." Pushing up onto her hands, Jude met Diana's gaze over her shoulder. "Just fuck me already." When Diana lifted an eyebrow, she added, "*Please.*"

Eyes sparkling, Diana dragged Jude backward onto the dildo, only stopping once her butt sat flush against Diana's groin and the entire toy was socketed inside her fluttering vagina. Jude moaned, angling her face toward the class so they could witness the pleasure Diana was giving her. She tightened her grip on the blanket as strong hands seized her around the waist and shoved her forward—away from Diana's warm body and nearly off the dildo altogether—then cried out in ecstasy at the swift reintroduction of every inch she'd asked Diana to wield.

A hand swept beneath her chest, cupping her breast ahead of another deliberately forceful thrust. "I can feel how tightly you're squeezing me." Diana grabbed her right butt cheek and spread her open, exposing her anus to the cool air and her heated gaze. The hand on her breast vanished, a loss Jude barely had time to register before it reappeared in the form of one lone fingertip—generously coated in lube—that delved into the valley of her buttocks to confidently trace the outline of her smaller, untouched hole. "You like feeling full. Don't you?"

"Yes." Jude hung her head to concentrate on not finishing too quickly. She was already unbelievably close, especially for not yet having touched her own clit. That was her usual road to orgasm while getting drilled from behind, an indulgence made necessary by how rarely she got off on penetration alone. But with Diana it was different, and why wouldn't it be? Sex with Diana was always different, shattering old standards to establish new ideals Jude feared no other woman could ever uphold. "I'm not gonna last much longer."

Diana disappeared entirely, leaving Jude to ache for her return. When the gentle pressure on her butthole intensified by a degree, Jude's desperate body rewarded the request by opening up to draw Diana's fingertip inside. "Is this okay?" Diana stopped moving. "I'd like to slide my finger all the way inside your tiny little asshole, sweetheart, and fill you up completely...but only if you want that, too. Only if it'll help you come." She repositioned the dildo at Jude's sopping vagina, then paused, awaiting consent.

In light of what Diana planned to do to her the following weekend, Jude wasn't about to refuse the chance to practice. "Please. I want you to."

"Want me to what?" Diana inched forward with her hips, parting Jude's labia with the bulbous head of the dildo. The fingertip lodged inside her anus remained locked in place, stubbornly denying the pleasure Jude knew would come if only she gave the right answer. "Say it."

"Fill both of my holes." Jude burned like wildfire, in awe of how effortlessly Diana commanded her body, and how wholly gratifying it felt to let her. "*Take me.*"

"Yes, ma'am."

Jude pitched forward slightly as Diana eased into her narrow rectum, then exhaled, forcing herself to relax. She needed to prove she was game for anything, that she could handle the physical demands of what could be the last workshop she'd ever attend. Without knowing whether Diana still intended to cancel the class on lovemaking and intimacy, Jude had to assume that Anal Sex 101 was to be their final professional interaction, which meant it might also be her last chance to persuade Diana that their chemistry was too explosive to relegate to a classroom and too precious to squander due to fear.

Diana smoothed her palm over Jude's shoulder blades, instantly soothing her tense muscles. "Talk to me, sweetheart. Tell me what you need."

Pulsing around Diana's finger, Jude arched her spine as an enticement. "I need you inside my pussy again...I need to feel you *everywhere.*"

This time there was no taunting, only the roaring satisfaction of Diana re-entering her with a ravenous growl. Jude's head shot up and she gasped, thunderstruck by the unreal lack of emptiness—and completion— brought about by the claiming act. On the verge of orgasm for the second time that evening, Jude fought to hold off the inevitable but couldn't stop her thighs from quaking at the skillful rhythm of Diana's shallow, controlled thrusts.

"Like this?" Diana sank deeper on every stroke, hitting spots Jude never knew existed. "You're so hot, baby, so hot and tight and wet...and so sweet for letting me take you like this. I've fantasized about having you doggy style for way too long and sliding my finger into your sexy little ass…you have no idea."

Jude dropped her head, curtaining her face with her hair so no one would see how bittersweetly Diana's pillow talk had landed. She knew the dialogue was only that—dialogue, crafted for a performance, signifying nothing. Diana's words were an example for their coupled students to aspire to, but that was all. They didn't mean anything in the real world. They weren't even personal.

But damn if they didn't make her heart swell anyway.

The hand on her butt traveled around her hip, leaving a trail of gooseflesh in its wake. Bending low over Jude, low enough that her magnificently bare tits danced across Jude's sweat-dampened shoulder blades, Diana seized her erect clit between two fingers and tugged. "It's okay, darling. Lie on your belly. Let me do all the work."

Jude's arms accepted the offer first, collapsing beneath her until she rested on her forearms, head buried in the space between. Her knees surrendered next, but Jude didn't fall because Diana didn't let her. Instead, she guided Jude's unsteady lower body to rest on the thin mattress, handling her as delicately as old dynamite. The hand on her clit didn't falter throughout this transition, jacking its distended length in sync with both Diana's pounding hips and her wiggling finger. The latter of Diana's twin instruments of pleasure initiated Jude into a staggering new world of bodily delights, one she'd scarcely imagined. No one had ever performed that particular act with this much care, with this attention to what satisfied *her*. Never had she met a woman talented enough to tend to her so thoroughly, who made her feel like she might have three orgasms at once.

"That's right, baby." Diana kissed Jude's temple, whispering into her ear. "Will you come with me inside you? I want you to squeeze this dildo so hard I feel it in *my* clit. Can you do that for me?" She hastened the hand between Jude's thighs, and Jude moaned, grinding away helplessly. Diana nuzzled a sensitive patch of skin behind her earlobe, then kissed Jude's flushed cheek. "You *want* to come, don't you, sweetheart? You want to come all over my big, fat toy while I've got it buried deep inside you." Her hips canted sharply, sending the dildo into *precisely* the right spot. "Fucking you like no one else ever has. Isn't that right?"

"Yes," Jude hissed from between gritted teeth. Her whole body shook, thrown into orgasm by Diana's intimate proximity and the dirty, beautiful words being murmured into her ear. "I'm coming for you!" Jude cried, flooded with irrational panic over not having asked permission first. "Diana, fuck—"

"Don't stop," Diana said, moving more slowly as Jude contracted around the dildo. "Take everything you can from me." She drew back, kissed Jude's shoulder blade, then plunged all the way inside her again. "Let me feel what this does for you. Your little noises make me so wet, Jude. So wet for you, and so *hot*."

Encouraged, Jude whimpered on every contraction of her inner muscles around the finger and toy. When Diana angled to hit her favorite spot, seemingly from memory, Jude raised her head, crying out as she fell into a second, even stronger climax before the first had subsided. Her eyes sprang open and she groaned, undone by the vision of raw, distinctly feminine carnality playing out before her. Women of various colors, shapes, sizes, and abilities were represented, each one working hard to satisfy their partners within their own personal seduction scenes. The reminder that she and Diana weren't alone—that they were in fact working—sobered Jude in a productive way, enabling her to ride out the remaining waves without dissolving into the tears that had gathered.

Once she could take no more, Jude clutched Diana's forearm. "Enough. I can't...stop. I'm done."

Diana had already frozen in place. "What should I remove first?"

"Your finger," Jude muttered, strangely bashful given what they'd just done—for a crowd of spectators, no less. "Slowly."

"Of course." Diana nibbled on her earlobe, distracting Jude while she delicately extracted her finger at the pace set by Jude's reflexively constricting sphincter. "Was it good for you?"

Jude laughed at the absurdity of the question. She had to. "Don't be stupid."

Fully extracted, Diana chuckled along with her. "May I take that as a 'yes'?"

"Well, you *did* just fuck me better than anyone else ever has." Coming up on her elbows, Jude composed her face, then glanced backward to reward Diana with a satisfied grin. "It was *beyond* good, Diana. Obviously."

Even smirking, Diana exuded an aura of vulnerability Jude didn't know how to interpret. Maybe Diana wasn't as stoic as she liked to pretend? Or maybe that was Jude's stubborn optimism talking, trying to fool her into believing the impossible could one day come to pass if only she said and did the right things. Eyebrow raised, Diana grasped Jude's hips possessively. "This one, too?" She eased the dildo out a couple of inches, waited a beat, and—when Jude didn't object—buried herself to the hilt once more. "Or not yet?"

Tempted as she was to go for a round two, Jude didn't want to risk missing the opportunity she'd been promised. "Depends. Do you still intend to let me have a turn? Because if yes, that's what I *really* want… to fuck you."

Diana's nostrils flared. After the scantest hesitation, she withdrew from Jude's vagina and let go of her hips. Jude barely had time to miss her before Diana was turning her over, then urging her to sit so they were face-to-face. Without speaking, Diana rose to lower the tight, boy-short-style harness around her ankles. Stepping out of the get-up, Diana kicked the toy aside, then bent—oh so provocatively—to rummage through her oversized purse for a much-larger object than Jude had anticipated. When Diana introduced her preferred toy to the class, Jude's pussy clenched and she whimpered, awed to have climaxed without being touched.

"If you don't like wearing a harness, or simply desire an even more direct connection to your partner, consider investing in a strapless dildo like this." Diana outlined the features of her toy with the finesse of an experienced salesperson. "The bulb-shaped end goes into the wearer, allowing her to penetrate the receiver with the angled shaft." She lowered the dildo and checked Jude's eyes. "Would you be comfortable wearing this for me? If not, I brought my other favorite dick as a fallback option."

Jude shook her head, intoxicated by the idea of fucking Diana skin-to-skin without any barriers to separate them. "Sure. I've actually…worn one before." She licked her lips, hoping like hell her body would respond when called upon to perform. She'd done all right with a strapless dildo in the past, both times she'd tried, but Diana was no ordinary lover. She knew it was naive or even crazy to think, but Jude couldn't vanquish her belief that any given sexual encounter they had might somehow sway Diana's opinion on dating for real. If Jude proved to be the best lay of her life, why *wouldn't* Diana want to lock her down for the long run? Womaning up, Jude got onto her knees and gestured for Diana to join her on the blanket. "Help me put it in?"

"I'd be delighted." Diana knelt in front of her. "Go ahead and spread those pretty legs for me one more time."

Jude set her knees apart, hyperaware of the unbelievable slickness coating the insides of her thighs. Diana positioned the bulbous end of the toy at Jude's pleasantly sore entrance and waited. Jude braced herself until she feared she might go mad, then realized that Diana wanted her consent—or maybe to hear her beg. Covering her bases, Jude said, "Go ahead. The faster you get that thing inside me, the sooner I'll get inside *you*. And I need to be inside you…please."

Diana's eyelids drifted shut ever so briefly, but even that admission of desire was enough to send Jude's heart into joyful rapture. Regardless of what Diana might say or do, not all of what Jude felt was unreciprocated. Holding her gaze, Diana carefully worked the toy into her vagina as Jude bore down against the invasion. Breathing out once the bulb was fully seated, Jude ignored the faint aftershocks triggered by its presence to address Diana's needs instead.

Catching her wrist before she could retreat, Jude tugged Diana closer. "Ready?"

"Honey, you have no idea." Diana captured Jude in a sensual kiss and, at the same time, latched onto the shaft end of the embedded dildo to pump its length with her fist. The motion dragged a trio of strategically placed ridges across Jude's clit, threatening to distract her from the mission at hand.

Time to take control or else lose it entirely. Tearing away from Diana's lips, Jude grabbed her by the upper arms and placed her on her back in the center of the blanket. "Spread your legs," she said, climbing between Diana's creamy thighs as they fell open. "I'm going to fuck you until you come. Think you can handle that?"

Diana writhed beneath her. "Yes." She moaned, and undulated to bump her clit against the firm shaft. "I want you so bad. *Fuck me.*"

She didn't wait to be asked twice. Hauling Diana's right knee up to her chest, then aside, Jude revealed her shiny, dark-pink opening and wedged the tip of the strap-on against it. Before going further, Jude lowered her chest to Diana's and reveled in the glory of their stiff nipples coming into contact for the first time. She reached between their lower bodies, steadying the toy in her hand before entering Diana with a smooth, confident thrust. Diana threw her head back and moaned, nearly bringing Jude to a premature finish right then and there. Somehow she held on, teeth gritted in determination as she sought to prove that she could also fuck Diana better than anyone else ever had.

"*Yes,*" Diana gasped, in what was either an Oscar-worthy performance or else sincere, next-level bliss. "Oh, you feel fucking *fantastic.*"

Jude wondered how long it had been since Diana was last taken this way. Not since before Ava's accident, surely, so at least six weeks. No doubt she needed this and was counting on Jude to deliver. Stirred by the thought that she was the only one permitted inside Diana now that Ava was otherwise engaged, Jude wrenched Diana's arms above her head and pinned her to the blanket. "Is it all right to hold you like this?" She kept her grip loose in case the answer was no.

"Quite all right." Diana squirmed, playfully testing her strength. "I hope you're okay with a little resistance." She attempted to free her wrists from the fingers encircling them, but Jude clamped down tighter.

Jude ended the faux rebellion by sliding into Diana, burying the toy until she felt the stiff point of Diana's clit thrumming wetly against her mound. Diana's fingers spasmed on the blanket and she choked out a moan, yet her body strained upward for more. Jude stared into the blue eyes that had dominated her fantasy life for the past year, entranced by the satisfaction that flared within them every time she moved. Without thinking, she dipped her head and pressed her tongue into Diana's open mouth, initiating an impassioned kiss that had them groaning as one. Jude gradually slowed her energetic rhythm, going almost completely still except for the restrained rocking of her lower body as she continued to grind against Diana's clit. She freed Diana's left wrist to caress the side of her face while they made out, consumed by desire that burned hot enough to incinerate every last inhibition she possessed.

When Jude liberated Diana's other wrist to trace her taut jawline tenderly, Diana wrenched her head aside with a breathless gasp. Her eyes slammed shut, and her hands flew up to brace against Jude's chest, a reaction that made Jude freeze mid-stroke as ice-cold terror ripped through her veins. "Diana?" she asked, waiting for the safe word she was sure she'd provoked. "Are you—"

In an impressive show of strength and sexual mastery, Diana reversed their positions by forcibly rolling Jude onto her side, then her back, without breaking their intimate connection. Once on top, she pushed herself into a seated position astride Jude's motionless hips. Looking out at her students—presumably to avoid eye contact with the assistant who'd apparently pushed her too hard—Diana said, "There are lots of fun positions you can achieve with a strap-on. This might be my favorite. When I ride my partner, we're both stimulated." She rolled her hips to demonstrate. "She's teased with friction and given the visual treat of seeing me take what I want." She repeated the indulgent motion, gaining steam on each iteration. "As for me, I'm able to decide whether I'm fucked hard or soft, fast or slow, shallow or deep. I'm able to maintain ultimate control over my own pleasure. For me, this is *the* ideal position if you're new to penetration, or at all intimidated by the size."

Following Diana's lead, Jude shook off the aftermath of their strange moment to reassert her cool with a typically smart-ass remark. "I'm not complaining." She settled her hands on Diana's waist, content to let her set the pace. "There are few things I love more than a gorgeous pair of bouncing tits."

"What luck." Eyelashes fluttering, Diana lowered her eyes to Jude's. She jerked her hips, shamelessly vamping for what Jude assumed was their audience's benefit. "Want to put your hands on them?"

Jude flexed her fingers around Diana's waist, itching to do exactly that. "Yes, please."

"Then do it." She dragged Jude's hands up to her chest, centering the palms over her turgid nipples. "Touch all you want, sweet pea. *However* you want." Diana's lips curved into a smile, and her hips picked up speed. "As for what I'd like from you..."

Jude whimpered at the delicious scrape of Diana's wiry pubic hair against her clit on every enthusiastic surge of her lower body. "*Anything, Di. Just ask.*"

Bending, Diana muffled Jude's noises with a firm hand over her mouth. "No more talking. Can you do that for me? I don't want any distractions from how perfect you feel."

Jude nodded, unsure what to make of the request but determined to honor it just the same. Sighing at the fiery imprint of pebbled nipples digging into her palms, Jude surrendered to her employer's will, biting her lip to stay quiet while Diana got herself off. Every now and then she'd jut her hips upward to counter a particularly forceful thrust, but for the most part Jude focused on running her hands absolutely *everywhere*, cataloguing the wonder of Diana's nude form through a tactile journey of exploration that began at her gloriously full breasts and ended with her miraculous ass. Jude held on to the warm, shapely bottom that had been making regular contact with her naked lap, squeezing, separating, then smacking—anything she thought might turn Diana on, might make her *come*.

Anything that might change her mind about falling in love.

CHAPTER TWENTY

Just three days later, Diana fiddled nervously with her phone as she tried to decide whether she was about to make a huge mistake. She and Jude hadn't spoken since Saturday night, shortly after fucking each other's brains out with their favorite dildos, and Diana found herself more hesitant than usual to initiate contact. She assumed Jude felt the same, or else she'd most likely have heard from her by now. Over text, if nothing else. It wasn't as though they'd talked much outside of class before last week, but with the recent evolution of their friendship into a potentially casual sexual relationship...well, Diana had expected their change in status to yield more immediate benefits. On the contrary, Jude seemed more skittish than ever. She'd barely spoken during the drive home on Saturday and hadn't reached out since, even though Diana knew she'd spent every night at home, blessedly alone.

Had she upset Jude somehow? There'd been that one awkward moment during their last fuck, when Diana had seized control to reverse their positions and escape the heart-pounding intimacy of Jude's naked, full-body embrace and her searing, toe-curling kisses. She'd sensed Jude's well-hidden disappointment and regretted not being able to grant her free rein to do anything she pleased. Jude was the most exciting sexual partner she'd ever had—kinky yet inexplicably innocent, responsive in ways Diana hadn't anticipated outside her wildest dreams, and with a body that fit against hers as though designed for that purpose alone. She wanted nothing more than to willingly give herself to Jude, to be swept away by her youthful, fervent hunger without hesitation or fear, to lose her awareness of how even the most exhilarating connection could turn rotten eventually...but alas, there was no escape from the prison Janine had built around her heart. Diana was who she had become, a fact she'd repeatedly tried to hammer into Jude's head so as not to lead her on.

Then again, maybe Jude *wasn't* upset. Maybe she was simply waiting for Diana to make the first move, too gun-shy to start testing the expanded boundaries of their tenuous friendship. Diana brought up Jude's cell number for the umpteenth time, staring at the screen while all the old, familiar arguments against love, romance, and basic human connection rang out in her head. Fucking Jude wasn't *meant* to be about love. It wasn't even about basic human connection, most of the time, beyond the purely physical. The most compelling reason to see Jude outside of class was that sex with another person gave her access to pleasures she couldn't experience on her own. Like having her pussy licked—or better yet, licking pussy.

"Shit." Diana brought a finger to her lips, wetting the tip with a flick of her tongue. Caution urged her to return the phone to its charger and go to bed, but her stubborn libido sent her thumb to hover indecisively over the call button. Grasping for a rationalization, *any* rationalization, to explain why she had to touch base with Jude at nine o'clock on Tuesday night, Diana practiced a few opening lines slash excuses. "Just wanted to check in after this weekend…make sure the workshop went all right for you…that you enjoyed everything we—" She switched gears as the path forward solidified in her mind. "How'd you feel about the butt stuff? Hope it was okay…I figured, you know, with next weekend on the horizon…" She breathed out, then lowered her thumb to the call button. "We need to practice."

Jude let out a shaky breath, simultaneously stunned, relieved, and terrified about the date Diana had just proposed. "Practice?" Her mind reeled, thrown into chaos by Diana's not entirely unexpected suggestion that they have sex in Jude's apartment, alone and away from prying eyes. Only half listening to Diana explain how she wanted to be sure Jude enjoyed receiving anal sex before they attempted to demonstrate for other wary first-timers, Jude tried to imagine what it would be like to have Diana in her bed. Would her walls finally come crashing down? Would their connection feel even stronger without an audience there to inhibit them?

"Jude?" Diana's concerned tone snapped her into focus. But before Jude could answer, Diana offered the get-out-of-jail-free card she'd never wanted. "There's no pressure to attend this workshop if you don't want to. If you'd prefer to skip this one, I'll understand."

"No!" Jude's face heated at her wildly frantic denial. But the thought of missing their last paid engagement flooded her with panic. For all she knew, that could be the end in more ways than one. "That is, I made a commitment. I'm not about to leave you hanging."

"If you'd rather fuck me in the ass, we could do that instead. I'll teach you how." Diana hesitated, then murmured, "It's your choice."

Jude's hand floated to her forehead, pressing down firmly as though that might help organize her half-formed, rapidly cycling thoughts. "Uh… to be honest, I liked the butt stuff on Saturday. A lot, kind of…I think." She burbled nervous laughter, then cringed at the sound. "I mean, so much was happening. But I came super hard, like…harder than usual." She cleared her throat, lamenting that everything she said came out sounding so insipid. "I'm starting to think that anal penetration gives me incredibly intense orgasms…but it'd be nice to know for sure before the workshop. If for no other reason than to figure out how much I can handle before we let other people watch."

"Yes, it only seems right to offer you a proper first time without the pressure to perform for an audience." Diana paused, breathing audibly enough to raise goose bumps on Jude's arms. "Plus, this'll be a great test of the whole fuck-buddy concept. I'll come to your place with some toys…and we'll see how it goes." A long silence stretched out between them. Finally Diana asked, "You in?"

"When?" Jude asked. She'd planned to spend the next few evenings writing, but who was she kidding? Her concentration was shot—and had been for over six weeks by this point. Without waiting for specifics that wouldn't matter anyway, she said, "Hell, yeah, I'm in."

CHAPTER TWENTY-ONE

Taking a deep breath, Jude plastered an exaggeratedly easygoing smile across her face and answered her door. "Hey." She stepped aside to let Diana into her apartment, noting the bold journey of her neighbor's gaze as it meandered down, then back up, her barely clad form. Shutting the door behind Diana, Jude swallowed at the inevitable wave of self-consciousness that crashed over her. "Sorry I didn't get dressed. Once I finished executing your, uh...pre-game instructions—" Literally, Diana had emailed paragraphs of educational text about how to prepare her body for tonight's lesson. "It seemed silly to put my shirt and pants back on only to take them off again a half hour later."

Diana glanced backward without breaking her stride. "Don't apologize. You look delicious enough to devour."

Jude blushed, the reaction embarrassing her even more than Diana's compliment. She assumed the skin above the cleavage-baring neckline of her satin camisole had also flushed pink, though she didn't dare check. "Shame we have other plans this evening."

Diana set the bag she carried on the coffee table and gave Jude a sultry wink. "Actually, *my* plan begins with licking you all over. As I tell my students, oral attention ought to be considered a prerequisite for any serious attempt at anal penetration. The recipient needs to be as aroused as you can reasonably make her. Every single time."

Impossibly wetter from Diana's shift into teaching mode, Jude couldn't fathom being any more aroused than she was already. It might literally kill her if Diana tried. Still, what a way to go. "I doubt that'll be strictly necessary," Jude said, "but I'm not inclined to refuse such a generous offer." She cleared her throat, approaching the couch, and

Diana, on wobbly legs. "I've been wet for you all day." Every day, her mind corrected. Every day *for months*—but Jude kept that fact to herself. "The entire ritual of getting *this* squeaky clean for you was…far more erotic than any activity involving an enema has the right to be."

Diana's fond laughter loosened the tension between Jude's shoulders, helping her relax enough to close the distance between them. She came to a stop well within Diana's reach—no more than a foot away—and shyly met those enchanting blue eyes. A good-natured smirk ghosted over Diana's full lips as she traced the tip of her index finger along Jude's jawline, then bent to capture her mouth in a brief but intimate kiss. Backing away, she whispered, "I'm glad you're excited. I am, too."

Jude struggled to maintain eye contact, unable to hold Diana's steady gaze for more than a second or two before looking away. A warm hand closed around hers to offer an encouraging squeeze, enabling Jude to further relax despite the butterflies stampeding inside her stomach. Like a puppet whose strings Diana controlled, Jude raised her head and stared longingly at the woman standing before her. "I'm for sure excited… but also nervous. Like, *mildly* nervous." She fidgeted with the hem of her camisole, afraid to alter Diana's opinion about the wisdom of this date with less than total confidence. "Especially with you standing there looking at me like that."

Diana grinned. "Like what?"

"Like I'm the dessert you've been craving."

Eyes sparkling, Diana raised Jude's hand to her lips and kissed the knuckles. "But that's exactly what you are, my darling." She tugged Jude in front of the center couch cushion, then searched her eyes. "Should we do this here or in your bedroom? I'm fine either way. Whatever's most comfortable for you."

Startled by the realization that Diana meant to jump right in, Jude debated only a moment before making her choice. "Bedroom. This couch isn't great to fuck on."

If she hadn't been standing so close, Jude might not have noticed the nearly imperceptible tightening of Diana's jaw or the jealousy that shadowed her expression for less than a second before a carefree smile replaced it. "Lead the way."

Jude took Diana into her room, slowing considerably as they reached the bed. Her heart thumped so hard she just *knew* Diana could hear its rapid, staccato beat against her chest wall. Noticing the bag in Diana's hand, she tilted her head. "What did you bring?"

Diana emptied the contents onto her mattress, then sat beside the heaping pile of plastic, latex, and silicon, displaying each item to Jude one at a time. To start, she held up a clear, pump-action bottle overlaid with dark-purple text. "First and foremost, lube."

Perhaps the biggest bottle Jude had ever seen, in fact. She voiced a retort she hoped would make Diana laugh. "And lots of it."

"Damn straight." Diana pointed the bottle at Jude before tossing it aside to seed a new pile. "Your anus can't naturally lubricate itself. As it's already a much narrower opening than you're accustomed to..." She flashed Jude a patient smile and patted the mattress next to her hip. "There's no such thing as too much lube. I promise, Jude, if we do this right—taking it slow, going hot and heavy on foreplay, applying handfuls of slippy stuff—I can bring you pleasure beyond any you've ever known. Anal sex shouldn't hurt or cause any sustained discomfort, all right? If something I'm doing feels unpleasant, I need you to tell me at once. No stoic silence. I never want to find out after the fact that you chose to grin and bear a sex act you didn't enjoy. Understand?"

Jude sank onto the edge of the bed, reassured by Diana's sincere concern for her physical safety. "Yes, ma'am."

Diana showed her a sealed silver pouch. "These are brand-new, purchased especially for you." She unzipped the top and extracted a tiny silicon plug, then tilted the pouch to reveal three additional plugs of varying size concealed within. "We'll start small and gradually work our way up." Diana swapped out the toy in her hand for the largest of the set, offering it for Jude's inspection. "Six inches long, one-and-a-half inches in diameter at its widest point."

"Damn," Jude breathed. Until that moment, she hadn't appreciated how even the most reasonably sized dildo could intimidate in another context. She returned the toy to its pouch, suddenly doubting whether she was truly up to this task. "My pussy says no problem, but I'm not sure my butthole agrees."

Diana winked, zipping the pouch and setting it aside. "It's entirely possible we won't get that far. You may decide you've had enough after one or two sizes, which is absolutely acceptable...and fair." She scooped up one of the remaining items, a familiar pair of shorts she dangled from her fingertip. "If we *do* proceed past the trainers, maybe you'll ask me to wear this."

Jude licked her lips, darting her gaze from the harness to the silver pouch and back again. "Yeah," she whispered, cotton-mouthed from a heady mix of adrenaline, anticipation, and conflicted unease. "I'd like that."

"The final plug has a flared base that'll fit my harness. So at some point, if you want—and I mean *only* if you want—I could strap it on and penetrate you like that." Diana surprised Jude by ducking her head, as though sheepish to have broached such an advanced topic. "I only brought it along because you'd mentioned...before, you know, that you might want to try—"

"I do." Jude exhaled evenly, squeezing the base of her neck to relieve its tightness. "If possible."

Diana showed her the last object on the mattress. "This would be another alternative. Slightly longer, but also slimmer than the largest plug." She handed Jude a rather narrow dildo that also featured a flared base. "No need to decide right now. Let's see how you feel once I've warmed you up."

Jude returned the dildo to Diana, grateful and covered in goose bumps. "Thanks." She nibbled on her lower lip, debating how to best communicate her current state of mind. "While I *am* nervous...I do trust you, one-hundred percent. I can't think of anyone I'd rather be with for this first time."

Diana drew Jude's hand onto her lap and laced their fingers together. Her shimmering eyes hinted at some level of emotion about Jude's heartfelt words—emotion she hid behind an amiable smile. "I'm glad you feel safe. It's important to me that you do." With that, she changed the subject completely. "Do you have a TV in here? Or a laptop that plays DVDs?"

Jude attempted to process the seemingly random query. "I guess a laptop?" Blinking, she scanned the room to verify the validity of her unthinking answer. "I usually keep it on the floor between my nightstand and the bed. Why? What are we watching?"

"Smart girl, keeping television out of your bedroom. Your willpower puts mine to shame." Diana kissed Jude's hand, then released her to grab a plastic case Jude hadn't noticed from the edge of her discard pile. She handed the disc to Jude with a cheeky smile. "Do you like porn? Not that this is *porn*, per se. Personally, I consider this one more instructional than strictly titillating, but...still, it *is* titillating. And informative."

Jude read the title on the case's spine, then studied the cover image of an attractive, brimming-with-confidence, middle-aged brunette and her eager, fresh-faced co-star. "Are you asking if I want to watch, or telling me I should?"

"I'm saying I'd like you to watch, sweetheart, for me." Without warning, Diana grasped the hem of Jude's camisole and yanked it off over her head, leaving her bare above the waist. "It'll turn me on to hear you witness someone else's first time while I prepare you for yours."

Jude's nipples hardened in the cool air. She resisted the impulse to cover her breasts, aware of how silly that would be, given Diana's mission to acquaint herself with the least-traveled region of Jude's body—a body she'd already explored on multiple occasions. *Thoroughly.* Casting aside her shyness, Jude positioned Diana's hands over her breasts, sighing at the warmth of her palms against the stiff tips. "It's chilly in here," she muttered, bashfully. "Your hands are warm."

Diana chuckled, then gave Jude a kiss that both curled her toes and torpedoed any hope of softening her nipples. Jude leaned into the ardent touch, wishing to somehow get closer, to erase the stubborn distance Diana insisted on keeping between their hearts. Clad in only pajama shorts now that her camisole was on the floor, Jude blushed at the wetness that trickled out of her to stain the crotch and coat her inner thighs. She ended their kiss when Diana's hand landed on her knee, causing the nipple she'd abandoned to harden painfully. Diana sighed against her lips, then wrapped her arms around Jude's waist to haul her onto her lap.

Jude died a little when her sodden shorts came into contact with Diana's warm thighs. "I'm getting your pants wet."

"Excellent." Diana wrapped one arm around Jude's back and maneuvered the other between her thighs. "Means I'm doing something right."

Jude didn't say so out loud, but Diana was doing *everything* right. As her blunt fingernails tickled their way across the crotch of her shorts, Jude had to remind herself that what they were doing was strictly business—or, at the very least, unromantic. Also, that even if they were friends, sort of, Diana saw her mostly as a mere sexual outlet, a warm body to ease the loneliness of turning away from real, reciprocal love.

Deft fingers crept beneath the leg of her shorts and stroked the inside of her thigh, an exquisite tease that compelled Jude to open her legs for greater access. Diana caressed the tender flesh bordering her outer labia, then murmured into Jude's ear, "I like having you on my lap."

Shaken, Jude hooked her arms around Diana's neck and cuddled closer. She rested her head against Diana's, closing her eyes with a contented whimper. Earnestly, she whispered, "I like being here."

Diana's hand moved farther into her shorts, the clever fingers gliding along her labia before parting them to dip into the liquid heat pooled at her entrance. Jude stopped breathing for a few, exhilarating heartbeats, then, when she could stand it no longer, gasped raggedly for air. Chuckling, Diana kissed her forehead affectionately. "Deep, even breaths, sweetie. I don't want you passing out."

Self-conscious about her over-the-top reactions, Jude wished for the casual cool—and easy confidence—she'd cultivated before Diana's impromptu job offer turned her life upside-down. In less than six weeks, she'd become a shell of the self-possessed person she'd once been, hollowed out by unrequited love and weary from the struggle to constantly manage her own expectations. No other woman had ever made her so afraid to say the wrong thing or disappoint in any way. Abashed by how wantonly she hungered for Diana's love and approval, Jude marveled that her new friend didn't perceive her true feelings each and every time they touched.

"Jude." Diana ran a finger between her inner labia. "Relax for me, baby. I'll never fit inside that snug little ass if you don't."

Jude exhaled at length, recalling the advice from one of Diana's articles. "I know." She inhaled, then breathed out, determined to collect herself before Diana deemed her unfit for meaningless, no-strings-attached anal sex. "I really am trying."

"It's all right." Diana removed her hand from Jude's shorts, then took her by the shoulders and looked into her eyes. "How about you go grab that laptop so we can get some foreplay going?"

Get it going? She'd been lingering on the precipice of orgasm since their first kiss. Jude didn't know how much more she could withstand before she surrendered to the inevitable. "Okay, but fair warning…it won't take much to make me come."

"Challenge accepted." Diana helped Jude off her lap, holding onto her waist until she could stand on her own. "I plan to give you as many orgasms as I can tonight. The more excited you are, the more receptive your anus will be."

Jude staggered to her nightstand to retrieve her laptop from the floor. She put it on the bed in a hurry, not trusting herself to carry her most prized possession—and writing companion—while hobbled by a dangerously out-of-control libido. "Here?"

"Sure." Diana handed over the DVD. "Go ahead and put this in for me. Then take off your shorts and lie down on your belly so you can see the screen."

Jude executed her instructions to the letter, trembling at every step. By the time she'd stretched out on her stomach to watch the opening scene of Diana's instructional film unfold, she was so relieved to be off her feet that she forgot to wonder about Diana's next move. She jolted at a light touch on her ankle, then moaned at the feeling of skillful hands running their way up the insides of her thighs. Jude parted her legs without being asked, thrilling at the heat and pressure of Diana's body as she settled into the space between.

On-screen, the middle-aged performer addressed the camera, introducing her younger co-star and explaining how this would be the attractive redhead's first anal experience. Jude's heart rate accelerated at the tickle of Diana's silky hair along the backs of her thighs, then her unguarded ass. When Jude's buttocks clenched reactively, Diana murmured, "Relax," and dragged her tongue through the crevice between her tense cheeks.

Jude yelped, caught halfway between ecstasy and hilarity. "*Relax?*"

Diana delved deeper with her tongue, painstakingly circling Jude's anus before she paused to answer. "You heard me." Securing Jude's wrists, Diana moved her arms behind her back and positioned the captured hands on her own quivering bottom. "Spread those cheeks open for me, good girl, and *relax*."

Still skeptical about that last bit, Jude held her buttocks apart, gasping when Diana buried her face with a hearty moan. "Oh, fuck," Jude breathed into the comforter, transported by the unique bliss of having her ass eaten by professional sex therapist Diana Kelley. "*God,* that feels absolutely fucking *fantastic*." She whimpered pitifully when the heat of Diana's mouth vanished.

"Keep your eyes on that laptop, young lady." Diana licked the tight ring of muscle, then stuck her tongue just past the outer rim. She stayed there for only a second, until Jude attempted to raise her hips and draw her farther inside. Retreating, Diana brushed her lips over Jude's white knuckles and chuckled. "I want you to see what you'll be begging me to do to you later. Pay special attention to how well the younger actress takes instruction and *relaxes*."

With effort, Jude lifted her head to watch the action on-screen. Both actresses were sprawled upon what appeared to be a king-sized bed, their bodies entwined in a mirror image of her and Diana's positions. The older woman lapped at her younger counterpart's puckered opening so voraciously Jude's pussy contracted, unleashing fresh wetness for Diana to collect on her fingertips and redistribute around her slick anus. Jude pushed her butt up into the air, eager for Diana to resume her prerequisite oral attention—and so much more.

Jude watched the older actress sneak a hand beneath her co-star's hips to tease her labia and clit, the caresses noncommittal enough to avoid bringing about climax. Her young protégé squirmed beneath her ministrations, a nearly continuous stream of mewling noises spilling from her open mouth as her mentor's tongue worked diligently around and inside her presumably loosening hole. Jude echoed the redhead's lewd moans when Diana entered her once more, patiently tonguing her ass like they had the rest of their lives to get there. It felt so utterly decadent to lie there and passively receive such an intimate, undoubtedly one-sided act—decadent, and deliciously naughty—that Jude could barely think, let alone worry.

To her surprise, the tension began to melt away.

"There you go," Diana drawled, sliding her fingers from Jude's labia to the entrance of her vagina. "You're doing so well, darling. Do you like how it feels?"

Enraptured by the sight and sound of the redheaded actress spasming in release, Jude whispered, "It's wonderful."

"Would you like it if I put my finger in here?" Diana traced around her drenched opening, heightening Jude's anticipation. "If I made you come with my tongue inside your ass?"

"*Yes.*" Jude arched, searching for the completion her filmed counterpart had been granted. She tracked the aftermath with keen eyes, fixated on the brunette as she continued her lesson by carefully inserting a lube-covered finger into the redhead's willing sphincter. Jealous of the elation etched across the younger woman's face, Jude broke down and begged. "Please, fuck me. Make me come."

Diana's fingers glided into her pussy without resistance, instantly honing in on the magical spot she'd first mapped during the vaginal-massage workshop. Her touch was electric, triggering pulse after pulse of bliss to course through Jude's legs, her abdomen, her pussy, her clit. Just when she was certain she couldn't keep going, Diana drove her tongue deep inside Jude's ass, setting off a climax so explosive she feared she might pass out. Unable to keep her head up any longer, Jude laid her cheek on the comforter, sobbing at Diana's relentless pursuit of her pleasure. The euphoric torture lasted for minutes, one orgasm bleeding into another until, at long last, Jude begged for it to end.

"Wait." Jude grasped Diana's hair, pulling weakly. "Stop. I need a break…" She whined, conflicted by Diana's instant compliance. "A quick one. Then we'll keep going."

"That's the spirit." Diana shifted to lie on top of her, venturing a hand between Jude's thighs to cradle her slick, swollen vulva. Kissing behind her ear, Diana murmured, "You really are something else, baby girl. I love how you taste…how you sound…how you feel around my fingers when I'm getting you off…" Diana nibbled her earlobe, then curled her free hand around the slender column of Jude's throat. "Watch them, sweetheart. See her take that plug for her mistress?" Diana urged her head back, tightening the fingers on her neck until Jude stared directly at the performance Diana meant for them to emulate.

The brunette had finished seating a small plug inside the redhead's anus. Devilishly, she touched a vibrator against her prone lover's clit, making her jump, then howl. Jude's pulse quickened when Diana's fingers parted her labia to tease the sympathetically throbbing bundle of nerves concealed within. Kissing her temple, Diana murmured, "Let's watch together."

A needy whimper escaped from deep in Jude's throat when the brunette escalated the encounter, cautiously dragging the plug out of her partner's anus, then pushing it back in. The redhead's mouth fell open, but no sound emerged. Instead, her body quaked as she succumbed to a violent climax. Chasing the same joy, Jude rocked against Diana's hand, mindlessly humping the fingers and palm that brought her so much pleasure. When Diana ventured deeper between her labia to swirl around her opening, Jude pleaded, "Keep going."

Diana sank part of her finger into Jude, then stopped. Pressing down on Jude's clit, she drew fast, focused circles around the swollen tip, a maneuver that rewarded her with a handful of cum in just under a minute. Diana rumbled laughter. "Are you *always* this easy, Ms. Monaco?"

Too immersed in their scene to practice proper self-censorship, Jude admitted, "Only with you." Blinking, she allowed her eyes to stay closed for a full ten seconds before forcing them back open. She'd lost all perspective on matters relating to Diana Kelley and thus had no way of knowing whether that response would be taken as harmless flirting or alarming devotion. Covering, Jude said, "I mean, obviously. You *are* a trained professional." To distract from her stupidity, she commented on the steadily progressing filmed encounter. "Wow. Someone's confident."

Diana chuckled, kneading Jude's vulva as she peered over her shoulder at the screen. "They move faster than I plan to."

"I hope so." Jude's eyes widened at the steady insertion of a plug she judged to be almost twice the length and diameter of the first one the redhead had been asked to accommodate. The sight made her clit twitch, as did the genuine rapture on the redhead's face. Lingering uncertainty aside, Jude yearned to experience the same forbidden delights. "But I think I'm ready for that first plug now." Moaning as the brunette actress wiggled the large plug within her lover's ass to deliver a shallow, gentle fucking that left the redhead spasming on the bed, Jude said, "I want this, Diana. Between your tongue and this movie...I *need* you in my ass." She rolled her hips into Diana's flattened hand, whimpering, "Give it to me, please."

"Can you be patient for me, baby?" Diana drove her crotch against Jude's upturned butt, pantomiming the kind of fuck she hoped to eventually receive. "She's about to penetrate her with the strap-on."

As promised, the brunette rose from the bed to secure a harness around her hips. A dildo roughly the same length as the one she'd just discarded jutted from the center O-ring, bobbling dauntingly as she approached the waiting redhead. Jude glanced backward, meeting Diana's desirous stare with an imploring pout. "It's not like I've never seen anal porn before. I know—"

Diana shushed her. "Listen." She applied slight pressure to Jude's neck, forcing her to watch the instructions being given by the actress on-screen. "You might learn something."

Scowling, Jude bucked in frustration. "You know, I *did* read every piece of literature you sent. Really. It's all about relaxing my pubococcygeus muscles...right?"

"Look at you!" Diana bit her earlobe. "Doing your homework like a smart girl. Aiming for teacher's pet?"

Jude shivered at the steamy breath on her neck. "I wanted to please you."

"Oh, you please me. So very, very much." The lips on Jude's neck curled into a wolfish smile. "Shall I close the laptop and take over your training from here on out?"

Jude practically sobbed. "I wish you would."

Diana reached over her shoulder and snapped the laptop shut. "It's okay, sweetheart. I'll take care of you." She rolled off Jude's prone body, then gave her butt a rousing pat. "Get up. I want you facedown across my lap for this next part."

Dazed, Jude sat up to watch Diana scoot to the edge of the bed and set her feet on the floor. Despite her bones turning to jelly, Jude somehow mustered the strength to crawl across the mattress and join her. "You don't have to worry about whether I'm aroused enough for this." She knelt beside Diana, running her hand over her labia to collect a fraction of the unreal wetness pooled there. "I'll need to strip the bed after we're done. And do laundry."

Diana quirked an eyebrow at the shiny digits Jude showed to prove her readiness. "Impressive." Making eye contact, she bent to sample the tip of Jude's middle finger with her tongue and gave a hearty, approving moan. Backing away, she asked, "Did you make that for me, baby?"

Jude's stomach fluttered ecstatically at Diana's repeated usage of that endearment in particular—first added to her lexicon during their strap-on workshop—even if the sweet pet name also left her more confused than ever about how Diana truly felt. "All for you," Jude whispered, chagrined by the truth. She hadn't slept with anyone else in over three weeks and didn't intend to break that streak anytime soon. Sex without Diana not only sounded boring, but almost painful to contemplate. Concerned Diana would perceive all that messy, internal conflict simply by looking at her face, Jude crawled over Diana's thighs before she was invited to do so. Resting her cheek on the comforter, Jude sighed in relief. "I'm ready."

Diana laid her hand on Jude's butt, calmly caressing the swell of her left cheek with her thumb. Vibrating from head to toe, Jude closed her eyes and bit the inside of her cheek, afraid Diana might mistake her lovesickness for genuine fear about taking it in the ass. She tried to relax her muscles, starting with her jaw, shoulders and sphincter, but she wasn't sure such a feat was even possible anymore. As though to prove that point, Diana's hand moved lower, the thumb dipping into the crevice between Jude's buttocks. On instinct, Jude sucked in a startled breath and flinched away.

"Jude."

Shit. Eyes clamped shut, Jude silently chastised herself for sabotaging an experience she was desperate to have. "You surprised me."

Jude launched a staunch defense of her traitorous body. "I'm not freaking out or having second thoughts, okay? I'm just…"

"On a hair trigger. It's okay." Diana wiggled the thumb she'd planted between Jude's butt cheeks. "Your safe word is laundry. I trust you to use it if necessary."

"I will." Jude exhaled, sagging as the threat of losing Diana's touch diminished. "You know I will."

Diana's thumb paused its coy exploration for a fraction of a second, more than long enough for Jude to notice. Before she could apologize for invoking such a fraught memory, Diana replaced her thumb with what Jude guessed was an index finger. She circled the perimeter of Jude's anus, a feather-light caress. "You've done an outstanding job of making lots of wetness for me, but I'm going to apply more lube anyway. Shall I warm it with my hand first?"

Simultaneously touched and turned on, Jude folded her arms beneath her head to get comfortable for the penetration. "Yes, please."

"As you wish." Jude heard the bottle uncapped, then squeezed. "I'll start by slipping a single finger into your anus. I want to make sure you like the sensation before we break out the training plugs."

When Diana's hands disappeared again—ostensibly to gather lubricant—Jude mourned their absence with a heavy sigh. Sheepish about her own lack of discretion, Jude decided to fill the silence before Diana could. "You're incredible at this." Face hot, she explained. "Taking care of me. Making sure I'm okay." She swallowed when Diana pried her buttocks apart to smear a large dollop of lube across her cum-slicked anus. Whimpering, Jude said, "All of it."

"You're not so bad, either." Diana used her finger to circle the perimeter of Jude's puckered hole, then carefully inserted the blunt tip. "I love how tight you are around my finger." She wiggled the digit to elicit a loud moan, then forged deeper, sinking into Jude until her knuckles rested against Jude's bottom and she had nowhere left to go. "You have such a fierce grip on me, sweetheart. Can you try to relax?"

Jude scoffed at the notion for the second time that evening but cut her amusement short when her anus reflexively clamped down on the invading finger. Intent on obedience, Jude entered a semi-meditative trance, focusing inward to achieve the improbable. "I'm trying."

Within seconds, her muscles slackened enough to allow the free movement of Diana's finger—in, out, in, out—as it established a steady cadence that left Jude gasping for more. Diana snorted, patting Jude fondly with the hand that wasn't fucking her. "That's my girl."

Ignoring the praise so Diana wouldn't feel how powerfully it hit her, Jude mumbled, "Feels heavenly."

"Ready for the first plug?"

Jude answered without thought. "Bring it on."

CHAPTER TWENTY-TWO

D iana exhaled to steady her nerves, then slowly extracted her finger from Jude's mouthwatering ass. Grabbing the toy from the silver pouch she'd left behind her hip, she pumped yet more lube onto her fingers to thoroughly coat its length from tip to base. The first trainer was a scant four inches long and merely one inch at its widest point, so she had confidence her precocious partner could endure its insertion. Despite her intermittent bouts of anxiety, Jude clearly craved this experience, and Diana's touch.

Unfortunately, Jude's fear of misstepping was every bit as transparent as her desire. More than once, Diana had sensed Jude's fear of reacting in a way that would cause Diana to stop what she was doing, if not leave altogether. So although Jude had promised not to hesitate with her safe word, Diana couldn't shake her concern about her young friend's stubborn need to please.

Knowing she'd never forgive herself if she hurt the woman on her lap, Diana conducted one last check-in. "Jude…" She parted Jude's shapely cheeks with her left hand and positioned the tip of the plug against her anus with the right. Painting deliberate, suggestive circles around the rim, Diana said, "If you do need to use your safe word, that doesn't mean our night together has to end. Not if you don't want it to. Got it? I need to make sure you know that you're allowed to push pause. It won't freak me out or make me leave. I promise." To prove she wouldn't stop until Jude commanded it, Diana applied pressure to the base of the plug, savoring Jude's moan when her butthole opened up to suck the tip inside. "Do you understand what I just told you?"

Jude gave a semi-frantic nod. "Don't be afraid to use my safe word. I won't, I promise." She reared back to try to force the toy deeper, whimpering when Diana prevented the attempted takeover by moving with her. "Please, Diana. Fucking *do it* already. This foreplay is *bullshit.*"

Heady from her power over sweet, sexy, creative Jude, Diana ventured farther inside her slim rectum, coming to a stop as Jude groaned at the introduction of the widest point. "Relax," she murmured like a broken record. "Relax, darling, and bear down." She felt Jude consciously heed her advice and beamed as the plug continued its unhurried journey into her anal passage. "That's it! You're doing an amazing job, sweetheart. I'm so proud of you."

Jude shuddered as the plug slid the rest of the way inside and her anus constricted around the narrower base. "Ohh..." she breathed. Hips jerking, she humped Diana's lap in a blatant hunt for friction. "That's... it feels..." Hoping to inspire some elucidation, Diana gave the plug a glacial twist, wiggling the base carefully from side to side. Jude's fingers twitched on the comforter, and she moaned. *"Unreal."*

Diana smiled, chest tight from the unmitigated joy of seeing Jude experience that much ecstasy. Her satisfaction wasn't about having caused it so much as being there to savor the result. Seeing Jude happy made her happy. Period. Stirred by feelings she didn't want to entertain, Diana fondled Jude's labia while removing the plug halfway, then driving it back in. "Rub your clit, honey. Keep that pussy slick for me while I'm fucking your ass."

"Fuck," Jude whispered, trickling hot juices onto Diana's roving fingers. "Maybe...get the next plug. Before..." She gasped. "Before I come...again."

Jude's right hand moved between them, bumping rhythmically against the juncture of Diana's thighs. Wishing she'd removed her pants to benefit from the modest friction, Diana disregarded her rising hunger to attend to Jude. She reined in her libido, then eased the first plug all the way out. "As you wish," she said, trading the toy in her hand for the next size up. She applied a generous serving of lube to the new plug—all four and a half inches of it—before placing it between Jude's firm cheeks. "Tell me when."

"Now." Jude strained upward. "Please."

"Don't stop jacking off that fat clit, good girl." Diana's lips twitched at Jude's predictable moan in response to what was quite possibly her favorite phrase, at least when it came to eliciting a vocal reaction. "And rela—"

"*Relax,*" Jude mimicked in a singsong tone. "Aye aye, ma'am."

Chuckling, Diana pinched the underside of Jude's left buttock. "Don't you sass me, young lady."

Jude squeaked, dissolving into giggles Diana couldn't help but echo. Her heart filled with affection and oh-so-serious desire, but rather than shut out the resulting euphoria, Diana chose to bask in it. For a moment, maybe two, but no more than that. She couldn't *let* Jude become more than that. Waiting for the laughter to subside, Diana replaced the rounded tip of the toy with her index and middle fingers, then slid into Jude's willing asshole with a moan.

Jude gasped. "That isn't the toy."

Diana stopped at her second knuckles, just in case. "That's two of my fingers inside you, darling. Still okay?" She waggled the tips almost imperceptibly, glad for the abundant lubrication to enable her frictionless motion. "Or would you rather stick to plugs instead?"

When Jude's anus contracted around her embedded digits, Diana groaned at the perfect tightness of the youthful body draped across her lap. She stroked her thumb along the curve of Jude's left buttock, wishing for the briefest moment that things could be different. That *she* could be different—more innocent, even naive.

Interrupting her lapse into melancholy, Jude said, "I like having you inside me. Just…go easy, okay?"

"Always." Diana hadn't planned on doing any vigorous fucking under the guise of practice. This workshop was meant to be a gentle, patient initiation into previously unexplored realms of bodily pleasure, *not* a hard-core physical challenge. Even if they did advance all the way to strap-on sex, Diana didn't anticipate a lot of thrusting on her part. Just kissing, and grinding, and whispering naughty words into Jude's delicate ear. "I won't even move, if you don't want me to."

"You can move," Jude whimpered, a weak protest that hit Diana directly in the clit. "Slowly."

Taking Jude at her word, Diana sank her fingers a half inch deeper, fluttering them faintly as she settled into place. "I think you're ready for that plug. What do you say?"

Jude's chest hitched, and her hand hastened on her clit. Fluttering around Diana's vibrating digits, she moaned, "I say *yes, please.*"

"That's the spirit." Diana swapped her hand for the lube-coated second plug. Without giving Jude's sphincter the chance to constrict, she smoothly guided the toy into the space left by her fingers. This time, Jude's body welcomed the invasion, swallowing the widest part of the plug with little visible effort. Diana opened her mouth to deliver some well-deserved praise, but Jude interrupted with a throaty shout and a series of powerful orgasmic convulsions. Grinning, Diana gave the plug a minute wiggle that seemed to intensify the orgasm, until finally Jude's hand stopping moving and she collapsed in an exhausted heap.

"Holy fuck," Jude mumbled into the comforter. "What the fuck?"

Diana laughed, thrilled to have reduced her sexually well-versed assistant to foul-mouthed ineloquence. "My, my. Ms. Monaco, I do believe you *love* taking it in the ass."

Jude turned her face to the side. "So it seems."

"How are you feeling?" Diana released the base of the fully inserted plug to give Jude's butt a friendly rubdown. "Tapped out, or capable of more?"

"*Eager* for more." Jude strained to catch Diana's gaze over her shoulder. "Maybe you should get the harness. I think I can handle it now."

Diana caressed Jude's bottom soothingly. "You're still one plug away from graduating to the strap-on. The next trainer is one and a quarter inches in diameter. Both the strap-on and the final plug are one and a half."

"Do the third trainer, then." Jude squirmed, her restless hips pleading for more. "I can't wait to feel your body on mine."

Diana offered a compromise. "Why don't you get on the bed for this next part? I'll lie next to you."

"Yes." Without removing the plug, Jude made her way off Diana's lap and up to her pillow. Hugging it to her face, she lay on her belly to await Diana's arrival. "May I..." Jude exhaled. "Ask a favor?"

"Of course." Diana stood to clear space on the bed for the main event. "What's up?"

"I want..."

Jude's palpable nervousness brought Diana to a hesitant standstill. Whatever the request, Diana didn't want to refuse. She prayed she wouldn't have to. "Tell me."

"Will you take off your clothes, too?" Jude glanced over her shoulder, so vulnerable it took all of Diana's willpower not to crawl up the mattress and shelter her nude form in a loving embrace. "I want to feel your skin against mine."

Diana had walked into Jude's apartment with the absurd notion that her clothing was akin to protective armor, thus staying dressed was the easiest way to keep her heart safe. And yet her hands flew to her shirt in an instant, thumbing open the buttons before her brain could formulate a more pragmatic response. "Sure." Bothered by the blistering heat in her already flushed cheeks, Diana turned away from the bed, first dropping her shirt onto the floor, then unclasping and discarding her bra in the same spot. Undoing her fly, she stole a quick look at the bed—where Jude was once again riding her hand. Diana groaned and stepped out of her jeans, then kicked them aside. She left the panties on.

Jude sucked in a shaky breath as Diana climbed onto the mattress, then sighed tremulously when she lay flush against her side. On task, Diana pumped more lube into her hand, then liberally coated the third plug before shifting her attention to the toy still buried between Jude's slippery cheeks. Rotating the base a full quarter turn, Diana withdrew the first inch, then sank half that length back into Jude's tense opening. "Relax," she whispered, not caring if Jude rolled her eyes. She jostled the plug within Jude's rectum, doing what she could to loosen her up. "Tell me when you're ready for that upgrade."

"Now." Jude used her sphincter muscles to encourage a faster extraction. "Before I make myself come again."

Swapping the toy in Jude's anus for its slightly larger counterpart, Diana wobbled the new plug to and fro until she'd worked the first of its five inches into Jude's receptive bottom. Then she stopped, requiring a bit of active participation to continue. "Back into it, sweetheart, when you want the rest."

Jude flexed her hips to take in another inch. She paused only millimeters short of the plug's widest point, groaning. "Wait."

"You're nearly there, baby. Another inch and the hard part is over." Diana kept her wrist steady, letting Jude decide where to go, and when. She bent to kiss Jude's parted lips, then her eyelids. "But only if you want it."

Jude blinked to reveal hazel eyes that glittered with pure determination. Diana leaned back, making space for Jude to resume the arduous journey onto the biggest toy she'd ever tried to take. "*Fuck.*" Jude's voice cracked as she bore down on the silicon length, rocking her lower body until—at long last—the rest of the plug disappeared into her increasingly greedy butthole. "Fuck!" she repeated, shouting this time. "Oh, fuck...*Diana.*"

Resting her palm on the flared base, Diana stroked her pinkie finger over Jude's tender bottom. "Like a pro." Then, unable to resist, she pressed a soft kiss to Jude's temple. "Still good?"

"Uh-huh." Jude held her lower lip between her teeth, nostrils flaring. "*Yeah*."

Tickled by Jude's newly limited vocabulary, Diana asked, "So don't stop?"

"Only if you want to make me cry."

"*Never*." Diana's whisper came out more impassioned than intended.

Jude drove her hips against her self-pleasuring fingers, keening for more. "Please let me feel your body. Get on top of me."

Tantalized by the suggestion, Diana didn't think before acting. She got up and caged Jude's body with her own, dragging her swollen clit across the silicon base between Jude's butt cheeks before thrusting against her insistently. "Feel me in your ass?"

"Yes," Jude hissed. She bucked to counter Diana's next thrust. "You're so *big*."

"And this is just a warm-up." Licking the edge of Jude's ear, Diana whispered, "My real cock is even bigger."

Jude stopped moving, and breathing, until Diana kissed her neck to calm her. "*Relax*."

"I don't know how, with you." The words barely carried to Diana's ears, words she sensed Jude hadn't meant to say aloud.

Diana bowed her head, ashamed of the anxiety she'd created with her commitment-phobic, hypersensitive, sometimes grumpy ways. Week after week, Jude had shown up and given her all. She'd kept every promise, honored every boundary, and inexplicably brightened Diana's life in ways she'd spent the past five years convincing herself weren't possible. Jude deserved more than to always be on edge. She deserved to be worshipped, and adored, and protected. She deserved to *relax*.

Diana brought her face alongside Jude's, registering the heat of the cheek touching hers with remorse. "You don't need to be afraid," she breathed. "I'd rather die than hurt you, Jude. I…like having you around."

A muted sob burst from Jude's throat, compelling Diana to follow her instinct. She turned her head to draw Jude into the deepest, most passionate kiss she'd shared with anyone in over a decade, a kiss that devastated her so completely she feared she'd never truly recover. Overwhelmed by an unexpected rush of what felt like love, Diana broke away from the mouth she dreamed of losing herself in for hours, gathered Jude in a possessive embrace, and came all over the flawless butt of the girl next door. Jude's heartbeat thumped rapidly against Diana's forearm during the entirety of her remarkable orgasm, an intoxicating reminder of how profoundly her attraction was reciprocated. Their chemistry was straight-up nuclear, with the potential to evolve into even more. That should've frightened Diana, but tonight she reveled in the thought. Being with Jude felt too right not to occasionally let go and enjoy the ride.

"*Please.*" Jude danced her lower body between her busy hand and Diana's crotch. "Will you try the strap-on? I can't wait anymore."

She knew Jude had to be getting tired, plus…well, Diana didn't want to wait anymore, either. If Jude wasn't adequately primed to accept the increased size, then the strap-on simply wasn't meant to be—tonight, at least. They could always revisit this challenge in the future. Until then, the rest of this encounter was Jude's to dictate.

Diana left Jude with a hug and a kiss on the crown of her head, clambering off the bed to don her favorite boy-shorts-style harness and the slim dildo. Making sure Jude could see the lube she'd squeezed into her palm, Diana fisted the shaft between her legs to spread it around. When Jude's wide-eyed gaze traveled from the toy to her hooded stare, Diana tilted her head and smiled. "Show me how you play with your pussy when you're all alone at night. Get yourself as close as possible, but don't you *dare* come without permission."

Eyes open and locked to Diana's face, Jude raised her butt into the air to reveal the furiously moving hand beneath her. Diana went to the foot of the bed for a better view, spending long, reverent minutes admiring the deliciously wet pussy and shapely, inviting bottom on display. "Beautiful," she said, entranced by what she saw. "Sweetheart, do you have a vibrator somewhere nearby?"

"Nightstand, bottom drawer." Jude nodded vaguely with her chin.

Diana opened the nightstand to retrieve one last tool for the job. She chuckled as she grabbed a remote-controlled bullet vibe, then the cold metal chain tucked beside it. "Are these *nipple clamps*, sweetie?" She met Jude's coquettish smile, grinning wolfishly. "Another time, maybe."

Cognizant of the dwindling patience in the room, Diana tossed the nipple clamps into the drawer and knelt on the mattress behind Jude. "Lie flat, baby. You'll be more comfortable that way." Diana couldn't stop the endearments from flowing off her tongue, a veritable waterfall of helpless affection. What did Jude think? Was she sending mixed signals again? *Let's face it: probably.*

Cooling her tone, Diana said, "First things first. Let's get that trainer out of you so I have somewhere to put my cock." She maneuvered her hand between Jude's thighs to push the cylindrical, vibrating bullet into her vagina, fucking her only briefly before withdrawing and leaving it behind. Step one finished, she clicked the remote to start the vibration at its lowest setting, sending a perceptible jolt through Jude's sweat-dampened body.

"Ohh…" Diana sensed Jude's fingers stop on her clit as she contended with the new stimulation. Moaning low and loud, Jude said, "I can *definitely* come again."

Exactly as Diana had hoped. Gratified by the result of her improvisation, she grasped the base of the plug and twisted carefully. "Help me, okay? Like I taught you." She tugged just hard enough to encourage Jude's sphincter to expel the invading object, then dropped the lube-soaked plug over the edge of the bed. Coming forward on her knees, Diana placed the strap-on dildo between Jude's buttocks and rasped, "Spread it open."

Jude complied, abandoning her clit to grab a butt cheek in each hand and wrench them apart. Satisfied with the abundance of lube—both natural and man-made—dripping from Jude's every orifice, Diana touched the head of the dildo to her more relaxed anus, then retreated, then touched her again. Nudging harder each time, she eventually managed to fit the first half inch inside. "Good girl," she said, straining for a view of Jude's face. "How is it? Any pain?"

"No." Jude said. "But please, may I rub my clit again?"

Did Jude have any clue what it did to her when she asked for permission? "Yes, baby."

Diana guided Jude's hand beneath her hips, leading Jude to breathe a grateful "*Oh.*"

Taking that as a sign, Diana edged forward with the dildo, then paused to wait for Jude's vocal consent. "Tell me when."

"Keep going. Don't stop unless I tell you to."

Diana heard the resolve in Jude's voice and knew the moment had come. She steadied the base of the toy with her left hand and held onto Jude with the right. Millimeter by millimeter, Diana crept forward, tingling with delight at the sensation of Jude's sphincter opening up to permit her entry. Expecting to stop at least once before she hit bottom, Diana suddenly found herself buried to the hilt in Jude Monaco's lush, quivering ass.

The enormity of what she'd just done, and of what this moment would represent in the annals of Jude's personal sexual history, hit Diana hard—far harder than she'd imagined a casual fuck ever could. Consumed by emotions she didn't care to examine, Diana flattened herself against Jude's back and cradled the trembling body she rested inside, listening to Jude moan at the nearly imperceptible rocking of her hips.

"Diana..." Jude undulated beneath her. "Talk to me, please."

Sensing Jude's desperation, Diana grabbed the remote and turned the vibration up a notch. Then she captured Jude's wrists and stretched her arms above her head, holding her against the bed while she whispered into her ear. "I'm fucking you in the ass."

"*Yes.*" Jude gasped.

"Not a virgin anymore, are you?" She licked Jude's neck. "Thank you for this gift."

Jude's entire body quavered. "It was always yours to take."

Diana drew back an inch or so, then brought their lower bodies flush, relishing Jude's guttural cry at her careful thrust. "Glad I asked, then."

"Me, too."

Diana wondered if she genuinely meant that. With all the bullshit she'd put Jude through, was she honestly still grateful for her offer of paid sex? *Well, why not?* Diana wanted to believe her. *That's a substantial extra income for a struggling author, and our sex is top-notch.* She brushed her lips over Jude's shoulder, then the corner of her eye. Then, without meaning to, Diana opened her mouth...and out poured her heart. "You really are so beautiful, Jude. Your body, your writing...your soul." Releasing Jude's wrists, she threaded their fingers together and surged against her ardently. "I could stay inside you like this forever."

Jude fell apart, sobbing into the mattress as her body convulsed ecstatically. Diana closed her eyes, then lowered their arms beneath Jude's chest so she could hold Jude tight and offer comfort during the powerful climax. The orgasm—or orgasms, Diana couldn't tell—stretched on for minutes. Every time she felt certain Jude was nearly finished, that her pleasure was dwindling, she'd let out another roar as her body came back to life. Diana murmured into her hair throughout the violent eruptions, praising her every way she knew how. Nuzzling Jude's damp neck, Diana told her how proud she was, how impressed.

Then finally, Jude shouted, "Stop! No more!"

It wasn't her safe word, but there was no mistaking Jude's tone. Diana cut power to the vibrator and ceased moving. "You okay?"

"Yeah." Jude's shoulders were shaking—with mirth, Diana soon realized. Thank goodness. "Except my clit can't take anymore…and my butt is pretty well over it, too."

Amused, Diana raised her upper body off Jude's and eased back an inch. "Help me."

Jude expelled the toy without any problem. "Damn, that feels weird."

"Indeed." Diana stood to remove her harness, then tossed it, the attached dildo, and the other stray items into her bag. Time to pack up. "But before the weirdness, it's actually rather magical. Don't you agree?"

Jude's hand brushed over the seat of her panties, making Diana jump in surprise. She whirled around to find her breathtakingly nude assistant looking up at her as though Diana were an oasis surrounded by endless desert. "Those were the best, strongest orgasms I've ever had."

Unable to help herself, Diana brushed a lock of hair away from Jude's eyes, then caressed her cheek. "Good."

"Please…" Jude moved her hand between Diana's legs but didn't make contact with the soaked panties. "*Ma'am.*"

Jude knew exactly what buttons to push, didn't she? "Yes, sweetheart?"

"May I give you an orgasm, too?"

She already knew she wasn't strong enough to refuse, but Diana needed Jude to work for it anyway. "You did, my darling. You must've felt me getting off all over your tight ass?"

"Yes, but…" Jude's imploring stare melted the last of her resistance. "Please, may I do it again?"

Diana knew she needed to leave—soon, before this got even messier—but she lacked the will to deny either of them what they both craved. Planting her right foot on the corner of the mattress, she yanked the crotch of her panties aside. "Go ahead."

Jude ducked her head and wrapped one arm around the back of Diana's thighs, then used her free hand to part Diana's labia and lick between the slick folds. Sighing against Diana's wetness, she lapped up her copious juices like a ravenous wildcat. Diana pulsated against Jude's silky tongue, knees buckling. The arm around her thighs tightened, a valiant but only somewhat effective attempt to keep her on her feet.

"Shit." Diana forced Jude's head away from her crotch, then grabbed her arm to haul her off the bed and onto the carpet. "Kneel." Trading places, Diana sat on the mattress and opened her legs, then curled her hand around the back of Jude's neck to drag her forward. "Get me off fast. No teasing, or I'll stop you and take care of it myself."

"Yes, ma'am," Jude said, the words muffled by the labia in her mouth. She did precisely as Diana asked, sucking her clit between pursed lips and batting it with her expert tongue. Jude's moans reverberated through Diana as she worked her over with infectious, diligent enthusiasm.

Diana reclined on one elbow, fingers curled around the back of Jude's neck to maintain the illusion of control. "Look at me," she commanded, and when Jude did—raising bright, hopeful eyes for her to drown in— Diana shattered to pieces in her warm, wet mouth. The orgasm was superb, building and building until it couldn't possibly get any more intense, then building some more. Diana thrashed against Jude urgently, seeking out and taking every last thrill she could wrench from the talented tongue on her clit. Hating that Jude could make her feel so much more than anyone ever had, even Janine, she clasped the head between her thighs and fucked Jude's gorgeous face, full of conflicted, vehement anger and unwelcome love. Finally, when she felt like she might burst, Diana shoved Jude away and slammed her legs shut. "That's enough."

Jude toppled bare-assed and panting onto the floor. She gave Diana a tentative smile, licking the cum off her lips. "I could've stayed *there* forever."

The callback to her overly intimate pillow talk sobered Diana in a heartbeat, engaging the part of her brain responsible for self-protection against emotion-fueled stupidity. But before she could get up and flee, Jude climbed onto the bed, then Diana's lap, and drew her into a heated kiss. Afraid of the hurt she would inflict by pushing Jude off, but even more terrified of being seduced into staying the night, Diana broke away with an apologetic wince. Taking Jude by the upper arms, she carefully deposited her onto the mattress at her side. "Unfortunately…forever's not an option."

"Then how about a few more minutes?" Jude placed her hand on Diana's inner thigh but made no attempt to touch her vulva. "I bet I could give you another. I'll do whatever you want."

Though she still hadn't fully recovered, Diana forced herself to stand and collect the rest of her scattered supplies. The offer was too tempting. *Jude* was too tempting. Wanting to be clear but not rude, Diana joked, "Still horny after the dirty, *filthy* things I just did to you? My, my. I'm thinking it's lucky I just trained you to be a highly shareable fuck toy, Ms. Monaco, because it appears there's no sating *this* sex kitten."

"I don't have to touch you again. Just…" All of a sudden Jude sounded like a lost, stoic little girl, desperate to show a brave face even if she didn't feel that way on the inside. Diana's heart clenched, and she turned away, tucking the bottle of lube into her bag before she gingerly knelt to gather her clothing from the floor. Jude watched her calculated escape with sad, resigned eyes. "I have some chocolate-chip-cookie-dough ice cream in the freezer. Maybe we could talk for a few minutes? Like a debrief."

Diana went still, unsure how to respond to the seemingly innocuous invitation. Eating ice cream wasn't inherently intimate, but where Jude was concerned nothing felt safe. Every interaction they had lured Diana deeper in love and farther from the core tenets keeping her safe in a world where women like Janine hid in plain sight. Did she truly believe that ice cream with Jude, or even another orgasm, would inevitably lead her back into misery and abuse? Not really. No. But then she'd never imagined Janine assaulting her, either.

"I'm not trying to be pushy." Jude's smile appeared forced. "Promise. I just—"

"Jude." Diana didn't let her finish, afraid to be won over. "You aren't pushy, and it's fine that you asked. I don't think it's a smart idea, that's all. I hope you understand."

Jude's defeated, watery nod suggested that she didn't. "Sure. I get it." She folded her arms over her chest, hiding her bare breasts from view. "Well, thanks for coming over. This really did make me feel better about Saturday."

And worse about everything else, judging by your face. Diana hated to leave Jude distraught, but this was supposed to be the first test of their joint ability to have casual, unpaid, obligation-free sex. She refused to let either of them fuck up, because the thought of losing this tenuous friendship was more excruciating than any pain Janine had ever inflicted. Short of losing Ava or her aging parents, Diana couldn't imagine anything worse. *I'm already in too deep.*

The realization propelled Diana to the bedroom door. "I'll text you, okay? We'll touch base before the workshop, debrief and all that, maybe tomorrow. Or early Saturday. We can hash out the details later. Okay?"

Twisting at the waist, Jude watched her go with a dejected nod. "Sure."

"You were amazing tonight, Jude." Unreasonably, Diana didn't want to leave without seeing Jude smile one last time. No doubt because she'd never felt like a more giant, irredeemable jerk. "Even better than I'd imagined."

Jude seemed almost stung by the compliment. "Thanks," she said, looking away from the door as she hugged her upper body even tighter. "You, too."

Worried she was only making things worse—and that she might crumble and end up staying after all—Diana told herself she could make her apologies over text later. Still, her feet refused to move until she'd offered a weak justification for the hasty exit. "I'm not leaving because I *don't* care about you. You know that, right?"

"I know." Jude sniffled, then unpeeled her fingers from her arm to wave her out the door. "Go, Diana, really. I'm fine." She glanced at Diana, a familiar spark in her eyes. "I just need a few minutes to recover. Then I'll most likely take a bath and sleep like a baby until tomorrow afternoon."

Diana laughed, relaxing at Jude's lighter tone. "Brilliant plan. Maybe I'll do the same."

At the momentary curve of Jude's lips into a subdued smile, Diana flashed an over-wide grin and walked out the bedroom door. Her grin faded the instant she crossed the threshold, then vanished entirely as she tossed on her clothes and fled like the coward she was.

Jude waited until she heard the outer door of her apartment click shut, then collapsed into a pathetic heap at the edge of her bed. Emptiness far too vast to comprehend washed over her and, with it, heartache of a magnitude she hadn't suffered in years. Not since her mother chose her dickhead boyfriend over the daughter she'd spent ten years raising on her own, letting Jude run away from home to grow up far too soon. Her chest ached as though Diana had literally ripped out her heart to take home with the rest of her toys. Despite still registering Diana's presence deep inside her pleasantly sore ass, the distance between them had never felt vaster.

Jude surrendered to the tears that flowed, craving some measure of release after all she'd just experienced. She'd been fucked in the ass, legitimately, and loved everything about the way it made her feel, except for the aftermath, when Diana ran like usual. But what had she expected? Diana had always been clear about what she wanted from their association. Sex, maybe even pseudo-friendship, but nothing too familiar. Sharing ice cream after an evening of transcendent, life-altering sex had never been a possibility. Why did Jude's foolish heart keep tricking her into thinking it was—or could be?

You really are so beautiful, Jude. Your body, your writing...your soul.

Gasping at the memory of Diana's impassioned declaration, Jude dug her nails into her arms until she punctured the skin. She needed her physical pain to supersede the emotional, because blood was easier than a fractured heart. If Diana was so adamant that they avoid intimacy, if she didn't want their sex to be personal, why *say* stuff like that? Why whisper words no one else ever had—meaningful words, words that made Jude feel special—like she actually meant them? Didn't she understand how deeply that cut? How it made her inevitable retreat a thousand times more excruciating for the lovesick fool left in her wake?

Because, yes, Jude *was* a fool—a fool Diana seemed perfectly content to tease.

A fool who couldn't take it any more.

CHAPTER TWENTY-THREE

Diana slid into the driver's seat of her car, shutting the door to watch Jude settle into the passenger side. Her lovely assistant had barely spoken since the workshop ended, offering only a handful of syllables in response to the small talk Diana attempted to initiate while they packed up to leave. Having finally reached the privacy of her vehicle, she intended to force whatever conversation Jude seemed determined not to have. "Hey." She touched Jude's arm, triggering a perceptible flinch. "Sweetheart, are you okay?"

Jude stared straight ahead at the parking garage wall, steadfastly avoiding her curious gaze. "I told you I'm fine." She rested her head against the seat and closed her eyes. "Just tired. Butt sex takes a lot out of me."

"You're not beating yourself up over not being able to take that last dildo, are you? Because I totally understood. It's a lot harder to relax with all those people watching. You were right to stop me, and honestly, it was valuable for the class to witness such a strong example of the receiving partner knowing and communicating her limits. I was seriously proud of the way you handled the situation. As far as I'm concerned, tonight was an unqualified success with or without the strap-on." Diana waited for a response that never came, wishing she knew how to penetrate the barrier Jude had thrown up. "If this mood you're in *isn't* about the strap-on, then please tell me what's got you so upset. I can't fix it if I don't know what's wrong."

Snorting, Jude muttered, "You couldn't fix it even if you did."

Diana broke into a cold sweat. What the hell had *happened*? They'd met early that morning at the diner down the street from their apartment building for pancakes and a hushed debrief of Thursday's meeting, and while the conversation hadn't been overly effusive, Diana had assumed the public venue was to blame. Driving to the workshop together that evening, they'd sung along to Queen on the radio, rocking out harder than Diana had in what felt like an entire lifetime. They hadn't done a lot of talking then, either, but she'd seen no sign of a yawning chasm opening up between them. Yet now she seemed to be standing at the edge of a horrific abyss, unable to fathom how she'd created such a tremendous distance. Tonight's sex hadn't exactly lived up to their practice session, but had Jude really expected it to? Why get so bent out of shape about less-than-perfect sex, anyway?

Was this even *about* tonight?

Afraid she already knew the answer—and why Jude doubted her ability to repair what was broken—Diana said, calmly, "Why don't you let me be the judge of that?"

Jude sighed, then whipped around to pin Diana with a borderline accusatory stare. "So what's the story with that last workshop you originally asked me to do? How to Make Love, I think you called it? You never bothered to mention if I still needed to be available." Hackles raised at Jude's confrontational tone, Diana took a measured breath before she answered. "You're right, and I'm sorry. Even with all my proselytizing to clients about the importance of communication, mine isn't always the greatest."

Jude scoffed. "Understatement."

Ignoring her bait, Diana went on. "I decided to change the topic and offer refunds to anyone who requested them. Only one couple took me up on that. I sent them a voucher to attend a future session free of charge, for their trouble. You know, on top of the refund. So anyway, yes…if you're free, I'd love your assistance next Saturday."

Jude's eyes glittered strangely, hinting at myriad ways this conversation could unfold—none of them good. "Care to let me in on the subject matter before I answer?"

"Facesitting and femmedom." Diana mustered an impish grin, aiming to win Jude over with their reliably incendiary sexual chemistry. "I assumed you would approve. As far as who gets to be on top…that's your call."

Jude stared at her without a trace of humor, looking at least a decade older than she had at breakfast. Her pretty face conveyed an alarming mix of frustration, sadness, and defeat, all of which caught Diana entirely off guard. Even more unsettling was the pure and utter *exhaustion* with which Jude regarded her, as though she'd already given up on Diana altogether. After a heavy pause, Jude confirmed her sick intuition. "Actually, I think I'm done. I think…" Her nostrils flared, the momentary crack in her armor revealing an inner torment she couldn't quite hide. "I can't do this anymore, with you. Sorry."

The abrupt end of whatever they'd been doing crashed over Diana like a tsunami, sweeping her into a dark, treacherous whirlpool of hopeless panic and despair. That Jude would simply cast her aside, and that she actually *gave a shit*, ignited a fiery rage inside her that kicked her defenses on at full blast. "Is this about the other night?" She loathed the venom in her voice, yet couldn't hold back a mean-spirited little jab. "Because I wouldn't stay and eat *ice cream*?"

Blinking rapidly, Jude faced forward in her seat, then curled up against the passenger door to hide the tears Diana knew she'd elicited. "Just take me home, please."

"With pleasure." Diana started the car, exhaling to clear her head before she backed out of the spot. A couple of blocks into their commute, she'd calmed enough to offer a more measured response. "Listen, Jude…I really am sorry for whatever I did to upset you this badly. If you *are* angry about Thursday night, and that ice cream, you should've told me this morning at breakfast. If only so I could've apologized before fucking you again. *Especially* in the ass." She didn't *want* to scold Jude, exactly, but she in no way appreciated the knowledge that she'd spent the past few hours inside the anus of a woman who apparently hated her guts. "No wonder you had trouble back there. You must've been incredibly tense."

"I was all right." Jude hesitated, then sighed. "Maybe I should've talked to you at breakfast, but it felt safer to wait until after the workshop. I didn't want to ruin everything and screw over your students in the process."

Diana's mind spun. Ruin *everything*? Flummoxed, she asked, "Ruin the workshop…over *ice cream*?"

Jude huffed, indignant for reasons Diana still couldn't discern. "This isn't about ice cream, okay? It's about taking care of myself." She hesitated, then said, "Of my heart, more than anything."

Diana tightened her fingers on the steering wheel. "How many times, exactly, did you swear to me you'd be okay with casual sex? More than once, for sure, but I'll admit…I lost count after a while."

"You're right. I *did* tell you I was okay to keep things casual—and usually I am. I really thought I could..." Jude's voice wavered, threatening to cool Diana's simmering resentment. "Except it turns out I can't, and I feel terrible I didn't realize it from the start. I honestly tried not to get attached, but...you've made me feel *so much*. I sincerely wish you didn't, believe me, but...here I am. I've fallen for a woman who will never reciprocate my feelings. A woman so averse to intimacy she can't even stay and chat for a few minutes after screwing me in the ass for the first time. Who was willing to leave me naked and alone after the most transformative, taxing—physically *and* emotionally—sex I'd ever had. That's not 'casual,' Diana. It's cold. And you know, maybe if you weren't so loving at other times, calling me 'baby' and 'sweetheart' and... and telling me how *beautiful* my writing and my soul are—" She took a shuddering breath. "Maybe this wouldn't hurt so much. Maybe I wouldn't even care."

If the car hadn't been in motion, Diana might've slammed her own head against the steering wheel from the burst of self-hatred that exploded inside her. She *knew* she'd gone too far that night, that she'd said too much. She'd long been prone to heartfelt declarations during moments of shared passion but had assumed Jude knew her well enough by now to understand that no matter what was said during sex, her policy against love and relationships remained in force. But now she realized how stupid that assumption had been, and selfish. Jude had never hidden her infatuation. Of course Diana's words mattered—every last one.

Diana sniffed. "You're right. I shouldn't have said those things to you." Trying to justify her lack of impulse control, she deflected the blame to the worst possible target. "I only wanted to make you feel good. To help you relax."

"Oh, so that's why you fill my head with bullshit? For *my* sake? To help *me?*"

Angry to have been cast as the villain for an arrangement they'd both agreed upon, Diana snapped, "Have I given you any reason to believe I want more from you than casual friendship with benefits? And by the way, calling you beautiful doesn't count, because of course you are, and I'm *positive* I'm not the first woman to tell you so."

Jude didn't speak for almost a full block. She found her voice when Diana stopped at the intersection, muttering a dejected, "I guess you haven't. That line about wanting to stay inside me forever..." She shrugged listlessly. "I get that it was just a thing to say."

Diana had to bite her tongue, literally, to stop the truth from pouring out. It *hadn't* simply been something to say. Unable to alleviate Jude's dismay, she opted instead for additional self-defense. "I feel like I've been incredibly upfront with you from the beginning."

"You have," Jude mumbled.

"You told me you understood, that you would be satisfied with an occasional fuck and no strings attached, that you'd respect my boundaries." Diana's throat constricted, and her vision went blurry. "You promised you wouldn't betray my trust. I thought we were *friends*."

"So did I." Sniffling, Jude wept quietly into the sleeve of her jacket. "But a real friend would've stayed with me that night. A few minutes longer, at least. A friend would've seen how much I needed her there and *stayed*."

"Fine. I'm a shitty friend." Diana wiped the moisture from her eyes, glad for the light traffic. Driving didn't exactly feel safe in her current state, but pulling over wasn't an option when it would mean trapping herself in the car with Jude even longer. "You want to end things over ice cream? Great. Thanks for proving my theory that fucking a millennial isn't worth the inevitable, kindergarten-level *bullshit* your generation seems to thrive on."

Diana regretted her derision even as she spat out the spiteful insults, but she was *mad*—so, so mad at Jude for fucking up an uncommonly gratifying friendship, at herself for not being more sensitive to Jude's feelings, and perhaps most of all, at Janine for creating a monster capable of reducing sweet, artistic, kind-hearted young Jude Monaco to silent, heartrending tears. "It would've saved us both a shitload of trouble if you'd been clearer about your feelings, like I was crystal fucking clear about mine."

She expected Jude to lash back—wanted her to, in fact—but instead Jude nodded. "I know. I *should've* been more honest...with you, and myself. But I'm a dumbass. A stupid, horny dumbass. I thought having sex with you could be enough. That I'd sate my curiosity about the woman who's played the lead role in my sex fantasies since the day she moved in and ideally put this ridiculous crush to rest in the process. Unfortunately, that's not how things worked out. You were...so much *more* than I imagined. Not just sex with you, although obviously...I mean, *obviously*..." Jude breathed out at length, as though fighting not to let whatever memory her brain had chosen to supply distract her. "You've made me feel safe, and supported—and, and *seen*." She barked helpless laughter. "Sometimes you also make me feel like shit, but that's a different story. That's Janine haunting us from the past."

If not for the even-keeled delivery, Diana would've erupted at the Janine comment—but Jude's restraint inspired her own. Jaw tight, she replied, "No, *that's* the cold bitch I've never denied being. The one only a dumbass would fall for."

"That's me." Jude rubbed the lingering tears from her eyes. "Look. All I know is that I can't keep lying about how I feel. You want this to be casual, but it's not. Not for me. That means I can't pretend not to give a shit about whether you stay for ice cream. Because I *do*."

Stunned by how badly she *did* want to fix this mess they'd made, Diana asked, "What if I worked on my friend skills? Meaning, no more taking off immediately after sex. And trying harder to consider your feelings before choosing my words."

"Diana…" Jude's apparent reluctance to go on hinted at what she planned to say.

"Fantastic." Pissed off to have gotten involved with a woman who had zero compunction about luring her into a pseudo-friendship under false pretenses, Diana mentally closed the door on the idea of Jude being anything other than her next-door neighbor and the second-worst mistake of her sexual life. "We're done, then. Thanks for subbing for Ava. Your help was very much appreciated. It was nice knowing you."

"Diana." Jude sounded desperate not to dissolve into fresh sobs. "Believe me, the last thing I want is to stop seeing you, but…I also don't want to be alone for the rest of my life. I'm not like you, okay? You may only need a casual friend who's willing to fuck you on occasion, but I happen to want the fairy tale. I'm sure that's silly or naive of me, but it's true. One day I hope to find a woman who loves me and sets me on fire. Someone I can love back just as fiercely. It doesn't feel right to lead you on with casual sex when I know that's not what I want anymore…and that I'll end things with you the second I meet the right woman."

Diana ground her teeth, seething at the agony Jude had chosen to inject into her well-ordered life. How many times had they talked through their respective positions before reaching this point? Had Jude listened to *anything* she'd said over the past six weeks? "I never asked for a commitment, Jude. That's the whole point."

"True, but I saw how upset you were after Ava told you she wanted to be monogamous with Katrina. When you suddenly realized you were alone, like for real *alone*, you weren't happy about it, were you? Despite your many protestations to the contrary." Diana tried to interject, but Jude steamrolled over her with another load of psychoanalysis. "It's clear you *do* want a lover in your life, but she can't have any expectations. She can't get too close. Maybe I *could* be that person for you a while longer… and maybe I should, because this sucks—turning you down *sucks*—but eventually, I will want more. And I don't want to hurt someone I care about to get it."

What do you think you're doing now? Diana stifled the comeback, knowing it would be unfair to say that aloud. Instead, she asked, "You didn't consider any of this before we decided to sleep together on our own time? Surely you knew then that this 'fairy tale' romance fantasy was your ultimate goal? Why this sudden altruism about not wanting to hurt me once you inevitably find your hypothetical lady knight in shining armor?"

"I won't pretend this is entirely selfless. As much as I don't want to hurt you, I also don't want to hurt myself anymore, either. Being with you, but without *being* with you…rips me apart inside. I'm so tired of being sad, Di. Tired of not being able to write because I'm sad. Tired of waiting for someone who'll never feel the same." Jude sucked in a sharp breath, bending at the waist to drop her head into her hands. "It's killing me. If I'd known how bad this was going to feel…I don't know."

Diana glowered out the front windshield, lamenting that she'd *paid* for this heartbreak. "I should have never hired you."

"Don't say that," Jude choked out.

"It was a mistake." Gritting her teeth, Diana muttered, "I've got a real knack for those."

Jude released a tremulous sigh, then shook her head, defeated. "You know what's the saddest part? How badly I *do* want to keep fucking you, still, because this idiotic voice inside my head won't stop whispering that maybe, you know…*maybe.* Even after everything. But that would be bad for both of us, and I think you know it, too." She dropped her hands but kept her face lowered. "I regret telling you I could be content with just sex. I didn't intend to mislead you. I just…thought I'd be able to handle it."

"Sounds like this was a real learning experience for you." Diana had never been more relieved to turn onto their street or eager to eject Jude from her car and life. "Glad to have provided the fodder."

"Diana…"

"Stop saying my goddamn name," Diana snapped, fully aware of how immature she sounded. "It's no big deal. I hired you to do six workshops, maybe seven, and you did six workshops. We only slept together once outside of class, strictly to practice. Now you don't want to work for me anymore, and you don't want to sleep with me either. Wonderful. Let's move on."

"I'm so sorry, Diana, for all of this. You were so adamant about avoiding drama, and here I've poisoned your life with a big fat dose of it. I don't blame you for feeling like you were right all along." Jude paused, and for a moment neither of them spoke as Diana drove into the lot. But then, likely prompted by the impending end of their time together, Jude blurted one final slap across the face. "'I'm not leaving because I *don't* care about you.' Isn't that what you said? Same applies here. As much as I love you and want to see you happy, I can't get trapped in this place with you. I have bigger plans, and a brighter future, than anything you can offer."

Diana backed into her assigned spot and parked, but left the engine running. "Does that conclude your little speech? Or did you want to keep going? Maybe tell me more about how sorry you are, and how bitter and lonely and pathetic you think I am."

"Diana—"

"I said *shut the fuck up* with your goddamn *Diana*s." The reprimand exploded out of her in a loud roar. Instantly shamed when Jude flinched away, Diana dialed down her volume and snarked, "Like you actually give a shit about me, or my feelings. Go on. Get out of my car. Leave me alone."

Jude unbuckled her seat belt, hands visibly trembling. "We obviously need time apart, but maybe at some point…" Warily, she turned to face Diana head-on. "Maybe someday we could try to be friends. Just without the benefits."

Diana dismissed the idea with an exaggerated roll of her eyes. "I don't need a friend, thanks. Especially not a lying brat who has trouble keeping her pants on."

Jude recoiled as though she'd been physically struck, then reached behind her hip to clumsily open the passenger-side door. "That works out great, then, because I actually don't have room for a bitter old shrew in my life, either."

"How serendipitous." Diana drummed her fingers on the steering wheel to hold off the emotional breakdown she felt coming. "Now would you kindly get the fuck out of my vehicle?"

Jude scrambled out of the passenger seat but hesitated to close the door. After a moment of apparent indecision, she bent to peer into the car with a difficult-to-read frown. "You aren't going upstairs?"

"Where I'm going is none of your business." Diana had no idea where she'd land for the night, but sure as hell not upstairs with Jude. "Right?"

"Fair enough." Jude straightened, finally in position to close the car door. "Just…be safe tonight, all right? Please."

"Because you *care?*" Diana sneered. Her pain was too raw to temper, and also, she needed Jude to storm off so she could fall apart in peace. "How sweet. Now shut the door and walk away…before I get ugly."

Muffling a sob, Jude shot back, "Too late." She slammed the car door with a growled "*Bitch.*" With that, Jude did precisely as Diana had asked, even if it wasn't what either of their hearts wanted.

She walked away.

CHAPTER TWENTY-FOUR

Lying facedown on her couch, Jude sobbed into her favorite throw pillow like a teenager suffering her first broken heart. She felt ridiculous crying over a relationship she'd always been told would never happen, but there was no other way to ease her agony except to let it escape however her body demanded. Anyway, she *was* ridiculous. The past month and a half proved it.

Diana had been right. Naked utterings aside, she'd never given Jude any reason to believe their relationship could transcend the staunchly casual, sometimes paid arrangement they'd both agreed upon. That Jude had gone ahead and developed feelings anyway was her own damn fault. Despite Diana's slight thaw over the past six weeks—evolving from her hard policy against any sort of fraternization, to a tentative friendship, to embracing the additional benefits that could accompany such a friendship—she'd never wavered on the question of love and dating. She'd *always* been clear about what she desired: sex, and *only* sex.

Being a dumbass, Jude had simply failed to listen.

And now she was useless, too depressed to sit up and play video games, let alone work on her novel. Jude tried to remember the last time she'd written more than a few words. *Fat lot of good this workshop money does me when I've just murdered my creative spirit on the altar of unrequited love.* Her sobbing intensified.

A knock on the door saved her from drowning in a puddle of her own salty tears. Jude sat up, blinking as she looked around in a daze. After the second knock, she forced herself off the couch and onto unsteady feet. She opened her mouth to call out, then snapped it shut, afraid the unexpected visitor might be Diana—but even more afraid it wasn't.

"Jude?" Her knees turned to water at the soothing timbre of Katrina's voice. "Honey? I'm letting myself in, all right? With my key."

Spared from having to drag herself across the room, Jude dropped onto the couch with a heavy sigh. She moved to wipe away her tears for the hundredth time, then stopped. Why bother? They'd surely return as soon as Katrina asked her what was wrong. When her apartment door swung open a moment later, Jude greeted her cousin with a feeble wave. "Hey."

"Shit." Muttering, Katrina locked the door and rushed to the couch. She sank down next to Jude, taking both her hands in a fretful grip. "What did Diana do?" When Jude didn't answer, Katrina gave her fingers an insistent squeeze. "Honey, what did she *do?*"

Embarrassed to have caused such alarm, Jude shook her head, eyes clamped shut to delay the inexorable flow. "Nothing."

"She's obviously done *something.*" Katrina let go of Jude's hands to haul her into a warm hug. "Ava got a call maybe a half hour ago—right after your workshop ended, apparently—from Diana, asking to come over. I could hear her over the speakerphone, and she was *not* okay. She was actually so distraught that Ava suggested I come here and check on you to make sure you were okay."

Jude buried her face in Katrina's shoulder, grateful for a friendly place to leak despair. "Diana hates me."

Katrina snorted and tightened her arms. "I doubt that very much."

"Believe me...after tonight, she does. But I couldn't keep pretending I didn't care that she barely treats me like a friend unless we're actively fucking." Jude cried into Katrina's shirt, sheepish about being this undone by a breakup she'd initiated. "So I told her I couldn't have sex with her anymore, and now she hates me."

"First...anyone who hates you for not having sex isn't worth fucking in the first place." Katrina rubbed big, calming circles over her back. "Second, Diana does *not* hate you." Kissing her hair, Katrina rocked Jude gently within the protective embrace. "I have that on good authority. You may have broken her heart, and I imagine she's disappointed to lose you as a sex partner, but I *promise* she doesn't actually loathe you."

Jude bit her lip, embarrassed by how badly she wanted to believe that. "You didn't hear her, Kat. She was furious."

"Because you're refusing to play by her rules." Katrina eased away to meet Jude's watery gaze. "And she isn't ready to lose you."

Jude attempted to scoff, wary of allowing a single shred of her foolish hope to survive the night. Yet deep down, she still couldn't believe that Diana didn't feel anything for her at all, even if only faint affection. Pillow talk might be meaningless to an extent, but those tender sentiments came from *somewhere*. Of the myriad ways Diana could've helped her relax, of all the words she might have chosen, she'd decided to not just compliment Jude's body, but also her cherished creative soul. *Who delivers lines like those to a slut she doesn't care about?* Based on what little she knew about the woman, not Diana Kelley.

Hesitant to be fooled again, Jude asked, "Do you say that because *you* think I'm too awesome to lose, or because Ava told you Diana actually felt that way?"

"Both. Ava genuinely believes Diana is falling for you. I'm somewhat sworn to secrecy about this subject, but...you deserve to know that much. Diana is guarded about her feelings, even with Ava, but she's said—and done—enough to convince Ava that you're special to her in some way. According to Ava, that you two have been sexual outside of class is hugely significant. Even more so because you live next door, which massively heightens the potential for drama."

"Case in point," Jude mumbled, miserable about being trapped within what felt more and more like a no-win situation. "I don't know how I'm going to deal with running into her at the mailbox, or the elevator—or God forbid, the laundry room—after the fight we had." Overwhelmed by how thoroughly she'd destroyed her reasonably happy existence thanks to one wrongheaded move, she hugged Katrina tighter. "Maybe I'll move. It wouldn't be terrible to find a cheaper place."

"Do me a favor and hold off on making any big decisions for at least a week. Maybe two." Katrina pushed a damp lock of hair away from Jude's eyes. "Let's see what happens first."

Jude knew that was good advice but argued anyway, mostly for the sake of arguing. "It's not like Diana will change her mind. Anyway, even if she *did* forgive me for getting involved despite having feelings, that won't make it any less painful to see her around. If anything, it'll be worse. Not to mention...if I have to hear her through the wall, you know, fucking some other woman..." She swallowed. "I might actually puke."

"I understand." Katrina smiled carefully. "But you should still wait."

Slipping from Katrina's embrace, Jude reclined against the arm of the couch, grumbling, "Yes, Mom."

"Look, you need to give Diana time to process. It sounds like you dropped a real bomb on her tonight." Katrina pulled Jude's socked feet into her lap and started a gentle massage of the soles. "Okay, so she had a shitty, knee-jerk reaction. That doesn't mean she won't come around once she's had a chance to think about what she loses by letting you go."

"Diana doesn't give a shit about losing me." Jude glowered as the very worst of her dark thoughts rose to the surface, even the ones she didn't fully believe. "All she cares about is having a warm, wet cunt available at her convenience. That's it. She's pissed she lost two sex partners in the same month, not depressed that Jude Monaco won't be in her life anymore."

"You make her sound so indifferent." Katrina traced a fingernail along the arch of Jude's foot, making her jerk, then snort. "Which is *definitely* bullshit. If Diana felt it was worth the personal risk to be with you outside a professional setting, she clearly isn't indifferent. But I think you know that."

"Do I?" Jude wasn't ready to relinquish her negativity. "I'm halfway decent at sex. She was horny." Throat raw, she said, "The end."

"Right. Because Diana couldn't possibly find another woman willing to go to bed with her." Katrina pinched Jude's big toe. "Therefore she was forced to settle for her lesbian next-door neighbor."

Jude knew how to convince Katrina of Diana's lack of concern— even if doing so would compound her misery a thousand fold. "Want to know how much Diana cares? Last Thursday, she came by my apartment so we could rehearse for tonight's workshop, which was Intro to Anal Sex, by the way, if you were curious."

Katrina didn't flinch. "Was that your first time having sex outside work? I mean *physical* sex. I know about the dirty texts and listening to each other through the wall and all that."

"You do?" Jude hadn't shared any of those details, which implied that Diana had confided in Ava about their minor indiscretions. What did that mean, if anything? "But yeah, that was the first time." Her voice caught as she reflected on the seminal event. "And *my* first time. Having anal sex, I mean. On that level."

"Okay." Katrina's pleasant tone carried no judgment. "How was it? For Diana's sake, I hope she made the experience positively wonderful for you."

"Oh God, Kat…" Jude drew in a tremulous breath before surrendering to a fresh round of tears. "The sex was *unreal.* I've never felt anything like it before. Pleasure upon pleasure…upon *ecstasy*." She shivered at the memory of Diana holding her and whispering those beautiful lies, as the dildo in her ass and the vibrator inside her sent her to heaven for minutes on end. "The last time I came that night, Diana was on top of me, and inside me, whispering in my ear."

It took all her strength to repeat the meaningless praise that had ushered their non-relationship toward its demise. "She said…I really was *so* beautiful. My body, my…my writing. My *soul*, even. She said she could stay inside me forever." Hiding the quaver in her voice with bitter laughter, Jude spat, "What a fucking joke when less than ten minutes later I was begging her to stay—only a few more minutes, so we could talk about what I'd just experienced—and she barely treated me like a friend. Meaning she couldn't run away fast enough. I've never slept with someone who made me feel so worthless. I don't ever want to feel that way again."

"I understand why you were hurt, truly, but…" Katrina appeared to wage a brief internal battle before unexpectedly leaping to Diana's defense. "Don't you think it's possible that Diana bolted because she *does* return your feelings? It sounds like you had an unbelievably intimate encounter. I'd guess far more intimate than she anticipated. For me, it's more plausible that the woman who called you a beautiful soul simply panicked about where 'a little longer' might lead, as opposed to 'she just doesn't give a fuck.'"

"This wasn't the first time we've had intimate sex." Cheeks hot, Jude said, "From my perspective, that is."

"But it *was* the first time without some sort of protective buffer. Like, say, a room full of horny ladies to study your every move?"

Jude shrugged, still hesitant to believe Diana's words. "How can someone be so terrified of after-sex ice cream that their only recourse is to abandon a friend who clearly isn't okay?"

Katrina bit her lip. "Listen, I'm not sure how much Diana has told you about her past—"

"I know about Janine." Jude reconsidered that claim. "A little. I know *a little* about Janine."

"From what I've heard, Diana's ex is a complete piece of shit. Manipulative, cruel, even abusive—in more ways than one." Katrina stroked Jude's feet, holding the stare she received in response. "Ava wonders if she still suffers from post-traumatic stress. That would make sense, given that Diana once confessed that she feared for her life during

Janine's worst rages. A relationship like that has to create a lasting impact, right? Living for years with someone you fear might actually kill you one day?"

Jude lowered her gaze, reminded of the lingering pain caused by the man her mother had favored over her. "I know those scars don't automatically vanish once you're away from whoever inflicted them. I just…I *needed* her, Kat. And she damn well knew it."

Katrina nodded. "Well, if you can't cope with the arrangement you and Diana made, you're right not to stay in it for her sake. At the end of the day, your first obligation is to your own mental health."

Jude tipped her head, agreeing without feeling. "I know. That's why I told her I couldn't help out at next weekend's workshop. Or see her in any capacity, at least for a while." Her nostrils flared. "Possibly forever." Voice breaking, she whispered, "She was *livid*, Kat. Just…*enraged*."

"She's hurt," Katrina said. "You know she is."

"She's angry I agreed to casual sex I didn't actually want. She realizes, as I do, that I could've been more realistic about my feelings from the word go. She told me right away that she wasn't open to any type of relationship, ever. Meanwhile, I *knew* I wasn't satisfied with long-term casual sex as a lifelong aspiration." Jude's jaw quivered. "I deceived her, basically, so I could sleep with her. And now she knows it."

"Listen to me. 'Casual' implies a distinct lack of lifelong commitment. That you agreed to a no-strings-attached arrangement without intending to sleep with Diana forever shouldn't cause you any guilt." Katrina scooted closer, seeming eager to offer comfort even if unsure how. "Weren't you always honest about having a crush? Don't beat yourself up because those feelings deepened over time. You couldn't have predicted Diana would warm up or allow you closer. How could you have known that your relationship would become more intimate than Diana told you it'd be? You promised not to push for anything other than casual sex, and you didn't. When you realized you needed more than Diana was able to give, you got out. Rather than nag her for more than she wants to give, you chose to walk away. You kept your word."

"The other interpretation would be that I got Diana emotionally invested in a new sexual relationship, only to cut ties less than two weeks later. Lured her in, then shoved her away." Jude's stomach turned at the thought of how her behavior had reinforced Diana's distaste for personal entanglements. "Leaving may have been the right call, but that doesn't excuse the fact that I did something shitty. After working so hard to convince her I would be content with whatever she was willing to give, however little that might be…" Swallowing her self-disgust, Jude dabbed at her flushed, tear-streaked cheeks. "She looked *so* betrayed, Kat. And I just feel ashamed, and embarrassed, and stupid…but most of all, unfair. Diana told me exactly what she wanted. I'm the dumbass who refused to believe her."

Katrina tugged her into another desperate embrace. "You're not a dumbass."

"No?" Sinking deeper, Jude reached into the past to bolster her self-flagellation. "I seem to recall you saying otherwise when I used to sell myself to pay the rent."

"Jude." Katrina wove her fingers into the hair at the base of Jude's skull, cradling her closer. "I'm sorry for the stupid shit I said back then. I was scared for you, that's all. You were doing your best in a bad situation. Your mom was the dumbass, forcing a seventeen-year-old to fend for herself."

Uninterested in rehashing the manner in which she had escaped her wretched childhood, Jude kissed Katrina's hair and mumbled, "I love you."

"I love you, too." Katrina relaxed her grip. "Also, I couldn't help but notice that you just acknowledged Diana's emotional investment in whatever you two were doing." She paused to allow for a rebuttal, but Jude had lost the energy for that particular crusade. "Drop the 'she doesn't give a shit' crap, will you? We both know that's not true."

Baffled by Katrina's compassion for all parties, Jude asked, "Why are you sticking up for her?"

"Because I have empathy for both of you." Katrina drew back to look Jude in the eyes. "Also because Ava loves her, and Ava is one of the best people I've ever met. And…" She blew out a nervous breath. "And because if Ava asks me to marry her one day…I think I will."

Jude's mind boggled. "*Seriously?*"

Katrina met her incredulity with a solemn nod. "I love her, Jude. I think…the same way my mom and dad love each other."

Having witnessed the unshakable bond between their joint love-and-marriage role models, Jude instantly gleaned how Ava had become this important to Katrina, this quickly. "That's wonderful, Kat. Congrats." She tried in vain to extinguish the envy simmering in her gut. "I'm glad my time with Diana amounted to something." Her chin wobbled. "For someone."

Katrina pouted in sympathy. "I'm sorry to have somehow stumbled upon exactly what you'd hoped to find with Diana, essentially by accident. I feel awful that my happiness had to come at your expense."

Jude shook her head, chastened by Katrina's unselfish recognition of her point of view. "I'm thrilled for you. I mean it." She managed a weak chuckle. "After all those losers you've dated—"

Katrina poked Jude in the side. "There haven't been *that* many losers."

"True." Jude winked, enjoying the lighthearted affront she'd caused. "One reason among many I'm elated to have introduced you to someone who excites you this much. I know you've always wanted a love like your parents'. A lofty goal, admittedly…but one I'd endure any amount of heartache to help you achieve." She laced her fingers through Katrina's and mustered a genuine smile. "You saved my life when my mother wouldn't. Who knows where I'd be if you hadn't taken me in? You always made sure I was safe…and *writing*. I would do anything for you."

Katrina blinked, causing twin tears to roll down her cheeks and meet at her chin. "Thank you. I just wish I could do something for you. Find some way to get through to Diana—"

"No." Jude shook her head emphatically. "Please, just let this go. For me."

"Whatever you want." Katrina searched Jude's eyes, her expression shadowed by guilt. "Will you do something for me in return?"

Jude assumed she already knew what Katrina wanted. "Don't start apartment-hunting until after next weekend?"

Nodding, Katrina lifted Jude's hand to her lips and sprinkled light kisses across her knuckles. "Pretty please." She moved Jude's palm to rest against her warm cheek, a gesture of affection that brought fresh tears to Jude's eyes. "If Ava and I *do* end up together, life will be so much easier for everyone if you and Diana are able to stay on good terms. Suddenly moving out would almost certainly throw fuel onto an already raging firestorm."

Jude snorted. "I'm not sure why you think Diana *wouldn't* be relieved to see me leave, but like I said, I'll do anything for my favorite cousin. Even if what you want from me totally sucks."

"That's my girl." Katrina released her with a final kiss on the cheek, then stood. She turned toward the kitchen with an expression of steely determination. "Now for the most important question of the night: cupcakes, brownies, or Rice Krispies Treats? You choose, I'll make, and we'll spend the rest of tonight pigging out in front of British baking-show reruns."

Grateful that Katrina had refrained from offering ice cream, Jude grabbed her hand for one last, adoring squeeze. "Rice Krispies Treats. If marshmallows and butter can't fix this, nothing will."

Katrina's answering grin was tinged by sorrow. "Nothing but time." She stroked Jude's hair, radiating love. "Give it time."

CHAPTER TWENTY-FIVE

Diana startled awake, excruciatingly aware of not being in her own bed. She relaxed at the sight of Ava's kind brown eyes returning her stare and sighed as her muscles unclenched by a degree. The soreness in her eyes as she blinked away the sleep brought back her memory of the previous evening in a sickening rush. The workshop. Realizing something felt off with Jude, then confronting her about it in the car. Their argument during the drive home. Kicking Jude out of her car in the parking lot and driving away in tears. Pulling over only three blocks away to text Ava through uncontrollable sobs and also berate herself for being an even stupider version of the woman who'd once wasted six years of her life trying to please a jealous, abusive, narcissistic asshole. After that, showing up at Ava's apartment after ten o'clock, wildly upset but unprepared to share the gory details. And finally, drifting off into a troubled sleep haunted by bad dreams she'd already forgotten, comforted by the close proximity of her one true friend.

"Good morning," Ava murmured, grazing her knuckles over Diana's cheek. "How'd you sleep?"

"Like shit." Diana yawned and let her eyes slip shut. "Don't wanna wake up."

"I know, sweetie." Ava tenderly fingered a lock of her hair. "But you can't stay in bed forever."

"Why not?" Grumbling, Diana opened one eye and scowled. "It's warm, and cozy, and you're here."

"All true." Gently, Ava said, "On the other hand, this'll get mighty awkward when Katrina shows up for our next unpaid—and highly unconventional—physical therapy session. As I've been fantasizing about going down on my lovely caregiver for approximately seventy-five of the seventy-six minutes I've been awake, that moment could arrive far sooner than you think."

Diana sighed at the blatant reminder that Ava had landed herself a hot young girlfriend to fuck—while bedridden with a broken spine, no less. "I'll go," she said, sitting up. "I appreciate you letting me stay the night. Tell Katrina I'm sorry for crashing your party."

"Wait." Ava latched onto Diana's forearm before she could leave. "Not until you tell me what happened."

Wishing she could believe her own lies, Diana feigned nonchalance. "It's honestly not that big a deal. Jude unexpectedly announced that she wanted to quit, and then we argued, and for some reason the entire situation made me *way* overly emotional...I'm sure because I was tired. And hormonal. At any rate, I'm feeling one-hundred percent better after sleeping it off."

"Cut the bullshit." Ava's harshness caught Diana by surprise, making her heart temporarily race. "Seriously, *enough*. Stop acting like you don't care, when we both know you do. Now, please explain why you spent a solid hour crying in my arms before you finally passed out last night? What in the world did Jude say to leave you in that state?"

"Nothing." Diana tugged her arm from Ava's grasp. "Just that she was done and can't have sex with me anymore. Because she doesn't do casual now. With every other woman in the Bay Area, sure. But not with me." She huffed, annoyed by Jude's seemingly inevitable immaturity, but even more so by her own failure to avoid the heartache she'd long known their association would bring. "She thinks she has feelings for me. Real ones. The kind that apparently make it impossible for her to accept that I don't want to hang out and eat ice cream after we're done fucking."

"Why not?" Ava quirked a good-humored smile. "Post-orgasmic ice cream is the bomb."

"Because we're fuck buddies. And I'd put us at about ninety-percent fuck, ten-percent buddies." Diana shifted as her discomfort grew, tempted to simply get up and leave Ava's apartment. *It's not like she can chase me if I do.* Ignoring her worst instincts, Diana touched Ava's wrist but avoided her gaze. "It would've been too intimate if I'd stayed." Not quite under her breath, she admitted, "It was already too intimate."

"Meaning?"

Diana threw her hands into the air. "Meaning I should've kept my damn mouth shut so I didn't talk to her one way, then treat her another.

Honestly…I can't blame her for being upset. Of course, I did last night… blame her. Even snapped at her. Called her a child for getting bent out of shape over a bowl of ice cream…except I knew it wasn't about the stupid chocolate chip cookie dough. She was upset because I might as well have told her I loved her. Whispering into her ear about how beautiful she is… some pseudo-romantic nonsense about 'your body, your writing, your soul.'" Diana grimaced. How had she let herself spin so out of control? "Naturally I was inside her ass at the time—her *first* time."

Ava admonished her with a frown. "You're telling me you fucked that girl in the butt—becoming the very first person to ever enjoy that privilege—while whispering a bunch of sweet, poetic nothings into her ear…then *berated her* for being wounded that you refused to stay and talk afterward? Keeping it real, Diana…you can be such a *jerk* sometimes. Never more so than when that false sense of security of yours is threatened."

"I know," Diana mumbled, too drained to defend the indefensible. "How could anyone ever love what I've become? This cold, frightened, empty shell of a person Janine used up and left behind."

"*Wrong.*" Ava tapped Diana's thigh with her fingers. "I told you, I've had more than enough of that horseshit. You're lovable, because *I* love you. Fucking deal with it."

Warmed by her best friend's steadfast loyalty and unfailingly foul mouth, Diana placed her hand over Ava's. "Yeah, but you're grandfathered in—*not* a jab at your age, by the way. Just, you knew me before. You love the Diana I used to be."

"No, sweetie, I love *you*. Then and now. That's why I hate seeing you close yourself off from the world, and slowly self-destruct, over a woman you had the courage to leave over five years ago." Ava placed her free hand atop Diana's knee, likely anticipating another attempt to flee the frank chat. "We've gone over this before, Di—more than once—but this time I'm begging you to *listen*. If you can't find a way to yank your head out of your ass and reclaim the life you've mistakenly convinced yourself Janine stole away, well…there's a more than decent chance you really *will* lose Jude. Forever."

"I don't want a girlfriend," Diana muttered, while trying to imagine for the first time how a relationship with Jude might look. Would they find anything to talk about, or was their connection purely physical? Could Jude cope with the burden of having an older, undeniably damaged girlfriend? Was there any real chance she'd stick around after meeting the Diana she rarely revealed to other people—a beaten, scared, silently defiant, lapsed true romantic who wanted more than anything to find refuge in the arms of someone she trusted without fear? If so, would that be enough to restore her faith in love?

Was she about to lose the love of her life?

That's exactly the sort of fairy-tale mentality that led me to Janine. Unable to dwell on the later years of their relationship without inviting more tears, Diana let her thoughts return to her most bittersweet memories: those of Janine as the dashing, intensely romantic older woman who'd once treated her like a princess—and sometimes even a queen.

Looking back, her ardent suitor had perhaps been a little *too* perfect. For the first year Janine's smile had never slipped as she spent her days effortlessly placing Diana in the center of her universe with a mere glance, or caress, or heartfelt declaration of undying love. Even before the smiles began to tighten, then fade, Diana had detected hints of Janine's jealously possessive nature. At first, she'd rationalized her new girlfriend's grumpiness about her favorite low-cut shirt and irritation with the woman who'd smiled at Diana on their way out of the bakery as proof of Janine's devotion to their storybook romance.

In hindsight, she realized she'd ignored warning signs because she'd so badly wanted to believe in Janine's all-consuming version of romantic love. To admit she'd been wrong about the person she'd told all her friends was the love of her life, then extract herself from such a powerful force of nature, ended up being the hardest thing Diana had ever done. So hard it took her half a decade to accomplish.

She couldn't afford to waste any more years on another misguided delusion.

"Jude isn't Janine." Addressing her unspoken anxiety, Ava repeated the now-familiar refrain with admirable patience. "Think about it, Di. They couldn't be more different. Jude is younger than you, and sweeter, and she respects your limits. She could've lied about her feelings, or tried to change your mind about dating, but she didn't. She let you go because that's what you claimed to want. She also doesn't share Janine's hang-ups about your sexuality."

"Right now, she doesn't. Who's to say she won't change her mind once we're together?"

"Anything is possible, I suppose. But doesn't that seem unlikely? Thanks to your paper-thin bedroom wall, I happen to know that Jude's always been…somewhat promiscuous. We're talking about a girl who agreed to let her next-door neighbor—a near-stranger thirteen years her senior—eat her out in front of a crowd of attentive women, for cash. Then signed up for more." Ava's words carried the slightest undercurrent of exasperation. "Can you *seriously* envision Jude screaming at you for showing off a little cleavage? Or flipping out because a stranger dared to glance your direction?"

Of course not. But that didn't make her feel any safer. "I swore I'd never give someone the power to hurt or control me again. You act like five years is such a long time, but I still can't imagine being comfortable enough to show weakness in front of someone who isn't you. Even if Jude and I dated for the *next* five years, I don't know that I'll ever be able to trust her intentions. So why ruin what I've managed to rebuild? Why set myself up for even more nights like the one I just endured?"

"Because it will be tragic to spend the rest of your life regretting that you didn't." Ignoring Diana's eye roll, Ava delivered a final, emotionally devastating argument. "What if being with Jude is precisely what you need to heal? Even if a relationship didn't work out...hell, even if she turns out to be a brat who breaks your heart...I wonder if this is how you finally get past Janine. Spending time with a beautiful, sexually submissive younger woman will help prove to you that not all potential love interests are jealous and cruel. Also, that your life is far from over." She paused for effect. "Unless you choose for it to be."

Diana's breathing faltered as she contemplated the agony of never again being with Jude. Never making her smile, or come. Never finding out her favorite book, or movie, or if she preferred dogs over cats—assuming she even liked animals at all. There was so much Diana didn't know, literally thousands of secrets she felt reluctantly compelled to uncover, and Ava wasn't wrong. Unless she could muster the bravery to change her ways, Jude would eventually disappear from her life forever. It wouldn't take long before Jude met someone new, someone young, and less broken, and infinitely more willing to risk it all for the possibility of true love. A kindred spirit. Whatever remaining affection Jude felt for her sad, lonely neighbor would evaporate, and she'd leave behind this chapter of her life without a backward glance. Abandoning Diana to her solitude.

Exactly like she purported to want.

Groaning, Diana admitted, "Fine, you're right. I *don't* want to lose Jude. But I'm terrified of being fooled again." The confession scraped against Diana's already raw throat on its way out. "What if we're both wrong about her? What if this is the worst advice you've ever dispensed?"

Ava chuckled. "Highly doubtful. But look, if Jude *does* end up being a literal nightmare, just dump her ass. Kick her to the curb." She touched Diana's shoulder, waiting for eye contact before she said, "Don't ever forget what a strong, resilient, badass survivor you've become, my love. One who refuses to take shit from anyone, especially the women invited to share your bed."

Diana's nose scrunched from her effort not to cry. She nodded, ducked her head so Ava wouldn't see her visible anguish, then bent to wrap her arms around her best friend's motionless body with a grateful sob. "I love you."

"I love you, too." Ava stroked her hair as though comforting a small, terrified child. Perhaps she was. "Do me a solid?"

Certain she knew what Ava wanted, Diana said, "I guess."

"Ask Jude out to dinner. On a real date, somewhere nice. If that goes well, ask her out again. Then again, for as long as you're happier with her than you would be without her. If that's only a week or two, great. Other fish, blah, blah, blah. But at least you'll have *tried*."

"And if she decides to end things with me?" By now it felt like arguing against destiny, but Diana didn't know how to give up this fight and welcome the pain and heartbreak she sensed looming in her future. "What if I do fall in love with Jude, only for her to finally realize that she's been sucked into the orbit of a bitter, ill-tempered old woman overburdened by more baggage than anyone should be forced to shoulder at the tender age of twenty-six? She may want to be my girlfriend now, but reality *will* set in at some point."

"If that happens, then you'll do some crying, and we'll drink wine and eat a pan of brownies—maybe two—while you tell me what a crap friend I was to force this issue. I assume you'll also swear off dating again for a while." Ava tickled her ribs. "Until another woman captures your attention."

Diana shook her head against Ava's shoulder. "Nope. Not interested."

"That's what you said about Jude, too."

"Jude's different." It terrified Diana to admit how much. "Or she was supposed to be. I only…" she exhaled. "Wish she hadn't pushed. Everything was going so well."

"Not for Jude." Ava rubbed Diana's shoulder, the fond caress in sharp contrast with the bluntness of her truth-telling. "Apparently."

"No." Diana struggled to swallow past the lump in her throat, unable to shake the memory of Jude's stricken expression as she'd packed up her butt plugs and bolted out the door. Or the weary, aged look in Jude's eyes when she'd ended their work partnership, along with whatever else they'd been doing. "I should've known better. What the fuck is wrong with me?"

"Nothing you can't overcome." Ava patted her. "You screwed up. Sucks, yeah, but it happens. Even to me. Just yesterday, I snapped at Kat for misplacing my favorite lighter. Turns out it'd gotten tucked beneath my pillow somehow, by me, I'm sure. What matters is how you proceed *after* a screw-up. What'll it be, Di? Will you double down out of pride, run away from the situation altogether, or get your shit together and beg forgiveness to the fullest extent of your abilities?"

Diana knew what she was supposed to say but struggled to verbally commit. She wasn't convinced she'd be able to follow through. "Is that what you did? Beg forgiveness?"

"Damn straight that's what I did. For over thirty minutes, in fact." Ava's confession took on a wicked edge. "Kat did a bunch of research on safe positions for spinal patients, and we found this fantastic one for oral. I may have been the one apologizing, but it ended up a win-win."

Diana wanted nothing more than to go home, knock on Jude's door, and spend the rest of the day on her knees begging for a second chance. *One date, huh?* She weighed the suggestion in her mind, marveling that Ava's request wasn't nearly as unpalatable as the thought of saying good-bye to Jude forever. *If things don't work out, or she isn't who I think, I can always end things.* She'd done it before and could sure as hell do it again. *And if Jude breaks my heart...* Diana snorted, shaking her head at herself. *At least I'll know I still have one.*

Raising her head from Ava's shoulder, Diana stared down into her best friend's hopeful gaze with the slowly growing certainty that her life was about to shift in a major way. "Promise you'll let me blame you forever if everything goes to hell?"

"Absolutely." Ava drew her into an excited hug. "As long as you promise to be sweet to Jude no matter what happens. You know, since your girl happens to be *my* girl's baby cousin. Assuming Kat doesn't get over her crippled old lady fetish anytime soon, you're bound to see each other in the future." She pinched Diana on the hip, managing to draw out a giggle. "My plan is to treat Kat like the goddess she is and pray she'll continue to overlook my shortcomings."

"What shortcomings?" Diana raised up to give Ava a smile she genuinely felt, to the depths of her soul. "You're the perfect woman, mostly, and Kat is one lucky nursemaid."

Ava pinched her butt this time, and Diana barely resisted the urge to squirm away laughing. Worried about jostling Ava, she carefully caught her friend's wrists and pinned them to the mattress, immobilizing her without force. Ava frowned without trying to break free. "No fair. You know I can't fight back."

"Hello?" Katrina's cautious greeting echoed through the apartment.

At the unexpected sound of her entrance, Diana scrambled off the bed with the guilt of an illicit mistress caught in flagrante delicto. It was an extreme reaction, but also wholly instinctive, triggered by years of being accused of infidelity she hadn't committed. At first she thought Ava's wide-eyed gasp was an echo of her own fear but swiftly realized that she'd done exactly what she hadn't wanted and injured her friend. "Shit." She sank back down on the mattress and touched Ava's shoulder. "Shit, I'm *so* sorry. I didn't mean to hurt you."

"What happened?" Diana backed off at the alarm in Katrina's voice. Rushing to the opposite side of the bed, Jude's cousin sat beside Ava and grasped her hand. "Poodle, are you hurt?"

Despite the agony etched onto Ava's face and the lingering threat of being labeled a cheater and breaking more than her best friend's back, Diana couldn't suppress her tickled laughter. "*Poodle?*"

Ava recovered enough to flash her a dirty look. "Long story. Now hit me up with some pain relief, you clumsy dork."

"What happened?" Katrina repeated the query, combing her fingers through Ava's hair while Diana opened the nightstand drawer to fish out a freshly rolled joint. "Did I interrupt cuddling, fighting, or fucking?"

"Cuddling." Seemingly anxious about Katrina's reaction, Ava scanned the younger woman's face. "Diana had a rough night. She's still a bit on edge."

Taking over, Diana said, "I'm sorry. I don't know why I reacted like that. Ava broke the news of her monogamy to me weeks ago, and I'd never disrespect either one of you by attempting to seduce an honest woman." To vindicate Ava of any suspicion her paranoia had created, Diana made a major admission.

"I'm actually here because I'm falling in love with your cousin. Ava's been talking me down, and offering counsel, since I woke up. You just missed her making me promise to ask Jude out on a real date, just one, to see how it goes. Oh, and I've been warned to treat Jude well regardless of whether I manage to pull my head out of my ass, as we'll apparently be seeing more of each other in the future." She smiled, hoping Katrina would accept her lack of interest in competing for Ava's love and affection as genuine. "On account of how well things are going for the two of you."

"They are." Katrina briefly lowered her loving gaze to Ava's face, then challenged Diana with a direct stare. "So? Don't leave me in suspense." She arched a well-manicured brow. "Are you really going to ask Jude out?"

Diana swallowed. "I think so." She shook out her hands, stunned to feel exhilaration more than nervousness at the thought of returning to Jude with her tail tucked. Jude might reject her apology and decline a date, but at least their last interaction wouldn't involve Diana verbally flaying her for setting perfectly reasonable boundaries to protect both their self-interests. If nothing else, perhaps Diana could walk away from this mess a bit wiser and a whole lot less awful to those she cared about. Maybe that would make the pain of sabotaging things with Jude worth *something*. Or maybe not. Uncertainty crept in. "Unless you think it's a bad idea."

Katrina's eyes narrowed. "It's only a bad idea if it's not *yours*." She pursed her lips. "By which I mean, please wait until you're sure about what you want before asking Jude anything. She's heartbroken enough as it is. Teasing her with the impossible would be unforgivably cruel."

Humbled by the report on Jude's wellbeing, Diana asked, "Have you seen her?"

"Last night. And again this morning, briefly, before leaving for my shift with Ava." Katrina refused to blink. "She feels guilty about upsetting you. Really, for getting involved at all. Even if you don't want to take her on a date, I'm sure she'd appreciate knowing you don't blame her for everything that happened. Because she sure blames herself. To be fair, though, she was only trying to honor your wishes and not push."

"I know." The unwelcome agony Jude had inflicted simply hadn't let her admit that at the time.

Cracking a reluctant smile, Katrina said, "Luckily, you seem to be fairly irresistible. I've never known Jude to feel so strongly about anyone. Especially this fast."

For the second time that morning, Diana discovered she was more excited than afraid about prospects that would've terrified her only a few short weeks ago. "No matter what, I'll make sure Jude knows this wasn't her fault. You have my word."

"Thank you." Katrina nodded cordially. "I do hope the apology goes well and everything works out. You'd make a fantastic couple."

Diana swallowed her instinctive, self-deprecating retort about not feeling the same. "That's very gracious of you, considering how standoffish and short-tempered I've been during most of our interactions."

Katrina waved off the semi-apology. "It's fine. I get it."

Diana studied Ava's face, wondering how much dirt she'd divulged to her young lover and what secrets, if any, Katrina had passed on to Jude. Ava met her inquiring eyes without any trace of guilt—just impatience. "Incidentally, still waiting on that joint."

Diana lit up and passed the patient her medicine. "Your highness."

"Literally." Ava took a greedy hit before circling back to the discussion of Diana's newly resurrected love life. "When do you think you'll see Jude? Today?"

"I don't know." Diana checked Katrina's eyes as Ava sucked in another long toke. Reading her unspoken warning, she said, "Like Katrina says, I need to wait until I'm sure."

"Until you're sure you're ready to *try*," Ava said, gesturing for Katrina to agree. "Right? No one's asking for a lifetime commitment. Only an open mind about where a date could lead."

"Right. Be sure you're ready to *try*." Momentary indecision gripped Katrina's face, and she added, "But I wouldn't wait more than a week, *maybe* two, before initiating some sort of conversation. Jude deserves to be let out from under the guilt she's piled onto herself."

Diana nodded, aching for the kind young woman silly enough to fall in love with the likes of her. "Understood." She paused to take stock, then stood. "I'll leave. You two enjoy your day."

"We will." An untroubled grin spread across Ava's face, evidence that the plant was working its magic. "Enjoy your soul-searching."

She almost never did. Still, with each step Diana took toward her car—and home—her heart became more and more certain about what it wanted. It wanted her to try.

It wanted *Jude.*

CHAPTER TWENTY-SIX

Jude paused her video game at a crucial moment in the most arduous boss fight she'd taken on yet, annoyed at whoever dared to knock on her door. After three days of struggling and mostly failing to write through her depression, she'd discovered her ideal therapy: immersion within a punishingly difficult, combat-driven adventure. Having to focus on her character's every action and reaction made it impossible to wallow in self-pity, let alone obsess over her decisions and whether they were right or wrong. She was sick of thinking about Diana. All she wanted was to slay digital demons. Fuck thinking. Fuck *hurting.* She scowled at the peephole as she approached the door.

Most likely Katrina was checking in again, but even the prospect of time with her best friend couldn't pull Jude out of her funk. While she loved Katrina dearly, the girl wasn't all that into watching Jude play video games. She would prefer to chat, no doubt, but Jude was all talked out. They'd discussed the situation with Diana every day that week, yet come Thursday afternoon, Jude still felt like shit. Hence she was giving up on chitchat. Only wanton digital carnage could heal her now.

Wondering how offended Katrina would be if asked to kindly go home, Jude peered through the peephole as her visitor knocked a second time. The sharp rap of knuckles against wood punctuated the thunderclap of emotion that detonated inside Jude at the sight of Diana's nervous, mildly distorted features on the other side. Jude jerked away like she'd been burned, and in a sense, she had. Five minutes ago, she'd been safely ensconced inside a beautifully grotesque fantasy world, but now the source of her heartache was here to drag her back into reality. A mixture of resentment and guilt coursed through Jude, compelling her to back away from the door. Even if Diana *had* come to apologize, Jude wasn't certain she was strong enough to hear her yet. She definitely didn't have the strength to rehash her own mistakes.

Not expecting persistence, Jude jumped when Diana spoke through the door. "I know you're in there. I heard you pause your movie."

Jude bit her lower lip, then said, "Video game."

"Whatever it was, it sounded terrifying." Diana paused. "Maybe I'm less so?"

Jude wasn't so sure. Without weighing the consequences, she called out, "I don't think I'm ready to talk to you yet."

"Even if I'm here to tell you how sorry I am?" Diana lowered her volume. "I know I made mistakes, major ones. The worst of which was not staying for ice cream. I should have. A real friend *would* have."

Sighing, Jude opened the door. She didn't want what sounded like sincere remorse to become a spectacle for their neighbors. When she saw what Diana held, Jude clutched her chest and sucked in a startled breath. "Why is Karen here? If you're asking me to pet-sit…I don't know. I have my limits."

"No." Diana glanced down at the clear acrylic enclosure she carried and the four-inch, pink-toed tarantula stuck to its side—its *inside*, thank God—with a flustered, self-conscious expression. "I guess I didn't…" She exhaled and met Jude's gaze. "Need to bring her along. I seem to have a knack for totally bananas ideas that feel solid right up until you open the door."

Confused why Diana would ever think to bring her tarantula for a visit, yet oddly charmed that she had, Jude defied her own anti-spider policy by asking, "Would you two like to come inside?"

Diana slowly broke into a smile. "I can take her home first, if you want." She gestured at her own apartment door. "It's not far."

"That's all right." Jude moved aside to let Diana pass. "Just keep the cage closed."

"Always." Diana walked to the couch and set Karen on the coffee table next to Jude's still-glowing controller. Nose crinkled, she regarded the frozen image on-screen. "That *is* terrifying."

"Says the woman lugging around a giant, boxed spider."

"Touché." Diana rubbed her hands together, then pointed at the couch. "Do you mind if I sit? I don't have to stay long, if I'm interrupting, but I need to say a few things before I chicken out. And before I…" She licked her lips. "Lose you forever."

"Diana…" Jude's heart rate sped up even as she privately warned herself against optimism. *All she wants from you is sex. She'll ask you to reconsider and promise to be a better friend. But don't you dare say yes. You know that'll never be enough.* "Please don't." She paused, stunned by the tears that immediately sprang to Diana's vivid blue eyes. "Not unless you mean it."

Diana sat on the edge of the couch and gestured for Jude to join her. "I mean it."

Dubious but intrigued, Jude tentatively sank onto the farthest cushion. "I forgive you for not staying that night. I knew what we were doing, and…shouldn't have taken it so personally."

"Jude, stop," Diana said, scooting closer. "Why *wouldn't* you take it personally? What happened between us *was* personal, and intimate, and…" She paused, briefly closing her eyes. "Life-changing. I meant everything I said when I was inside you, sweetheart. It was unfair to whisper that kind of adoration into your ear, then skip out before you'd even recovered. I didn't do it to be cruel, though I'm sure it must've felt that way. I just… couldn't not tell you how I felt. It was only after, when you asked me to stay, that I realized how transparent I'd been. I got scared…so I ran."

"You did." Empathy washed away the last of Jude's anger. "And I understand why. It wasn't your fault."

"Of course it was." Diana tightened her fingers on her knees. "Don't you ever make excuses for my bad behavior. Not *ever*, you hear me?"

Jude nodded, sensing how important her agreement was to Diana's peace of mind. "Fine, you were a jerk. But I knew what I was getting into with you, didn't I? You were never unclear about what you wanted. My holding onto the hope that I could change your mind was every bit as unfair as what you did."

Diana dropped her head and sighed. "So we both fucked up. To be fair, though, how could we have known?"

"Known what?" Jude's palms began to sweat.

"That I would return your feelings."

For a moment, Jude couldn't breathe. Couldn't even think. She could only stare at Diana in disbelief. When Diana opened her mouth to keep speaking, Jude whispered, pleadingly, "I said don't."

"And I said I mean it." Inching closer, Diana held out a trembling hand. "Please, Jude. I'm trying here. Let me?"

Jude didn't know what to say. Despite Katrina's optimism, she'd refused to entertain the fantasy of Diana experiencing an epiphany capable of swaying her negative opinion of romantic love. Wishful thinking had only ever gotten her into trouble. Jude hesitated to celebrate the apparent change of heart, even straight from Diana's mouth. The past five days had been some of her longest, yet Diana's turnaround felt awfully fast, given her formerly unshakable determination to stay single.

Quietly, Jude asked, "What's changed?"

"I have." Diana reached across the center cushion to place her hand atop Jude's. "This week has been miserable without you. You'd think because we regularly go days without seeing each other, five measly nights couldn't possibly hurt this much. But it's been torture, mostly due to knowing that if I can't get past what happened with Janine enough to finally ask you out—like on an actual date—then I'll have lost you." Choking up, she whispered, "And I really, *really* don't want to lose you."

Jude shook her head, stunned by the raw emotion in Diana's heartfelt confession. Afraid she'd somehow bullied her into a relationship she didn't truly want, she murmured, "Di..." She snapped her mouth shut, unsure how to compromise on this particular issue. It destroyed her to reject the most soul-stirring sex of her life, but for the sake of her mental health—and by extension, her writing—Jude had no other choice. "I didn't quit to try to change you. While I can't imagine the courage it took for you to come here and say all of that to me, I don't want to go out with you when you're asking only because I basically blackmailed you into it."

"No, Jude..." Diana tightened the grip on her hand. "I'm asking because it only took being disconnected from you for a few dozen hours to realize that never knowing where our chemistry might've taken us scares me even more than the idea of taking you on a real date. Just one, to see what happens." Her throat moved, hinting at the anxiety she surely felt. "I'll buy you dinner at the restaurant of your choice. Unless you'd prefer I pick the venue. Whatever pleases you."

Jude couldn't pretend to care about food in the face of Diana's surreal shift in attitude. "What about our age difference? I thought you were too old, or I was too young."

"Maybe we are." Smile wavering, Diana ran her thumb along the inside of Jude's wrist. "But one dinner isn't a commitment—for either of us. If it doesn't work out, then at least we'll know for sure."

"And if it does?" Jude steadied her voice, then admitted her worst fear. "I can't go down this road with you unless you're prepared to deal with the aftermath of a potentially epic date."

Exhaling, Diana turned to the coffee table and put her hand on Karen's enclosure. Jude watched in horror as the tarantula reacted to her presence by slowly crawling toward the lid. "I brought Karen along as a reminder, and as proof, that I've faced my fears before. While I won't always get things right, and I'll definitely make mistakes, and perhaps even panic now and then, I know I can face them again. And I *want* to, for you."

Jude was losing the will to argue against an outcome she hadn't dared to dream would ever occur. Without taking her eyes off the roving spider, she curled her hand around Diana's thigh to give her a fond squeeze. "One date. We'll split the check."

Diana's tremulous inhalation drew Jude's attention away from Karen and onto the unintentionally suggestive placement of her hand. Latched onto Diana's thigh scant inches from the inner juncture, Jude shivered at the familiar heat warming her skin. She hadn't meant to be so forward, but based on Diana's body language, the contact wasn't unwelcome.

Diana whispered, "Let me compensate you for the pain and suffering. One fancy meal is the very least I can do."

Again, Jude sensed how important this was to Diana. She bowed her head in acceptance, but said, "Only if you let me pay for our second fancy meal together. Assuming the first doesn't end in disaster."

Diana dissolved into a vaguely giddy smile. "I admit, it's hard to imagine it will."

"You sure that doesn't freak you out?" Jude traced her fingertip along the seam of Diana's pants, journeying closer to the concealed pussy she longed to finally claim for her own. "The possibility of *more* than just one date, to see how it goes?"

"Of course I still have my doubts—and brief episodes of mindless terror—but I'm telling you, Jude, from the bottom of my heart…" Diana released a shaky breath as Jude paused her exploratory caresses no more than a millimeter from her crotch. "I'd rather be afraid with you than safe without you."

Jude opened her mouth, but no sound escaped. She'd never dreamed of hearing such a sweetly romantic sentiment from the woman who'd treated committed relationships like the ultimate anathema. The turnaround broke her brain…to the point she started questioning the very nature of reality. She took her hand off Diana's inner thigh, eliciting a disappointed whimper she hadn't expected. Shaken, Jude asked, "Why me? I mean, I know we have great sex—"

"The *best* sex."

"Really?" Jude had assumed that within the pantheon of Diana's lovers, she likely ranked high but surely not at the top. She'd been positive that Ava reigned supreme, courtesy of her extensive knowledge of Diana's every curve and crevice. Suspicious, Jude asked, "Like, *really* or…"

"*The best*," Diana repeated. "We have the hottest, most satisfying sex I think I've ever had. Not only that, but you're gorgeous, and smart, and talented, and compassionate, and funny, and while you may be young, you're not immature, and…" She stopped to breathe, flushed from the heartfelt speech. "You couldn't be more different from Janine. The more I get to know you, the more I see that—and that difference is exactly what I need."

Jude finally understood. She was to serve as Diana's path to healing. "I can see where I'd be an ideal palate cleanser. A non-threatening way to prepare for your next serious relationship." While she appreciated Diana's one-day-at-a-time mentality, she had to weigh whether her heart could handle whatever came of 'just one date'. The odds were decent their relationship would go nowhere, that whatever friendship they might salvage would be irreparably harmed by the attempt to turn blistering sexual chemistry into a legitimate partnership. Yet to know Diana more genuinely, to perhaps even kiss her without reservation, was a dream Jude couldn't bring herself to turn down.

But before she could accept, Diana's smile faded, and her gaze fell to the floor.

"I'm not interested in a palate cleanser. I wouldn't…" Diana sighed. "I never would've come here if I weren't serious. I'm telling you that I enjoy spending time with you and having sex with you, and so I'd like to get to know you better. And to let you get to know me, too. I have no idea what'll happen after that, and I can't make any promises, but I can tell you that I don't consider you a rebound or practice for the real thing. I've had a couple of flings since Janine, and that's not what this is." She raised her watery eyes to Jude's. "Unless that's all *you* wanted it to be."

Jude watched the uncertainty sweep across Diana's face and, for a few, heart-stopping moments, wondered if she was about to run away for the second time. Hoping to stop her, Jude held Diana's thigh even tighter and higher than before. Diana sank her teeth into her lower lip, then pressed her fingers against the racing pulse in Jude's wrist. Neither spoke, staring into the other's eyes.

When Jude was certain she had Diana's full attention, she ended the tense standoff by leaning forward to brush their lips together. Rather than deepen the kiss, she backed away so Diana could both see and hear the sincerity of her words. "I'm too damn old to waste my time on yet another fling. I'd rather find something that'll last for a while. A relationship to invest in...and build on." She rubbed her thumb over Diana's slacks. "Besides, you're not exactly fling material. Too much of a 'real thing' vibe coming off you. That's why...well, I need to know that you feel the same. Or *could* feel the same...someday."

"I do." Her incredulity plain to see and hear, Diana laid her open hand against Jude's cheek and exhaled. "I don't know how I ever looked at you and saw anything but a remarkable woman I'd be proud to have on my arm. Lucky for me you're so patient and forgiving."

"Only with those rare people I'm *seriously* determined to win over." Jude turned to kiss Diana's palm. With a goofy smile, she added, "So... you, basically."

Adorably, Diana reacted to the compliment by cracking a coy grin. "Told you I'm lucky."

Past her need for therapeutic demon-slaying, Jude glanced at the television, then Diana. "I know you're looking forward to buying me a real dinner, and I *totally* want that, too, but..." She pointed at her cozy pajama pants, then plucked her Wonder Woman T-shirt away from her chest. "It's been a rough few days, so I'm not all that excited to get dressed up and go out *tonight* or anything, but..."

Jude's heart stuttered as she plunged headlong into the first test of Diana's new attitude. "Would you care to hang out for a bit? If you're not in the mood to talk, we could watch a movie. Or television. Or eat some ice cream." She regretted that last suggestion the second it passed across her lips. Entering damage-control mode, she forced a lighthearted smile. "I won't be upset if you say no. I know you'll likely need some space after a conversation this...monumental. Rest assured, I *am* a big-enough girl that I can wait to see you again."

"Okay," Diana said. "Yes. Let's talk some more." She caught Jude's free hand and laced their fingers together, leaving Jude's other hand a hair's breadth from her crotch. "I don't want to go home, either."

"Yeah?" Relaxing, Jude observed her close proximity to Diana's pussy. The bold contact didn't seem to upset Diana, but she also wasn't pushing to act on it. "Cool. May I ask you a question?"

"Go for it."

Jude flexed her fingers on Diana's thigh. "How do you feel about sex?"

"Personally, I love it." Diana winked. "You?"

Jude dug her blunt nails into Diana's sensitive skin, eliciting a girlish squeal. "Sex forms one third of my holy trinity of pleasure, alongside writing and video games. But you know that's not what I meant." Sobering, she loosened her grip. "You want to take me out and get to know me for real, but…" Unsure what she hoped to hear, Jude addressed the Tyrannosaurus rex in the room. "How does sex fit into this new plan? Or doesn't it? I know we've already fucked, what, a half dozen times? But were you thinking we'd put a moratorium on trading orgasms until one or more of these 'actual' dates have played out, or…" She left the alternative unsaid. "I'll obviously respect your decision either way. I'm open to whatever."

Diana sat forward, causing Jude's fingernails and first knuckles to rub against her warm center as she shifted position. "Trading orgasms is what brought us together, sweetheart, and being inside you connects me like nothing else. As sex is one of the most efficient ways to create intimacy and trust, and we're already pretty great at doing it…I don't see a reason to postpone that aspect of our relationship. Why? To prove a point?" She halted her gradual advance inches away from Jude's face and blinked. "But if you'd prefer to suspend our sex life until we figure out whether there's anything else between us…I'm also open to whatever. Whatever *you* want."

Jude expelled a jerky breath. Although she appreciated Diana's willingness to spend time in her presence even without the promise of ecstasy given or received, she loathed the thought of willingly giving up the one ritual to have reliably knocked down the barriers between them— even if only temporarily. "As long as sex isn't all we're sharing, I don't want to stop, either."

"Excellent." Diana closed the remaining distance between them to give Jude a reverent peck on the lips. Then, rather than deepen the kiss, she backed off to look Jude in the eyes. "Maybe after we talk for a bit, you can help me practice for that workshop I never should've canceled. In case we decide to reschedule it."

Shakily, Jude whispered, "How to Make Love?"

Diana's nostrils flared as she gave a solemn nod. "Let me teach you?"

"Yes." There was almost nothing Jude wanted more. Except— "After we've talked."

CHAPTER TWENTY-SEVEN

Four hours after working up the guts to ask Jude on their first date, Diana exercised her grit for the second time as she took her new love interest by the hand and led her next door. Head spinning from all the fascinating new details she'd learned during their sprawling, in-depth conversation on Jude's couch—covering their early childhoods, memories from high school, and other formative life experiences—Diana couldn't recall ever wanting anyone so acutely. Jude's fingers trembled in hers, proof that she wasn't the only one to register the weight of what they were about to do. Diana's request to make love in *her* bed had obviously shocked Jude, yet she hadn't hesitated to agree despite a visible spike in her anxiety.

"You okay?" Diana murmured as they entered her bedroom. She felt as though she were ushering a virgin to her deflowering, so pronounced was Jude's shaking. "Just a reminder that we don't have to do this tonight, if you're not ready."

Jude laughed, tightening her fingers on Diana's. "Given where we were and what we were doing exactly one week ago this evening, I don't know why I'm so nervous."

"Because 'this' is entirely different than that?" Diana stopped at the foot of her bed, facing Jude to hold both her hands. "Don't get me wrong. Being able to introduce you to anal sex was insanely hot...and so, so passionate. Really, it was one of the most intimate experiences of my life—despite me doing my best not to let it be. Tonight, though..." She let go of Jude's hand to brush a lock of hair away from her glittering eyes. "I'm not holding back."

Swaying, Jude grabbed onto Diana's hip to regain her balance. "Di," she breathed. "Please..."

Diana wrapped her arms around Jude's waist and drew her into a protective embrace. "Come here."

Jude's arms looped around her neck without further prompting. She clung to Diana fiercely, their hearts pounding in sync. "Don't ever shut me out again, all right? I can handle whatever you're willing to give…and I won't make you regret it."

The longer they spent together, the less Diana could imagine sweet Jude morphing into a vicious, younger version of her psycho ex. Where Janine had always been a highly skilled wearer of masks, Jude's expression was perpetually open and guileless, conveying exactly what she felt, when she felt it. Breathing in her scent, Diana curled her hand around the base of Jude's skull and held her as close as she could. "At this point, I think I worry more about your regrets than mine."

"Don't." Jude kissed Diana's hair, the only place her lips could reach. "Assuming we don't discover any fatal incompatibilities going forward, I'll never wish I hadn't taken this chance with you. I like you so much, and I've wanted you for ages…" She nuzzled Diana's neck, sighing. "Even if we never make it past a second date, I'm thrilled to be trying at all."

Diana rocked Jude gently back and forth, then held her by the shoulders and took a step away. Reflecting Jude's adoring gaze with one of her own, she said in a husky voice, "Why don't we take off our clothes and get into bed? While I'd love to keep holding you like this forever, I suspect this'll get even better once we're lying down with your bare skin on mine."

Jude shivered as she reached for the hem of her T-shirt. "I suspect you're right."

Stopping Jude before she could disrobe, Diana asked, "May I?"

"Of course." Jude raised her arms above her head, waiting for Diana to remove her top. When she did, groaning at the naked breasts she uncovered, Jude's nipples puckered into stiff peaks. Diana winced with Jude at the ache she could only imagine, then bent to suck one turgid nipple into her mouth while warming the other beneath her palm. Gasping, Jude grabbed a handful of Diana's hair to keep her where she was. "Yes, like *that*."

Diana smiled as she licked and soothed Jude's nipple with her tongue and fingertips. Jude moaned and arched against her, triggering a torrent of wetness to soak Diana's panties before she'd even been touched. Matching Jude's moan, Diana nibbled on delicate flesh that refused to soften, then brought her fingers together to capture the tip of the other, less-aroused breast. Jude's hips bucked and she cried out, seemingly close to orgasm already.

Jude tugged on Diana's hair. "We're supposed to lie down, remember?"

"I do." Diana straightened, staring into Jude's eyes while loosening the drawstring at her waist. Determined not to speed through an encounter this monumental, she knelt before Jude to nuzzle the spot where her quivering thighs met, then deliberately lowered her pajama bottoms to the floor. She mumbled praise for Jude's cooperation and tickled the screen-printed crotch of the Princess Leia panties she'd just uncovered. "Invoking your inner badass?" Nodding at the T-shirt pooled on the floor nearby, she said, "Wonder Woman *and* Princess Leia. That's quite the pair."

Jude chuckled, folding her arms over her naked chest with a one-shouldered shrug. "They were clean. I'm embarrassed to admit how much time has passed since my last visit to the laundry room."

Diana straightened, guilt tugging her mouth into a frown. "Not because you were afraid to see me there, I hope."

"Nah." Jude's failed attempt to sound blasé gave away the truth. "Just lazy."

"Mmm-hmm." Advancing slowly, Diana kissed each of Jude's eyelids, then her nose, then her lips. That accomplished, she reached behind Jude and gave her bottom a fond pat. "Get in bed, sweetheart. I'm right behind you."

Jude released a quiet, conflicted whimper but obeyed anyway. Flinging her body onto the mattress belly first, she rolled over to watch Diana unbutton her shirt. "You *do* know how ridiculously stunning you are, right?"

Diana gave her an indulgent wink. "The girl with the golden tongue."

"It's true, though." Posture relaxing, Jude laced her fingers behind her head. "You're like an old-fashioned movie star. Those blue eyes, that thick, gorgeous hair...I've dreamed about running my fingers through your hair, literally."

Diana discarded her shirt onto the floor, then unhooked her bra. Smirking, she asked, "Old-fashioned because I'll turn forty in a few weeks?"

Jude appeared distressed to have potentially caused real offense. "No! Because..." She hesitated, then stared down at her hands. "Because you possess this classic, timeless beauty that's always reminded me of a youngish Elizabeth Taylor. If you must know." Unable to meet Diana's gaze, she took a deep breath and said, "I'll tell you this one more time, Di, before I spend the rest of tonight *showing* you: your age is the least interesting thing about you. Your confidence, your compassion, your loyalty to Ava, your courage—with spiders and people—your uncanny ability to know exactly what my body needs, usually before I do..." Raising her eyes to Diana's, Jude slipped her hand into her panties and stroked the hidden pink folds Diana thirsted to rediscover. "Those things matter. What year you were born doesn't."

"Nineteen seventy-eight," Diana said, half-convinced that Jude would at long last understand the chasm she intended to leap once she pointed out the entire decade plus between their birthdates. "In case you hadn't done the math."

"So?" Jude shrugged and slowly tilted her bent knee to the side. Rubbing circles over what had to be her clit, Jude narrowed her eyes at Diana's clothed lower body. "Come on, Di, keep going. Show me what panties *you* wore for this occasion."

Diana battled an unfamiliar ripple of self-consciousness as Jude's appraising stare swept across her naked breasts. She forced an amused chuckle and unbuttoned her jeans like she hadn't a care in the universe. "I'm afraid they're not as cute as yours."

Jude inhaled audibly when Diana lowered her pants to lay bare the partial dishonesty of that claim. While the lacy black briefs sported no logos or likenesses of fictional heroines, their seductive design included a heart-shaped opening in back that lovingly framed her exposed buttocks for Jude's visual consumption. Turning in place to offer Jude the complete picture, Diana kicked her jeans at the hamper and lowered herself onto the bed.

"Liar." Jude continued to play inside her own panties as Diana stretched out alongside her. "That's the sexiest article of clothing any woman has ever worn. Throughout all of history."

It was becoming increasingly difficult to convince herself that Jude didn't really mean the things she said. Nothing about her neighbor's endearingly dopey, lovestruck manner came across as anything less than genuine—including the growing stain on the sodden crotch of her underwear. Emboldened by that unmistakable evidence of a mutual desire, Diana kissed the corner of Jude's mouth, then snuck a hand into her panties to still the slick, busy fingers on her clit. Pressing her lips fully against Jude's, she whispered, "How about saving the rest for me?"

"Yes, ma'am." Hands rising in acquiescence, Jude bit back a grin and looped her arms around Diana's neck to lure her into another kiss. "Anything you want." She bit down gently on Diana's lower lip, then licked the tender flesh with the tip of her tongue. "*Everything* you want."

Overwhelmed by the dirty, wonderful ideas her brain supplied in response, Diana broke away to gulp in a few lungfuls of much-needed air. As soon as she'd caught her breath, she folded Jude into a tight hug, eyes clamped shut against the long-forgotten emotions coursing through her overheated body. "Oh God," she whispered, and nothing else. There was no way to articulate the sea change taking place inside her previously guarded heart.

Jude rested her hand between Diana's shoulder blades, a simple caress that managed to impart tremendous comfort. Relieved by the loosening of her muscles, Diana rewarded Jude with a reverent squeeze. Jude squeezed back, molding her entire body to Diana's as though to ensure they could never be separated again. "You're right, this *is* different. Already, it's…" She shuddered, cuddling closer. "It's so *much*. Diana…are you really okay to do this tonight?" Jude's timidity hinted at a newfound apprehension, no doubt stemming from Diana's regretful past words and actions. "Our whole situation is still so new, and fragile—"

Diana pressed her tongue into Jude's mouth to silence whatever argument she'd been attempting to make. Once Jude surrendered, sagging against her with an utterly delicious moan, Diana ended their kiss and whispered, "Yes." She rolled Jude onto her back, then nudged open her thighs to settle between them. Sighing as Jude's breasts came into contact with her own, Diana stared into the pretty hazel eyes of the woman who'd single-handedly thawed her heart. "I'm okay with this. Are you?"

Jude nodded, though her expression remained tense. "I just need you to be sure. All right? It would be devastating if we fucked things up by moving too fast."

Though Diana burned to ride Jude's thigh and worship her pretty breasts, she knew it was important to listen to what was being said, then offer a thoughtful response. "Jude, sweet pea…I know what it means to do this with you right now. Our sex has always been intense, but this time it actually means something. Emotions will be involved. Hell, one of us may even cry." She smiled, wishing she could coax the same out of Jude. "I'm prepared for all of that. I wouldn't have invited you to my bed if I wasn't."

Jude's head bobbed again, but without much conviction. "As long as we're not moving too fast—"

Diana stopped Jude's fretting with a passionate kiss. Groaning at the ecstasy of Ms. Monaco's talented tongue, she didn't pull away until the need to breathe forced her to retreat. Once she'd regained her breath, she whispered into Jude's ear. "I'm dying to show you what I wish I were brave enough to say. May I?"

"Yes." Already in tears, Jude whispered, "But only if you swear we'll really go on that date. No matter what."

"No matter what," Diana vowed. She lifted her head to stare into Jude's shimmering gaze. "We're having a nice dinner at a fancy restaurant no matter *what* happens between us tonight. After all the soul-searching I had to do just to knock on your door, even falling hopelessly in love won't change my mind." Jude's eyes widened, and she went completely still. If not for the heartbeat hammering against Diana's breast, she might've been a statue. Seeing the impact of her words, Diana marveled at her own newfound conviction. The past five days of heartbreak, solitude, and regret had clarified her priorities in ways she'd never anticipated.

Moved by the memory of losing Jude, however fleetingly, Diana murmured, "I want you too much to give you up that easily."

"I want you, too." Seemingly awestruck, Jude clutched Diana's shoulders and strained to reach her lips. "Show me."

Diana slipped her left hand behind Jude's neck to invite her into another soulful kiss. She allowed her right hand to trail down the side of the delectable body beneath her, stopping to grab Jude's shapely hip and tug her closer. Their tongues slowed, the mood shifting as Diana ground her pussy into Jude's thigh, and Jude swallowed the resulting cry of pleasure with a heartfelt moan. Diana pushed her knee higher between Jude's unsteady legs, massaging the prominent clit hidden within her drenched panties. Sucking on Jude's bottom lip, Diana asked, "Think we can come like this?"

Jude's tongue swept over hers, hips bucking against the rhythmic pressure of Diana's knee. She released a plaintive whimper when Diana retreated beyond her reach to wait for an answer. "Yes," Jude begged. "*Please.*"

High off the thrill of making Jude want her so unashamedly, Diana felt her hips surge, and she dove back in for more. Jude answered the quickening movement of her lower body with sharp, desperate counter-thrusts that not only hinted at her desperation, but also how out of control she clearly felt. It made sense, given that Diana had just flipped her sense of reality inside out with this willingness to treat sex as a true emotional exchange. Jude's world had to be spinning—fast.

Moving her lips to Jude's neck, Diana soothed it between nibbles. "Easy, baby. Let's go nice and easy, and make this last."

Jude dragged her crotch up and down the length of Diana's bare thigh. "But I'm so close."

"Seriously? Our panties are still on." Diana gushed at the news. "Overachiever."

"I blame you." Jude tangled her fingers in Diana's hair and hauled her up for another round of kissing. "For being everything I've always wanted."

In a flash, Diana was also close—and done with nice and easy. "I suppose we do have all night…"

"Yes, ma'am." Jude licked her earlobe. "*All* night."

"And tomorrow morning." Diana grinned at Jude's palpable astonishment at having been invited to sleep with her, literally, for the first time. "If you're into that sort of thing."

"Waking up to a seduction by Diana Kelley?" Jude rolled her hips, vibrating with satisfaction. "*Yeah,* I'm into that."

Finally ready to eradicate every last boundary standing in their way, Diana paused from riding Jude's thigh to ease off and sit at her side. Before Jude could vocalize the protest in her eyes, Diana said, "May I take off your panties? I want to feel your fat clit sliding across my skin."

Jude lifted her hips to allow Diana to remove her underwear, then watched as they were tossed onto the floor. "Take yours off, too?"

Diana already had her thumbs hooked beneath the waistband. "Absolutely." Less interested in teasing than in reclaiming her spot over Jude's nubile form, Diana shed her panties without any ceremony, then got up to wedge her knee between silky thighs already parted in anticipation. "I want you to feel how wet you've made me." Laying her full weight atop Jude's receptive curves, Diana positioned her slippery labia against the muscular thigh she was straddling, then rotated her hips to smear her juices across Jude's sweat-dampened flesh. "Feel how badly I want you? How much you mean to me?"

"Di…" Jude grabbed a handful of her hair and, yanking roughly, shoved her leg against Diana's throbbing clit and frantically humped her back. "I've never…no one's ever…"

She didn't have to finish for Diana to swell with pride. Capturing both wrists, Diana pinned Jude's arms above her head and placed her lips next to her ear. "Except me." A week ago, this dialogue would've frightened Diana. Tonight, every word felt essential. "Use my body to get off. Just let go, baby, and I promise I'll take care of you."

Three forceful thrusts later and Jude came with a shuddering moan. Her hips jutted erratically through spasm after spasm of pleasure, coating Diana in a thick layer of hot, sticky, well-earned cum. Moved by Jude's wholehearted enjoyment, Diana raised herself up on her arms for leverage and drove her clit insistently against Jude's tense, trembling upper thigh. Releasing one of Jude's hands to hook an arm behind her neck, Diana pulled her up and into a steamy kiss that nearly triggered her own climax the instant their tongues touched. It took only a few seconds more for Diana to finish, propelled into an earth-shattering orgasm by the physical and emotional perfection of touching Jude without having to hide.

Jude's free hand latched onto her flank, the nails digging in a little deeper every time a fresh contraction rolled through her twitching frame. Returning Diana's kisses with a perfect mixture of lust and affection, she raised her knee to provide more surface area for Diana's pleasure. "Don't stop." Jude gasped, flexing the fingers of the hand Diana still had pinned against the mattress. "Don't stop, don't stop, *don't stop! Fuck...* Diana!"

Diana's tears gathered, then fell—treacherously—at Jude's full-throated embrace of their emotionally charged joining. A fat droplet landed on Jude's cheek, eliciting a giggle amidst her fervent moans. As the last vestiges of Diana's climax faded, she watched the saline track its way along Jude's delicate jawline and drip onto her addictively kissable neck. With a self-deprecating smirk, Diana muttered, "Who decided to chop onions?"

Jude beamed. "Dork." She wiggled her captive fingers against the mattress. "May I borrow this hand for a few? I want to hold you...using both arms, preferably."

"Sure." Diana drank in the glorious vision of Jude's flushed cheeks and chest, her tousled hair, and the ethereal light in her wide, adoring eyes. Unhanding her delicate wrist, Diana wrapped Jude in a bear hug and rolled them onto their sides. Jude threw her arms around Diana to hold her in a mutual embrace. Diana's head swam at their physical closeness and at her growing fondness for the woman in her arms. Their lovemaking had stirred emotions she hadn't felt in years, reminding her of all the beauty she'd been determined to give up forever. Unable to put words to the seismic shift inside her heart, Diana relied on familiar dry humor to break the silence. "So was it good for you?"

Shoulders hitching, Jude sniffled and tugged Diana closer. "Shut up."

Taking pity on Jude's fragile state, Diana kissed her temple and whispered, "It was perfect for me."

"Diana..." Jude hesitated, then released an explosive sigh. "I *will* fall in love with you. You know that, right?" When Diana attempted to move to check Jude's face, the arms around her shoulders locked her in an iron grip. Unable to see Jude's expression, she could only listen to the rest of the rambling speech pour out in a single breath. "I may already be in love with you. Even though, yes, I realize we barely know each other. It doesn't matter. Whether this ultimately goes anywhere or not, I..." She exhaled, then whispered brokenly, "Are you going to be okay with this if I end up loving you?"

Diana answered from the heart. "As long as you're okay with me taking things one date at a time." She petted Jude's hair, noting the subtle sag of the body against hers. To reassure Jude of her honorable intentions, she said, "Only until I'm marginally more confident you aren't too good to be true. Once I get there, I'll be all in." Hugging Jude closer, she murmured, "Between you and me, I don't expect that to take very long."

"I hope not." Jude loosened her grip, allowing Diana to rise and stare down into her eyes. "I want to give you all the time you need, but—"

"You're not getting any younger?" Diana teased.

Snickering, Jude muttered, "I'll show you young." She delivered on the threat by strong-arming Diana onto her back, reversing their earlier positions. Wrenching Diana's arms up to the headboard, she laced their fingers together to pin her down. "Tell me, *ma'am*, how might a whippersnapper like me convince a dignified older lady such as yourself of her noble—if not *entirely* pure—intentions?" Jude released Diana to snake her right hand between their bellies and caress her sensitive labia. "What if I let you come in my mouth? I could crawl between your thighs and lick your clit until you're shaking and begging me to stop. Would that help?"

Happy that Jude didn't seem inclined to push for more than she was prepared to give, Diana quipped, "It sure wouldn't hurt." Then again, it wasn't *exactly* what she'd envisioned doing next. "But first, I wanted to ask—" She was reluctant to voice the request on the tip of her tongue. After a brief pause and the gathering of her nerves, Diana said, "I still haven't found anyone to assist me at this weekend's workshop. Are you willing to help me again, or..." She stared into Jude's bottomless hazel eyes. "Would you rather our relationship remain strictly personal?"

"Facesitting and femmedom, wasn't it?" Jude's tiny smile widened into a massive grin. "What kind of loser says no to that?"

"Does that mean you're in?" Relief didn't describe how Diana felt. Though she wasn't ready to admit it to Jude, she *really* didn't want sex with anyone else. "Top or bottom?"

Jude didn't even pause to consider. "Bottom."

Flipping them over to retake her place on top, Diana straddled Jude's hips and delved into her mouth for a lingering kiss. "That's my girl," Diana whispered after they eventually parted. "I knew I could count on you."

Jude flashed her a naughty smirk. "To start, that is."

"Meaning…" Diana licked her lips, intrigued by Jude's tantalizingly unspoken suggestion. "You want to take turns?"

"Only if you do." Jude nibbled teasingly on Diana's chin. "But you know, I *have* always wanted to sit on your face."

She required no further convincing. "I'd be more than delighted to let you."

"Right on. But first…" Jude brought her hand down sharply on Diana's butt, a powerful smack that set her clit on fire. "Sit on mine."

"Yes, ma'am," Diana drawled. Before obeying, she tucked Jude's hair behind her ear, then teased the lobe with her teeth. "About that dinner…how's six o'clock tomorrow sound?"

Jude cut off her air supply with an earnestly powerful embrace. "Like a *date*."

EPILOGUE

One Year Later

Elated to have survived an overly contentious, last-minute emergency couples' counseling appointment, Diana unlocked the door to her new apartment and entered the sanctuary awaiting her. She stepped across the threshold, shoulders loosening at the unexpectedly familiar smell of home. Engaging the deadbolt behind her, Diana shed her coat and strolled into the living room slash gaming den—only to stop dead at the wondrous sight of her beloved kneeling on the rug they'd recently picked out at Ikea, clad in a low-cut camisole and nothing else. The stress of her afternoon melted away in an instant. Diana grinned. "My, my. *Someone* missed me."

Jude answered with a vigorous nod, fingers laced behind her lower back in perfect submission. "All day long."

Diana raised a skeptical eyebrow. "I've only been gone two hours. Remember how hard I made you come in the shower before I left?"

"Yeah, but..." Jude's lower lip poked out in the mock pout Diana continued to adore. "I didn't get to return the favor. Not before you put on that skirt, and those *pantyhose...*" Her gaze ran up and down the length of Diana's professionally attired frame before settling in the vicinity of her crotch. "I've been dying here all alone. I even tried to distract myself by writing you a super-short dirty story."

"Aww." Diana sauntered forward to tower over Jude's pleading pose. "I can't wait to read it."

The last story Jude had gifted her was the single greatest piece of erotic literature Diana had ever consumed. Never before had prose made her that wet or provided anywhere near enough fuel for a subsequent four straight hours of energetic fucking—an achievement Diana had taken tremendous pride in at almost forty-one. Jude's energy certainly kept her young, if slightly sore, and she was grateful. Both to Jude for revealing herself as the unlikely love of her life and to Ava for strong-arming her into opening her heart to the possibility of another romance. Hell, Diana was even thankful for Katrina. If not for her sexual healing, Diana may never have found a reason to move beyond the safety of her arrangement with Ava.

And that would've been a shame, because Diana was so, so happy about all the ways her life had changed.

Caressing Jude's cheek, Diana murmured, "I love you."

"I love you, too." Jude beamed as though she'd never heard those words before, when in fact, Diana had been saying them for months. "Now may I please suck on your clit? *Pretty* please?"

Diana put her purse on the arm of the nearby couch and lifted her skirt to reveal that the pantyhose Jude had been admiring covered an otherwise bare pussy. Having guessed that Jude would be in the mood to finish what they'd started, she'd foregone wearing panties altogether. Taunting, she said, "You seem to be enjoying these too much for me to take them off."

"You don't have to." Jude wet her lips, then pressed her open mouth against Diana's nylon-covered crotch. She swiped her tongue up the length of her protected labia, pressing firmly enough for Diana to register a delightful twinge from her hidden clit.

Concluding that Jude had nothing more to say, Diana grasped the back of her head with one hand, pulling her in. She shoved her other hand down the front of her pantyhose to spread her labia and expose her swollen clit to Jude's searching tongue. "Lick it."

Clearly trying her best, Jude whined and lapped at Diana with hunger that bordered on desperation. "Please...ma'am..." She stretched her mouth open wider, enveloping Diana's sopping labia. After a moment, Jude released her with a whimper. "I can't get my lips around your clit."

"Poor baby." Diana loosened her grip on Jude's hair and withdrew the hand from her pantyhose to search through her purse. "I have just the thing." She rustled around briefly, then retrieved a folded pocketknife and extended the blade. Jude watched, rapt, as Diana offered her the sharp edge. "Cut a hole in my stockings wide enough for your mouth. *Carefully.*"

Nodding, Jude took the pocketknife and raised her solemn eyes to Diana's face. "I won't hurt you."

Diana wrapped a lock of her girlfriend's hair around her finger, tugging affectionately. "I know."

"Thank you for the trust." Jude held the blade away from their bodies and, after nodding for Diana to lift her skirt out of the way, leaned forward to plant a reverential kiss between her legs. "And your permission."

Diana clung tighter to her skirt as Jude used two fingertips to pinch the nylon directly above her clit and yank it away from her skin. Bringing the tip of the blade to the thin material, Jude made a deliberate cut with a cautious flick of her wrist. Diana watched the process unfold in silence, marveling at how she always felt safe with Jude—even in moments of stark vulnerability. "Of course I trust you," she murmured, stroking Jude's cheek with a steady hand. "You're my good, sweet girl."

A sunny smile broke across Jude's pretty face, evidence of how much the praise meant. "And you…are my queen." Jude widened the hole in Diana's pantyhose with another conscientious slice. Then she let go of the material, allowing the nylon to snap in place around Diana's pussy while she folded and put away the knife. "My brave warrior queen."

The cool air tickled Diana's exposed flesh, making it impossible to ignore the well-placed opening Jude had crafted for her greedy lips and tongue. Lowering her hand between her thighs, Diana toyed with the engorged clit Jude appeared frantic to taste. When Diana groaned, throaty and satisfied, Jude licked her lips and sighed with longing. Hint taken, Diana removed her index finger from atop the slippery nub and rested it on Jude's bottom lip. After a brief stare-down, Diana invaded Jude's mouth for a thorough tongue bath. "Are you prepared to serve your queen?"

"Yes, your highness," Jude answered, throwing herself into the impromptu roleplay with gusto. "In whatever way you require. My body is yours to command."

Diana shivered, thrilled to hear such a proclamation from Jude's earnest pink lips. "That's why you're my favorite lady-in-waiting."

Jude chuckled, a momentary lapse she immediately corrected by tilting her face toward the floor. "I regard you highly as well, my queen."

A grin spread across Diana's face at the proper, wholly in-character response. "After you've finished pleasuring me, I plan to bend you over the arm of the couch, eat out your soft, yummy cunt, then stick a few fingers in one or both holes and fuck you until you can't come anymore. Would you like that?"

"I'd love it."

"Good. So will I." Diana turned, then walked backward until the backs of her thighs bumped against the arm of their new couch. "In the meantime…" She sat on the arm, sparing her aging knees the strain of staying upright while in thrall to Jude's otherworldly tongue. Beckoning her lady-in-waiting closer, Diana placed her hands on either side of the opening that framed her pussy and spread her labia to display the engorged clit within. "You know what to do."

Jude shuffled forward on her hands and knees, eyes locked on her goal. "Yes, my queen." She flashed Diana a wicked grin and lowered her mouth between her legs. "Like you taught me."

Bracing herself against the sofa, Diana glanced up at the ceiling as Jude's lips encircled her clit and her tongue laved the throbbing head into a stiff point. Her legs wobbled, instantly validating her decision to use the couch for support. "That's nice," Diana murmured, a massive understatement. "I like that a lot."

Jude nodded and mumbled, incoherent words whose vibration unleashed fresh juices to soak her cheeks and chin. When Diana shuddered, then hissed an exultant curse, Jude pursed her lips and sucked. "Ah!" Diana shouted, swiftly overcome by ripples of climactic pleasure. "*Fuck*, you…" She gasped for air. "*Bad* girl."

Grinning, Jude moved her tongue against Diana through multiple orgasms and one near collapse. Finally, right as Diana began to wonder how much more she could withstand, Jude ended the delicious torture. Sitting back on her heels, she beamed at Diana, wet-cheeked and full of pride. "I thought you said I was *good*."

Diana flattened her hand against her chest to track her hammering heartbeat as she slowly came down from the tremendous high of Jude's expert-level cunnilingus. "That was before you decided to finish me off in under two minutes." She admonished Jude with a faintly scolding frown. "You know I prefer to savor your attentions."

Jude offered a regretful shrug. "I know you do, my love. But—and I hesitate to even bring this up, given how fucking hot you are and how badly I want to keep servicing you—we're supposed to meet Kat and Ava for dinner tonight. In about forty-five minutes, in fact." She managed to sound even more apologetic than she looked. "Remember?"

Diana hadn't, but details began to surface in her sex-addled brain. "Right, because they're finally back from their honeymoon." Her disappointment about having to cut their encounter short warred with the excitement of seeing their best friends after two weeks without any significant contact. "And we miss them."

"Exactly." Jude held out her hands, and Diana grabbed hold, helping her to her feet with a powerful tug that landed her in Diana's waiting arms. She kissed Diana's nose, then her lips. "Sorry we ruined your pantyhose for a quickie."

"Entirely worth it, I assure you." When Jude slipped from her embrace to move toward their bedroom, Diana gripped her arm to prevent her escape. "Where are you going, young lady?"

"Oh." Jude went limp. "I assumed we were getting dressed to leave."

"I don't think so." Drawing Jude against her chest, Diana rotated their bodies to put Jude between her and the couch. Then she spun Jude around, guiding her to lie over the arm so her bare bottom was easily accessible. "I told you what would happen once you finished pleasuring me, and I'm nothing if not a woman of my word."

"You think we have time?"

"You're not the only one who knows how to get her girlfriend off in under two minutes."

"True." Jude wiggled her butt enticingly. "Guess you'd better get to work, then."

Pleased by Jude's assertiveness, Diana dropped to her knees and brushed her tongue over the snug opening she yearned to slide her fingers inside. She moaned at the flavor she loved more than any other, then grabbed a handful of Jude's ass and squeezed. Setting her thumb atop the puckered opening between Jude's cheeks, Diana paused long enough to whisper yet another "I love you"—to be sure Jude truly knew—before showing her exactly how much.

It took one minute, forty-two seconds flat.

Jude admired Diana across the table, in awe of how difficult it still was to tear her eyes away from the open, relaxed, unambiguously *happy* face of the woman she loved. After one year of committed monogamy and close to three weeks of official cohabitation, she'd expected the shine to start wearing off. Yet she'd never felt more dedicated, more passionate, more *psyched* to spend her days alongside anyone. The crush she'd developed during her stint subbing for Ava was a pale shadow of how she felt after spending nearly every day of the past twelve months together.

The more time she spent with Diana, the more reasons she found to love her.

Beneath her girlfriend's initially brusque exterior lurked a compassionate, playful, generous spirit who genuinely cared about her clients and the lucky few souls whose friendship she chose to accept. As a romantic partner, Diana treated her as an equal in their daily lives, yet never hesitated to indulge Jude's most depraved sexual fantasies free of judgment or self-doubt. She always knew just what to say to bolster Jude's creative self-confidence and chase away the doubts that occasionally threatened her ambition. On a more surface level, Diana liked a lot of the same music, television, and literature that she did. They *clicked*.

As for her beloved's flawless tits, well, Jude considered them a bonus. A perfectly proportioned, expertly showcased, eye-catching bonus.

"It appears that we've lost Jude." Katrina communicated her disapproval with a long-suffering sigh.

"Somewhere in Diana's cleavage, I think." Thankfully, Ava sounded more amused than annoyed by Jude's inattention to the happy couple's animated retelling of their last day in Prague. "Can't say I blame her. Ignoring that view is no small feat."

Blushing, Jude defended her own nonexistent honor. "I was just taking a moment to appreciate my girlfriend's *smile*, thank you very much." She ducked her head, then flashed Diana a sheepish grin. "Mostly."

"You go ahead and admire whatever part of me you want, sweetie." Diana quirked a smile and raised the bottle of beer in her hand to her succulent lips. "Makes this old lady feel damn special, having you stare at me like that."

"Like I have eyes?" Jude picked up her fork to take a bite of the salad she'd largely ignored. "And a pulse?"

"More like you want to climb inside her pussy and live there forever," Katrina snarked. She stuck out her tongue in response to Jude's mock-threatening scowl. "Trust me, I'm the one who has to see your face while you're doing it."

Laughing, Ava grabbed Katrina's hand and gave her fingers a fond kiss. "My wife has a real way with words, doesn't she?" She pressed Katrina's knuckles against her cheek, gazing at her as though they were the only ones in the room. "One of her many prodigious talents."

The goofiest grin spread across Katrina's dopey, lovestruck face, both warming Jude's heart and inspiring her to weaponize the blatant hypocrisy on display. "Looks like I'm not the only one susceptible to distraction by a sexy older woman."

"Back off," Katrina countered in a jovial tone. "We're newlyweds who just spent two weeks fucking our way across Europe. The occasional trip down memory lane is inevitable. If you and Diana ever decide to tie the knot, I'll cut you some slack on the boob-ogling front for, like, a month. Two, tops. After that, I make no promises." Eyes alive with mirth, she added, "Consider it part of your wedding gift."

Every muscle in Jude's body went rigid at the audacity of Katrina's teasing. She knew Diana loved her, and oh God, did she ever love Diana back, but they'd never discussed making things legal. Jude refused to touch the subject with a football-field-sized pole, and Diana had never mentioned it either. Not even when Ava had proposed to Katrina, causing both their cell phones to blow up with excited text messages as they were perfecting their sixty-nine technique for a future workshop. Nor at their best friends' intimate wedding ceremony in the redwoods, where they'd both shed joyful tears that the women they loved were so in love with each other. It was Diana's conspicuous silence on the subject of marriage that made Katrina's careless ribbing so frightening. While she was confident that Diana hoped to stick with her long-term, Jude still wasn't entirely sure how the love of her life would react if cornered or pressured for more than she wanted to give.

At a loss, Jude could only croak, "*Katrina.*"

"Allow me to apologize on behalf of my legally wedded spouse," Ava piped up. She put her hand on Jude's wrist to impart a supportive caress. "We'll blame jet lag for this one."

Katrina glanced at Jude, then Ava, then Jude once more—this time with regret. "She's right. I *have* been struggling to adjust. Jumping that many time zones was tougher than I thought." She frowned and stole a look at Diana's inscrutable face. "Ignore me, please. I get cranky when I'm off my regular schedule."

Diana snorted and jabbed Ava with her elbow. "See what happens when you rob the cradle?" She winked at Katrina, eyes sparkling.

"Uh-huh." Ava gave Jude's arm an amiable pat, then retaliated to Diana, "At least mine was born *before* the nineties."

Jude cringed. *Must* Ava point out how much younger she was than everyone else? "Boy, it sure is wonderful to have you two home. So, when's the next trip? Soon, I hope."

Under the table, Diana trailed her foot up the back of Jude's calf. When Jude reluctantly met her gaze, Diana greeted her with a soft smile. "Don't worry, sweet pea. I'm not freaking out, and I'm still one-hundred percent devoted to you *and* this relationship. All is well."

Embarrassed to have Diana not only recognize her real panic but also address it in front of the group, Jude nodded and looked down at her salad. Katrina rested a timid hand on her back, rubbing gentle patterns along Jude's spine. "Hey," she murmured under her breath. "I really am sorry about what I said. I wasn't trying to upset you. I was just…being a dumbass, basically."

"Another of my blushing bride's prodigious talents," Ava dead-panned, drawing laughter from around the table—even Jude. "Granted, one she very rarely demonstrates. Ninety-nine percent of the time, Kat is a brilliant, angelic, saint of a human being."

"She has to be, to put up with you." Delivering the jab in an untroubled tone, Diana traced the toe of her high-heeled shoe over the inside of Jude's knee, then maneuvered between her thighs to follow the seam leading to her crotch. "Nice save, by the way. After that 'brilliant' and 'angelic' stuff, there's no way Kat'll remember how you started off by calling her a prodigious dumbass."

"See. That's *my* talent." Ava smirked. "Charming my ass out of the proverbial doghouse." She shot Jude a warm smile, then reached for Diana's arm. "Do you think I could talk you into accompanying me to the restroom? I'd love to empty my bladder before our entrees arrive, and the girls would probably appreciate the chance to patch things up in private."

"Certainly." Diana tossed her napkin onto the table, then hesitated, searching Jude's face. "If Jude will remember how much I adore her, and how desperate I am to be with her, the entire time we're gone."

Diana's sincerity brought Jude to tears. "I will."

"Then okay." Diana stood and offered her arm to Ava, helping her onto her feet. "We'll be back in a few. Until then, play nice."

"Yes, ma'am," Katrina said, in a legitimately contrite mutter. "I already feel like enough of a jerk as it is."

"You're not a jerk." Diana granted Katrina a friendly smile. "Let's be real. It's not like I've never considered the possibility of making an honest woman out of Jude one day." Shifting her focus to Jude's gawping face, Diana flushed, then lifted her shoulder with fairly convincing nonchalance. "As far as I'm concerned, well…never say never. Right?"

Jude had no clue how she could still be breathing. How, when Diana had just implied she might want a bond to last the rest of their lives, was Jude conscious at all? Struck silent, she nodded dumbly—and kept on nodding until Ava tapped her cane on the floor to remind Diana of their mission.

Blowing Jude a kiss, Diana quipped, "As you can see, 'patience' has never been among Ava's many fine qualities." She curled her arm around Ava's and allowed herself to be led away from the table. "Save our seats!"

"Wow," Katrina murmured once their partners were out of earshot. "I've never seen Diana this high on life before. What did you do to her?"

"What *haven't* I done to her?" Jude cracked a grin, unable to stay angry in light of Diana's unprecedented future talk. "That's the real question."

Katrina snorted. "So the sex remains adequate?"

Jude laughed heartily at the understatement. "Our sex is unreal—and somehow only gets better as time goes on."

"*Right?*" Lighting up, Katrina leaned closer and whispered, "Our last evening in Venice, Ava gave me *seven orgasms*! All in a single night! I'm not sure I'd ever achieved seven orgasms in a single *week* before Ava." She shook her head, apparently in disbelief. "So far, married sex has been even more awesome than engaged sex. I remember thinking when we first started fooling around, chemistry this amazing can't last. Mostly because we'd die if it did. And yet…what we were doing then was *nothing* compared to what we've got going on now. All that practice is really paying off."

Tickled to hear Katrina's exuberance about a topic her cousin hadn't always felt comfortable discussing, Jude invited her to bump fists before pulling her into a one-armed hug. "You're welcome."

"For introducing me to my soul mate by way of your kinky part-time job?" Katrina held Jude tighter. "Yes…*thank you.*"

"It was my pleasure, truly." Jude released Katrina to have another sip of wine. "You know, if we hadn't had the two of you as role models—"

"You mean catalysts?"

"Both." Jude raised her glass for an impromptu toast. "If not for your decision to finger an injured, helpless client in an ethically questionable attempt to ease her embarrassment about your sort-of accidental voyeurism, who knows where Diana and I would be today? Quite possibly nowhere."

"Instead, you're practically pre-engaged." Katrina clinked their glasses together. "Thanks to me and my ethically questionable fingers."

She extended her index and middle digits, then used the tips to paint lewd circles in the air. "*You're* welcome."

"I suppose that means we're even." Jude plucked a slice of apple from the salad and popped it into her mouth. "Or forever indebted to one another."

"Either way." Katrina put down her empty glass and gave Jude a hopeful smile. "So you aren't mad at me anymore? Because I'm willing to grovel if you are."

Jude shook her head. "I'm not mad." She chomped another bite of salad, re-energized by Diana's positive reaction to Katrina's gigantic mouth. "She said, 'Never say never.' You heard that too, right?"

"I did." Katrina folded her arms over her chest and leaned back in her chair. "Remember how worried you were about moving in together? Sure looks to me like I was right. Diana *doesn't* hate living with you, after all."

"Yeah, yeah, you were right." Jude rolled her eyes and shoveled more spinach into her mouth. "I wouldn't get used to it."

"I'm already used to it." Katrina threw her arms around Jude for another enthusiastic hug. "On that note, may I offer another piece of advice?"

Jude rested her chin on Katrina's shoulder, sighing. "If you must."

"Have more faith in Diana. She made up her mind about you a long time ago." Katrina pinched Jude's hip, then kissed her hair. "I'd be floored if she ever let you go. Ava would, too."

"Ava would too, what?"

Katrina backed out of their hug to arch a meaningful eyebrow at her wife's return. "Nothing."

Diana dragged her chair away from the table, then stopped. "Hey, Kat? Would you mind if we traded seats for a while? I'm feeling the need to stay close to my favorite girl right now."

Katrina leapt to her feet, stumbling in her eagerness to comply. "Yes! Fabulous idea."

Ava greeted her spouse's arrival on the opposite side of the table with a lingering kiss. "I missed you," she purred, sex dripping from her words. "Did you miss me?"

"Always." Pink-cheeked, Katrina watched Diana sink into the chair she'd abandoned with her body angled toward Jude. "So, enough about us. How are things with you guys now that you share an address?" Leaning closer to Diana, she shielded her mouth to whisper conspiratorially,

"Have you gotten used to the way Jude's socks never *quite* make it into the hamper? Because I sure didn't."

Diana chuckled, reaching to take Jude's hand from her lap and carefully interlace their fingers. Moving their joined hands to rest at the juncture of her own thighs, she answered in a suggestive undertone. "Without going into *too* much detail, let me assure you that Jude possesses her own laundry list of prodigious, even *miraculous* talents. Skills like those more than make up for a few scattered socks and the odd backward-facing toilet-paper roll."

Katrina blurted laughter. "That's right! Jude claims she can't remember the correct way to put it on the holder."

"Yes, because 'why would anyone care about something so trivial? With all the problems in this world, who has time to worry about proper toilet-paper installation?'" Diana stroked her thumb over the inside of Jude's wrist. "But she *is* super cute."

"As a button," Ava drawled, doffing an imaginary cap in Jude's direction.

"Seriously, though, I can't get too upset about any of Jude's idiosyncrasies after the hell I went through with my ex." Diana raised their clasped hands to her lips, kissing Jude's knuckles tenderly. "If that relationship was a nightmare, then being with Jude is a dream come true."

"Awww." Ava and Katrina cooed in tandem, to which Ava added, "Fuckin' cheeseball."

Katrina admonished her wife with a literal slap on the wrist. "You hypocrite. Shall I read our friends the love poem you wrote for me during the flight home?"

Ava's face turned uncharacteristically red. "That won't be necessary."

"Love poem, huh?" Diana sported an evil grin. "Do tell."

Gaining confidence from Diana's steadfast grip on her hand, Jude unleashed a zinger of her own. "I imagine it takes a true artist to compose a romantic limerick."

"Hardy har," Ava grumbled. "What do you say we go back to picking on Jude now? That was fun."

Their harried waitress arrived with their entrees at long last, sparing the next victim of the group's friendly teasing. Everyone stopped talking while their meals were being distributed, but when Katrina turned to Ava and whispered into her ear—making her smirk, then chuckle—Diana scooted closer until her chair touched Jude's and their faces were inches apart.

"Hi," Diana whispered, then pecked Jude on the nose. "Ava said I needed to make sure you knew that I want our relationship to be the last one I ever have. Also, that I'm planning to love you for the rest of my life. You, and nobody else." She released a shaky breath, then straightened to gaze at Jude with a bold, loving smile. "You *do* know that...right?"

For perhaps the first time since she fell for the sex therapist next door, Jude let her entire body relax, and she breathed freely. Secure in the knowledge that her feelings were far from unrequited, Jude found her answer at the bottom of her heart. "I do."

THE END

About the Author

Meghan O'Brien is the author of ten lesbian romance/erotica novels published by Bold Strokes Books, including *Thirteen Hours* (2009 GCLS Award, Lesbian Erotica), *Wild* (2011 Rainbow Award, Best Lesbian Novel), *The Night Off* (2012 Rainbow Award, Lesbian Erotic Romance and 2013 GCLS Award, Lesbian Erotica), *The Muse* (2015 Foreword INDIE Bronze Medalist, 2015 Lambda Literary Award, 2016 GCLS Award in Lesbian Erotica), and *Her Best Friend's Sister* (2018 GCLS Award, Erotica and 2017 Foreword INDIES Silver Winner for Erotica). She lives in the Bay Area with her wife, Angie; their son; and a motley collection of lovable pets.

Books Available from Bold Strokes Books

All of Me by Emily Smith. When chief surgical resident Galen Burgess meets her new intern, Rowan Duncan, she may finally discover that doing what you've always done will only give you what you've always had. (978-1-163555-321-5)

As the Crow Flies by Karen F. Williams. Romance seems to be blooming all around, but problems arise when a restless ghost emerges from the ether to roam the dark corners of this haunting tale. (978-1-163555-285-0)

Both Ways by Ileandra Young. SPEAR agent Danika Karson races to protect the city from a supernatural threat and must rely on the woman she's trained to despise: Rayne, an achingly beautiful vampire. (978-1-163555-298-0)

Calendar Girl by Georgia Beers. Forced to work together, Addison Fairchild and Kate Cooper discover that opposites really do attract. (978-1-163555-333-8)

Lovebirds by Lisa Moreau. Two women from different worlds collide in a small California mountain town, each with a mission that doesn't include falling in love. (978-1-163555-213-3)

Media Darling by Fiona Riley. Can Hollywood bad girl Emerson and reluctant celebrity gossip reporter Hayley work together to make each other's dreams come true? Or will Emerson's secrets ruin not one career, but two? (978-1-163555-278-2)

Stroke of Fate by Renee Roman. Can Sean Moore live up to her reputation and save Jade Rivers from the stalker determined to end Jade's career and, ultimately, her life? (978-1-163555-162-4)

The Rise of the Resistance by Jackie D. The soul of America has been lost for almost a century. A few people may be the difference between a phoenix rising to save the masses or permanent destruction. (978-1-163555-259-1)

The Sex Therapist Next Door by Meghan O'Brien. At the intersection of sex and intimacy, anything is possible. Even love. (978-1-163555-296-6)

Unexpected Lightning by Cass Sellars. Lightning strikes once more when Sydney and Parker fight a dangerous stranger who threatens the peace they both desperately want. (978-1-163555-276-8)

Unforgettable by Elle Spencer. When one night changes a lifetime... Two romance novellas from best-selling author Elle Spencer. (978-1-63555-429-8)

Against All Odds by Kris Bryant, Maggie Cummings, M. Ullrich. Peyton and Tory escaped death once, but will they survive when Bradley's determined to make his kill rate one hundred percent? (978-1-163555-193-8)

Autumn's Light by Aurora Rey. Casual hookups aren't supposed to include romantic dinners and meeting the family. Can Mat Pero see beyond the heartbreak that led her to keep her worlds so separate, and will Graham Connor be waiting if she does? (978-1-163555-272-0)

Breaking the Rules by Larkin Rose. When Virginia and Carmen are thrown together by an embarrassing mistake they find out their stubborn determination isn't so heroic after all. (978-1-163555-261-4)

Broad Awakening by Mickey Brent. In the sequel to *Underwater Vibes*, Hélène and Sylvie find ruts in their road to eternal bliss. (978-1-163555-270-6)

Broken Vows by MJ Williamz. Sister Mary Margaret must reconcile her divided heart or risk losing a love that just might be heaven sent. (978-1-163555-022-1)

Flesh and Gold by Ann Aptaker. Havana, 1952, where art thief and smuggler Cantor Gold dodges gangland bullets and mobsters' schemes while she searches Havana's steamy Red Light district for her kidnapped love. (978-1-163555-153-2)

Isle of Broken Years by Jane Fletcher. Spanish noblewoman Catalina de Valasco is in peril, even before the pirates holding her for ransom sail into seas destined to become known as the Bermuda Triangle. (978-1-163555-175-4)

Love Like This by Melissa Brayden. Hadley Cooper and Spencer Adair set out to take the fashion world by storm. If only they knew their hearts were about to be taken. (978-1-163555-018-4)

Secrets On the Clock by Nicole Disney. Jenna and Danielle love their jobs helping endangered children, but that might not be enough to stop them from breaking the rules by falling in love. (978-1-163555-292-8)

Unexpected Partners by Michelle Larkin. Dr. Chloe Maddox tries desperately to deny her attraction for Detective Dana Blake as they flee from a serial killer who's hunting them both. (978-1-163555-203-4)

A Fighting Chance by T. L. Hayes. Will Lou be able to come to terms with her past to give love a fighting chance? (978-1-163555-257-7)

Chosen by Brey Willows. When the choice is adapt or die, can love save us all? (978-1-163555-110-5)

Death Checks In by David S. Pederson. Despite Heath's promises to Alan to not get involved, Heath can't resist investigating a shopkeeper's murder in Chicago, which dashes their plans for a romantic weekend getaway. (978-1-163555-329-1)

Gnarled Hollow by Charlotte Greene. After they are invited to study a secluded nineteenth-century estate, a former English professor and a group of historians discover that they will have to fight against the unknown if they have any hope of staying alive. (978-1-163555-235-5)

Jacob's Grace by C.P. Rowlands. Captain Tag Becket wants to keep her head down and her past behind her, but her feelings for AJ's second-in-command, Grace Fields, makes keeping secrets next to impossible. (978-1-163555-187-7)

On the Fly by PJ Trebelhorn. Hockey player Courtney Abbott is content with her solitary life until visiting concert violinist Lana Caruso makes her second-guess everything she always thought she wanted. (978-1-163555-255-3)

Passionate Rivals by Radclyffe. Professional rivalry and long-simmering passions create a combustible combination when Emmett McCabe and Sydney Stevens are forced to work together, especially when past attractions won't stay buried. (978-1-163555-231-7)

Proxima Five by Missouri Vaun. When geologist Leah Warren crash-lands on a preindustrial planet and is claimed by its tyrant, Tiago, will clan warrior Keegan's love for Leah give her the strength to defeat him? (978-1-163555-122-8)

Racing Hearts by Dena Blake. When you cross a hot-tempered race car mechanic with a reckless cop, the result can only be spontaneous combustion. (978-1-163555-251-5)

Shadowboxer by Jessica L. Webb. Jordan McAddie is prepared to keep her street kids safe from a dangerous underground protest group, but she isn't prepared for her first love to walk back into her life. (978-1-163555-267-6)

The Tattered Lands by Barbara Ann Wright. As Vandra and Lilani strive to make peace, they slowly fall in love. With mistrust and murder surrounding them, only their faith in each other can keep their plan to save the world from falling apart. (978-1-163555-108-2)

Captive by Donna K. Ford. To escape a human trafficking ring, Greyson Cooper and Olivia Danner become players in a game of deceit and violence. Will their love stand a chance? (978-1-63555-215-7)

Crossing the Line by CF Frizzell. The Mob discovers a nemesis within its ranks, and in the ultimate retaliation, draws Stick McLaughlin from anonymity by threatening everything she holds dear. (978-1-63555-161-7)

Love's Verdict by Carsen Taite. Attorneys Landon Holt and Carly Pachett want the exact same thing: the only open partnership spot at their prestigious criminal defense firm. But will they compromise their careers for love? (978-1-63555-042-9)

Precipice of Doubt by Mardi Alexander & Laurie Eichler. Can Cole Jameson resist her attraction to her boss, veterinarian Jodi Bowman, or will she risk a workplace romance and her heart? (978-1-63555-128-0)

Savage Horizons by CJ Birch. Captain Jordan Kellow's feelings for Lt. Ali Ash have her past and future colliding, setting in motion a series of events that strands her crew in an unknown galaxy thousands of light years from home. (978-1-63555-250-8)

Secrets of the Last Castle by A. Rose Mathieu. When Elizabeth Campbell represents a young man accused of murdering an elderly woman, her investigation leads to an abandoned plantation that reveals many dark Southern secrets. (978-1-63555-240-9)

Take Your Time by VK Powell. A neurotic parrot brings police officer Grace Booker and temporary veterinarian Dr. Dani Wingate together in the tiny town of Pine Cone, but their unexpected attraction keeps the sparks flying. (978-1-63555-130-3)

The Last Seduction by Ronica Black. When you allow true love to elude you once and you desperately regret it, are you brave enough to grab it when it comes around again? (978-1-63555-211-9)

The Shape of You by Georgia Beers. Rebecca McCall doesn't play it safe, but when sexy Spencer Thompson joins her workout class, their non-stop sparring forces her to face her ultimate challenge—a chance at love. (978-1-63555-217-1)

Exposed by MJ Williamz. The closet is no place to live if you want to find true love. (978-1-62639-989-1)

Force of Fire: Toujours a Vous by Ali Vali. Immortals Kendal and Piper welcome their new child and celebrate the defeat of an old enemy, but another ancient evil is about to awaken deep in the jungles of Costa Rica. (978-1-63555-047-4)

Holding Their Place by Kelly A. Wacker. Together Dr. Helen Connery and ambulance driver Julia March, discover that goodness, love, and passion can be found in the most unlikely and even dangerous places during WWI. (978-1-63555-338-3)

Landing Zone by Erin Dutton. Can a career veteran finally discover a love stronger than even her pride? (978-1-63555-199-0)

Love at Last Call by M. Ullrich. Is balancing business, friendship, and love more than any willing woman can handle? (978-1-63555-197-6)

Pleasure Cruise by Yolanda Wallace. Spencer Collins and Amy Donovan have few things in common, but a Caribbean cruise offers both women an unexpected chance to face one of their greatest fears: falling in love. (978-1-63555-219-5)

Running Off Radar by MB Austin. Maji's plans to win Rose back are interrupted when work intrudes and duty calls her to help a SEAL team stop a Russian mobster from harvesting gold from the bottom of Sitka Sound. (978-1-63555-152-5)

Shadow of the Phoenix by Rebecca Harwell. In the final battle for the fate of Storm's Quarry, even Nadya's and Shay's powers may not be enough. (978-1-63555-181-5)

Take a Chance by D. Jackson Leigh. There's hardly a woman within fifty miles of Pine Cone that veterinarian Trip Beaumont can't charm, except for the irritating new cop, Jamie Grant, who keeps leaving parking tickets on her truck. (978-1-63555-118-1)

The Outcasts by Alexa Black. Spacebus driver Sue Jones is running from her past. When she crash-lands on a faraway world, the Outcast Kara might be her chance for redemption. (978-1-63555-242-3)

Printed in the USA
CPSIA information can be obtained
at www.ICGtesting.com
JSHW082152140824
68134JS00014B/197